A LIGHT COMEDY

Eduardo Mendoza was born in 1943 in Barcelona, where he now lives. He spent some years in New York where he worked at the United Nations as an interpreter. After making his literary debut with *The Truth about the Savolta Case* (rated by *El País* one of the three best Spanish works since 1975), he went on to write other novels, including *City of Marvels*, selected by the Paris review *Lire* as the best book they had read that year, and *The Year of the Flood*. His works are translated into many languages.

Nick Caistor has translated many French and Latin American films for television, works as a producer for the BBC Latin American service, and edited two Latin American short story anthologies. Authors whose work he has translated include Osvaldo Soriano, Juan Carlos Onetti, Sergio Ramirez, Ulises Ponce de León, and the Portuguese Nobel laureate José Saramago.

Eduardo Mendoza

A LIGHT COMEDY

TRANSLATED FROM THE SPANISH BY
Nick Caistor

V

VINTAGE

Published by Vintage 2003

2 4 6 8 10 9 7 5 3 1

Copyright © Eduardo Mendoza 1996
English translation copyright © Nick Caistor 2001

Eduardo Mendoza has asserted his right under the Copyright, Designs and Patents Act, 1988 to be identified as the
author of this work

The song on page 417 features in Carlos Clavería's *Estudios
sobre los gitanismos del español*, C.S.I.C., Madrid, 1951

This edition has been translated with the financial assistance
of the Spanish Dirección General del Libro y Bibliotecas,
Ministerio de Cultura

First published in Spain with the title *Una comedia Ligera* by
Editorial Seix Barral, Barcelona

First published in Great Britain in 2002 by
The Harvill Press

Vintage
Random House, 20 Vauxhall Bridge Road,
London SW1V 2SA

Random House Australia (Pty) Limited
20 Alfred Street, Milsons Point, Sydney
New South Wales 2061, Australia

Random House New Zealand Limited
18 Poland Road, Glenfield,
Auckland 10, New Zealand

Random House (Pty) Limited
Endulini, 5A Jubilee Road, Parktown 2193,
South Africa

The Random House Group Limited Reg. No. 954009
www.randomhouse.co.uk

A CIP catalogue record for this book
is available from the British Library

ISBN 0 099 44898 X

Papers used by Random House are natural, recyclable
products made from wood grown in sustainable forests.
The manufacturing processes conform to the environ-
mental regulations of the country of origin

Printed and bound in Great Britain by
Bookmarque Ltd, Croydon, Surrey

CHAPTER ONE

I

That summer it was all the rage for women to make bobbin lace. Besides that, it was a summer like any other: the days were long and hot, the nights cool and damp; the skies were radiant, cloudless, deep satin blue; there were also, as every summer, sudden squalls, as violent as they were short-lived. By contrast, the previous winter had been bitterly dark and icy; the people of Barcelona had been forced to endure it stoically, warming themselves at rug-covered tables with charcoal smoking in the braziers beneath, passing the time by exchanging with each other the tiniest details of their humdrum lives – because those were quiet times, with few amusements, in which the days and hours dragged past in the dull monotony of long hours at work or never-ending domestic chores. While the men spent most of their time at the office, occasionally working, but more often chatting with their colleagues, doing crosswords or filling in lottery numbers, at home the women fought their lonely drudgery by listening to soap operas, competitions or music programmes on the radio, or drowning out the noise of their steaming irons and pots and pans by crooning the words to sad songs that told of hearts betrayed and cruelly broken.

Order, moderation and harmony were all-important. Discretion and elegance were the supreme virtues, while good manners were to be observed at all times and on every occasion. Men gave up their seats for women on the trams or trolleybuses and doffed their hats whenever they walked past a church. Vehicles stopped for a passing funeral and people crossed themselves when they left home or set out on a journey. In those days, religion played a crucial rôle in offering people support and comfort: everyone knew that all their deeds, words, intentions or thoughts were implacably judged by an all-seeing God, but also knew that when things went wrong or they faced misfortune they could count on divine aid, either directly or through the intercession of the Holy Virgin or the countless male and female saints listed in the calendar. Receiving the sacraments, attending Mass or novenas, spiritual exercises, sermons, night vigils and a whole range of other pious activities took up a fair part of the hours of the day, especially for women. They were not only the main target for this complicated mix of religious fervour and ceremony, but also its chief beneficiaries, since any woman who had not found herself a husband by the time she was thirty could find consolation and interest for the rest of her days only in the assiduous practice of religion. This meant that the care of one's soul through religious rites was extremely intricate, and priests were a necessary presence everywhere. It was also common for the rosary to be recited by the whole family together. No-one wanted to stray from the straight and narrow for any reason: at the back of everyone's mind was the troubling memory of a recent past when the lack of religion and anti-clericalism had first of all given rise to every kind of excess, and then led inexorably to those terrible years when the city had been submerged in violence, pillage, want, and fear. Nobody had been safe from acts of revenge, crass mistakes, even outbursts of violence, and many had found themselves deprived unfairly, but irrevocably, of their freedom, or their lives. In those dreadful years, as if in a biblical scene, thunder and lightning, fire and brimstone had smitten the city; the streets were witness to bloody political feuds; and

2

dreadful crimes were committed under cover of all the confusion. A chorus of lamentation rose day and night from the smoking ruins.

Now, however, the bitter memory of those years nestled only in dark corners, and the consequences were felt in only a few aspects of life. Although the authorities did their utmost to resolve serious supply problems, bread, beans, lentils, chick peas, meat, sugar and oil were rarely seen at the tables of the poor, while due to the high cost of building materials, new immigrants to the city had to live in flimsy adobe-and-tin shacks, thrown up in chaotic fashion in districts lacking all services, schools or clinics. They were to be found usually on wasteland unfit for human habitation: dried-up riverbeds and sandbanks, or steep hillsides where year in, year out, the violent autumn rains caused floods and, more often than not, fatalities. There were also large numbers of unfortunates who, unable to find work or even afford one of these filthy shacks, wandered the streets begging by day and sleeping at night under public benches or in trucks parked on the outskirts of the city. But these minor problems were not so serious as to disturb the proper functioning of the city, or the hushed conformity of its inhabitants, keen to secure peace and quiet at any cost. The men had suffered so badly that now their greatest wish was to earn a more-or-less decent wage, pay their bills, talk politics with as little controversy as possible, argue about bullfighting and football and tell racy jokes. The women never took part in these violent, daring or salacious discussions – it was they who had to bear the brunt of showing the moderation and propriety demanded by the moment. In those years, their chief concern seemed to be domestic help, which was increasingly hard to find, did not know the meaning of hard work, and got cheekier by the day. Apart from this worrying and annoying topic, most of the lengthy if discreet women's talk revolved around the exchange of recipes, secrets and tips about cooking, and above all clothes – because at that time, while always displaying a proper sense of decorum, women were expected to pay a great deal of attention to their appearance. In this realm the Paris fashion houses acted as benign dictators: in the year in question, skirts had to be worn bell-shaped or with pleats on the bias; waists had to be narrow, shoulders broad; dresses had collars, and necklines were squared-off; gentle colours were a must, and silk, shantung, surah and piqué were the fabrics to wear. Although some magazines suggested it, no self-respecting woman would have dared wear a skirt any higher than the calf, put on slacks, or leave off her stockings on hot summer days. At Easter and Corpus Christi a *peineta* and a shawl were still *de rigeur*. The church authorities frowned on all this frivolity, which they saw as contravening the dignity and modesty every woman should show, and which only led to an expenditure that sat ill with the shortages still experienced by the less favoured in society. But the clergy's reasonable objections fell on deaf ears. And anyway, this and similar concerns became irrelevant with the sudden arrival of the unbearable summer heat, making the asphalt shimmer by day and keeping everyone from sleeping at night. As soon as the school year was over, Barcelona families moved out to their charming summer residences to escape. Well-off families spent the summer on the coast; those with lesser means, in the mountains. Some rich people even had two summer houses, and switched between the seaside and the mountains, arguing that although the imperatives of fashion made it essential to be seen at the beach, the mountain air was much better for the body and refreshed the mind – a consideration as accurate as it was unnecessary, since at that time wealthy people enjoyed enviable good health.

So it was that from St John's Day at the end of June to the

Feast of la Merced in late September, women, children and maids abandoned the city and set themselves up in the summer resorts, transporting with them huge bundles of luggage strapped to the roofs of their cars. Their husbands, kept by their jobs in the city from Monday to Saturday (the five-day English week had been heard of, but not adopted) bore their loss as best they could, lunching and dining in cheap restaurants, filling the gap left by an empty home in café get-togethers or in a double bill at any cinema that had Carrier air-conditioning. There, protected from the asphyxiating heat, they slumped in the lumpy back-row seats, and as soon as the lights had gone down and the first strains of the official newsreel blared out, tried to doze off, mostly in order to avoid falling under the perverse spell of the romantic films of the period, which were heady love stories with gorgeous *femmes fatales* capable of arousing waves of desire with their gaze, laughter and dancing, leaving every man's heart aching and his soul ablaze. They slept because they did not want anything to disturb their lives' peaceful calm, and the temptresses on the screen posed a threat from which none of them felt secure; women like that were the root of all evil, disaster and strife.

2

Emerging from a dense fog, the stage doorkeeper rushed out of his box as soon as he saw Prullàs come in. He greeted him with a great show of respect, smiling as he did so to show two rows of large, ill-defined teeth. He was carrying a clay candleholder with the stump of a candle in it because, he said, the electric light kept coming and going. Although restrictions had been lifted some time ago, a slight overload in demand, an uncertain distribution network, or any other problem could – and in fact did – lead to numerous blackouts every day. At that moment, however, the light in the theatre foyer was working, and a bulb shone a cone of yellowish light onto the newspaper the doorkeeper had spread over the shelf in his hideaway. He slid the bolt on the foyer entrance to make sure no-one could steal into the theatre while he was not there, then set off down the corridor without paying any attention to Prullàs, who was protesting that there was no need for him to move. "I know the way, Bonifaci, I'm not going to get lost."

But the doorkeeper waved the candleholder as if to draw the newcomer's attention to the value of this humble gadget. His gesture seemed to say: if the light went off suddenly, as it has been doing all afternoon, what would become of you? So the two of them made their way down the corridor until they came to another narrower one without doors or windows.

"It's not just us," the doorkeeper said, still leading the way. "When the light went, I ran out into the street: the whole block was in darkness, and the street was pitch-black, so it must be a general power cut; it's probably a transformer."

"Probably," Prullàs agreed, more from sympathy than conviction. A couple of days earlier, in similar circumstances, the porter at his apartment block had blamed the blackout on "the atomical bomb". The press, radio, and cinema newsreels had recently been full of the explosion of an atomic bomb in the Nevada desert; now splitting the atom and chain reactions were terms that no-one understood but were on everyone's lips. Prullàs had been surprised and annoyed that his porter had said "atomical" instead of "atomic" to him, it merely showed the man's carelessness. But here was Bonifaci, an avid reader of the evening papers, offering a much simpler and more local explanation for the power cuts. Although neither of them knew the real reason, and were merely talking for its own sake, Prullàs nevertheless silently praised Bonifaci's more restrained and homespun imagination.

All of a sudden the wall-lights in the corridor started to flicker. "What did I tell you, Don Carlos!" Bonifaci exclaimed, and asked him to be so kind as to take the candleholder while he searched for a match. Bonifaci's decision was immediately vindicated: no sooner had he spoken than the lights went out completely, and the corridor was left in darkness. Bonifaci struck the match. He lit the candle with it, then, shielding the wavering flame with his hand, set off again at full tilt down the corridor; as he carried the light off, the walls seemed to open to make way for him, then to close again at once behind his back. Noticing this strange play of light, Prullàs felt as if he were following Bonifaci on a journey through time. He remembered that during the terrible war years, Bonifaci had, for a while, been something of a voluntary fireman. He had fashioned himself a uniform out of the theatre wardrobe: a cardboard helmet dyed scarlet and a red jacket adorned with tassels and buckles originally intended to emphasise the comic effect of the ritual appearance of a fireman in the bedroom of a bawdy farce. Now, though, Bonifaci was wearing a simple grey overall. The corridor finally led to the proscenium, which was dimly lit by lights from the stage.

"I'll leave you here, Don Carlos, if you've no further need of me," Bonifaci whispered. "Have a smoke, Bonifaci," Prullàs said, offering him a cigarette that the doorkeeper lit from the candle flame. As he did so, Prullàs slipped the packet into the man's overall pocket. The doorkeeper protested, but Prullàs cut him short with an imperious gesture: "Go on, go on."

Bonifaci left, pleased with himself. By the light of an oil lamp placed on a table at the front of the stage, a man was carefully studying some typed sheets of paper, his back to the stalls. The stage was lit by a few low-volt lights fed by a generator that was spluttering quietly in a corner somewhere. Between the director and centre stage where the actors were moving about, there was a patch of shadow, out of which their voices carried in disembodied, harsh tones.

JULIO: I've been giving it a lot of thought, Cecilia, I've weighed up all the possibilities, and the only solution is murder.

CECILIA: Murder! But, Julio . . .

JULIO: Yes, Cecilia, that's right. We have to murder Todoliu. And sooner rather than later.

CECILIA: You mean . . . with our own hands?

JULIO: Yes, darling. There are some things you can't leave to the maid.

CECILIA: And you say it has to be soon?

JULIO: Tomorrow afternoon.

CECILIA: Oh, botheration! I'll have to cancel my hair appointment. Couldn't it wait till Wednesday?

JULIO: No, no: it has to be tomorrow. I've thought it all through, it's all organised. It can't go wrong . . . (*A doorbell rings*) Heavens! What was that?

CECILIA: Calm down, Julio; it was only the doorbell.

JULIO: The doorbell? Who on earth can that be? Were you expecting someone?

CECILIA: No, but we'll soon find out. The maid has gone to open.

LUISITO: (*coming on stage*) I say, Who . . . who . . . Julio: is water animal, vegetable, or mi . . . mi . . . mineral?

JULIO: Who's asking?

LUISITO: It's the co . . . co . . . competition on the radio. What would you an . . . an . . . answer?

JULIO: Well, I'd say water is . . . wet air!

LUISITO: Oh, Julio . . . how cl . . . how cl . . . how clever you are! (*Exit*)

JULIO: That poor brother of ours gets dumber by the day.

CECILIA: I hope him being here doesn't spoil our plans for . . . you know what.

JULIO: For the murder? No, not a bit. In fact, he's one of the keys to my plan!

CECILIA: Luisito is?

JULIO: Shhh, someone's coming!

MAID: (*entering*) The fiancé's mistress . . . I'm sorry, I mean the mistress's fiancé is here.

CECILIA: (*in alarm*) My fiancé? Enrique? Here? At this time of day? That's impossible. Did he say why?

MAID: No, ma'am. He simply said he wanted to see you. He's waiting for the living-room. I mean, he's waiting for you in the living-room.

CECILIA: Very good. Tell him I'll be down in two shakes.

MAID: (*Curtsies and leaves*)

JULIO: That's all we needed!

CECILIA: What can have got into him? We're in trouble if he gets wind of what we're up to . . .

JULIO: (*angrily*) Nobody but you could have got lumbered with a policeman for a boyfriend!

CECILIA: How was I to know? When we first started going out, he didn't mention it. And anyway, he's in the secret police . . . Besides, what's wrong with being a policeman? Some of them are decent people.

JULIO: Yes, they are, stupid, but we are criminals and we're in the midst of planning a murder, aren't we?

CECILIA: Oh my, that's true: isn't that a coincidence? But listen, Julio, couldn't we commit the murder, then let Enrique find out who did it? That'd give his career a real boost.

JULIO: Oh, yes, and boost us all the way to the scaffold!

At this point the director called a break, and Prullàs took advantage to ask him: "How's it all going?" "As you can see," the other replied. Prullàs thought the director did not look in good shape generally despite his mountain suntan. The two of them were whispering as if not to disturb the actors. This brought a protest from the leading lady, who was still in the bright circle of light onstage. What were the two of them up to? What were they plotting behind everyone's back?

"What brings you to these parts?" the director asked, without raising his voice and ignoring the insults from the stage. Prullàs looked at him in surprise, but before he could say anything his companion complained that it was ghastly; sometimes it was such a complete disaster, it seemed everything was conspiring against them. The play didn't work, the actors were performing like beginners, the jokes weren't funny, and to cap it all, there were the blasted power cuts, he moaned.

"Pepe, you know I'll do all I can to help," Prullàs said. "As you can see, I came as soon as I got your message." "What message are you talking about?" the director asked curtly. "I didn't ask you to come; I don't need you here. This play is giving me enough headaches as it is." "Didn't you phone my home number this morning? And leave a message saying you wanted to see me urgently?" Prullàs asked. Even before he had finished speaking, both of them realised how the mistake had arisen, and who had provoked it. "Ah, I see, it was all a misunderstanding," Prullàs said. "I'm sorry I interrupted you, I'll be on my way."

Without another word, he stood up and headed across the stage for the exit. As he crossed the area lit by the floodlights he stood momentarily blinded. He heard a voice asking why he was leaving and what had gone on between the two of them, but all he replied was that they should meet up in the bar opposite after the rehearsal. He tried to say this as softly as possible so no-one else in the cast would hear. He could just imagine all their eyes fixed on him.

Before he had reached the corridor leading back to the foyer, the director caught up with him and apologised: he hadn't been feeling well for several days now. "I don't know what's the matter with me," he murmured; "I'm sorry for what I said to you." "I didn't hear a thing, Pepe," Prullàs said, putting his arm around the director's shoulders; "we can talk about the play some other time. And don't worry about the dialogue: if there's anything we don't like we can change it, and that'll be that. You know as well as I do that 'Arrivederci, pollo!' isn't exactly Calderón de la Barca." "That's true enough," the man replied. He seemed on the verge of tears. Prullàs felt a sudden surge of sympathy for his friend. "That's what we've always done, Pepe: we've managed to turn any old rubbish into a hit, and this time'll be no different, you'll see." "Of course," said the director.

3

"It's amazing how long the days are now, Don Carlos: it's almost nine and you can still read the paper without having to put the lights on," the waiter said.

Four tables, eight metal chairs and two parasols stuck in the pavement made up the improvised bar terrace, embellished and marked out from the rest of the city street by half a dozen earthenware pots where a few desultory shrubs struggled for survival. A sour smell of wineskins floated out from the interior of the bar. Prullàs agreed with the waiter. He was always surprised to see it was still light when he came out of the theatre, he said. But where would we be without the subterfuge of shadows?

The waiter did not seem inclined to follow that particular train of thought. He had been a waiter all his life; he had three sons, and each of them in turn had become a waiter in bars or restaurants around Barcelona. "I suppose we can get used to anything, Don Carlos," was his only comment.

Prullàs sat at a table with a good view of the theatre stage door, and ordered a beer and a plate of anchovies in vinegar. Then he called over the bootblack, who had been hovering in the background without getting involved in the conversation, and gave him some change to go to the nearest newspaper kiosk and buy an evening paper, a sporting gazette, and a bull-fighting magazine. When he came back, Prullàs made a present of the sports paper to the waiter. He glanced at the photos in the bullfighting magazine before handing it to the bootblack. One of them showed the moment after a bullfighter had been spectacularly gored: the bull was nowhere to be seen, only the wounded fighter being dragged to the exit by his team. It was a poor quality photo or reproduction: the contrast between sunlight and shade had been reduced to a uniform greyness which gave the tragedy a sordid, clinical aspect. The caption pointed out that the goring had not been serious; a few moments later the matador had come limping back into the ring and had finished his performance to the cheers of the crowd. Prullàs began to flick through the newspaper. He was hoping to make the wait less burdensome, but in fact could feel himself becoming increasingly anxious. Even though he thought he had come out of it all right in the end, his row with the director had left him hurt and confused. So now he stared at the newspaper headlines without taking in a word, and heard without listening as the bootblack aficionado went on about how nothing had ever been the same since that dreadful afternoon in the arena at Linares, Don Carlos.

At long last the theatre door opened and Mariquita Pons emerged into the street. Prullàs folded the newspaper, stood up and waved to her. The actress waved back, and came across to meet him. Her slender form, the apparent simplicity of her clothes, and the bustling way she walked all made her seem still young; this first impression faded as she came closer. On this occasion, though, the soft evening light continued the magical effect of the footlights.

It's always the same, thought Prullàs, I see her and I don't recognise her. Outside the theatre, she looked ordinary. There was nothing about her that seemed to justify the enthusiasm she could arouse in an audience, he reflected. It's as if she can not only change her expression at will, but her entire body, even her height. Perhaps that's the secret of her success, her ability to trigger fantasies whenever she likes, thought Prullàs as he watched her walking over to his table. Who is she really? he wondered: a famous actress approaching the end of her youth, whose only wish is to please and be loved by her public? A mature woman who shines in the salons thanks to her charm and vivacity? Or each and every one of the characters she is able to bring to life on stage with such conviction? She's a paradox all right! I'd love to know which of them I've been involved with all these years: perhaps it's a mixture of all three; perhaps it's a fourth one that only I know; perhaps it's none of them, simply yet another character in her repertoire.

The waiter, who had come over as soon as she sat down and ordered a plate of grilled prawns and a vermouth with soda, treated her respectfully, but was plainly not in awe of her; the actress cannot have wasted an ounce of her enormous capacity for seduction on him, thought Prullàs.

As if reading his thoughts, Mariquita Pons crossed her legs, offering a glimpse of her graceful knees. "What happened between you two?" she asked. "That's what I'd like to know, Kiki." He had been collaborating with Gaudet for years; of course, there had been the inevitable frictions between an author and his director, and these had sometimes led to violent arguments, insults and even threats. But now Prullàs said he felt the director really had it in for him, adding that perhaps it was all due to worries about his health. Mariquita Pons agreed with him. The actors, too, were depressed by this sudden change in attitude from a director they had all worked with so often in the past. But, she added, that wasn't the reason why she had summoned him: in fact, she wanted him to take her to the pictures that evening. "If, that is, you're not ashamed of being seen on the arm of this middle-aged adolescent," she said, pointing at herself.

Prullàs would not so easily be distracted from the object of his annoyance. "I can forgive him the insults," he growled, "but I don't know why he had to say the jokes were no good." "If you take me to the pictures, I'll tell you," she replied. "Tell me and I'll take you." The famous actress adopted a mocking expression. "No sir, first the pictures." "What about your husband?"

"He's in Madrid," she said, accompanying the word "Madrid" with a disdainful shrug, as she always did. Although her parents were from Valencia and she herself, thanks to the quirks of fate, had been born in Havana, she was brought up in Madrid. It was there she had launched and enjoyed most of her artistic career. But then she had married a Catalan and gone to live with him in Barcelona, and this had affected her brilliant position. She invariably played the lead part in Prullàs' thriller comedies, and this brought her success in Barcelona and, when touring, throughout Spain, but the great dramatic roles seemed to be reserved for actresses based in the capital, where the theatre had always carried more weight. Nor had she received many offers from the film industry, apart from a few small and uninteresting parts in costume dramas. Thinking of this always depressed her. "I renounced fame for the sake of a man who now spends all his time on business in Madrid," she would say.

"What picture did you have in mind?" Prullàs asked her. In reply, she took a handbill out of her bag and showed it to him. Prullàs read: HER ONLY LAW WAS HER DESIRE. Underneath this bold statement appeared the faces of Bette Davis and Olivia de Havilland. "A fine pair of hags you're taking me to see!" he protested.

4

When they left the Cristina cinema to walk back to Prullàs' car in Rambla de Cataluña, the famous actress hung on his arm. It was a sultry night, without a breath of air. The film dialogue was still buzzing inside his head:

Gimme another drink, Mitch.
You've already had enough, Peggy. Why don't you go home?
Go on, Mitch, there's a good boy. Just one more and I'll be on my way, I promise you.
What's the matter? Have you seen Mr Morton again?
Oh, Mitch, why is it that all the interesting men are married?
Perhaps you should look elsewhere, Peggy.
Like in Mrs Merryweather's shop, you mean? Forget it, Mitch. I wasn't born to have a mother-in-law and four or five kids. Anyway, what's wrong with having a bit of fun?
Maybe there's more to life than fun, Peggy.

"Take me for a drink, Carlos; I'm thirsty and starving." Prullàs said nothing. He didn't like to be seen in public with Mariquita Pons: she was so well-known they could not stay anonymous, but he could hardly refuse her request. A beggar came lurching up, as if about to confide a huge secret in them. "I've got the woife in bed with teebee," he muttered. Prullàs gave him a coin and the beggar staggered off gabbling incomprehensible words of thanks. The actress seemed still caught up in the film. "Admit you liked it," she said. "No," Prullàs replied. "Bah, you're just saying that because you don't approve of films in general." "Of course not," Prullàs retorted, "what is there to like? Everything in them is false; I don't know how you can take them seriously; I don't know how anyone can take talking photographs seriously. You're right, Kiki, I can't bear films, and especially American ones. In American films everyone has names you can never remember and lives the whole year round in rented summer houses. What's so good about that?"

"They help you dream. Ordinary people like to dream they live in a two-storey house with a porch, garage and a garden. They also like to dream they're not called Pérez or García, but have some foreign name: they think having the name can transport them far away from their work, their house, their family, everything they find unbearable. People live with a continuous film being shown inside their heads; every now and then they have to interrupt the show and make contact with reality again, but as soon as they can, they switch off the lights once more and slip back into the film they themselves are writing, directing and starring in." "Well, I've absolutely no wish to be called Broderick Crawford, and even less to have the mug he has," said Prullàs.

When they came in to the Terminus restaurant, the head waiter did not betray any signs of familiarity, but quickly led them to a table on its own in a discreet corner. Once they were safe from prying eyes, he greeted them effusively and asked after their health. Prullàs ordered a glass of cognac. The same for me, Luis, said the actress. "You just told me you were hungry and thirsty," Prullàs said when the waiter had left their table. "Well, I thought cognac was thirst-quenching and filling at the same time," she joked.

As he sipped his brandy, Prullàs returned to the problem that had been worrying him for hours. Was it true the rehearsals were as stuck as the director claimed? And if so, what was the reason? Was it down to the director's health problems? Mariquita Pons nodded. "It's possible," she said, "but there's also the fact that the play stinks," she added.

Prullàs gulped down the rest of his drink. Raising his voice, he retorted she was only saying that to get her own back because he had pulled her up for her stupid, unjustified love of the cinema. "Go on, go to Hollywood and see if they give you the part of a sheriff in some Western!" Mariquita did not take offence, merely saying she couldn't understand why he was so angry. After all, he had asked her opinion, and she had given it. Of course, if he preferred blind praise to the truth, there were plenty of people who would oblige, because if there was one thing there was more than enough of in their accursed profession, it was flatterers and toadies, she said. Then after a pause: "I tell you what I think, straight out; I say what I mean, whether you like it or not; and anyway, you can't be so upset or you wouldn't be trailing after me the whole time the way you do." "Don't you believe it, Kiki, I trail after all women, on principle. And I never pay the slightest attention to what you say. So go on, why does 'Arrivederci, pollo!' stink so much?" "Because the plot is forced, the characters are unbelievable, and the jokes are older than Methuselah. Is that enough for you?" "Enough, but wrong," Prullàs protested. "The plot is ingenious, the denouement is a complete surprise, and the jokes are so funny I find myself laughing out loud whenever I hear them."

"Then you're the only one who does, darling." She put her glass on the table, sighed, and after a while, added: "For the love of God, Carlos, who on earth in this day and age would make a character out of someone with a stammer? That went out in the last century."

"All right, I admit I've never tried to break any moulds," Prullàs replied. "But after all, Luisito is a classic figure, part of a long and noble tradition: he's the Fool, who's been around in our theatre since the Golden Age. He speeds the action up when a scene is dragging, and helps fill blank moments. That's what he does in my play: there's a ring at the doorbell, the maid goes to answer, everyone falls silent, waiting to see who this surprise visitor might be; it's then that the fool makes his appearance: he brings some humour to the proceedings, and gives time for the maid to get back."

"Have it your own way, but don't shout so, everyone is looking at us," Mariquita warned him. And then added: "I'm tired, take me home."

5

Prullàs slept till mid-day. He shaved, had a shower, got dressed and phoned Gaudet. At the other end of the line, the director's voice sounded thick with sleep, as if he too had woken up late, but he immediately accepted Prullàs' invitation. "Thank God you're not still angry with me for yesterday evening," he said. "No, I'm not, but I will be if you keep on talking nonsense," Prullàs said, and then hung up.

He had breakfast and took his time reading the morning papers. It was plain from them that the silly season was in full swing. Most of their correspondents and regular contributors were on holiday, and those left in charge – either because of a lack of decent stories or because they felt their readers didn't want the summer truce broken – filled the pages with light items of little lasting interest. Most of the news seemed to be about popular fiestas or bullfighting, strange events, inexplicable phenomena, peculiar inventions, or, as a last resort, the discovery of some enormous vegetable or other. The analysis and comment pages were in the hands of stand-in writers, who gave their pronouncements on everything under the sun as the mood took them, and expressed the most banal ideas as vehemently as if they had succeeded in coming to the most trite conclusions almost by magic. The international news that morning concerned the sighting of a flying saucer above the Nevada desert, and the re-opening of the Nuremberg Trials. As time had gone by, these trials – which at first had created great expectations – had lost their attraction once the most notorious prisoners, those whose images were enough to stir memories and provoke the most violent and conflicting sentiments, those who had been accused of unimaginable acts of the most dreadful perversity, had all been judged several years earlier, and their sentences summarily carried out. Now judges appeared confused as to what legislation it was they were supposed to be operating under, and even seemed unsure as to the legitimacy of what they were doing, hearing the cases of lower-ranking officials and ordinary citizens, who had committed acts during a tumultuous period that were more matters for their individual consciences than for the deliberation of nations. The more serious newspapers questioned whether it made sense to declare guilty those who had been merely carrying out orders from their superiors, or had simply carried out their allotted tasks efficiently and precisely but without ill-intent or hatred, unaware of the consequences their actions might have on third parties caught up as they were in an unforeseeable chain of consequences which they could not in any case modify. This debate had been going on for years, and in practice seemed to be resolved more in accordance with what the victors considered right than with any objective moral argument. Deep down, Prullàs did not really care. On this particular day, however, the news was more interesting, because the person in the dock was none other than a figure known and admired all over the world, the descendant of a famous dynasty whose name was almost mythical: Alfried Krupp. The fame of the Krupp family went back to the sixteenth century, when an ancestor of the man now being tried in Nuremberg had begun to make weapons for the Thirty Years' War. Ever since those far-off times, no large-scale war in Europe could have taken place without the Krupp family's contribution. More exactly, they had devoted four centuries to producing and perfecting artillery pieces. This was not the reason, however, why Alfried Krupp now stood accused. Nobody blamed him for making weapons as such, but for placing his colossal industry and immense fortune at the service of the wrong cause.

Prullàs left his apartment and called in at the corner bookshop. This was a place with low ceilings, walls lined with dark wooden bookshelves, and a parquet floor. A back room contained a small printing press, where the local people had their visiting cards and headed paper made up; in the spring months, the press was busy from morning to night printing First-Communion cards and wedding invitations. The shop also sold school stationery. There was always a powerful smell of paper, ink, school erasers and glue. In spite of the tremendous heat and the almost unbreathable atmosphere, Prullàs enjoyed being there: it was a quiet, soothing place.

"Aren't you going on vacation?" he asked the woman who came to serve him. She cast her eyes to the ceiling. "*El meu marit!*" she exclaimed. Her husband had been an intellectual: twenty years earlier he had signed a Futurist manifesto and had published a book of poems that was not without merit, even though the poems in it had little to do with the principles outlined in the manifesto and a lot in common with the stereotypes it held up as anathema. He was also a great drinker, with the result that instead of becoming the *poète maudit* as he might have wished he ended up sodden and invalid, an occasional victim of the most terrible fits. Before collapsing into this pitiful state he had married someone from the same part of town, a quite unattractive, naïve girl with no education at all. A few years later, it was she who had to run their business, which the entire family, including her drunk husband's mother, depended on, as well as take care of the house and look after him. The only help she had came from their only daughter, whom Prullàs had known since she was born, and who had been given responsibilities since the age of six. Now she was ten years old, she promised to turn out as capable and as unattractive as her mother.

"What new books d'you have?" Prullàs asked, gesturing towards the shelves. The woman shook her head sceptically. The summer months were pretty dead when it came to new titles, she said. But, she went on, she had just finished reading a book by Bernanos which had come out the previous winter, and which she had been very struck by. Prullàs nodded. "What about *The Long Shadow of the Cypress*, by that newcomer from Valladolid?" For strictly commercial reasons, and without being aware of it, the poet's wife over the years had become something of an expert in contemporary literature. Because she had no pretensions, Prullàs valued her judgment highly. He bought a novel by Pearl S. Buck for Martita and two copies of the latest Simenon novel.

Despite all this, Prullàs arrived early at Parellada. He sat at a table on the terrace in the shade of a tree and ordered a vermouth with olives. He began to read one of the novels he had bought, but Gaudet arrived before he could finish the first chapter. "It looks promising," he commented; "here, I bought you a copy."

He gave the spare copy to his friend, who thanked him without enthusiasm and put it in the left pocket of his bush jacket. He then started idly looking round at all the adjacent tables, which had begun filling up with locals. The dove man had set up his cart opposite the restaurant terrace. It was crowded with doves: either to distinguish them from ordinary pigeons, or to make them more striking, he had dyed the craws or the underside of the wings of some of them in bright colours. When released, they fluttered all round the dove man and, at a signal from him, settled on his arm or on a metal ring on top of the cart. Occasionally, to the delight of his spectators, a dove would disobey its master's orders and settle instead on his hat; it was all too obvious, however, that this mistake was not only planned, but carefully rehearsed. The whole thing was not much of a spectacle.

"Going back to yesterday evening . . . " Gaudet started to say. "Forget yesterday, for Heaven's sake!" Prullàs exclaimed, not giving him time to finish the sentence. Gaudet retreated into a hurt silence; he had obviously prepared a short speech of apology, which Prullàs' magnanimous attitude had deprived him of. Guessing at why his friend was so upset, the author said: "Oh, all right, if it makes you feel better to say you're sorry, go ahead, and then we can move on."

Gaudet responded with a vague gesture that appeared to mean: bah, let's not make it into a meaningless ritual. "But what's wrong with your health, Pepe?" Prullàs asked when he realised the matter was going no further. Gaudet frowned. "I don't know," he blurted out. "I haven't been feeling well for months, but I haven't the faintest idea what it is." Prullàs asked if he had seen a doctor. "Yes, I went to see my family doctor; he used his stethoscope, took my blood pressure, tapped me all over, and looked at some X-rays. But he couldn't find anything."

"So much the better," said Prullàs. "If it really is nothing, so much the better, as you say. But if that's so, why do I get these symptoms?" Gaudet sighed. "It might be just fatigue," Prullàs suggested, "or maybe you're worried about something; something you're not even aware of, but which is gnawing away at you. Nerves attack you where you least expect it, y'know." Gaudet gave a smile. "That's what the doctor told me." Then he added, without a pause, that for no apparent reason he couldn't sleep at night. "D'you think it could be just nerves?"

A dove which had been fluttering close by had landed on a nearby table and knocked over a mug of beer with its wing. The dove man came rushing to the scene of the crime, at a loss for words. I should make you pay for the drink! the aggrieved customer shouted at him. The dove man could only respond with a timid gesture that suggested: you are perfectly right, of course, but I'm a poor beggar, and all I can offer you are my apologies. The waiter wiped up the spilt liquid with a cloth and signalled to a colleague to bring another glass of beer as quickly as he could.

"You know me better than anyone, Carlos," Gaudet went on after the incident was over. "I've never been one to complain. But now, for some unknown reason, I feel completely depressed. I'm not interested in what I do; my work is a real burden. I feel as though I'm not doing anything useful, as if I've made all the wrong choices. My entire past seems useless and empty. And the idea that some illness or other might be causing this depression scares me. Not because it might be fatal. At worst, I'll die a few years sooner than I was due to go anyway, and that's not too serious. When I was born, nobody promised me I'd live to a ripe old age. Not even that I'd reach the age I am now. How many people do we know who haven't made it this far! What really frightens me, Carlos – and you're the only person I can say this to – is the thought of being ill, of having some chronic illness for ages, of being incapacitated. Because if the end doesn't come quickly, who will look after me?"

"Don't tempt fate," said Prullàs; "deal with problems when they crop up, don't worry so much about them beforehand. As for the emptiness of your life, what can I say? You're well-loved and admired in your profession; you've had lots of successes and will have many more. O.K., so you're going through a bad patch at the moment, and you're depressed. Don't take it to heart: it'll vanish just as suddenly as it appeared. Try to look on the bright side and don't let your dark thoughts get in the way of your work."

"Ah, so now finally you're showing the real reason you're concerned," the director laughed. "If I kick the bucket, who's going to put on the sketches for idiots you write? Don't worry, my friend, 'Arrivederci, pollo!' will be a triumph, and we'll celebrate it reaching a hundred performances right here. It's a good play. I know Kiki has been going on at you. Don't listen to any of her criticisms: she just wants us to pay more attention to her and less to the play. Of course, there are a few details that need looking at, like the stammering fool for example, but overall it works. It's just that the actors haven't found the right tone yet. Kiki herself isn't as relaxed as she usually is: D'you know if something's been bothering her lately?" "On the contrary," said Prullàs, "I know her well, and can tell you that everything is going fine for her at the moment." "Well then, don't give it a further thought," the director said, "you know what women are like." "No, I certainly don't. Do you, Pepe?"

*

Gaudet closely studied the menu the waiter had brought him. After a great deal of hesitation, he eventually ordered some boiled cod. Prullàs asked for Russian salad, stuffed aubergines, and kidneys tossed in oil. The sky had suddenly clouded over. The dappled patches of sunlight that had filtered through the trees onto their tablecloth had completely disappeared. "While we're on the subject of women," Prullàs went on, "who on earth is the girl who plays the maid in 'Arrivederci, pollo!'? I've never seen her before." "Me neither, she's a new recruit," the director said; "and I think exactly the same of her as you do, but what can I say?" "Is she someone's protégée?" Prullàs wanted to know. "She's been recommended," was Gaudet's laconic reply. "She's pretty and very keen." "She can't speak her lines to save her life," said Prullàs; "and she walks as if she has wooden legs." "You're wrong about the legs: there's nothing wooden about them, and perhaps that's the problem," Gaudet said. "But you shouldn't exaggerate: she's still shy, and her part isn't an easy one; it needs someone who's bright and cheerful, and you know how hard that is to achieve on stage. If you want, you could talk to her: she's no fool, and she's trying her best."

"No, no," said Prullàs, "I prefer to leave her in your capable hands. And anyway, I was planning to go to Masnou to spend a few days with my family, even though they're having a fine time without me: the children don't miss me, and although Martita hardly stops complaining, she's really enjoying it too. I'll only be gone a few days, as long as I can stand it."

The dove man was coming round the tables, holding out his dropping-stained hat. Prullàs tossed a banknote in and the street artist walked away, bowing his thanks. "Didn't you give him rather a lot?" asked Gaudet, who wasn't exactly famous for his generosity. "Who knows whether we won't end up like him some day!" Prullàs sighed.

When he arrived home, Sebastiana informed him that Señor Poveda had just left. He sat here waiting for the master, but since the master didn't come, he left, she said. Although the maid had opened the window as wide as possible, Poveda's peculiar smell still hung in the air of the hall. "I reckon that gentleman has a screw loose," she added. Sebastiana had a receding forehead, a flat nose and her eyebrows were a thick unbroken line; she had a rough, almost animal physique, but her eyes were lively and intelligent. "Did he say if he was coming back?" Prullàs asked.

"Yes, at two," said Sebastiana. "Will the master be eating in this evening?"

"I don't think so; I'm planning to go to Masnou this afternoon. For now, I'll be in the study; if Señor Poveda reappears, call me; if anyone else comes, tell them I've gone out."

The study was stifling. Prullàs pulled the blinds down, and left the balcony shutters half-open. Even though there wasn't a breath of air, it seemed cooler in the shade. He took off his jacket, tie and shoes, stretched out on the sofa, and immediately fell asleep. When he awoke, he had been so deeply asleep that at first he didn't recognise his own room. A pale orange light filtered through the blinds. He drank some fresh water from a jug hidden behind the curtain. Then he lifted the blinds and went out onto the balcony. The clouds were gone, and the sky was tinged with reddish streaks. Beneath the tree branches he could hear the intermittent rumble of traffic. He went back into the study, switched the lamps on, and phoned Mariquita Pons to tell her about his lunch with Gaudet.

"He seemed rather strange," he told her, "worried about his health and depressed; he looks out of sorts and he hardly eats." "His doctor said he couldn't find anything wrong with him," the actress replied. "That's no guarantee," Prullàs pointed out. "Doctors often get it wrong; it seems natural to me that he's nervous about it." "Don't defend him, Carlos, health isn't simply an illness waiting to be diagnosed." "That's all we need! The problem with Pepe is that he hasn't got over the death of his mother, Flavia. He was very attached to her, and now she's gone, he feels the whole world on top of him. He'll get over it, and he'll probably even come out of it stronger. Until then, just be patient."

Sebastiana put her head round the study door to announce that Señor Poveda had just arrived. "Tell him I'll be right there," Prullàs said, covering the mouthpiece of the phone with one hand, and then told Mariquita Pons, "I'm sorry, Kiki, I have to go, there's a visitor here to see me."

"And no ordinary visitor," she said, laughing: "Poveda." "Yes, how d'you know that?" "Because he's just been here, and he told me he'd called on you, and seeing you weren't in, he was thinking of going back." "Oh, that's too easy!" Prullàs said, and went on: "I'm off to Masnou for a few days, Kiki, I'll ring when I get back." "Say hello to Martita from me and enjoy yourself, but don't do anything silly."

The smell of the haircream that Poveda smeared on in huge quantities wafted through the curtain that separated the hall from the left side of the apartment, where the study was. "How are things, Poveda?" he asked.

With his weedy build, bony frame, wrinkled sallow skin and lifeless gaze, Poveda looked like a worn-out, bedraggled bird. Perhaps to counteract this shabby and lugubrious air, he sported a thin moustache designed to give himself a virile appearance; on closer inspection, however, it was clear the moustache was not real, but had been pencilled on in two lines above his upper lip.

27

"Ah, Don Carlos," he replied, "I'm still recovering from the shock – something incredible has just happened to me and which I must tell you about, if that's all right. What happened was that in response to an appointment, I presented myself at the home of a very distinguished lady who is well-known throughout the city, but whose identity discretion forbids me from mentioning . . . , well, no sooner had I arrived than the maid flung in my face that her mistress could not see me because she was indisposed, to which I replied I was sorry indeed to hear this, that there was nothing further from my mind than wanting to be a nuisance, and that I would gladly return the next day or whenever best suited her mistress. Hardly had I got these words out when a door was thrown open and the lady in question came in, face like a basilisk, and before I had time so much as to offer her my greetings she stared me up and down and boomed out: 'Tell me, my good man, how on earth do you dare go around wearing a tie like that? Take it off straightaway, Poveda, take it off!' I obeyed and undid my tie – what else could I do, Don Carlos? – and gave it to the aforementioned lady. To my complete amazement, she got hold of each end and yanked it so violently it snapped in two. Who could have suspected such physical strength in such a delicate creature? And that was that – what d'you make of it all?"

"No precautions are ever enough in the face of a temperamental woman, Poveda," was Prullàs' only comment. "That's as may be, but the truth is, I feel naked without my tie," Poveda replied.

"We'll see what we can do about that in a moment," Prullàs said, openly casting a worried look over at the wall clock. "For now, let's see what you've brought me."

Poveda bent down, and with obvious effort lifted a concertina bag up onto the side table and carefully placed it between a pair of candlesticks. While he was struggling with the clasps, he commented that the prices had gone up slightly. "I know it's not something that worries you, Don Carlos, but I feel obliged to tell you. You're a gentleman and I know you will react as such, but I've found myself in a number of situations I prefer not to recall, and with people who are well-known in this city of ours!"

As the case opened, a large, fat fly buzzed out. Without paying it the slightest attention, Poveda pushed one of the candlesticks aside and started to lay out the things he had brought: three cartons of Camels, four pairs of stockings, several packets of razor blades, two car headlight bulbs, half-a-dozen English pencils, a small bag of sugar, two tins of coffee and a roll of film.

"I think that's all you asked me for," Poveda said, proudly surveying his miniature bazaar. Then, rolling up his eyes as though something had brought an old fantasy back to his memory, he added that he had brought something else he was sure would interest him, even though it was a bit expensive. He had spent a lot of money on it, thinking he could sell it to the lady whose fury he had just felt the force of, he said, but after the tie incident he had not dared offer it her. Poveda gazed down in ecstasy at the tiny box nestling in the palm of his hand. "*Arpège*! the perfume of the most refined . . . and most seductive women!" he whispered while he flapped his other hand theatrically to try and drive the fly away from his face.

"I'll buy it, Poveda, so you can spare me the speech," Prullàs said. When the transactions were over, he left Poveda on his own in the room, went to his own wardrobe, found a tie and brought it out to him. "Here, keep it, Poveda, I never wear it."

After much protestation, Poveda eventually accepted the gift. Then he said he had composed a satirical ballad "to that French woman". "You'll die laughing, Don Carlos, shall I recite it?" Prullàs dissuaded him. "I'm in a hurry," he said.

After the other had gone, Prullàs put everything he had brought into the study cupboard, with the exception of the stockings and a carton of cigarettes. These he put into a briefcase, along with the Simenon novel he had bought that morning. He slipped the perfume bottle into his pocket, added a wad of notes he had removed from the wall safe, told Sebastiana he was going, and left the apartment.

7

The caretaker stuck his head round the door between the front desk and his living quarters. "Shall I get your car out for you, Don Carlos?" "Yes, do, and put this case on the back seat, would you, Basilio. I'll be back in five minutes."

In a nearby store Prullàs bought two toy pistols and two fishing rods; at the news-stand he picked up *Billiken, Purk el hombre de piedra, Lecturas* and *Triunfo*. When he got back, the caretaker had parked the huge Studebaker outside the building and was flicking at the paintwork with a red duster. A starveling woman with a woebegone expression on her face came up to the two men and said: "I'm anaemic and have to sleep on the street." Prullàs gave her a couple of pesetas and got into the car.

By the time he was clear of the city, night had fallen. There was a line of slow, foul-smelling trucks that gradually diminished as he got beyond the industrial zone. He stopped at a highway petrol station and filled the car up, taking advantage of the halt to remove his jacket and tie and undo the top button of his shirt. When he set off again, he had to be extremely careful not to crash into donkey carts whose only warning lights were a tiny lantern hung on the back axle that gave off a dull red glow like an ember. As he came over the brow of a hill, the climate and the landscape both underwent a sudden change:

the smell of the sea was wafted into the car by a fresh, light breeze; the sound of waves breaking irregularly on the shore overlaid the steady hum of the car engine, and the horizon was dotted with lights from the fishing boats working off the coast. The highway ran between two lines of ancient, massive trees whose upper branches formed a tunnel of foliage.

Shortly before Masnou, Prullàs had to stop at a roadblock. A man dressed in farm clothes checked his papers by the light of a candle. He was carrying an old musket slung over his shoulder. Two other armed men watched from a nearby embankment.

It was past midnight by the time he pulled the car up outside the back door to the house. The only street lighting came from a single bulb dangling ineffectually from the top of a wooden post. It was so dark he was able to contemplate the myriad stars in a moonless sky. The silence of the sleeping village was disturbed only by the distant roar of the sea. He went in by the back door and found himself in a large, high-ceilinged shed that was both dark and damp. The feeble light from outside allowed him to make out the dim outlines of several bicycles, a table-tennis table, a garden bench, and a small dinghy propped on two trestles. He groped his way out of the shed and up the path that led through the vegetable patch to the house. The smell of hens and rabbits drifted over from their hutches. As he got into the garden proper, he could hear voices and female laughter. He found his wife sitting on the terrace with some-one he could not recall ever having seen before. On the marble table-top he could see coffee cups and two folded fans, which the cool of the night had made unnecessary.

"What a fright you gave us!" Martita complained; "when we heard footsteps we thought it must be a burglar."

Prullàs slipped on the jacket he had been carrying over his shoulder. He did not give his wife a kiss, feeling embarrassed at the presence of the unknown woman.

"Or a murderer," this intruder said. Then, noting how strangely Prullàs was looking at her, she laughed and added: "I'm Marichuli Mercadal," before Martita even had time to introduce her. She was a redhead, and the yellow light from the lamp that Prullàs' father-in-law had installed on the terrace, on the theory that its violent colour would drive away mosquitos and moths, gave the strands of her hair fiery gleams. Prullàs bent and kissed her hand.

"The fact is, we didn't expect you today. The children and my parents went to bed hours ago." Her explanation was hardly necessary: apart from the yellow light on the terrace, the rest of the house was in complete darkness, and all the shutters were closed. There was something oppressive about its total peace and calm, Prullàs thought. "And I'm only up because of Marichuli."

"I came in the early evening for a chat, but Martita insisted I stay to dinner; after that there was no stopping us . . . and as you can see, if you hadn't appeared, we'd have been here until cockcrow," Marichuli Mercadal said. She talked in a relaxed way, without the aggressive note of someone trying to hide a natural shyness.

"I would have been here earlier, but as usual, things got complicated," Prullàs said. "And then I had some fun with the militiamen on the way. They were bored, so one illiterate fellow took it into his head to read my papers from back to front. But anyway, don't let my presence disturb you: carry on talking, I'll go to bed." Martita asked if he had had supper, and he replied that he wasn't hungry. The visitor got to her feet and picked up her fan. "It's time for me to go to bed as well," she said. "No-one will be able to wake me tomorrow otherwise. Not that I have anything to do anyway," she added with a laugh. She took a canvas bag from under the chair, stuffed the fan in it, kissed Martita on both cheeks, and held out her hand to Prullàs. "A pleasure to meet you. I'll take you home," he said. "There's no point, I live practically next door," she protested. Prullàs insisted: "It's a very dark night, and the streets are deserted." "What d'you think might happen to me?" she asked. "Nothing, and I don't want anything to, that's why I'm going with you," he replied. "I'll be right back," he said to his wife. "I'll go on up to bed," Martita said; "if you're not quick, I'll be sleeping like a log. There's some food in the refrigerator, if you feel like a bite."

"I left the car in the back street in order not to disturb anyone opening the garage," Prullàs said; "I'll bring it round to the front." "There's no point," Marichuli Mercadal said, "I really do live close by: if you're determined to come with me, let's walk."

"You're very tanned," Prullàs said after they had walked a while in silence; "I thought the sun was supposed to be bad for redheads, but I can see that's not always the case."

"It's usually true," she replied. "Redheads normally have freckles and fair skin, and are very sensitive to the sun. But I'm an exception, perhaps because in spite of the doctors' warnings, I've always been out in the sun a lot. At any rate, this is the natural colour of my hair; I'm only saying that if your remark implied some kind of doubt on that score," she added, coming to a halt in front of an impressive iron gate.

"Oh no, I only said it because I'm curious about you," Prullàs replied. The gate hinges creaked. "D'you live all alone in this beach-hut, then?" he asked as the two of them walked through a garden, at the far end of which could be dimly made out the shape of a huge four-storey house complete with mansard windows and a slate roof. "No; there are the servants, our daughter, and her nanny," she replied, "and every once in a blue moon, my husband."

Prullàs slowed his steps. Even in the darkness, an air of

neglect was evident in the garden. "Am I to conclude your husband doesn't look after you?" he said. "Yes." "And you miss him?" "Sometimes I do, sometimes I don't."

"Marichuli, I reckon you're a flirt," Prullàs said on an impulse.

She stopped in her tracks. "How dare you say such a thing to me, Señor Prullàs?" He made no reply, but put his arms round her waist. "Please, Carlos, I'm a decent woman," she whispered. "Decent but passionate," he replied. "Oh, yes!" she sighed, pulling him to her with wild abandon.

My God, the things that happen to me, Prullàs thought to himself on the way back. His wife was waiting for him in bed, still awake. "The coffee must have woken me up," she said; "are you sure you don't want anything to eat?" Prullàs said he didn't. He had had a very busy day, a difficult journey, it was late, and he was exhausted. "Come here, I've missed you," she said, switching off the light.

"And I missed you," Prullàs said, switching the light on again. In the dark, he found himself troubled by images of Marichuli Mercadal leaning back on her garden seat, her hair tousled and her dark skin gleaming with perspiration.

"What d'you make of Marichuli Mercadal?" Martita suddenly asked. There seemed to be no hidden intention behind her question.

"Nothing in particular," Prullàs replied. "She seems like a pleasant, cheerful sort, easy on the eye; ah, and she lives in a very splendid house. What does her husband do?" And, without waiting for a reply, he added confidentially: "I don't think he should leave her on her own for so long, there are lots of rogues around." "You, to start with!" Martita said with a laugh. "Did she tell you that her husband left her on her own?" "Not in so many words, but it's what I gathered from our conversation. Am I wrong?"

"I guess not. To tell you the truth, I hardly know her. We've become good friends, but we haven't had the time yet to tell each other our life stories in any detail. But she does go everywhere on her own. And those low-cut dresses of hers certainly attract the looks. At any rate, her husband is much older than she is. He's an eminent surgeon, apparently; whenever he's not in the operating theatre, he's off at a medical conference somewhere or other. He travels a lot and is in great demand; so his wife has to look after herself."

"Why doesn't she go with him?"

"Because of their daughter," replied Martita. "According to Marichuli, she has a heart problem; she was born with a weak heart or something. They've taken her to all the best specialists, who've all said the same thing: that they can try to operate when she's older, but that at the moment there's nothing to be done. They've also been told that she may not live that long anyway, and could die before she reaches twelve. It's so tragic."

"How old is she now?"

"Six or seven. She's become great friends with our children. Their beach tent is next to ours, so from the first day here the children were playing together as if they'd known each other all their lives: you know how kids are. Alicia is very gentle and delicate, perhaps because of her illness; and that makes the situation even worse, if possible." Martita's eyes were glistening with tears of pity. "Let's talk about something else, shall we? Why don't you come to bed? You say you're exhausted, but you've been standing to attention there for about half an hour now."

"I was listening to what you were telling me. Would you like me to be one of those husbands who gargles while his wife is talking?" "What husbands are those?" Martita wanted to know. Prullàs finished undressing and switched off the light again. "I don't know, most of them." "And how would you know what most husbands do in their bedrooms?" she asked again: "D'you hide under their beds and spy on them?" "No, but I've seen it at the pictures." "Bah, what you see in films is nonsense, and d'you want to know why? Because the stories are written by liars and cheats like you. Anyway, come and give me a hug, and stop waving that thing at me like that."

8

As soon as they had finished breakfast, Martita and the children set off for the beach. "Why don't you come with us, papa?" "What's the hurry, I'll see you there later; if I go now I'll only get sunstroke." Left on his own, he found the Simenon novel in his bag, and suddenly remembered the bottle of French perfume Poveda had sold him, which he had brought to give Martita. He searched for it in the bag, then in his jacket pockets, and finally looked inside the car in case it had fallen out there during the journey, but without luck. It'll turn up, he thought; and if it doesn't, that's too bad. He took a deckchair out under the pine trees and sat reading, undisturbed apart from the arrival of his in-laws, who dropped in after ten o'clock Mass. They greeted Prullàs affectionately and asked him how things were in Barcelona. "Pretty much as usual: the anarchists have burnt down another three or four convents."

His mother-in-law crossed herself. "You don't change, do you?" she protested. "You know I don't find that joke at all funny, yet you're always repeating it," she said condescendingly. Martita's father chuckled to himself. He had always had a soft spot for Prullàs. Martita was an only child, and as such was heir to his fortune; this had always made the question of the person she married of the utmost importance to him: the greatest fear of his life had been dowry-hunters. And yet Prullàs, who by definition was bound to represent what he most feared, had incomprehensibly won him over right from the start. Given the circumstances, the wedding ceremony was held with the greatest simplicity in San Sebastián. Almost as soon as the religious part was over, the old man had whispered in his new son-in-law's ear: "You rascal, you're getting your hands on a tasty morsel there." This was said in a confidential, almost conspiratorial tone, as if only the two of them were aware of the auction that had been taking place at the altar. Prullàs never knew, and never tried to find out, whether by "tasty morsel" his father-in-law had been referring to Martita's personal charms or to the inheritance he was acquiring rights to thanks to their union. The previous evening, during his somewhat gloomy stag night, a friend of his had expressed the same idea in the following crude terms: "Lucky bastard, you're using one key to open two doors." Well aware that the advantages he was getting out of his marriage with Martita could cast doubts on the sincerity of his feelings for her, Prullàs had merely replied with a cold smile to this obscene suggestion; and he had responded in a similar way to his new father-in-law's remark the next day with a cautious laugh. To Martita's father, Prullàs was a playwright with an uncertain future and no family or fortune; known to live a chaotic life and to be a womaniser: the very image, in short, of an addle-brained wastrel. And yet somewhere inside himself, the older man had decided that this upstart was the man to make his daughter happy, and that was enough. Deep down, he was relieved his son-in-law was not going to continue his business and therefore become a possible rival. Even though he enjoyed complaining about how tired he was after so many years at the head of the firm and pretended to hope that someone would soon relieve him of all the burdens and responsibilities he had to bear, in fact he would have fought tooth and nail to defend every inch of his territory against anyone trying to take away even the least of his powers. But nor did he want to see the fruits of the labours of several generations, including his own, vanish into thin air at his death, and so he was consoled by the thought that when the time came, in the dim and distant future, his grandsons would be there to carry on for him. And it was thanks to Prullàs that he could face the future with such confidence and peace of mind. With the passing of the years, and against all expectations, this marriage that gossips had dismissed as a mistake and as detrimental to Martita's family and destined for a disastrous end was turning out better than if he himself had planned it down to the last detail. "Aren't you going down to the beach?" he asked. "No, I'd like to finish this book first," Prullàs replied; "what about you?" "Oh no, it's too hot and noisy," they replied. To their mind, the new fashion for seaside holidays had ruined what had once been quiet and picturesque spots. Prullàs finished his book and set off down to the beach.

The sun's rays fell vertically onto the sand, and the air seemed soaked in a milky glare of light. Children's shouts and the cries from gulls drowned out the sound of the waves. "Aren't you going in for a swim, Señor Prullàs?" a cheerful young voice said at his back. Turning round, he saw Marichuli Mercadal wrapped in a pastel-blue bathrobe. She was wearing her mane of hair up, covered in a flowery headscarf. "I had no idea last night how beautiful you would look in the sunlight," he said, kissing her hand. "Who are you looking for?" "For my family," he said; "Martita has my swimming costume and the key to our cabin." "She must be in your tent," Marichuli suggested. "That's the problem, I've no idea which one it is; they all look the same to me," Prullàs said, waving towards the rows of windscreens. "I'd better go with you," Marichuli suggested; "I wouldn't want you to end up in the wrong one and get mixed up with another woman; your tent and mine are next to each other." And then without a pause, she added: "Martita is wonderful, don't do anything to upset her." "And how do you suggest I do that?" Prullàs asked. "For a start, you could be more careful," she said, taking the *Arpège* bottle out of her bathrobe pocket. "The gardener found it this morning by the bench next to our swimming pool: how on earth can it have got there?" "I haven't the faintest idea. Perhaps the gardener put it there himself to incriminate an innocent man; they're not to be trusted, you know." "Was it a present for Martita?" Marichuli wanted to know. "Keep it if you like the perfume," he said. Marichuli came to an indignant halt. "Ah, no, I've no intention of keeping anything that belongs by right to Martita!" she said, emphasising each word. "How can such an obnoxious suggestion come from someone who's regarded as so intelligent and refined, from such a man of the world? Is this an example of the ingenuity which, according to the critics, is so much in evidence in your plays?" He stared at her without replying, and walked on across the beach. "So there'll be no repeat of last night?" was all he finally said. "Whenever you like, I'm free and at your disposal at all times," she replied with a smile that sought to be both timid and seductive, but which struck Prullàs as nothing short of crazy.

"Well, well, you go off at night together, and here you come the next day still together, what am I to think!" Martita exclaimed. "I caught him up to no good and brought him to you," Marichuli said. "The hot weather and sheer idleness can lead to a relaxation in manners and to concupiscence; at least, that's what the good father told us in his sermon today." "I didn't know today was a Holy Day of Obligation," Prullàs said. "It isn't," Marichuli explained, "but I go to Mass every day." "I didn't realise you were so religious," Martita said. "I wasn't until we learnt about our daughter," she replied. "Alicia," she said, turning to Prullàs, "has a congenital heart condition." "I know, Martita already told me, I'm really sorry," he said. Martita handed him his swimming costume and a large rusty key hanging from a wooden hoop. The number 14 was written on it. The cabin was full of Martita's and the children's clothes. How much simpler it would be just to come down to the beach in my costume like Marichuli Mercadal, he thought. When he got back to the beach tent, he found it had been invaded by children: his two sons, a skinny, ungainly boy who he remembered having seen in previous summers, and a dark-haired girl who he took to be Marichuli's sick daughter. She's not at all like her mother, except for the look in her eye, he thought. Marichuli was watching them from some distance away on a deckchair set up under her own tent. She had taken off her bathrobe and her scanty swimsuit attracted admiring glances. Prullàs winked at her; she stuck her tongue out in response. "Carlos, will you help me convince this tribe of savages?" Martita called out above a chorus of complaining children. "What do the tribe of savages have to be convinced of?" There was to be an open-air film show that night in the garden of the Social Club, and they all wanted to go, but Martita was against the idea: she was being a spoilsport, the children claimed. "What film are they showing," Prullàs wanted to know before pronouncing his verdict. "A musical comedy," Martita said. "And what's wrong with the children seeing it?" Martita's voice became serious: the film probably wasn't suitable for children; it was out in the open and the nights were damp, which meant they ran the risk of catching coughs or a cold; and they would be staying up too late. "Well, those don't seem like very good reasons to me," Prullàs said. "Viva papa!" the children shouted. "A fine ally you turned out to be," Martita said, shrugging her shoulders. "Papa, can Alicia come too?" his eldest son asked. Prullàs looked at her closely: nothing in her appearance or her attitude showed weakness or any other symptom of being ill; she seemed delicate but healthy, and despite obviously living surrounded by lots of loving attention, she didn't give the impression of being spoilt or moody. "You'd have to ask her mother," he said. So the children swarmed off to Marichuli Mercadal's tent, and won her consent without much difficulty. "But if you get tired or it gets cold, we'll go home and you won't say a word," she warned.

With the matter settled, she came to join the two of them. "Ow! the sand is burning hot," she squealed. "And how white you look in your bathing costume, Señor Prullàs!" "What, you're not on first name terms?" Martita exclaimed. "I thought you might have got to know each other a little better last night." Prullàs looked nervously at the two women, but both of them appeared quite calm and natural. "At night everyone looks the same," Marichuli said jokingly; "but in the daytime I'm rather in awe of him." She's a cool customer, Prullàs thought admiringly. "Well, it seems we've all agreed to go to the cinema this evening," Martita said. "What, they aren't going on their own?" asked Prullàs. "No way!" the two women exclaimed with one voice. "And since you're the one to blame, you are responsible for their physical and moral welfare. The local parish priest is always warning us of the dangers of the cinema," Marichuli said. "And what does your parish priest say about your bathing suit?" Prullàs blurted out. "Don't be so rude, Carlos," Martita said, horrified. Marichuli laughed out loud, with no offence taken. "I'm not showing anything that shouldn't be seen," she said. "I hate musicals," he said. "I think Xavier Cugat is in this one," Martita suggested. "All the more reason," he said. Marichuli jumped up. "I'm going in," she said, "who's coming with me?" Martita had laid out her towel and was busy applying sun cream to her neck and shoulders. "You two go; I want to see if I can get a bit of a tan." "What about you, Mr Nightbird?" Marichuli said to Prullàs, "are you coming or staying put?"

He woke from his siesta bathed in a light that the gauze of the mosquito net turned into a golden dust. The bed next to his was unmade and empty. He splashed his face and went out onto the terrace; his children were in the summerhouse absorbed in a game of chess. "Have you seen your mother?" he asked them. "I think she's gone to see if the hens have laid," the elder one said, without lifting his eyes from the board. To judge by the position of the pieces, both of them were employing somewhat unorthodox tactics.

Two brilliantly-coloured dragonflies, one red and one blue, were zigzagging over the swimming pool; at moments, they hung suspended in the air, poised over the water as though time itself were standing still; then suddenly, passing from immobility to rapid movement without a transition, they darted off in a new direction. Prullàs walked round several rows of lettuces, melons and cabbages, and came to a halt by a wooden shack. Peering through a crack, he could see Martita crouching down, searching for eggs amid the straw; in that position, her blouse hung open to show a shadowy cleavage whose whiteness contrasted sharply with the smooth tan of her arms and neck. The hens were up on their perches, looking down with apparent indifference at the outrage they were suffering. Prullàs opened the corrugated iron door, shut it quickly behind him, and silently threw himself on Martita. They collided so violently two eggs fell from her basket and smashed on the ground. "Have you gone crazy?" she exploded. Terrified, the hens began squawking and beating their wings, raising a cloud of dust, feathers and bits of straw. "Would you rather I use the hens for what I'm trying to do to you?" he joked. Martita struggled without much conviction. "Carlos, I forbid you to make love in the henhouse, it's dirty and it's humiliating." "No use trying to scream, wench, no-one can hear you from in here," Prullàs growled. "Heavens above," Martita giggled.

That night, Marichuli Mercadal appeared in the Social Club with her husband. "What a surprise!" Martita said; "Marichuli convinced us you wouldn't dream of coming." "I know, but I've abandoned all my principles to see Xavier Cugat," Doctor Mercadal replied. He was a tall, thin man with striking features and a relaxed, festive expression; he was grey-haired and wore rimless glasses and a bow tie. His wife could not hide the sense of satisfaction it gave her to be seen in public on the arm of such a mature and distinguished gentleman. Doctor Mercadal put down the three folding chairs he was carrying to kiss Martita's hand and shake Prullàs'. With his other hand, he was holding on tightly to his daughter, doubtless fearing he might lose her in the crowd. His fears were groundless, though, because everyone there were people they knew, all of them summer holidaymakers who had brought their own chairs to the evening's cinema performance. Alicia also seemed happy to be with her father, whom she no doubt saw only rarely; she was smiling and showing the gap where she had recently lost two of her milk teeth. The screen was a white sheet slung between two posts at the far end of the garden. Four lemon trees prevented most of the audience from getting a full view of it. A loudspeaker hung from one of them. When the film began, the sound from this speaker was so poor that the dialogue was incomprehensible, and on several occasions the soundtrack was out of synch with the images. Whenever that happened, some members of the audience protested, whistling and shouting for the organisers to do something; but the rest just laughed and applauded. "What d'you say if we escape to the bar?" Doctor Mercadal suggested to Prullàs some twenty minutes into the film. "Sounds like a good idea," Prullàs said.

"Two whiskies," the doctor asked the barman Joaquín, who was serving drinks oblivious to all the noise from the garden. "What d'you make of my wife?" he suddenly asked Prullàs. "I only met her last night," Prullàs replied, not knowing what to think. "I'm sorry for asking you your opinion point-blank," the eminent surgeon said; "of course, I wasn't expecting you to say anything more than you did – or perhaps I was. We always hope we'll get revealing answers to our questions, don't you think? My wife and I have seen several of your comedies," he added. "Both of us are great fans of yours. I'm sure she didn't tell you, because she's quite shy, even though she doesn't seem so; she finds it hard to confide in strangers: she's reserved, rather cautious . . . although I know she can be flirtatious, but don't let that fool you. And please don't get me wrong: I was not in any way suggesting you had formed a wrong or immodest idea of her. On the contrary, I know for a fact it's not so: Marichuli told me you were so good as to walk her home last night, and that you behaved like a real gentleman. Between the two of us – between myself and Marichuli I mean – we have no secrets. What was I saying? Ah, yes, that we had seen several of your plays and that we were great admirers of yours. Another whisky? Waiter, two more whiskies, please. D'you smoke? Smoking is good for the health: it calms the nerves and helps control blood pressure. I even smoke in the operating theatre. What was I saying? Ah, yes, that I admire your skill, but there's more to it than that. I also admire your psychological insight, the way you have of drawing characters from real life. And everything seems so light and casual, as it should be, without any pomposity. As you can see, I'm an observant spectator. That's why I took the chance of asking you about my wife in such a direct way just now, because I know you're someone who penetrates, as I said, and I thought you might have been trying out your talent on her. I'm sure you hate hypocrisy: that's obvious from your

44

plays. I feel the same. Sometimes I'm in the middle of an operation and I think: so much hypocrisy and all for this? I have a liver in my hands, and I can't get the thought out of my mind. And you're like me in that – correct me if I'm wrong. And so is my wife, because I've taken it upon myself to instil these ideas in her, as I have with my daughter, although in her case they're not going to be of much use, I'm afraid." He tossed down his second whisky, signalled to the waiter to fill his glass again, and stared at Prullàs with a vacant expression. "Unfortunately, the demands of my profession mean I cannot devote as much time as I would like to my wife and daughter, but that doesn't mean I don't worry about their well-being or their education, even from afar, because I'm much older than they are, and so have a lot more experience. As you may know, there are illnesses which are far more serious when they're developing than when they've come out into the open; however much the symptoms might shock us or distress the patient, in fact they are a release. There are psychological complexes which function in the same way. They can't be operated on, but they are real illnesses of the soul. The difference lies in the fact that they can't kill the soul, which is immortal, but they can kill the body. I'm afraid for Marichuli: not for her health, which is excellent, but whether or not she will survive. There are worrying precedents in her family. Her parents committed suicide; together, and in dramatic circumstances. I prefer not to say any more for the moment. But I am afraid for Marichuli, as I say; and my daughter is also ill; her case is different, but just as serious, just as serious. It's my duty to look after them both, but as you can appreciate, that's no easy task. Of course, I don't expect any solution from you, any advice or even any real reply; after all, I'm the doctor. I just wanted to talk to someone, and since I've seen your plays and know Marichuli thinks highly of you, I thought you might

45

at least be a sympathetic listener. But perhaps you're thinking I'm off my head, and you could be right. Can you hear Xavier Cugat, his violin, his orchestra, those rhythms of his? Perhaps he's off his head too, but that doesn't mean he can renege on his obligations as a human being, and nor can I. I love my wife and daughter with all my heart. The problem is that sometimes fate puts us in a position where neither our feelings nor our knowledge and experience are of any use to us."

10

"Well, the children had a wonderful time, and that's the main thing," Martita said. At that precise moment, the pendulum clock in the living-room struck two in the morning. "Just so long as they didn't catch the whooping cough," said Marichuli Mercadal. Her husband gave her a worried look. "Why d'you say that? Why did you mention whooping cough? Have there been any recent cases of whooping cough in the village?" "No; none at least that I've heard of," Martita soothed him. "This is a beautiful house," she went on immediately, "and it's decorated with exquisite taste; was it like this when you bought it?" "We didn't buy it, we're renting it," the doctor replied. "Right up to the last minute, we couldn't decide between the mountains and the seaside. Of course, it's much better for health in the mountains; the sea air is not good for you, it puts people on edge, and that's not to mention the harmful effects of the sun's rays on the skin; but still, here we are," he concluded, with a grin towards his wife which implied she was entirely responsible for the final decision, as he was always inclined to let her have her way. "Until three or four years ago, the house belonged to a foreign couple," Marichuli went on to explain as soon as her husband had finished speaking; "they bought and furnished it; perhaps that's why nearly everything in the house comes from outside Spain: the piano, clocks, lamps, and all the crockery too – the dinner service and the pots and pans. Apparently, these foreigners had intended to live here for the rest of their lives, but something must have happened to change their plans, because, as I said, about three or four years ago they stopped coming, and nobody ever found out why. They were middle-aged, very refined and well-educated, but not very sociable, as I understand it." "Ah, I know who you mean," Martita interrupted her. "I remember them very well from previous years. Every evening at sunset you used to see them strolling arm in arm, up and down the main street. They never talked to anyone, not even each other; they were so self-absorbed they looked like two blind people as they walked along." "At the end of April they put the house up for sale," Doctor Mercadal said, taking up the thread of the story again after Martita's interruption, "and a real-estate firm bought it, mostly for the land. Apparently these old mansions need a lot of work to maintain them, and a number of servants it's impossible to find these days; that's why no-one is interested in them any more. The company that bought it wanted to pull the house down and put up a block of flats in its place, but either they're in no hurry to start the project, or they don't have the funds necessary for such a big job, so for this season at least they decided to get some return on their investment by renting the house out. It was a lucky coincidence," he added, "because that was exactly the time we were looking for a house. But I thought you had already been here," he concluded. "No," his wife explained; "Martita has never been, and Carlos didn't come in when he brought me back last night; we only spent a few minutes chatting on the garden bench." "You're not much of a hostess!" Doctor Mercadal exclaimed.

*

47

When he learnt that the surgeon was to stay on indefinitely in the village, Prullàs decided to return to Barcelona.

"I thought you were going to stay until the village fiesta," Martita said when he told her of his plans. Her voice sounded sad, but there was no sense of reproach or annoyance in her words. "I know you get bored here, but I thought this time you were getting on well with the Mercadals." Lying back, Prullàs could barely make out Martita's silhouette by the dim light of the bedside oil lamp as she sat up in her bed. Towards the end of that spring, Martita had suddenly had a haircut in a French style which had not been very popular even in that country. Prullàs himself had poked fun at her when she came back from the hairdresser's, already somewhat taken aback at her own daring. "You look like a Benedictine monk," he told her. But now, the gauze of the mosquito net lent Martita's bare neck and shoulders a precious alabaster nakedness.

"I'll be back as soon as possible," Prullàs sighed, "but I've got to return to Barcelona now." "What's the matter? Is there a problem with the play?" Martita wanted to know. "You could say that; I'm a bit worried about Gaudet's health." "Ah, that loathsome fellow," said Martita; "I don't know how you put up with him!" "Don't say that," Prullàs replied. "Gaudet is . . . a bit special, but he's a good sort." And when this remark met only stubborn silence, he at once added: "D'you know I hadn't realised before tonight just how brown you are? Go on, make room for me in your bed." "Oh no," Martita exclaimed, hiding her head under the sheet.

Prullàs' efforts to make Gaudet and Martita get on with each other had always failed: they hated one another, and made no bones about it. Gaudet had been against Prullàs' marriage from the start. He had tried by every means to persuade his friend he was making a big mistake: Martita was a rich woman and her wealth would inevitably corrupt him, he had prophesied. "And if you think that kind of thing only happens to other people, you've already taken the first step towards your downfall," he added. Prullàs had laughed to himself at hearing such a warning from someone who had earned a well-founded reputation as a miser. Perhaps what Gaudet had said had reached Martita's ears, or perhaps she disliked him for other reasons.

Prullàs and Gaudet had been friends since childhood, when chance threw them together not only in the same religious school but in the same classroom. The whim of one of the priests meant they shared a desk for a whole year, possibly out of a malicious desire to mortify poor Gaudet, because there could not have been two more contrasting pupils in the entire school. Even in his youth, Prullàs was attractive, socially at ease and a live wire. He dressed elegantly and had an innate gift for people that had won him the sympathy not only of his fellow students but of the teachers too. Gaudet, on the other hand, was ugly and bony; he was always badly dressed in old, worn clothes, and always looked uncomfortable, shy and taciturn. The contrast between the two pupils, which proximity only served to emphasise, could not have been more unfavourable to Gaudet. It was made even worse by his mannered gestures and way of speaking, influenced perhaps by his mother, who in those days still struck the pose of a diva and put on a fake, exasperating South American accent. These peculiarities, together with the rumours about being born out of wedlock and the secret sexual habits attributed to him, made him the butt of all kinds of jokes and taunts. Insufficiently robust to cope with this general hostility, timid by nature and deeply ashamed of his origins and his own way of being, Gaudet tried in vain to go unnoticed, particularly at break-time, when his schoolmates' antipathy showed itself in humiliating words and deeds, some of them extremely violent physical attacks, which took place under the vague, indulgent gaze of priests, who,

49

deep down, felt even stronger and more virulent contempt for this wretched boy than his companions did. This was how things stood when one day, taking advantage of their teacher's momentary distraction, Prullàs whispered in his desk companion's ear: "Why d'you let them trample on you like that? Fight back." "I can't," Gaudet whispered; "there's too many of them, and I don't have the strength or the courage to take them all on; I couldn't even face up to one of them." Prullàs thought for a minute: the possibility that there might be no remedy against such abuses was new to him. "Tell your father and get him to come to talk to the priests," he suggested. "That's no good: the priests are on their side, and anyway, I don't have a father." "What about your mother?" "Yes, I have a mother, but I couldn't say anything to her: she would be mortified. She makes huge sacrifices to send me to a fee-paying school because she thinks I'll get a good education here and will meet people who could be useful to me; she tells me as much every day, so how can I tell her that so far I haven't learnt a thing, and that the only people I've met are hypocritical, cowardly brutes?" Prullàs smiled, and Gaudet blushed to the roots of his hair. "I shouldn't have said anything to you," he said quickly. "Please, don't repeat any of it," he begged. "Don't worry," Prullàs said, "I'm no stool-pigeon; but I think you're exaggerating a bit: some of the boys are cretins, but not all of them. And if you look at it another way, you could say you bring it on yourself: look at you, your hair, your nails, the way you dress . . . you've even got your fly undone, so how d'you expect there not to be stories about you?" Gaudet buttoned up his trousers and smiled slyly. "Perhaps they're not all just stories," he murmured.

These shared confidences had been the start of a friendship which over time had become important for both of them, but whose immediate consequence had been that Prullàs offered

Gaudet protection in his difficult situation and had helped make his schooldays more bearable. As it was, the director was to say many years later, only half-jokingly, I acquired a debt of gratitude that will be with me for the rest of my life. "Nonsense, Pepe," Prullàs retorted, "I've never thought of our friendship like an accountant." "Ah yes, magnanimity is the first right of the creditor, and having to put up with it is the first duty of the debtor." "Why are you so resentful, Pepe?" "On the contrary, Carlos, you're the one who can't stand the sight of gratitude," the other replied, "it's the most oppressive feeling, and the most uncomfortable position to be in. But what can we do? It's all due to an artificial, unjust situation that distorted our relation from the start, although it's of no importance now. D'you remember how at school those bullies used to attack me, and you sprang to my defence? By lending me help, your dignity came out of it reinforced, whereas mine suffered all the more. You weren't to blame, of course, although I always suspected you acted more out of vanity than anything else; but be that as it may, the situation was so humiliating, and the difference in our strengths was so great, that we became winner and loser long before the outcome of the battle was decided. Even if I escaped unscathed from some incident, it was obvious I was the one who had been defeated. But what does all that matter? We've more than made up for our losses since."

Prullàs never took these bitter recriminations seriously. He was used to them: Gaudet had a difficult personality, and the years had only served to accentuate his awkward traits rather than smoothing them out.

11

"Señor Gaudet has telephoned several times asking for the master and he told me to tell you that you should call him as soon as you got back, that it was urgent," Sebastiana said. "Apart from those messages, no-one has rung or been here," she added. "That's odd," Prullàs said. "Did he say what it was about?" "No, master; he only said to call, and not to go round to the theatre before you had spoken to him."

Ah, Prullàs thought, that's even more disturbing. He shut himself in his study and called Gaudet's house; when nobody answered, he dialled Mariquita Pons, again without success. He rang the bell, and when Sebastiana appeared instructed her to run the bath and bring him a beer: the heat and his anxiety at the telephone messages had made him thirsty. While Sebastiana was carrying out his instructions, he decided to phone the theatre. "Is that you, Bonifaci?" he asked of the voice which answered his call. "Yes, Don Carlos, what can I do for you?" the caretaker replied. He's not too bright, thought Prullàs, but he recognised my voice straightaway; it just goes to show everyone has their good points. He asked out loud: "Bonifaci, have you by any chance seen Señor Gaudet?" "Yes, Don Carlos, as I do every day, and not by chance but because he's here, in the theatre, rehearsing the play you yourself have written, which is sure to be a great success. Would you like me to go and find him?" Prullàs gave a sigh of relief. "Don't bother him now, Bonifaci," he said. "Just tell him to call me when the rehearsal's over; at my place, I won't move from here." As he was hanging up, Sebastiana came into the study carrying a tray with a small bottle of beer, a glass and a napkin. "Your bath is ready," she announced, leaving the tray on the table. Through the open balcony window the tinny sounds of a barrel organ could be heard. Prullàs took the beer with him into the bathroom, but the combination of hot water and cold beer didn't give him the pleasure he had anticipated. As he was drying himself, Sebastiana tapped on the bathroom door. "Señor Gaudet on the phone," she said. "Tell him I'll be right there, and not to hang up."

To avoid leaving the bathroom wrapped in a towel, he took one of Martita's bathrobes from a china knob. Besides exposing most of his calves, the robe was pink, and had extravagant frills at the neck and wrists. When she saw him, the maid burst out laughing. "I'll deal with you later!" Prullàs said, quickly locking himself in the study. He picked up the telephone, worried that the line might have gone dead, but Gaudet's calm voice answered immediately. "Did you call me?" the director asked. Prullàs said: "I called you at the theatre because I was told you were trying to find me. What's the matter?" "Nothing serious for the moment," the director said, "but it would be a good idea for us to meet. If you're free tonight and there's no problem, come to my place: I'm a bit tired, and I'd like to go home as soon as the rehearsal is over." "Will you give me something to eat?" Prullàs asked. "No, but you can go and have dinner nearby once we've had our talk, I won't keep you long." "Aren't you going to have anything?" "I won't be hungry," Gaudet said. "I'll have a glass of milk and some crackers before I go to bed." "You're crazy," said Prullàs.

That night as he was getting out of his car outside Gaudet's apartment, he realised he had not set foot there since Doña Flavia's death. He felt overwhelmed by memory, and could not help associating her loss with his friend's problems, as Gaudet appeared, looking more like a ghost than ever in the gloomy light of his entrance hall. You'll have to forgive me for receiving you like this, he said. He was wearing a pair of shabby slippers and grubby-looking striped pyjamas. His down-at-heel appearance fitted exactly with the heavy, lugubrious atmosphere of the apartment as the two men walked down the corridor. As they were walking past what had been Doña Flavia's bedroom, Prullàs slowed down; he peered in at the room through the half-open door. "Everything is exactly as she left it," said Gaudet when he noticed his companion's surreptitious glance. "I should have got rid of the furniture straightaway, and changed the wallpaper; but I didn't, and then I found it was impossible: as if touching anything would have been betrayed her memory. I know they're unhealthy thoughts; but I'm not about to justify them to anyone, let alone you, who knows how much I loved her. Come on," he added, "we'll be more comfortable in the living-room. How did you get on in Masnou?" Prullàs thought he could make out a vague smell of burnt candlewax, as if the funeral candles had only just been blown out. "Fine," he said absent-mindedly, "you know what it's like."

He sat in an armchair, and Gaudet took another one. Its springs urgently needed replacing. "I think you should do something about your furniture, Pepe," Prullàs said. "You're right," the director replied. "And couldn't we open a window? It's like an oven in here." "Oh no, if you don't mind," Gaudet said, "any draft goes right through me! Why don't you take off your jacket?" Prullàs did so, undid his tie as well, and unbuttoned his shirt collar. "What were you reading?" he asked, pointing to a pile of typed sheets on the edge of the table. Gaudet handed him the top one:

ANDRES: Don't hit her, father, she's not to blame. After all, what's a worker's daughter for if not to amuse the sons of the rich?

"Very edifying," he muttered, passing it back to the director, who carefully returned it to the pile. "What is it?" "As you can see, it's a manuscript I was sent yesterday; it's by a young writer who's aroused great expectations." "Great expectations?" Prullàs spluttered. "Who on earth finds great expectations in material like that?" Gaudet gave an offhand smile that seemed more to denote his physical exhaustion than any intellectual stance. "This is the theatre of the future, Carlos, whether you like it or not. People are fed up with your comedies of intrigue, they want to see real problems on the stage; it might seem strange to you, but that's how it is," he said. "You mean my theatre is old-fashioned? That I'd do better to retire? Is that why you brought me here?" Prullàs exploded. "O.K., I admit it," he said, "perhaps I should change my style. It doesn't seem too difficult: in the first act, we can have a beggar eating his own vest, then in the second an eighty-year old woman murdering her mother so she can buy a new set of false teeth."

Gaudet shrugged: he didn't want to argue, he said. "I'm sorry, Pepe," Prullàs went on; "I've got nothing against you, but I've had more than enough of all this nonsense. Of course the theatre has to renew itself, like everything else, but I can't stand this idiocy, this blind admiration for all the empty phrases from abroad, especially from France." "And what have the poor French done to you?" the director asked. "Nothing, they make my blood boil, that's all," Prullàs replied; "the French think that to suffer brings its own rewards. And their theatre is pure tosh: platitudes dressed up in wigs. Sartre, Anouilh, Camus, what a line-up!" "Oho, so now you're the great radical, I can see." "I'm no radical, I'm just a man of honour. Or do you want me to become a philosopher of disaster just for commercial reasons? Pepe, you're asking me to prostitute my pen! What would Doña Flavia say if she heard you?"

Gaudet burst out laughing: "Carlos, you use your pen to spray out lewd jokes and nothing more," he said, "and don't use the name of a poor dead woman to support the rubbish you're coming out with. My mother was a fine woman, but a dreadful actress; she had more than her share of enthusiasm and dedication, but she hadn't a clue about the theatre."

Doña Flavia claimed that in her youth she had been a famous actress, a *tragédienne*. Prullàs, who must have been twelve or thirteen years old when Gaudet introduced him to her, had looked more bewildered than convinced when he heard this affirmation from her lips. "Oh, but no-one in this country will have heard of my exploits, darling," she quickly explained, "because it was in the fabulous theatres of Buenos Aires, Havana, Montevideo and the other great cities of South America that my art shone at its brightest." The flat reeked of cats and was a complete mess; it was autumn and Doña Flavia was wearing a between-season coat that was faded and lumpy from having been so often in the laundry; despite this, she showed no signs of going out, as she also wore a pair of slippers and her hair was filthy and dishevelled. "In those wonderful days," she went on declaiming in Prullàs' honour, "I was always travelling, always on tour, from capital to capital, suite to suite, working myself to the bone, darling, the American way of life! I was never worried, I burned the candle at both ends: sometimes a car would be waiting for me at the airport to take me straight to the theatre, I would come down the plane steps already shouting 'Desdemona! Desdemona!' But I never complained, and I could have carried on like that for the rest of my life if the father of this scoundrel here hadn't crossed my path," she said, gesturing across at Gaudet, who was staring at her entranced, as though rather than hearing his family history he were in the audience at a star performance. "I appealed to a lot of people, darling, but I never had the slightest intention of catching a man; I cherished my freedom above everything else, and that had led me to disappoint more than one suitor. Oh, but that rake was different. One night, soon after we had started going out together and although it was high summer in the southern hemisphere, he asked me to close my eyes and slipped a silver fox stole round my shoulders. Silver fox, darling!" Not even Gaudet himself knew how this torrid romance had ended, nor the identity or the whereabouts of his father, whom he had never met. "All I know is that his name was Gaudet," he would tell everyone who asked him about it. As an adult he had gone behind his mother's back and started enquiries, but these had come to nothing and only produced more doubts than certainties. In the end, he was forced to admit that Gaudet might not even have been his real name.

"She's the person who gave me my love of the theatre," Prullàs said. "No-one had such a decisive effect on my life. I can still almost hear her, reciting those dreadful verses. I always knew she was getting it wrong, and yet I believed in what she was saying. Didn't you?"

Gaudet shrugged. "She was my mother," he said, "and you never believe your mother. Your father, perhaps, but never your mother. Anyway, a lot of water has flowed under the bridge since then." He shrugged again, and went on: "Almost every night, before I go to sleep, I read a play. Think of it: three hundred and sixty something plays a year; so I know what I'm talking about. And I tell you, Carlos: whether you like it or not, times have changed, and the theatre public with them. Today's public isn't as accommodating as the one we were used to: they want profound ideas, strong emotions: a new view of reality."

"Rubbish!" said Prullàs; "the public and I are old friends. I don't want to manipulate their emotions or change their view of reality: they can look at that however they wish. Who am I to tell them how to think? I know all about these kinds of ideas,

Pepe: rousing the public's awareness, shaking them out of their humdrum existence. Utter nonsense! The world is plagued with wars, misery, crises and cataclysms. All you need do is glance at the papers: our daily reality is tragic, a real emetic for their consciences. And if that's not sufficient to shake people out of their humdrum lives, why on earth do you expect four pretentious lines in the mouths of second-rate actors to achieve anything?"

"Because," the director butted in, "because they speak their language. Wars and disasters are the language of History; the theatre offers people their own language. No, Carlos," he added wearily, "I don't want you to prostitute your smooth-running pen; I just want you to keep abreast of the times. But don't listen to me," he hurriedly concluded, "I could well be wrong; after all, there's no theatre here, no culture, no nothing; this is a land fit for idiots, Carlos, and we're part of it."

A ring at the doorbell interrupted their conversation. "That's strange!" said Gaudet, "who can it be at this time of night?" "Don't worry, it's for me," Prullàs said, "I'll go." He disappeared into the dark corridor, only to reappear shortly afterwards followed by a waiter carrying a voluminous wooden box. The waiter deposited the box on a chair, took the lid off, and from inside took plates, glasses, knives and forks, a soup tureen, a dish covered with a domed silver cloche and a bottle of red wine, all of which he arranged on the table. He then announced he would return the next morning to pick up the used service, hoped they had a good meal, thanked Prullàs for the banknote he slipped into his jacket pocket, and left. "You might have told me," Gaudet exclaimed when the two men were alone again. Prullàs shrugged: "You seemed intent on my dying of hunger," he said by way of excuse. "I wouldn't have received the waiter in my pyjamas, and with all this mess," the director protested.

"Don't worry about it, waiters don't notice things like that," Prullàs said. "That's all you know," Gaudet retorted. "Bah, don't give yourself such airs, and let's see what they've sent us," said Prullàs, lifting the lid on the tureen: "Oh good, cold consommé, and what's under here?" Lifting the cloche off the dish, they discovered it was a chicken à la cocotte. Prullàs tied a napkin round his neck and picked up a knife and fork. "Let's get stuck in!" he said. After he had been eating for a while, he realised Gaudet hadn't even bothered to come over to the table. "Pepe, don't make me feel bad." "Don't insist, Carlos, it was a nice idea, but I can't eat." "Try a spoonful, you'll see how delicious the consommé is." "No, Carlos, don't insist, please." "What'll we do with all the leftovers?" Prullàs complained. "Flush them down the toilet." "Pepe, there are people starving out there," Prullàs said, "and not just in those plays you like so much, but in the streets too." "And d'you think that if I force down some consommé, they'll be any less hungry?" the director replied. "I can see you're in a good mood," Prullàs said, serving himself a glass of wine, "is that why you wanted to see me?"

Gaudet's face brightened up. Despite his protestations to the contrary, it was obvious he lived for his work; he was only interested in things to do with the theatre; anything else left him cold. "We have a problem," he said. "Serious?" asked Prullàs. "The problem itself isn't serious, but its consequences could be if it's not sorted out quickly and efficiently."

Prullàs could see his friend's face through the cloud of smoke from the cigarette he had lit as an act of defiance at the dinner; in the lamplight, his sallow skin and gaunt profile gave him an almost spectral look against the shadows of the corner of the room. If I heard tomorrow or the next day that he had died, I wouldn't be in the least surprised, Prullàs thought.

"D'you remember," the director began, "that a couple of

days ago you asked me about the new girl in the company? Lilí Villalba, the one who plays the maid in 'Arrivederci, pollo!' I told you she had no talent, but tried hard, perhaps the worst combination there is. I also told you she had a protector. Well, the day before yesterday he came to rehearsal. He got in the way for half an hour or more, then said he wanted to speak to me in private. I had to suspend the rehearsal and go with him to one of the theatre offices. When we were alone, he asked me how his protégée was getting on. I swear, I hesitated a good few seconds before I replied. I was thinking I'd be doing everyone a favour if I told him the truth. She has no talent, and never will, so why encourage hopes that in the long run will only be dashed? Wouldn't it have been a thousand times better to say to him: 'My dear sir, the girl is no use in the theatre, take her away and help us stop wasting time, dreams, and money?' Straight out. But I didn't dare: I was frightened, Carlos, I was a coward. As I already told you, he's an influential man. I was scared he might be annoyed and create problems for us. The result was I said what one always does: she's promising, she's got what it takes to be a great actress, it's too soon to see any concrete results, she's very young, and the theatre is a very demanding profession: effort, work, sacrifice, and so on and so forth. As you can imagine, I said it all in the flattest, most mechanical way possible, without ever lifting my eyes from my watch. And then, believe it or not, hardly had I finished my piece but he comes back with how what I was saying didn't surprise him in the least, how he always had a blind faith in the girl, and what he has seen in the rehearsal and my words had convinced him how right he was. I was dumbstruck he took everything I said so literally. Who would have thought it? Everybody likes to hear flattery, but only fools believe it. Wait, don't say anything yet, there's worse to come. So this fellow goes on and says – hold on to your hat! – he says, why don't we offer his protégée the role Kiki is playing in 'Arrivederci, pollo!' I stared at him as if he had turned into the wolfman in front of my eyes, but he didn't even notice the look on my face. He went on to say that his protégée is much prettier than Mariquita, and of course, much younger . . . that Mariquita is starting to show her age, and that she's far too old to be playing the role of ingénue . . . for the love of God, Carlos, swear to me not a word of this leaves this room! . . . and that, from what he had been able to observe, Mariquita Pons is not as good an actress as some people claim, and as she herself believes. And on that score at least he's spot on, because for a good while now Kiki can't get a thing right: she can't memorise a single line correctly, she's always daydreaming, and if anyone says anything to her, she bites their head off. Give me another cigarette, will you?"

While Gaudet lit up, Prullàs set to the chicken. The two friends sat in silence for a while. Then Prullàs wiped his lips with the napkin and said: "Don't be too hard on yourself; in your situation, anyone would have done the same." "This sort of thing shouldn't happen to me at my age," Gaudet replied; "I was stupid, I should have seen it coming." "So what did you say to him?" "Well, at first I was so dumbfounded I didn't know what to say; then eventually, in order to say something, I told him that what he was suggesting was impossible, because contracts had been signed . . . He wouldn't let me finish. 'Oh, if that's all there is to it, leave it to me,' he said. I realised the best thing to do was to end the conversation there and then, because it was becoming more and more complicated, so I promised him I'd give careful consideration to all he had said, and would contact him as soon as I had worked something out; then I begged him to excuse me because I had to get back to the rehearsal, and put him out on the street."

Prullàs thought it over for a few moments, then said: "D'you think the girl knows anything? I mean whether this Señorita Lilí Villalba, or whatever her name is, is behind all this." "I haven't the faintest idea," the director replied, "but I'd swear she knows nothing; at least, that's the impression she gives, and after seeing her act, I doubt whether she's much good at pretending." "Don't confuse talent as an actress with hypocrisy," said Prullàs. "Whatever," Gaudet replied. "The important thing now is to decide what we're going to do." "Wait and see," Prullàs suggested. "No, no way: this is a snowball, and if we don't stop it right now, we're the ones it's going to crush," the other man replied. "You have to go and see this rogue, find out what his intentions are, and try to talk him out of it: make him see that if things go much further, there could be a scandal. He's a well-known figure and he won't want trouble." "Ah, so that's where all this was leading," Prullàs exclaimed; "you mess things up, and now it's me who has to save your bacon." "As it says in Hamlet, 'Thou art a scholar; speak to it, Horatio'," Gaudet said. "Why me and not you?" "Because he wouldn't pay any attention to me; I'm only a theatre director, and I doubt whether he sees any difference between me and an usherette." "And d'you think he'd be more impressed by a writer of farces?" "Not in the least," Gaudet said, "but you're rich and you've married into high society, he'll listen to you." "Is he married?" Prullàs wanted to know. "No." "Too bad! If he's a bachelor, he'll be less worried about a scandal. Is he rich?" "I suppose so." "Hmmm; what else do we know about him?" "Not much: his name is Ignacio Vallsigorri, he's a businessman, he has friends in the best circles, and undoubtedly in the worst as well. Ah, and he often goes to the Jockey Club," Gaudet added. "How did you find all that out?" Prullàs asked. "I have friends too."

Prullàs thought it over for a minute before saying: "O.K., I'll see what I can do; are you sure you don't want anything to eat?" "I already told you I didn't," Gaudet replied, his voice taking on an edge of irritability, as before. "Well then, put the chicken in the fridge; tomorrow you can heat it up and it'll be an easy dinner. Or you could have it cold with mayonnaise. And remember, they're coming to collect the things." "I'll leave them out on the mat tonight," Gaudet said. "What d'you think is the matter with Kiki?" Prullàs wondered. The director shrugged his shoulders.

As soon as he got home he had a shower. He had sweated copiously, partly due to the heat in Gaudet's flat, but even more because of the way the visit had unsettled him: the strange atmosphere in the apartment, Gaudet's state of mind, and the bottle of wine he had drunk anxiously on his own had all contributed to his exasperation. And on top of all that, there were problems with the play, the actors, with everybody, he thought under the shower. Once he was dry and well dusted with talcum powder, he put on a clean pair of pyjamas, dragged a small armchair over to the open balcony window, sat down, lit a cigarette, and began to feel better. The flat was dark and silent; the streetlight sent yellow beams through the leaves of the trees. He stared for a while at the starry sky. Tomorrow without fail I'll sort it out, he told himself. A metallic noise out in the street obliged him to get up and lean over the balcony, once he had checked there was no-one around to see him in his pyjamas. Two municipal workmen in grey overalls and round flat helmets were connecting a hosepipe to a hydrant. When they had finished this apparently simple operation, which took them a considerable amount of time, the two workmen divided their labours: one of them seized the nozzle of the pipe and stood in the centre of the pavement; the other stayed by the hydrant, waiting for his companion's signal. The two of them were wearing high rubber boots to protect them from any splashing water. Prullàs stood watching them, and came in from the balcony before they began to hose down the street. Tomorrow morning I'll sort everything out, he repeated to himself before he fell asleep.

12

"A lady is asking for the master on the telephone. I told her the master was resting and she said that it didn't matter, that I should wake you."

The clock showed eleven. Prullàs jumped out of bed and put his robe on. Coming out of his bedroom, he ran into Sebastiana in the corridor. "Which telephone?" he asked. Sebastiana pointed towards his study. After he had gone in, she closed the door behind him. The telephone handset was on the table. "Hello," he said. "Is that you, Señor Prullàs?" asked a voice that was not Mariquita Pons'. "Who am I talking to?" he queried. "It's Marichuli Mercadal, d'you remember me?" the voice said slyly. "What a surprise! Where are you calling from?" "From Barcelona; I came down on the first bus; my husband stayed in Masnou with our daughter." Prullàs didn't know what to say, so a silence followed, which Marichuli eventually broke. "Don't you want to know why I came?" "I'm sorry, I'm still half-asleep," Prullàs said; "Tell me, what brings you here?" "To see you and spend some time with you, if you don't mind." "No, no, on the contrary; I'm surprised, that's all; the problem is . . ." ". . . that you're busy all day," she said. "I thought as much; it doesn't matter, I've got a thousand things to do as well," she went on; "we can see each other tonight; I want you to take me to the pictures." "Agreed," he said. "What excuse did you give your husband?" "Unfortunately, I could tell him the truth: that I had to go to the dentist, that I would take advantage of being here to do a few errands, and that I wouldn't be back till tomorrow; he seemed to accept it. But what's that to you?" "Nothing, I was just curious." "I'd like to make you more than just curious about me, but for now I'll make do with that. Meet me at eight at the bar at the Marfil. Are you punctual?" "As a watch," Prullàs said. "I'm not," she replied; "I'll tell myself we arranged to meet at seven." Her voice betrayed the excitement she felt at this adventure she was embarking on, and had organised down to the last detail. "Till eight then," said Prullàs. "Shall I make myself beautiful?" she asked. "Could you ever be anything else?" he said. "How little you know me!"

Prullàs had a shower, shaved, got dressed, drank two cups of coffee, and looked through *La Vanguardia*. A photo-spread showed Salvador Dalí in his house at Port Lligat. The world-famous painter's recent return to Spain, plus the fact that he seemed to have carte blanche to do and say the most ridiculous things, seemed to have endeared him to journalists, who the artistic genius with the twirling moustaches kept well supplied with news and gossip. And there were those who claimed to know from a reliable source that the eccentricities displayed by this picturesque character were nothing more than public-ity stunts, and that in his private life Dalí talked and behaved like a perfectly normal person. At Nuremberg, Alfried Krupp's trial continued its tortuous progress. Among the charges brought against him was a letter signed by Krupp, together with Siemens, Bosch, Thyssen and other leading representatives of Germany's heavy industry, in which they called on Hinden-burg to appoint Adolf Hitler as chancellor of their country. The defence's response was that the accused, on this as on every other occasion, had acted in good faith; that Germany was going through a difficult period, and that the accused had believed that only a man with the energy and powers of persuasion of the

Führer could set it back on track. And, the prosecution objected, had not the accused been aware that this individual was not merely a threat to the entire world, but that his declared intentions could lead Germany to complete ruin? No; at that moment, the accused had seen only the positive aspects of national-socialism, its ability to bring together the German people without regard for ideological or class differences. The accused recognised that he had observed an undertow of violence, a streak of hatred and fanaticism in Hitler's words, but he had thought these extreme ideas were simply part of his electoral rhetoric, perhaps the only way to make himself heard in all the confusion and tumult around him, that basically they were no more than propaganda boasts. It was pure patriotism that had led him and the other captains of German industry to propose a measure whose repercussions they had not the slightest inkling of at that point in history. Was it legitimate now to condemn as criminals or evildoers people who had acted in the belief they were contributing not merely to the good of their fatherland, but to its salvation? Was it right to humiliate in this way those who had felt moved by one of the most noble – if not the most noble – sentiments to be found in men's hearts?

When he had finished reading the paper, Prullàs went out. He had thought of walking to the new site of the Jockey Club, on the corner of Diagonal and Calle Balmes, but by the time he reached Paseo de Gracia it was so hot he decided to look for another way of getting there. He spurned the gas-powered taxi belching smoke at the rank, and instead got on a tram, which at that time of day was reasonably empty, and stood on the back platform. The conductor was moving up and down the central aisle of the tram, asking the passengers if they had paid. There were always some who avoided his demands by the simple expedient of stepping down at one end of the vehicle and getting on again at the other. As the tram advanced extremely slowly, anyone could execute this manoeuvre with no risk of being left stranded in the street. It was a kind of sporting cheating that many inhabitants of Barcelona indulged in with obvious delight, although occasionally their game ended in tragedy, especially on rainy days, when the road surface was slippery and caused falls that with bad luck could leave those involved with broken bones. That morning, however, the ground was dry, the sky was clear, and Paseo de Gracia was full of the perfume of flowers, except when motor cars swept by in a cloud of black, foul-smelling dirt. The Fantasia cinema was showing an adventure film starring Yvonne de Carlo and Sabu; the Savoy had a comedy with Danny Kaye and Virginia Mayo. Prullàs was wondering which cinema he could take Marichuli Mercadal to if she really wanted to go and see a film and he could not talk her out of it. He couldn't understand why women were so crazy for the cinema. I loathe it; films bore me without exception, he thought to himself, especially musical comedies, although I have to admit I like Danny Kaye, though I couldn't explain why. And Sabu? What can he be like in real life? he thought as he rode on the tram platform; what can he say to his wife in the evening when he gets home stinking of elephants? What about his children? I wonder if he takes them to see films where their father appears in a loincloth speaking only in grunts, and generally behaving like a retard?

He got off the tram in Diagonal and continued on foot. He had hardly gone two paces when a young man with shaven head, transparent ears and a scruffy beard stopped him and asked for some change: "Can you help me, sir, I got out of prison a week ago and can't find any work." Prullàs gave him some coins.

Although Prullàs was not a member, the doorman at the Jockey Club came out to greet him in a very friendly manner, and responded to his question by saying that he thought he had seen Don Ignacio Vallsigorri go upstairs some time earlier. He would most likely find him in the small reading-room on the first floor, he added. Prullàs climbed the staircase slowly and reluctantly; now that their meeting was imminent, the idea seemed ridiculous to him. On the ground floor of the club, a clock struck the four quarters of the hour. Prullàs poked his head round the door of an empty room, in the centre of which was a green-baize gambling table. One of the walls of this gaming room was entirely covered with a painting on a pastoral theme. Prullàs stepped out onto the landing once more, then went into the room next door, which turned out to be a spacious reading-room with papered walls, dark-brown leather armchairs, standard lamps and small, low tables strewn with untidy piles of newspapers and magazines. The sun filtered in through the half-closed shutters and cast golden stripes across the blocks of the parquet floor. The room had only one occupant. Prullàs sat in the armchair next to this man, picked up a magazine from the table, and began to leaf through it. He cast sideways glances at his neighbour: he was a bald, stocky, rather vulgar-looking man wearing a rather grubby pinstripe suit. He had taken off his tie because of the heat, and it poked out of the left-hand jacket pocket. He was using a handkerchief to mop the sweat off his top lip.

"This is the worst time of day," Prullàs murmured, using the pretext to start up a conversation. His neighbour looked at him warily. "What's that you say?" "I was saying that this is the hottest part of the day," Prullàs repeated; "when the temperature is at its highest." "Oh, yes," the other man said, putting the handkerchief away in his trouser pocket; "Yesterday it reached twenty-eight degrees and I wouldn't be surprised if it went even higher today, and then there's this blessed humidity!" "What can you expect? We're in the dog days." "Yes, that must be it," the bald man replied, burying himself in his reading once more.

The two of them read in silence for a few minutes, then the man lifted his eyes from the magazine, stared directly at Prullàs, and said: "I've no idea how this affair in India will end." "Yes, everything's in turmoil since they assassinated poor Gandhi," Prullàs agreed. "And not content with that," the other man replied, "they threw his ashes into the Ganges; it's a barbaric custom, one that those of us who believe in a future life find repulsive. We're lucky all that is going on so far away from us." "Yes, that is an advantage," Prullàs concurred; "it's not easy to see how what's going on in India could affect us." "Not directly at any rate," the other man said, "but let me tell you this: it's my view that the way things are nowadays, nothing can happen in the world without it affecting all of us to a greater or lesser extent. Things aren't like they used to be: before, whatever happened in a country stayed within its frontiers; a country could be going up in flames, without its neighbours even noticing. But that's not possible nowadays, whether we like it or not, we're all part of a larger community: the world community, and increasingly things will be as I've described them to you," he concluded. "I can see you're very well informed, Señor Vallsigorri," Prullàs said hurriedly before the other man returned to his reading. "Well, I'm one of those who likes to know what's going on, and to know where I stand," the other replied, with a show of false modesty.

Prullàs did not know how to take the conversation further, so there was a renewed silence. Prullàs was racking his brains but could not think of a natural way to return to a conversation that had begun so promisingly; not only did he feel incapable of any kind of improvisation, but he also felt unusually abashed, doubtless because of his distaste for this artificial situation. He was on the point of admitting defeat and making good his escape when his neighbour noisily folded the paper he had been reading, slapped it down on the table and exclaimed, with somewhere between a bellow and a sigh: "What a mess things are in this world God has created!" Prullàs' face creased in a grimace that was intended to show agreement but seemed more like a lack of enthusiasm. Since he could think of nothing better to say, he quickly retorted: "Wouldn't it be better to say in this God-forsaken world?" This banal phrase appeared to greatly please the other man, who remarked that it summed up his entire philosophy of life. People were born traitors and so were countries, he intoned, nodding gravely.

"What can one do?" Prullàs replied. "When it comes down to it, we can't be responsible for what happens outside our own home." The stranger concurred, and added that in today's world, everything came down to ambition. That, in his view, was the cause of such upheavals and violence.

"Quite right," Prullàs said, "that's the root of the problem, as you say: ambition . . . and women."

The stranger leant back against his antimacassar and lifted his eyes to the ceiling. "Ah, women!" he murmured, pulling a face at the pink nymphs gambolling in the paintings there. "The little devils!"

"Ah yes, you may say so, my friend Vallsigorri, you may say so, but how hard it is to resist their temptations!" Prullàs said.

A cautious look crept over the other man's face, as it had when speaking of Gandhi's murder. "Not for me it isn't," he said. He stared Prullàs straight in the eyes and assured him that the woman hadn't been born who could make him lose his head, still less loosen his purse strings, he added with pride.

"Oh, come now, Señor Vallsigorri, you're among friends now," Prullàs replied, gently tapping the other man's knee; "among friends and gentlemen; nothing we say to each other will leave here, so you don't have to pretend to me."

"I'm afraid I don't catch your drift, sir."

"Well . . . there's no secret about your affection for a certain young actress, one of our theatre's most promising talents, although still somewhat green, I'm sure you know whom I'm talking about," said Prullàs. "No, sir, I haven't the slightest idea," the other man replied curtly, "I don't know what you're talking about, I don't know where you heard this slander, nor where your insinuations are leading; and above all, I don't know why you insist on calling me Vallsigorri when my name is Requesens."

"Ah, so you're not Don Ignacio Vallsigorri?"

"Obviously not!" the other man spluttered.

"In that case," Prullàs stammered as he rose from his armchair, "it's equally obvious I've made a dreadful mistake, Señor Requesens; I must beg your pardon and ask that for courtesy's sake you consider that I never said a word. Forgive me, and good day to you," he murmured as he picked his way towards the door.

"A good day to you too," the other man grumbled.

Quickly and without much appetite, Prullàs ate a set lunch at the bar of the Granjas La Catalana in Diagonal, and then walked back all the way to his apartment. By the time he arrived he felt so sticky that he told Sebastiana to run him a bath, which she bluntly refused to do. A bath so soon after lunch could be very harmful, she argued. So Prullàs had to do without. He telephoned Gaudet. "Well, did you see him? Did you talk to him?" the director wanted to know as soon as he recognised his friend's voice at the other end of the line. "Don't, Pepe, I prefer not to think about it, it was so embarrassing!" "But did you see him or not?" "Yes, I mean . . . no; anyway, I made a complete fool of myself; I'll tell you all about it when I come to rehearsal."

13

He tried a siesta, but it was so hot he could not sleep; he tried writing, but that was impossible too. In the end, he sat by the balcony to get the best of the breeze and read a Hammond Innes novel until five. At that point he had a wash, put on clean clothes, had the car taken out of the garage, and drove to the theatre. Gaudet was pouring the contents of a sachet into a glass of water, which at first turned milky then immediately returned to its usual transparency. Prullàs gave him a quizzical look, to which the director responded by pointing to his stomach. The heat in the auditorium was stifling.

"Carry on from where we left off," Gaudet shouted: "Act One, Scene Three! Todoliu and the maid enter!"

TODOLIU: So your master and mistress are not at home?

MAID: No, sir. They left after lunch and didn't say when they would be back.

TODOLIU: No matter, I'll wait. (*He sits down, takes a cigarette from a cigarette case and lights up*) I haven't seen you here before, have I? Are you new here?

MAID: Yes, sir. I was just passing the feather duster . . . Sorry. Yes, sir, I only started here a week ago. But this isn't my first position.

TODOLIU: Is that so?

MAID: Yes, sir . . . no, sir. Before this I was a maid for the Countess of Vallespir, until the poor dead lady . . . Sorry. Until the poor countess died in tragic circumstances.

TODOLIU: Ah, yes, I remember. The newspapers were full of it. A bloody and apparently motiveless crime, wasn't it? That must have been a terrible experience for you.

MAID: Yes, sir. Just imagine, there I was passing the feather duster over the countess's silver when I heard a blood-coddling . . . crudling . . . I'm sorry, somehow I can't say that word.

"Blood-curdling," Gaudet said without raising his voice, "but if you can't manage that, try something else: dreadful, terrible, horrifying, anything so we don't have to interrupt the rehearsal every ten seconds, all right?"

The young actress shrugged her shoulders and assured him that she was doing all she could to memorise her rôle; at home on her own she could recite it perfectly, but as soon as she got to the theatre, she didn't know what happened to her, she explained. She said this without the slightest sign that she was worried or upset by it, as if it were something that simply happened and in no way compromised her work. Prullàs was uncertain whether to put this down to her lack of self-awareness or to her sense of security at having a powerful backer. "Ten minutes' break, then we'll start from the top again!" Gaudet ordered the actors, "and someone go and tell Doña Mariquita: she must be in her dressing-room!" Prullàs gave his friend a brief account of what had happened in the Jockey Club. Gaudet listened with a scarcely-concealed glee. As Prullàs was coming to an end, the prompter came and joined them. He had been so hot in the prompting box, he said, that he'd almost fainted a couple of times. Prullàs offered him a cigarette. "Long time no see, Señor Mas!"

The prompter was known to everyone as Señor Mas. Nobody had the faintest idea what his first name might be. Absolutely everybody called him Señor Mas, including his wife, his daughter and her children, who were known as the grandchildren of Señor Mas. Señor Mas was an excellent professional, a real institution in the Barcelona theatre world.

"We were talking about Señorita Lilí Villalba," Gaudet said.

The prompter blew a column of smoke up towards the ceiling. "Ah, yes, Señorita Lilí Villalba," he sighed. "She couldn't get a line right if she tried, but she has a pair of legs that take your breath away. I've been in this profession more than 30 years now, Don Carlos, and I've seen a bellyful of actress's legs from my box; and I can tell you that the pair in question are the tops; take it from an expert. When it comes to breasts, I'm no expert," he added, "but legs, now there I do know a thing or two. I've seen the calves, the thighs and a little bit higher of all our Spanish actresses." "We'd better get back to the rehearsal," Gaudet cut in; and then, to Prullàs: "Why don't you stay on, and then we can have dinner together? This time I'll pay." Prullàs looked at his watch. "I can't today, Pepe, I have an appointment, and I must go; thanks for the invitation, though."

The bar at the Marfil was empty when he arrived. Although he was not a regular, the waiter seemed to know him: he asked how he was and served him a glass of sherry before Prullàs could even order. Prullàs concluded he must be confusing him with a frequent customer. Before he could set things straight, the waiter served him a wide choice of *tapas*: stuffed olives, fresh anchovies in vinegar, and slices of ham, cheese and salami. Prullàs had made a solid start on them by the time Marichuli came into the bar. Although he had last seen her less than forty-eight hours earlier, he was impressed by the way she looked: the sudden transfer from beach to city, the colour of her skin and her way of walking all gave off a vibrant sensuality; even the dress she was wearing seemed superfluous. "I tried to be on time, so you wouldn't find me ugly," she said as she clambered up onto the stool next to his. "So women become ugly if they arrive late?" "In the eyes of those who have to wait for them," she replied. The waiter greeted her as familiarly as he had done

Prullàs, but when the latter asked if she came often to the bar, she said she didn't. The waiter meanwhile had brought them fresh *tapas*. "If we eat all this, we won't want to dine," Prullàs said. "So much the better," she replied; "that way, we won't be late for the cinema." "Are you so keen to go to the pictures?" "Of course, you don't think I came to Barcelona to see *you*, do you?" "What about your dentist?" "Oh, that's a different kind of love. Look, this is the film I want to see," she went on, opening her handbag and pulling out a faded handbill in which the sour features of Bette Davis announced: "HER ONLY LAW WAS HER DESIRE". Prullàs' heart sank as he read it. "They say it's fantastic!" Prullàs couldn't bring himself to tell her he had seen the film a few days earlier with Mariquita Pons, still less what he had thought of it then. He handed the paper to Marichuli, who put it back in her bag. "D'you collect them or something?" Prullàs wanted to know. "Alicia does; she has more than a hundred already and says she wants to reach a thousand," she explained. All of a sudden, a sad look stole over her face, and Prullàs quickly changed the subject. "How did you get on at the dentist's? He can't have been too terrible, to judge by the way you're tearing into that salami." A cool breeze was blowing, so they walked down Rambla de Catalunya to the entrance to the Cristina cinema. As they arrived, a beggar woman came up to Prullàs and said: "Spare me some money, lucky man, you've got a woman there worth her weight in gold!"

Despite the *tapas*, when they were leaving the cinema Prullàs declared he was as hungry as a horse. The film had dragged on for so long, he said, that he felt as if he hadn't eaten for days. "Not so much a horse as a pig!" Marichuli taunted him. But Prullàs detected a note of doubt in her voice, and there was an uneasy look in her eye. It was she who had set up their meeting, with a boldness bordering on the shameless; during the film, she had taken and held Prullàs' hand, but now, as the night reached its climax, it seemed as though this vivacious woman was having second thoughts; her attitude now suggested she needed him to take the initiative. Prullàs was not happy at this prospect. If this situation continues, I'll soon find myself in an unholy mess, he thought; even someone as irresponsible as I am can see that. I wonder what she wants from me? Out loud, he said: "Come on, I'll take you home."

She did not contradict him, but let him take her by the arm and lead her to the exit onto Rambla de Catalunya. As they gained the street, he heard a teasing voice behind him calling out: "Good night, Señor Prullàs and co." He whirled round in time to see Mariquita Pons disappear among the crowd leaving the cinema with them. That's all I need, he said to himself.

14

The film had apparently dampened Marichuli's high spirits: she said barely half a dozen words in the whole journey from the cinema to her apartment in Avenida de José Antonio, between Calle Bruch and Calle Gerona. Outside her building, the pair of them maintained their reserve; she searched a long time in her bag for a set of keys, which she gave to Prullàs so that he could open the door for them. The hallway was in utter darkness. Prullàs lit a match, but the breeze immediately blew it out. All he managed to glimpse at the far end of the hall was a huge statue whose terrifying aspect was no doubt created by the flickering shadows the match flame had briefly thrown up before his startled eyes. "Come on, what are you doing?" she whispered. It was so dark it was impossible to tell where her voice was coming from, though to Prullàs it had the siren call of a shipwreck in thick fog. "I can't see a thing," he said. "Give me your hand." Hers was damp and cold. "It looks as though the light on the stairs isn't working," she said; "it's an old house and all the fixtures are antiquated. Come on," she said again, "it's only one floor." They groped their way up. As he began to climb the staircase, Prullàs stretched out his hand towards where he calculated the statue that had so frightened him must be. The tips of his fingers brushed against a marble shape. He waited on the landing while Marichuli opened the apartment door. Suddenly light from the entrance hall flooded the corridor. "Don't stand there in a daze, come in, there's no-one here."

All the furniture was covered in cretonne dustsheets, and the lamps with gauze; there was a musty, stale smell in the air. Prullàs did not know how to refuse her invitation, and she shut the door quickly and silently behind him; she didn't want the neighbours to hear them, still less see them coming in together at that time of night, she said. "Have you closed the flat for the whole summer?" Prullàs asked. "As you can see," she replied. "But I thought your husband was working in Barcelona." "He is, but with us away he stays at his mother's place; he can't stand being alone, especially when he's in one of his drinking moods. Don't be surprised that a man of my husband's age still has a mother alive: they all live a long time in his family. His grandmother lived to one hundred and three, and his uncle died at ninety-four when he fell off a horse while out hunting. It was because he was sure he had a good many years left that he decided to have children despite his age; what he couldn't know of course was that it wouldn't be him who would die prematurely, but our daughter: fate playing a dirty trick, as you see." "Is there no danger your husband might think of coming here?" "Why should he?" "To be with you." "Would *you* do that?" she asked. "I *am* with you," Prullàs replied.

As she switched on lights and he could see more, he discovered a whole set of rooms and corridors. "Go in there,"
Marichuli told him, pointing to a door. Prullàs did as he was
told, not suspecting for a moment it was a practical joke, and
found himself face-to-face with a skeleton. He cursed loudly,
and she burst out laughing. "Meet Matías," she said. "Very
funny," Prullàs replied, "who is he?" "Can't you guess? My
last lover: look what happened to him for trying to satisfy my
demands." When he had recovered from the shock, Prullàs
began to examine the room: there was a desk in the middle,
with a swivel chair; the walls were lined with bookcases full of
scientific books, and on the shelves themselves stood coloured
plaster casts of human organs. When Prullàs picked up a heart
to look at it, one of the ventricles fell to the floor. "Be careful,"
Marichuli said from the corridor. Prullàs picked up the piece
and put it back in the cast. "Is this where your husband works?"
he asked. "No, of course not, surgeons don't bring work home.
This is where he studies; doctors have to keep up-to-date;
progress doesn't stop, and nor do medical fashions. At the
moment hepatic diseases are all the rage, before that, it was
cardio-vascular problems, and so on. Are you going to spend
all night playing with body parts?"

Prullàs put the plaster heart back on its shelf, and tried
opening the desk drawers. Contrary to his expectations, they
were not locked; in them he found articles cut from magazines, pamphlets and handwritten documents, photographs
and diagrams. The centre drawer contained some money, a
bunch of keys, various identity cards and half a dozen family
photos, including one where Doctor Mercadal was in uniform,
his tunic covered with insignia and decorations. At the bottom
of the drawer Prullàs discovered a Luger pistol. Well, well, so
much for our doctor friend! he said to himself. He left everything as he had found it, shut the drawers and walked out of the

room. The corridor was deserted and in darkness. Prullàs felt a quiver of fear. What on earth was he doing there? he asked himself. He peered at his watch: a quarter to one. "It's really late," he said out loud, but there was no reply. He called out to Marichuli, but silence was the only answer. She's abandoned me, he thought; I'm all alone, locked in an empty house, with a skeleton for company: how ridiculous! The further he got from the study, where the light was still on, the more he found himself in a murky gloom inhabited only by shrouded pieces of furniture. Somewhere beneath all these covers there must be a telephone, he thought; I can phone Gaudet and get him to come and rescue me. But first I have to make sure that this crazy woman really has left me on my own trapped in here; why on earth could she have done it? He could think of several answers, each of them more far-fetched than the previous one: extortion, kidnapping, satanic rites. Am I a complete idiot? he wondered. Then he remembered the pistol in the drawer and realised he was on edge. He tried to see the funny side of the situation: any moment now Lon Chaney could leap on me, brandishing a sacred sacrificial dagger, he said to himself, with the cruel, slightly deranged laughter of María Montez in the background. He shouted again for Marichuli, and this time she replied quietly from behind him: "What's all this noise about? I'm not deaf." "I called you several times and you didn't reply," he said. "What were you doing?" "Nothing: when I saw you weren't following me, I went into the bathroom and with the tap turned on I couldn't hear you," she replied. "What did you find so interesting in my husband's study anyway, Mister snooper?"

Following the sound of her voice, Prullàs had discovered her in a rectangular room dominated by a tall, broad four-poster bed. Over the bedhead hung a mahogany crucifix, with an ivory Christ wearing a scarlet velvet skirt nailed to it. Marichuli was brushing her hair at a dressing-table full of pots and silver-ware, separated from the matrimonial bed by a screen. "We'll go into a guest room," she suddenly said; "this bed isn't made and anyway, this is sacred ground." She had changed out of her dress and was wearing a silk kimono that showed her tanned legs. Faced with this tempting vision, Prullàs immediately put the premonitions that had been troubling him out of his mind. He cleared his throat and was about to speak when she got in first. "The woman who said hello as we were coming out of the cinema is an actress, isn't she? A famous one." "Yes, Mariquita Pons," he replied, annoyed and confused: he had hoped she hadn't noticed the incident, or in any event, had not attached any importance to it. "And what is there between you two?" "Nothing, don't be absurd!" "There's nothing absurd about it: she's a very attractive woman, and doubtless very intelligent as well." "Two very good reasons for not getting involved with her," he replied jokingly, but then added in a more serious vein: "She's a good deal older than I am, she has a husband she's extremely happy with and who, as far as I know, she has never been unfaithful to; her husband is called Miguel Fontcuberta; and he's a good friend of mine as well. What's more," he added, "Mariquita Pons and I have worked closely together for any number of years, our relationship is strictly professional, and out of it has grown an entirely blame-less mutual affection; it may be that in a world so interested in gossip this has given rise to all kinds of stories, but there's no truth to them. Satisfied?"

Marichuli got up from her stool. She seemed thinner in her kimono, the bottom edges of which brushed against the tiles. Her look, which had seemed harsh and suspicious in the looking glass, was now luminous and passionate. "I don't care what you do," she whispered, "but don't talk to me like that. I'm not a bored housewife looking for an amorous adventure, and I'm not trying to occupy any special place in your heart or in your life. I'm wicked, that's all. I enjoy doing wrong. I'm shameless and perverse." Good grief, Prullàs thought, this is madness!

He still thought the same when he woke up with a start and didn't know what time it was or where on earth he was. A faint glimmer of light enabled him to pick out the frame of a closed balcony window and the shape of the pieces of furniture in the guest room. By his side, he could make out Marichuli's light, irregular breathing as she slept fitfully, tightly clutching her pillow. He got up stealthily, picked up his clothes strewn around the room, dressed, and spread the kimono carefully on the bed. He tiptoed out into the corridor, shoes in hand; this time, he had no trouble finding the door out of the apartment. On the landing, he put on his shoes. The silence in the building led him to suppose everyone else was away on holiday. He thought of Marichuli, all alone and unprotected in this huge empty block; he hurried on his way. Fortunately, he could open the front door from inside.

Outside, it was still night, and the city was sleeping the deep, untroubled sleep that precedes dawn. The streets were deserted and quiet. Mist threw a gauze veil round the streetlamps. His hair dishevelled, his clothes thrown on anyhow over his still-warm skin, Prullàs headed with all the guilty stealth of a spy for the spot where he had left his car. As he walked past the iron bars of a low window opening, he was enveloped in an overwhelming, cloying smell. Looking down through the grating, he could see a large basement room lit by a red glow; two men in caps and aprons were busy loading the four doors of an oven with the lumps of dough that another man, white from flour dust, was frantically kneading at the far end of the cellar. The heat from the oven immediately dried the sweat pouring from the bakers' faces and bodies, producing a small cloud of steam all round them. This was the only bakery in the neighbourhood that stayed open during the month of August. Nothing in the world would ever make me do a job like that, Prullàs thought to himself. From the belfry of the Salesas church the silence was broken by the sharp, stern clang of a bell striking four. A dog barked in the distance. A stooped nun emerged from a doorway in Calle Bruch. Probably she had spent the night at the bedside of a sick or dead person, and was returning to her convent for matins. Stepping out onto the pavement, she crossed herself as if she were venturing into the territory of infidels, and repeated the gesture as she passed Prullàs. For his part, Prullàs mistook the sign of the cross for a greeting, and bowed his head respectfully. Still engrossed in the voluptuous sensation of pleasure, he failed to realise how absurd he looked, even though somewhere deep inside himself he felt the first faint stirrings of concern about the unpredictable consequences of his rash adventure.

CHAPTER TWO

I

"No blackouts today then, Bonifaci?" Prullàs asked, seeing the theatre caretaker come out of his lodge without his usual candleholder. "That I couldn't say, Don Carlos, but if there are, I'm prepared," the caretaker replied, pulling a tiny candle butt out of his overall pocket. "Where's your candlestick?" "Oh, Don Carlos, I had it stolen a couple of days ago, and what makes me really angry is that it must have been someone from the theatre; you can't even trust your own colleagues these days!" He marched off down the corridor, and Prullàs followed behind; every now and then the caretaker slowed down to give a heavy sigh that managed to be both philosophic and asthmatic at the same time. "People can't be trusted, can't be trusted," he suddenly announced, as if drawn to this sad conclusion by all his sighing. "Still, you have to be kind to them," he added at once, with great conviction. "Isn't that a contradiction, Bonifaci?" said Prullàs. "Oh no, Don Carlos, I can't explain it," the caretaker replied; "but that's how things are." He really is a good man, thought Prullàs, a saint; if I remember, the next time I'm here I'll bring him a new candleholder; I'm sure we've got more than enough of them at home. They waved goodbye to each other backstage; the caretaker shuffled off back down the corridor, and Prullàs stayed concealed in the wings.

JULIO: Wonderful! Everything's going according to plan. In a few hours we'll have committed the perfect crime, and in a few weeks we'll be rich, Cecilia, rich! D'you know what that means? The end of debts, the end of begging, the end of turning jackets inside out. And we'll be able to eat lobster every day of the year!

CECILIA: There you go again with lobsters! I'm starting to detest them. As for the rest, you can say what you like, but I still have my doubts.

JULIO: Don't worry, my plan can't fail. Have you done everything I asked you to?

CECILIA: Yes, I called Enrique at the police station and left a message that Todoliu wanted to see him here at five on the dot, and I told Todoliu that Enrique would be here at five to talk to him. Not that I have the faintest idea what the two of them will talk about when they do meet.

JULIO: Well, about bullfighting, football and women, what else? The important thing is that Enrique sees Todoliu alive and kicking at five o'clock. And then, as soon as Enrique's gone . . . wham!

CECILIA: Good grief, how horrible! Couldn't we kill him without the "wham!"?

JULIO: That might be difficult, but we can try. And then . . .

(*The maid enters, out of breath and carrying her feather duster, closely followed by Luisito*)

MAID: I'm sorry madam, but yours truly is leaving this house straightaway. I'm dismissing myself! One may be poor, but I am honest, and what's going on in this house is beyond believe . . . belief . . .

CECILIA: But nothing's going on yet!

MAID: Nothing? D'you call nothing all the dishonest propositions yours truly has just had to put up with?

CECILIA: Oh, I see. (*To Luisito*) You ought to be ashamed of yourself! (*Slaps him across the cheek*)

LUISITO: But I . . . she . . . she . . . it . . .

CECILIA: And don't answer me back! (*Slaps him again*)

LUISITO: Ow!

MAID: No, Luis isn't the one to blame, poor thing! The person pursuing yours truly is Señor Todoliu.

CECILIA: Todoliu!

JULIO: Come on, tell us exactly what happened.

MAID: What happened is that this morning the feather duster . . . I'm sorry, yours truly was feathering the dust and Señor Todoliu comes up and starts talking to yours truly in a friendly way, and after a while straight out, without so much as a by your leave, he asks me if I'll go with him to the Côte d'Azur, he wants to take me.

CECILIA: Good god! and what did you say?

MAID: That yours truly won't be taken to the Côte d'Azur, the Costa Blanca, or any other coast, thank you very much.

JULIO: And how did he take that?

MAID: Very well. He told me that if I changed my mind, I should tell him, but I had to be quick about it, because he had his safe conduct signed and sealed, his bags packed, and that his train was leaving for the border at five on the dot.

JULIO AND CECILIA: (*with one voice*) At five!

"O.K.! that's enough for today," Gaudet shouted from the stalls. The actors quickly left the stage for their dressing-rooms, and Prullàs went down to his friend. "Things seem to be going better," he said. The director gave a sceptical shrug. "Have you been snooping long?" he asked. "Ten minutes, and I wasn't snooping; I stayed in the wings to avoid interrupting you."

"Fine," Gaudet replied as he scooped up his papers from the table. "He phoned me at home last night," he went on, with no explanation. "Who did?" Prullàs asked, "Ignacio Vallsigorri?" "Yes, but the real one, not the one you met," the director replied tartly. "For the love of God, Pepe, don't remind me what a fool you made of me." "It's not my fault, I didn't tell you start chatting to him." "All right, but what did the real Vallsigorri want?" "What d'you think? He wanted to remind me of our conversation the other day; you can't expect him to give up on his idea just because we didn't exactly rush to carry it out." "If Kiki had the slightest idea of what this is all about, she'd have burnt the theatre down by now, and us along with it," Prullàs said after a pause. "The best thing would be for you to talk to Señorita Lilí Villalba," Gaudet said. "Tell her how happy we all are with her, that's she's attractive and got a pretty face, and that if she's really interested in becoming an actress, what she has to do is work hard and let herself be guided, but that above all she mustn't try to run before she can walk, that any number of promising careers have been ruined by being over-hasty. Tell her she's very young, etc., etc., and that if she manages to learn her part properly, can improve her diction and do something about that ghastly accent of hers, it's highly likely the film industry will throw open its studio doors to her; that line never fails, and in this case it may well be true, if Señor Mas' reaction to her is anything to go by." Prullàs stared at his friend in amazement. "Quite frankly, I don't see why it's me who has to tell her all this, when you yourself have outlined it so convincingly." "Because she'll respect you, but be afraid of me," the director replied. "What if she isn't convinced?" "Then say the first thing that comes into your head, or if you like, strangle her: you have my full permission," Gaudet said. "I can't even remember her name," Prullàs protested. "Lilí Villalba," Gaudet replied, "Señorita Lilí Villalba."

On his way down the dark corridor to the dressing-rooms, Prullàs bumped into a stage-hand. To combat the intense heat in this confined space, the man was in his undershirt, although for some unknown reason he combined this with wearing a beret pulled down over his eyes. "Hello, Benito," Prullàs said. Benito was puffing and blowing; he was obviously suffering from the heat. "*Arriba España*, Don Carlos!" he replied, stepping to one side to let him past.

A printed card stuck with four tacks on the door of one of the dressing-rooms announced the name of its current occupant: Señorita Lilí Villalba. Prullàs knocked and went in without waiting for a reply. There was no-one inside; the lights round the dressing-table mirror were out, and only a yellowing bulb swinging on the ceiling gave off any light. There was the fusty smell of dirty washing in the room; a greasy turban and a moth-eaten, faded cape hung from a nail, while a cylindrical box stuffed with grimy wigs suggested macabre scenes of guillotining. "Señorita Lilí Villalba, are you there?" Prullàs whispered. His was the only image reflected in the mirror.

As he was on his way back to the stage to tell Gaudet of his latest failure, he noticed that the door to Mariquita Pons' dressing-room was ajar, and poked his head inside. A stifled cry greeted his intrusion. "What are you doing here?" he asked, taken aback not so much at finding Señorita Lilí Villalba somewhere she should not have been, as at finding her naked from the waist up. Although she had quickly folded her arms across her chest, she stood defiantly confronting the interloper; it was plain she was used to being stared at by men, and Prullàs, who had not expected such a spirited response in an embarrassing situation like this, was the one who was confused. "As you can see, I'm getting dressed." Prullàs turned from her and asked why she had come here to dress rather than in her own room. "I came here to have a shower," the young actress's voice informed him behind his back. "There isn't one in my dressing-room, and we've had no water at home for over a week now. Doña Mariquita left straight after the rehearsal," she went on. "I asked her where she was going in such a hurry, and she told me she had an appointment at the hairdresser's in five minutes and had no time for a shower, and that anyway she'd have a bath at home later because she had people coming to dinner; so I thought that if I came in here quickly and was careful, nobody would find out." Lowering her voice, she added: "You can check there's nothing missing."

Prullàs turned back to her; Señorita Lilí Villalba had finished dressing. He stared her up and down, trying to decide whether she was telling the truth or making fun of him. Yet when their eyes met, they both suddenly burst out laughing, as if the odd nature of this meeting had produced a subtle complicity between them. I know I was wrong, but by showing you my charms without meaning to, I've bought your silence, was what her laugh seemed to be saying, and this is our tacit way of sealing the agreement. "Who opened the door to this dressing-room for you?" Prullàs asked. "No-one, it was open." "That's a lie: the dressing-room doors are always locked." "Well, this one wasn't, see?" the youthful actress protested, switching off the lights and slamming the door shut on her way out. As she passed by him, the fragrance of her freshly washed skin and hair wafted over Prullàs. "Aren't you going into your own dressing-room for your bag?" he asked. "I don't have a bag, because I don't need one; when I'm not in the theatre I don't wear make-up, and I never carry money with me." "Do you always find someone to pay for you, Señorita Lilí?" he asked. "I've been quite lucky so far," she said, holding out her hand. "'Bye."

"How did it go?" the director wanted to know. "She seems like a reasonable enough person," Prullàs replied. "Did you talk about Ignacio Vallsigorri?" "No, not directly at any rate; I thought it was better to get friendly with her before grasping the nettle." Gaudet looked at him slyly. "And I can see who got stung," he cackled.

2

"Poveda's been here," Prullàs said as soon as he stepped into the hall. "Very clever of you, Watson," Mariquita Pons replied, holding two fingers to her nose; "but I bet you can't guess what he sold me this time." "How could I guess? It could be anything." "Well, say something, you're so perceptive." Prullàs made a few unenthusiastic suggestions. A lighter? No. Vitamins? No. Stockings? Cold, cold. "I give up," he said finally. The actress laughed: "A kitchen clock," she gushed, "come and see it!" "Where's your husband?" "In his mousetrap, reading the piles of papers he's brought back from Madrid," she replied, with a shrug of disdain.

"But this isn't a kitchen clock!" Prullàs exclaimed. "Oh, no, what is it then?" "A cuckoo clock." "It's all the same." "What d'you mean, the same? What would you know anyway? When have you ever set foot in a kitchen?" Prullàs had lifted the lid of a saucepan, and a thick cloud of steam enveloped the two of them. "Go on, out of here, and stop getting in my way," the cook grumbled. "I only wanted to know what you were cooking, Fina." "Stone soup is what you'll get, young man," the cook replied, waving her ladle at him. New to the household and timid as she was, the maid gave a delighted smile at this show of intimacy. "Carmen, don't stand there like a dummy. Put the éclairs into the fridge, will you, the ones Señor Carlos brought," Mariquita said. "It'll be a miracle they don't go off with this heat." The maid hurried to carry out her instructions.

She had recently started in the house, but Prullàs could see she had already come under the actress's spell: she had already unconsciously adopted her mistress's gestures and inflexions. "They're all the same; when they're outside the house, they must attract attention," Prullàs thought. "I'm sure they must look pretentious, stuck up or even slightly crazy to their friends."

Mariquita accompanied Prullàs to her husband's study, but remained in the doorway. "See if you can bring him back to the surface," she whispered. The allusion was apt: a lamp with a frosted glass mantle concentrated all the light on the desk, leaving the rest of the room submerged in an underwater gloom. "Miguel," she called out from the door, "Carlos Prullàs is here." Her husband lifted his head and blinked, as though her call had roused him from a profound state of indecision, although the sheets of paper he had been studying only showed long lines of figures. Is he really concentrating on those sums, Prullàs wondered, or is he miles away?

Miguel Fontcuberta jumped up and came to greet his visitor with open arms. "Carlos Prullàs, what a sight for sore eyes!" He was tall and athletic, though he was beginning to thicken at the waist. He was nearing fifty, was related to all the best families in the city, and was on the board of Barcelona Football Club. "How are things, Miguel? Off to Madrid again, I see." The two men slapped each other cordially on the back. "Oh yes, if you have to so much as sneeze these days, they need to authorise it in the imperial capital. But this time it wasn't such a waste: after sorting out a few bits of business I was taken to the Ventas bullring, and I saw Luis Miguel Dominguín offered two ears, and Pepín Martín Vázquez won one. And I still had time to see Benavente's latest play; that man's a genius!" "When you're ready, dinner is served," Mariquita said from the threshold.

Fontcuberta linked his arm with Prullàs' as they walked along the corridor. "Before I forget," he said, "if you're in Barcelona next Monday, and have nothing to do, stop by at Brusquets' place around eight, eight-thirty." "Brusquets?" Prullàs asked. "A friend of mine," Foncuberta explained, "a man with money and taste, as you'll see. He's having a housewarming party: not many people, just close friends. He especially asked me to invite you; apparently he's never met you, but he's an admirer of your work and wants to raise the tone of the occasion by having you there." "Are you going?" Prullàs queried. "Of course, and Kiki too," Fontcuberta replied. "In that case," Prullàs said, "how could I refuse?"

"That was a delicious meal and a lovely evening," he said again. "That's the third time you've said so, why all this flattery?" Mariquita asked. Fontcuberta had gone to bed, saying he was exhausted from his journey: it had been so hot he was unable to sleep on the train. If he closed the window in his compartment, he was fried alive; if he opened it, the noise was deafening and the soot went straight to the back of his throat. Prullàs guessed there must be some other reason for his retiring. During the meal, Mariquita had missed no opportunity to attack her husband and, faced with her hostility, Fontcuberta had withdrawn into his shell. Unlike other men, who are cowards in the outside world and get their revenge by being despots in the safety of their own homes, Fontcuberta, known to be ferocious in the business world, became a complete marshmallow when he got home. For those who knew him in these surroundings, it was hard to imagine that someone so meek, timid and slightly reserved could elsewhere be a cunning, tenacious and if necessary ruthless businessman . To see him with his wife, whose every whim he satisfied on the spot, whose orders he carried out to the letter, and whose changes of mood he tolerated with true stoicism, nobody would have dreamt that of the two of them it was he who had an iron side to his nature, whereas she was extremely fragile. Prullàs, blissfully unaware of the paradoxes of married life, always managed to completely misinterpret the situation. "What's the matter with your husband?" he asked. "Don't pay him any attention, he's just tired from the journey."

The new, shy maid served them coffee and brandy in the living-room. "Will madam require anything more?" "No nothing, Carmen, you can go to bed, I'll see to everything." The maid executed a clumsy curtsy and left, followed all the way by Prullàs' eyes, as he openly assessed her charms. "A useful acquisition," he commented, when she had shut the door behind her. "Where did you find her?" "They recommended her in the bakery," Mariquita replied, serving the coffee and cognac. "She's just arrived from her village and is little more than a girl; she's of an age to be my daughter, so leave her in peace, will you?" Prullàs sipped his cognac and smiled broadly: "I've not done a thing, Kiki!" "Oh, come on, you've spent the whole evening stripping her with your eyes; you ought to be ashamed of yourself!" "D'you think she noticed?" Prullàs asked. "Of course," she replied, "and anyway, *I* noticed, and I thought it was very ungallant of you."

Prullàs took her hand and lifted it to his lips. "It's a different kind of love, Kiki." The actress withdrew her hand and picked up her fan. "Sometimes I really feel I could strangle you," she said; "but if I haven't done it by now, I suppose I never will." "That's very generous of you," Prullàs said. "Lazy more like," she retorted. "After all these years, I've got used to you, like one does a physical defect."

Prullàs lit a cigarette and settled back on the ample cushions of the sofa. "We haven't known each other that long," he said. "At least, that's how it seems to me; perhaps it's that when I'm with you, the years are like days, and the days, seconds." "Very funny," the actress complained; yet there was a fleeting gleam of contentment in her eyes.

Prullàs' thoughts had already taken another direction. "D'you remember when we first put on 'All the Dead Are Called Paco'?" The actress put down the fan, placed a cigarette in her mother-of-pearl holder and allowed Prullàs to light it. "Of course, how could I forget?"

Mentioning the play took them both back to one spring night many years earlier in Madrid. Prullàs was just launching his first comedy and Mariquita Pons, in those days a young actress with a growing reputation, had decided to give a new, unexpected turn to her dramatic career and, against the advice of her agent, had taken the plunge and agreed to play the lead in the new playwright's work. Contrary to all expectations, the opening night had been a huge success. After the performance, when they had finished receiving the congratulations of all their friends and acquaintances, the author and his leading actress still felt too excited to go home to bed, and so had decided to carry on the celebrations. This was before Mariquita Pons had met Fontcuberta, and she had a boyfriend who was as charming as he was lazy; a professional scrounger, he was one part poet, one part revolutionary, and several parts ne'er-do-well: a characteristic representative of Madrid bohemia. Prullàs, who was already courting Martita, was on his own at the time, because her parents had refused permission for her to accompany him to Madrid, even though she had relatives there who could have put her up and kept an eye on her. Far from letting this depress him, Prullàs had managed to fix himself up with an elegant partner, a complete scatterbrain with intellectual pretensions. The four of them had ended up in the early hours of the morning at an open air dance-hall on the outskirts of Madrid, a trellis-covered place on the banks of the Manzanares, with long wooden tables and rough benches, lit by paper lanterns. They drank punch, danced *pasodobles* and Java waltzes to the strains of a barrel organ, and from a safe distance witnessed a fight between two young toughs. This consisted of a great deal of insults and verbal cut and thrust, defiant bragging and finally, the drawing of knives. Fortunately, things were resolved sensibly and nobody was hurt, but the incident left them all even more elated than they were before. Mariquita's boyfriend borrowed a guitar and sang a *bolero*, which everyone applauded; then the two women danced a daring *milonga* to a wild rhythm. They insisted Prullàs perform too, but he claimed he didn't know how to play the guitar, sing, and still less dance; when they wouldn't take no for an answer, he ended up reciting a romantic ballad by the Duke of Rivas, flinging his arms about and putting on a deep, bombastic voice. When he had finished, everyone cheered, and the two women kissed him simultaneously on both cheeks. By the time they got back to Madrid, day was dawning; a cold wind from the north was blowing, and the city roofs stood out sharply against the clear, calm blue of the sky. The walls of all the waste lots were covered with posters for the election campaign. Pranksters had defaced the stern features of Gil Robles and Largo Caballero. The elegant young woman clung to Prullàs' arm and declared for everyone to hear that she was going to vote for José Antonio Primo de Rivera. He was the only man who could save Spain from chaos, she claimed, and besides, he was so good-looking! In those troubled times, expressing open support in this way was extremely foolhardy.

"Whatever happened to that boyfriend you had then, Kiki?" Prullàs asked, interrupting the flow of images that flooded back to him from the past. "Manuel? You've got a good memory. For God's sake, Carlos, my love life hasn't been that rich," she exclaimed. "He was a charming rogue." "Did you hear anything more of him?" "Only indirectly: I was told he died in Burgos prison," she said. "What about that girl you were gallivanting with, the one who wanted to vote for José Antonio – what was she called?" "I haven't the faintest idea: it was only a brief and inconsequential fling." "Well, that night you seemed pretty infatuated with each other." "We were just having a good time. After all the fun, I took her home and we said goodbye at the door with a handshake." "That's all? You don't really expect me to believe that, do you?" "Of course I do. Her father was one of the blueshirt Fascists, always with a gun stuck in his belt." He gave a sad smile and added despondently: "How times have changed!"

"What's the matter, Carlos?" Mariquita asked. "Nothing." "You can't fool me, you're worried about something. Look, it's very late, why don't you tell me what it's all about, then you can go home?" Prullàs cleared his throat. "How did you get on at the hairdresser's?" he suddenly asked out of the blue. She stared at him in astonishment. "What hairdresser's?" "The one this afternoon; the one you had an appointment with, so you rushed off straight after rehearsals." "Good Lord! it's true, I'd completely forgotten about it," she exclaimed, automatically raising her hands to her head and tidying her hair. "When my husband's away I'm in another world, and when he comes back I don't know where I am: he drives me mad sometimes. But who told you about the hairdresser's anyway?" "That new girl in the play," he said. "Lilí Villalba." "Ah, her. I didn't know you were friends." "Until today, I hadn't even spoken to her; Gaudet was keen I that should go and see her after rehearsals," Prullàs said. "Gaudet sent you to talk to that miserable specimen? What on earth for?" she asked sharply. Prullàs realised he was venturing onto dangerous ground; at all costs, he must prevent her finding out about Vallsigorri's machinations. "I'm not too sure," he extemporised; "Gaudet says she's nervous, and he wanted me to try to calm her down." Mariquita smiled disdainfully. "And did you succeed in calming her?" "What is it, Kiki? Has there been some kind of argument between you and Señorita Villalba?" "Argument?" she murmured, "what argument?" "How should I know! I only come to rehearsals every once in a while," Prullàs responded; "but I get the feeling something's been happening with you lately, you're always so bad-tempered." The Princess replied that she only lost her temper with time-wasters: she did not specify whom she meant, but there was an impatient edge to her voice.

When they were in the hall, Mariquita Pons sighed and gave Prullàs a tender look as if, now that it was time to say goodbye, her anger had melted into a feeling of pity for him. "I can see that girl scored a hit with you," she said. Prullàs studied himself in the hall mirror: "D'you think she'll find me attractive?" he asked, half mockingly, but half seriously as well. The actress shrugged her shoulders. "All I can tell you is that she'll pretend she does; what more do you want?" Prullàs looked away from the mirror, smiled and shook his head sadly; she ran her fingers round the lapel of his jacket. "Be careful, Carlos," she whispered. "Señorita Villalba could lead you into trouble; you're better off sticking to your own kind, like that gorgeous redhead I saw you coming out of the cinema with the other night." "Trouble?" he asked, deliberately ignoring the Princess's reference to Marichuli Mercadal; "I don't understand: D'you mean that Vallsigorri fellow?" "Yes, that Vallsigorri fellow," she declared roundly; "I know him well, and he's not to be trusted; and he'll deserve whatever he gets," she murmured cryptically. She stood on tiptoe to give Prullàs a fleeting kiss on the cheek. "I worry about you, you know," she added, stepping back and pushing him gently towards the door.

Out of sorts and unable to sleep, he paced about his apartment when he got home. Who on earth can figure out women, he asked himself through clenched teeth; first there's that shameless hussy in the dressing-room, and now Kiki. What can she have meant by those veiled insinuations of hers?

3

Prullàs did not have to wait long to discover the meaning of her mysterious warning. Two days after his dinner at the Fontcubertas', Sebastiana interrupted him in the midst of breakfast to tell him he had an unexpected visitor.

Nothing was guaranteed to annoy him more. Like most night-owls, he woke up slowly, following a strict routine: he shaved, washed and dressed unhurriedly, and although his breakfast was usually frugal, he liked to linger over it, alternating this with a casual reading of *La Vanguardia* and a faithful commitment to completing the crossword. He found this the only way to shake off his morning lethargy without too much effort or disturbance. Good Lord! A visit at this time of day! Who on earth can it be?

Sebastiana gave an easy shrug. "Some trollop," she said. Prullàs gave her a disapproving look. "She must have given her name." "Lilí Villalba, or something like that," she muttered reluctantly, and then added with a note of triumph: "The early bird catches the worm." "When I need a pearl of popular wisdom I'll come and ask you," Prullàs said. "Until then, kindly be careful what you say." Sebastiana lifted her bushy eyebrows and pursed her lips. "All right, I didn't say a word, and see where that gets you," she muttered. "Shall I tell her to come in?"

Ignoring his maid's sarcasm, Prullàs thought about the situation: he would have preferred not to meet the young actress at home, but at the same time, the mere mention of her name had brought to mind such a vivid image of his recent encounter with her in the dressing-room at the theatre, that he couldn't resist the desire to see her again. "Tell her I'll see her as soon as I can," he said eventually.

He tried to immerse himself in reading the newspaper again, but it was useless; he swallowed the remains of his white coffee at a gulp, wiped his lips with the napkin, and got up. Passing the sideboard mirror, he straightened his tie and flicked his shirt cuffs. Then he went out into the entrance hall.

Señorita Lilí Villalba was sitting demurely on the edge of her chair waiting for him. When he appeared, she stood up and opened her mouth to speak, but said nothing. She was wearing a plain, discreet summer dress that had faded due to too many washdays. "Follow me," Prullàs said.

He led her to the study, showed her in, and closed the door behind her. Then he went and sat behind his desk and stared over at her. The desk itself, with its leather top and its bronze writing set, gave their meeting a decidedly professional tone, he decided. This idea made him more relaxed. While he was busy lighting a cigarette and pondering how to broach matters calmly, the girl suddenly started to speak. "Señor Prullàs," she began, "I came to ask you to forgive me for my silly attitude; the other afternoon in the theatre I was rude and childish; although the circumstances themselves were largely to blame, they in no way excuse my behaviour: when you took me by surprise, in a state of undress and committing a serious breach of theatre regulations, I was so taken aback that instead of admitting that I was doubly wrong, I reacted badly, like a stupid, insolent child; in short, I did the opposite of what I should have done. I simply wanted to tell you I'm sorry." With that, she fell silent again and dropped her head, as if the effort she had made to come out with such a speech had left her bereft of any more ideas or even words. A moment later, and still without raising her head, she added: "I'm sure this is just a trifling matter to you, but to me it was so important I had to come and tell you. I also know it was wrong of me to come to your home at this time of day . . ."

"That's true," Prullàs said, "it was wrong of you; but do sit down." He gestured forcefully at the chair she should sit in, but there was no anger in his words, and there was even a faint amused smile on his lips. "I know it was wrong," the girl immediately went on, without accepting his offer of a seat, "but I had no choice. During the day I have no free time: I have to be at the other end of Barcelona before long, in Clot. I have a part-time job in the packing section of a dairy factory there," she explained. Then after a pause she justified this apparently unnecessary explanation by adding: "You surely don't believe I live only on what I earn in the theatre, do you?"

"I thought . . ." Prullàs began, but pulled up short. The young actress blushed. "Señor Ignacio Vallsigorri is a great friend and is very generous," she said in a whisper; "I owe him a lot of favours, especially the fact that he opened the doors of the theatre world to me, but you can't really think that . . . " Prullàs cleared his throat. "Have you had breakfast?" he asked, trying to change topics. "Yes, before I left home; I'm used to getting up early. The truth is that what with the rehearsals and my work, I do miss out on sleep, but I'm young and very fit, and I always say to myself – I mean, whenever I think I've reached the point of exhaustion, I say to myself that some day, before I am no longer young and strong, I'll have made a name for myself in the theatre, and I'll be able to live on what I earn there; if that doesn't happen . . ."

"Do sit down," Prullàs insisted. This time, she did as she was told, and sat in silence. Prullàs looked at her, trying to make up his mind how much of what she had said was true, and how sincere her demure attitude was. Far from erasing from his mind their strange meeting in Mariquita Pons' dressing-room, seeing her sitting there in front of him now only served to reinforce the image, lending it an added, darker significance. "Have you really come here at this time of day to tell me that?" he asked her finally: "that you're sorry for what happened the other day in the dressing-room?" "Not for what happened, but for the way I behaved, as I told you; I wanted to get rid of the bad impression I must have made on you, that's all," she replied.

Once again there was a tense silence between them. All of a sudden she shuddered. Prullàs was afraid this might be the prelude to a bout of tears or hysterics, but when she finally spoke once more, it was in a calm voice. "I've already taken up far too much of your time, I'll be leaving; thank you for seeing me and again, I'm sorry for disturbing you in this way." Prullàs realised that if he said nothing, she would stand up, leave the flat, and the whole incident would be forgotten. The simple rhythmic sound of a metal bar struck against a tin pan drifted in through the open balcony window: to the beat of this rudi-mentary drum, the hoarse voice of a rag-and-bone man cried out: "*Es compren pells de conill!*" Prullàs said: "Why couldn't you have apologised at the theatre today or tomorrow, during a break from rehearsals? Did you really need to come here to tell me?" The smile gradually vanished from the young woman's face. "It was impossible in the theatre," she murmured. "You don't understand, of course; I mean there's no way you could understand, but that's how it is." "You're right, I don't under-stand," Prullàs said, trying to cover his unease by adopting a jocular tone: he was afraid of what she might say next. She looked down at her wristwatch and asked: "Can I steal a few more minutes of your time, Señor Prullàs?" "If I remember rightly, it was you who were in a hurry," he said. "Yes, of course, I'll be late for work," she agreed; "I'll have to find a good excuse . . . it'll be the first time, so I hope they won't fire me." "All right then, go on," he said.

"Well, you see, Señor Prullàs," she began, "when I told you

just now that I wanted to get rid of the bad impression you must have had of me from the other day, I was telling you the truth, but not the whole truth; I wanted to use the pretext of my apology to get to know you. Please don't interrupt: I know what you think of me, what you see me as; even though we hardly know each other, I know what you are bound to think of a young girl like me; believe me, I don't blame you for it; in your position, anyone would do the same." "You're very sure you can read my thoughts," Prullàs butted in. She smiled sadly. "I'm not so naïve I don't know what the people in the theatre think of me, nor so deaf I can't hear their comments when my back is turned. But don't get me wrong: I didn't come here to complain or defend my reputation; I'm not interested in doing either, and anyway, what use would it be?" "So, what did you come to tell me?" "Just this," she said. "The work I have in the theatre is important to me, I want to be an actress; I really want to be one, and I'm ready to do anything, to make any sacrifice to achieve it. It's not just out of a sense of vocation, I wouldn't lie to you. Best put all my cards on the table, Señor Prullàs, it isn't simply vocation. All I've known throughout my life were hardships and difficulties: my childhood was unhappy, but my life now is even worse, and the future looks so black I can't even bear to think about it. I'm not well educated or cultured; I'm not trained for anything, so how will I earn a living? For now I have the job I told you about, in the dairy: it's a monotonous, tiring job where I wear myself out every day for next to nothing, but even that really mind-numbing job is only temporary; I could find myself out on the street again at any time, and then what? I know what you're thinking: that I'm being melodramatic for no reason. When I arrived here and the person who opened the door to me told me the master couldn't see me because he was still having breakfast, I realised that whatever I told you would be useless: someone who lives in such a way simply cannot understand some things. Don't be offended. Those who haven't experienced poverty and real need imagine that they are simply ingredients in other people's lives; but for those of us who live in that world, poverty and need are the only reality for us, day after day after day, always the same, with no hope of change. If I didn't think that the theatre could pull me out of the hole I'm in, I think I'd end it all." She gave a deep sigh as she said this, buried her face in her hands, and in that position added: "I'm ready to do anything to get on." Then she quickly took her hands away, gave a winning smile and said: "But please don't misinterpret what I'm saying."

"Tell me how I should interpret it then," Prullàs replied.

"I know men find me attractive," she went on. Prullàs lifted his eyebrows at the unexpected twist the young actress's reasoning had taken, and when she caught sight of this, Lilí looked at him with a mixture of shyness and calculation. "I'm not flirting with you, I'm simply stating how things are; I know I have a good figure and pretty legs. I'm always being whistled at in the street, and I know what the looks men give me mean. I'm not shameless, but I'm no nun either; I think I've missed out on a lot, but I was given a lot too, and it would be absurd simply to accept all the bad things in life and not take advantage of the good – always provided," she added mechanically, "that there's nothing immoral in it."

"Don Ignacio Vallsigorri . . ."

"I wasn't talking about him, but I don't mind doing so," she said. "We met by chance, although doubtless that chance wouldn't have arisen if my legs hadn't been the way they are. As I already told you, he opened the doors to the theatre for me, and not just any doors, but the most prestigious ones: from one day to the next I went from being nobody to becoming part of a famous company, working with Doña Mariquita Pons and in a play written by no less a person than you." She said these words so enthusiastically that Prullàs could find no good reason for doubting that they were heartfelt. She was so caught up in what she was saying that she had got up from her chair and was pacing round the room. Then all at once, her youthful optimism seemed to desert her. She collapsed into the leather armchair and when she spoke again, it was in a weary tone. "I'm sorry I was so blunt," she said, "I had no intention of talking about myself like that. I came to try and improve your view of me, and now I'm afraid I've done the complete opposite. I'll be leaving now. I am sorry I interrupted your breakfast, thank you for being so patient with me, and I promise you I'll never set foot here again."

She got to her feet and Prullàs did the same. "I'll show you to the door," he said. "Don't trouble yourself," she said. "It's no trouble." Out in the hall, they shook hands.

The front door to the apartment was already open when Prullàs said: "You know, perhaps we should continue this conversation with more time . . . somewhere else . . . " Lilí Villalba blenched; the harsh light of the landing made her pale skin look even whiter. "What did you have in mind, Señor Prullàs?" Prullàs cleared his throat. "Nothing, just a passing fancy," he said, moving to close the door. Before he could do so, she said quickly: "In Calle de la Unión, not far from the Ramblas, there's a quiet spot I sometimes go to when I want to be alone; perhaps this afternoon after the rehearsal, I might call in there. The Hotel Gallardo. You can't miss it." She began to skip down the stairs without waiting for a reply and Prullàs, without giving one, pushed the door open.

Alone once more, he tried to return to his interrupted reading of *La Vanguardia*. The local news section reported a cruel event: the previous night, some heartless individuals had evaded the guards, cut a hole in the surrounding fence and got into the

Barcelona zoo, where they had killed a poor defenceless animal with catapults. As a result of what the authorities condemned as a shameful act, it had been decided to double the number of guards in the Parque de la Ciudadela, where the zoo was housed, especially since at sunset on several occasions recently, flashers had been spotted in its peaceful avenues. The Peters Sisters were performing in a Madrid variety theatre. And in Nuremberg, the charges against Alfried Krupp were piling up. He was accused not only of openly expressing his support for the national-socialist ideology, but of offering substantial material support towards the triumph of the dreadful party which embodied it. Irrefutable evidence showed that Krupp had contributed what in those days was the staggering sum of a million marks to help finance the Nazi electoral campaign. According to the prosecution, it was thanks to this contribution, and other similar ones from leading German families, that the Nazis had won the elections and come to power. It was only as a result of the unconditional support they received from powerful industrial and financial circles that the Nazis had been able to pay for their huge propaganda machine, which they had used to dupe the entire population, eventually leading them to their doom. The accused had not the slightest qualm in accepting all this. In fact, he told the court, it was Goering himself who had come round asking for money from the great families. Give without stinting, he had urged them; just think, if we win, you won't have to make any further contributions because there won't be any more elections in Germany for the next hundred years. Disgusted with the hypocrisy, indecisiveness and corruption inherent in the party system, this proposal had seemed to them not only justified, but above all, practical. And giving money to a party to help pay its election costs was not a crime, the defence lawyer hastened to add. When it came down to it, had the defendant not been acting according to the rules of the democratic process, and therefore was it not an inadmissible contradiction, an insult to logic, to classify as a crime against democracy the use of its own provisions, even if these were being employed to undermine democracy? Was this possibility not accommodated within the democratic system itself? the defence persisted. At this point one of the judges, a Justice of the Peace from Britain, had raised the following question: What would happen if in the course of a boxing match, for whatever reason, one of the fighters began to hit himself so powerfully that he knocked himself senseless? Could it be said that he had infringed Queensberry rules? And if so, on what grounds? Warming to the theme, another judge, an American this time, chipped in and recalled how in the far-off days of 1926, he had been present at the historic world heavyweight fight when – thanks to a highly controversial decision by the referee – Jack Dempsey had lost the title on points to Jim Tunney. Just as the speaker was preparing to launch into a description of some of the bout's more memorable moments, the president of the court, a Frenchman, had suspended the session due to the lateness of the hour.

4

"The people in the theatre all have it in for me," she said; "they have a grudge against me, and Doña Mariquita would love to tear my eyes out, I can tell." Prullàs was standing at the window, smoking a cigarette. "You should never speak ill of anyone," he said without turning round. "Curses have a way of rebounding on those who pronounce them." Although the weather forecast had predicted cloudy skies and isolated showers, until now the day had been clear and bright; just at this moment however, heavy clouds were closing in on the city, and the sound of distant thunder could be heard in the room. They get it right just when you least expect it, Prullàs thought. "You see," Lilí Villalba went on, "you see how I need someone to teach me these things? I didn't mean to criticise anyone, least of all Doña Mariquita: I worship her, I admire her as an actress and as a person; I'd give my life for her, I swear, and may I drop down dead right here if I'm telling a lie; all I wish is to continue at her side, learning my trade, so that one day I can be like her; please let her know that the experience is worth its weight in gold for me."

Prullàs stopped staring at the clouds and scrutinised the house opposite. All its windows were open, and the blinds lifted, yet it appeared deserted: the only sign of life was a goldfinch hopping about in a metal cage hanging from one of the window frames. In a shop window on the ground floor, which also seemed closed to the public, a printed notice read:

DOCTOR SOBRINO'S ANTIVENEREAL CLINIC.
SKIN DISEASES, GONORRHOEA, SYPHILIS.
PERMANGANATE WASHES.

"You tell her," he proposed. "Oh no, I wouldn't know how to, I find it hard to say what I really think, as you've just seen; when I try to say something sensible, it comes out sounding ridiculous." Prullàs turned into the room and smiled. "That's because you're so young," he murmured; "she'll understand." Lilí drew up her legs, wrapped her arms round them, and rested her chin on her knees; she had slender limbs but gave off an intoxicating sensation of youthfulness. This sight of her made up for the depressing room, the grubby sheets. "D'you really think she'll understand me?" she insisted disbelievingly. "Of course," he replied. Perhaps years ago Kiki was just the same, Prullàs reflected, perhaps she also had to go through something similar, spend time in rooms like this one; she would never admit it, but there's no reason to think it might not have happened.

Prullàs remembered he had heard the celebrated actress tell a story of how once during her early days, many years previously, in the crazy, bohemian Madrid of the Dictatorship, she had found work in a second-rate theatre troupe whose assistant director had the habit of concealing himself in the wardrobe of the actresses' dressing-rooms so he could watch them getting changed. All the actresses knew this, but the assistant director was a despicable, slanderous sort who for some unknown reason had a hold over the director and could ruin the career of anyone he took against. So the actresses preferred to ignore his presence in their dressing-rooms, and pretended they could not hear his panting among their dresses. Mariquita Pons had told this story in her own living-room to a circle of friends, and in front of her husband, and had not shown the slightest rancour or sense of shame, either because the years that had gone by since then had turned the episode into nothing more than an amusing anecdote, or because even at the time she had considered it perfectly normal and nothing to be ashamed of. Mariquita had also been brought up in an extremely tough environment, one of harsh poverty and little joy. Her exquisite femininity was a deliberate construction: she had decided to create that appearance and enjoy its benefits. By dint of struggle and daily effort, her personality now appeared to be one of delicate and spontaneous ease, with a finely-wrought sensibility; just how she had achieved it was by now of no importance whatsoever. On the other hand, Prullàs thought, the young woman he had just made love to in this grimy room at the Hotel Gallardo still had a long hard road ahead of her, full of doubts and dangers. Perhaps it's my duty to warn her, he told himself; and yet she's right of course – if she doesn't do this, what other choice has she got? It never so much as crossed Prullàs' mind that his behaviour was in any way akin to that of the lecherous, miserable assistant director who years earlier had spied on the young Mariquita Pons from the wardrobe. Prullàs considered himself a handsome, attractive man who had the added advantage of being famous; he thought it quite natural that women should fall into his arms without expecting much in return.

"But that doesn't mean that what I said isn't true," he heard Lilí say, as she carried on speaking in spite of the fact that he had fallen completely silent. "I know they whisper behind my back because I got into the company with a helping hand from Señor Vallsigorri, as if that were a crime. How else is someone like me to get on? The way I did it doesn't make me any different from them, and I'm not asking for any favours; on the contrary, I just want to be treated exactly like everyone else, I want to get on well with everyone, and for them all to appreciate me as much as I appreciate them. You tell her, please, tell them all I'm proud to be working with them, and that I know what a privilege it is to be under Señor Gaudet. Please, Carlos, talk to him and tell him I'm willing to do anything he asks of me, anything at all . . . tell him he won't offend me . . . and nor will you, you know."

Prullàs stared at her. He was wondering if this was a veiled invitation to something unmentionable, a hint of depravity. She gazed back at him quizzically. "Why are you looking at me like that?" No, he told himself, there's no mystery behind her words, but there's something perverse about her attitude. She knows what's expected of her, and she is willing to give it wholeheartedly, unstintingly and without prevarication. In many ways, she's still a child, with an innocent mind, but her whole being is corrupt. Perhaps in the world she's from, these things are viewed differently. But what about me, what am I doing here? He felt a vague sense of alarm spreading over him, the result more of a foreboding than of any rational response.

He had occasionally been involved in fleeting romances like this, but had known how to handle them discreetly, and end them tactfully at the right moment, in a way that benefited both sides, and without further consequences beyond the inevitable tears, protestations and recriminations. This time however, the situation was different and his instincts were alerting him to approaching danger. For the first time ever, he found himself caught up in an adventure with a woman who from the outset had taken the initiative, who was seemingly unconcerned about the difference in their ages, their rank or place in society, as if all that really mattered in their incipient affair was their mutual attraction. She combined the reckless attitude of a person sure she is bound to win, with the rashness of someone who stakes all she has on each throw of the dice, when her opponent has seemingly infinite resources.

A flash of lightning made him turn back to the window; there was a clap of thunder, and heavy drops began to spatter on the dusty street pavement. The goldfinch in its cage began hopping about, trying in vain to avoid the downpour. Botheration! Prullàs thought; I wanted to cut this short, and now I'll have to wait for the weather to clear. "Some day," Lilí was saying behind him, "when I'm famous and the journalists ask me how I started out, I can tell them it was thanks to you." Without noticing his wary glance, she went on: "Oh, Carlos, if only you could see me at night when it's too hot to sleep, tossing and turning in my bed while I imagine the most fantastic plans and ideas!" The rain began to beat on the windowpane. "Where are you leading me, you shameless hussy?" Prullàs said, closing the window and turning back to her. "Where do you want to go?" replied the girl.

The room was submerged in gloom. Prullàs lit a cigarette. "I don't want any problems," he declared. "I'm not going to cause you any," she protested. But it wasn't her he was thinking about: it was himself he was afraid of. I mustn't get carried away by my impulses, he told himself; remember, she already has a protector. And yet, faced with her youthful exuberance in the oppressive atmosphere of this stormy afternoon, and the kind of temerity he himself had once known but had later forgotten, he could not help fantasising about unattainable desires. Starting over! he thought, that siren song! He checked himself, and irritably drove such foolish thoughts from his mind. I'm impulsive and changeable; whenever a woman crosses my path, I inevitably lose my head; none of them has been able to completely dominate me, but they all seem to arouse the wildest emotions in me. Bah, that's the way I am and there's no point moaning about it or trying to change; the most important thing is not to deceive anyone. But how to stop them deceiving themselves, if that's what they want?

These thoughts inevitably led him to Marichuli. Until now, he had managed to fend off all memory of his ignominious flight, but now at last he began to feel remorse. It had been cowardly of him to abandon a woman at such a critical moment without so much as a word of explanation or at least a false promise which would have justified his actions in his own eyes at least. She did what she did for me, he said to himself; before we met she would never have dreamt of burning her boats in that way; however much she pretended to be unscrupulous, she's no adventuress, still less a whore; by choosing to forget the rules of decency she put herself at risk, whereas I simply humiliated her.

The heat in the room together with the sense of shame he felt suddenly left Prullàs short of breath. She doesn't deserve to be treated like a plaything, and I'm not such a heartless person, he concluded, and immediately decided he would go to Masnou the next morning, despite her husband's being there, and the astonishment his sudden arrival might cause. I'll have to be extremely careful in showing her that what happened between us was more than a mere game, but at the same time avoiding getting too involved with her and falling into the opposite extreme, he told himself. To Prullàs in the murky atmosphere of this cheap hotel room, these thoughts of Marichuli began to seem like some kind of life-raft.

"I'm in no hurry, but I know that one day you'll write a comedy just for me," he heard Lilí saying. Her mixture of ingenuousness and arrogance put him in a good mood again. He cast off the dark thoughts that had been preoccupying him, rinsed his hands and face in the iron washstand in the corner of the room, and went over to the bed, determined not to waste the extra opportunity the weather had offered him. "When you're famous I'll write a story for you about a young girl whose nose kept on growing and growing because of all the lies she told," he said.

5

Prullàs' speculations were not far from the mark. When she awoke and found herself abandoned by the man in whose arms she had committed such a sin, Marichuli Mercadal was overwhelmed by a sense of despair. The memory of what had happened was so sweet, and her feeling of loss so painful, that for an instant she thought she would lose her mind. Gradually she calmed down, but could not overcome her bitter sadness. Although she had no wish to think of the future of her relationship with Prullàs, she had no illusions: she knew she had only succeeded in creating a fleeting, shallow interest on his part, a mixture of curiosity and appetite, and that unless something extraordinary happened it would end with a fond farewell once summer was over. Perhaps it's best that way, she told herself resignedly; it would be madness to imagine anything else.

She returned to Masnou that same morning. When she arrived, an unstocked refrigerator, a film of dust on the top of a piece of furniture, knives and forks left out of the sideboard, and a few other details only visible to the expert eye of a caring housewife, signalled to her that the household management had suffered from her brief absence. She immediately issued the instructions necessary to re-establish order, and paid no attention to the concern expressed by Doctor Mercadal who, when he saw in his wife's face the obvious signs of a physical and emotional fatigue that he could only ascribe to her visit to the dentist's, prescribed complete rest and a course of streptomycin to prevent any possible infection.

In spite of all the summer distractions, Alicia had also missed her; she had been in low spirits, unwilling to eat, and had a bad night. All this greatly affected Marichuli Mercadal, and led her to see how ridiculous her flirtation had been; what had started out as an exciting adventure now seemed to her a sordid, dangerous and above all doomed adventure. I've been stupid, she told herself, yielding as I did to a senseless passion that not only threatens my salvation, but puts at risk the stability and welfare of my family; and the worst of it is, I have nothing to blame except my own wild, sensual nature. Resolved as she was to settle the matter once and for all, that afternoon the first thing she did was to visit the church, with the firm intention of cleansing her conscience. "Father, I cannot explain how the dishonest proposals of a perfect stranger, a married man, instead of meeting a clear rejection from me, somehow unleashed an uncontrollable torrent of passion; my soul burnt like tinder in a flame, and I gave him my consent," she whispered, kneeling in the confessional. "And a second time," she added, in an even lower voice, "it was I who sought him out."

The church was almost empty; it was late afternoon and

the gentle rays of the sun flared into life as they filtered through the stained-glass windows; through the half-open door of the church the high-pitched cries of swifts could be heard; the drooping flowers on the altar saturated the warm air inside with their sickly smell. "My child, what you have done is very wrong." But Marichuli barely heard the priest's instructive homily: evoking her disgrace and declaring her irresponsibility in such an open way had left her in an almost intoxicated state; the church began to spin around her. Fearful that she was about to faint, she crept out of the confessional. Perplexed, the father confessor stuck his head out of the drapes. "Don't go, Señora, I haven't given you absolution yet!"

She got out of the church by clinging on to the backs of the pews; out in the street she managed to stagger as far as a public fountain; there, the flow of cool water calmed her agitation, and she steadied herself and set off for home. She smiled back mechanically at the passers-by who said hello to her on their evening stroll. The next day, those same summer tourists had to leave the beach in a hurry when a cold damp wind suddenly sprang up, filling the horizon with dark, threatening clouds. Shortly afterwards, the same storm broke which a few hours later was to keep Prullàs longer than expected in the Hotel Gallardo.

Caught up as she was in all kinds of fears and forebodings, Marichuli could not help but see this drastic change in the weather as a fateful sign. For the first time in her life, she became frightened of lightning, and it was useless for her husband to employ all his knowledge as a scientist and all his patience as a doctor to try to prove to her that it was physically impossible for the family to be reduced to cinders inside the house. She lit a candle to Saint Barbara, and another to the Christ of Lepanto, and, deaf to the argument that there was more danger from these flickering flames near the curtains than from any atmospheric discharge, she summoned all the servants to this improvised altar and made them all say the rosary together. Before they had reached the second mystery, the storm ended, the sun came out, and a rainbow appeared in the sky. Faced with such a striking and dramatic confirmation, she could not hold back her tears. Her husband racked his brains to diagnose the reasons behind this unusual and extravagant behaviour.

The following day the usual summer weather had returned, and Marichuli Mercadal and Alicia walked down to the beach. On the way they had to step aside to make room for Prullàs' car. The sun was beating down so strongly on the Studebaker's bodywork that she couldn't make out who was driving, but she thought to herself: he's come back for me.

And yet over the next few hours, Prullàs made no attempt to get in touch: all his good intentions had evaporated as soon as he saw her. Have I gone crazy all of a sudden? he wondered; I should never have come; I've got more than enough problems already without going looking for more. If he could, he would have turned round then and there and headed back for Barcelona, but it was too late: she had already seen him, and such an extreme measure would only complicate matters still further. I'll go to our house, he thought; Martita and the kids will be glad to see me, and it will do me good to spend some days away from the theatre. And as for Marichuli, there's bound to be an opportunity to speak to her somewhere in public without it being too embarrassing.

In the garden he found his mother-in-law watering the hydrangea bushes. "Everyone else has gone down to the beach," she said. "Anyway, why are you here without telling anyone?" "Fleeing from the anarchists," Prullàs retorted; "they've taken Barcelona and now they're heading this way." The poor woman dropped the hosepipe to cross herself. She knew it was a joke, but her distress was real. "We had a good drop of rain yesterday," she said, once she had got over her fright; "but today, as you can see, there's not a cloud in the sky." "Yes, there was a downpour in Barcelona as well." "Aren't you going for a swim?" "Later on. First I have to go and make a phone call." He had left Barcelona in such a hurry, he hadn't even told Gaudet. He had a wash, changed clothes and walked up to the Social Club.

Compared to the glare outside, the club seemed to be in darkness; perhaps this was why when Prullàs went in he felt a pleasing cool, together with a mixture of smells that included both flowers and beer barrels. The first perfume came from the garden, wafting through the wide-open French windows; the second from the bar, where Joaquín, in a white apron, was busy drying a row of glasses and stacking them on the shelves. "What can I get you, Señor Prullàs?" "Don't let me interrupt you, Joaquín." The barman waved the wet and none-too-clean cloth he was carrying and said that he was there to serve clients. He was taking advantage of this slack time to clean up the place a bit, he said, while everyone was on the beach getting as pink as lobsters. Prullàs pointed to the far end of the room. "I only came to use the phone," he said.

Roller blinds kept the sun off this corner of the club-room, which housed the phone booth and the billiard tables. The names of the finalists in the summer competitions for billiards and snooker were chalked on a slate on the wall. Prullàs went into the phone box, pulled the door to, dialled 09 and waited a moment until he heard the operator's voice: he said he wanted Barcelona, gave Gaudet's number, and asked if there was much of a wait. The operator said no: fifteen or twenty minutes, in a tone which seemed to imply, "what else did you expect?" Prullàs hung up and went back to the bar. "Give me a vermouth and some stuffed olives while I'm waiting," he said. As Joaquín was spooning the olives out of a jar, the local village idiot made his appearance.

He had probably been hoping to find Joaquín on his own, because when he saw another person inside, his squat figure performed a few pirouettes against the light in the doorway. Joaquín waved his dishcloth to try and encourage him, but this only had the opposite effect. "Come on in, Roquet," he shouted.

The boy made his way across the room, head down and keeping close to the walls. Prullàs wondered how old he could be, because his features made it hard to tell: some of them made him look like a child, whilst others gave him a much older look, without any clue as to which corresponded to the real passage of time, and which to his mental deficiencies. He went by the name of Roquet el dels Fems, and the story in the village was that he had been abandoned by his parents – gypsies or foreigners passing through – not long after he was born. They had left him in a basket on the dean's doorstep, and on discovering the baby early one morning as he was leaving for his pastoral rounds, the dean had baptised him and decided to take care of him. "Have you brought what I asked you for?" Joaquín asked him.

The boy pointed triumphantly to a bundle of papers tied up with an elastic band. Although he couldn't read or write and lived on charity, Roquet el dels Fems earned some pocket money by running errands in the village: taking and fetching parcels, occasionally sweeping the pavements, or stoning stray cats to death. "Give Roquet some chips and a soft drink, Joaquín, they're on me," Prullàs said. The boy kicked his heels with delight and handed the bundle of papers to Joaquín.

Just then the phone rang, and Prullàs went to make his call. "Your connection to Barcelona, don't hang up," the operator said. Prullàs could hear the phone ringing at the other end of the line, then a distant voice asked: "Who's that?" He immediately recognised Mariquita Pons' voice, and thought he must have got the wrong number, even though he was sure he had given Gaudet's to the operator. Could it have been she who made the mistake? No, that was nonsense, he thought, holding the receiver away from him and staring down at the earpiece as though the answer to the mystery lay in that particular gadget. "Hello, hello, who's there?" the actress asked over and over.

At that moment, the door to the phone booth opened and Roquet el del Fems stuck his large head inside. Prullàs frowned sternly at him, but the boy did not see or perhaps did not understand this silent form of reproof. He held up a half-empty bottle of Orange Crush and stuttered: "Tha . . ank you . . . tha . . ank you." On a sudden impulse, Prullàs pushed the receiver against one of his flapping ears. "You speak," he whispered to him. Without betraying the slightest surprise, the boy shouted down the line: "Hello!" and then a few seconds later, added: "Who, me? I'm Roquet, Roquet el dels Fems! And who are you?" Then he turned to Prullàs and pulled a face. "I couldn't hear a thing," he said. "They must have hung up, but it wasn't your fault; you did everything you should have, Roquet," Prullàs consoled him. He took the receiver and asked the operator how much he owed, and what number she had dialled. The operator confirmed that she had called Gaudet. There could be no doubt then that Mariquita was at the director's apartment. Which, all things considered, is nothing extraordinary, Prullàs thought. And yet the idea made him uncomfortable in a way he could not explain, but found hard to shake off. What's going on behind my back? he wondered.

Preoccupied with these thoughts, he only realised once he was back at the bar that Joaquín had climbed onto a chair and was nailing a brightly-coloured poster to the wall. So that's what Roquet brought! he exclaimed. "The deliveryman gave him half a dozen to put up in the busiest places," Joaquín said, without taking his eyes off the poster; "Don't forget your vermouth, it'll be warm by now and weak." Roquet el dels Fems had polished off the chips and was staring greedily at the stuffed olives Prullàs had ordered. Prullàs pushed them along the bar towards him, and drank the vermouth while he took in what was on the poster. In its centre it showed a good-looking young man, dark-haired and with a thin moustache, in evening dress, covered from top to toe by a long white cape. His eyes were closed, eyebrows knitted, and the tips of his fingers were pressed or rested against his forehead in a gesture that implied the deepest concentration. In the background was the sketchy but unmistakeable figure of Mephistopheles; with a leering scowl, he stretched out the long, tapering fingernails of one of his hands towards the meditating magician, as if with this gesture he could endow him with supernatural powers or convey some arcane knowledge to him. At the foot of the poster was written:

THE DIABOLICAL DOCTOR CORBEAU
AND HIS AMAZING PHENOMENOLOGICAL POWERS
TWO HOURS OF EMOTIONS AND CONTACT WITH THE BEYOND
AN UNFORGETTABLE EXPERIENCE
NOT RECOMMENDED FOR CARDIACS

Joaquín had added to this another note written in his own handwriting, which announced in big letters:

SATURDAY EVENING AT NINE THIRTY
IN THE SOCIAL CLUB BILLIARD ROOM
ENTRANCE FOR THE PRICE OF A DRINK

"I've put the prices up specially because of the event," he explained. Prullàs told him how much the telephone had cost and asked him to add it to his bill. Then he left the club with

Roquet, and went into the nearby newsagent's, where he bought magazines for the whole family, and *Pulgarcito* and the latest episode of *Roberto Alcázar y Pedrín* for the children. Roquet el dels Fems gave the woman in the shop another of the Diabolical Doctor Corbeau's posters, and spent the money Joaquín had given him on a postcard of Rita Hayworth. "So you like the cinema too, d'you?" Prullàs asked him. "Nah," the fool replied, "only the girls!"

6

The arrival of Martita and the children woke him from an uneasy nap. "What a surprise, we didn't expect you till tomorrow!" Prullàs groped blindly on the floor for the copy of *Destino* he had bought at the newsagents'; he had started to read an article by José Pla from Amsterdam when he was overcome by a desire to sleep; with a dry mouth he tried to explain what had happened. "Are you sure you're all right?" "I had a vermouth on an empty stomach and it must have knocked me sideways," he reassured his wife, who was looking at him anxiously.

"Papa, papa! Tomorrow night there's a magician performing at the club! Can we go?"

"Yes, I saw the poster too," Prullàs said; "Roquet el dels Fems was taking them round the village. We had a drink together and a very interesting chat about our preferences in the film world," he added.

Martita's worried look changed to one of reproach. "Don't say things like that in front of the children, I've forbidden them to have anything to do with that rascal." Roquet el dels Fems was regarded as a public nuisance by the summer colony in Masnou; it was said he was forever trying to touch women's breasts, whether they liked the idea or not; and failing that, he would do the same to goats and cows; that he profaned the tombstones in the cemetery, and in general behaved in a brutish, reprehensible fashion. None of this was true. If he lost his temper, he would take it out on the person who had offended him, or whoever else happened to be within reach. In those cases, because he was heftily-built and had no notion of the harm his blows might cause, he could be dangerous. But these mad frenzies occurred less and less often as he grew older. Usually, Roquet el dels Fems was quiet, docile, polite, and extremely patient faced with all the taunts that the youngsters – and often adults as well – goaded him with.

"It didn't seem to me that it was a show suitable for children," Prullàs said. He looked across at his wife in the hope she would agree with him, but her face was noncommittal: she took it for granted that there could be nothing immoral about an evening of magic, and therefore could see no reason why the children should not go. "All right," Prullàs said, "but if halfway through I decide I don't like it, then we'll all leave."

Having got what they wanted, the children galloped off. Their mother's voice pursued them: "Shake your shoes before you go in or you'll get sand everywhere! Wash your hands! Don't drink from the tap!" She laid a hand on Prullàs' sweating brow. "What were you dreaming about?" she asked him. "I don't remember," he lied; "Perhaps about the diabolical Doctor Corbeau."

"Just a minute!" Doctor Mercadal shouted, waving his arms in the air. "Such an interesting discussion calls for something special. And in fact," he added, as though he had somehow known this was going to be an extraordinary occasion, he had put a bottle of French champagne on ice, a gift from a grateful patient. "I'll fetch it in a second, but you have to promise not to say any more until I get back. Marichuli, tell them to bring the champagne glasses!"

"I'll go and get them," she said; "the maids have no idea where they are." As she rose, the intense perfume she was wearing wafted through the pergola, obliterating the delicate fragrance of the jasmine and azaleas. Martita had tried several times to persuade her not to use the perfume: according to her, anything that was not an insect-repellent cologne only attracted mosquitoes. "They don't bite me," Marichuli had responded, "my blood's too bitter." But the scent drove Prullàs wild: he became so nervous he talked nineteen to the dozen, and during dinner he had not only knocked over his wine glass, but had twice dropped his fork on the floor.

That afternoon, Doctor Mercadal had turned up at Prullàs' in-laws house and without the slightest formality had invited Prullàs and Martita for dinner. "I thought you were in Barcelona," he said, "but my wife and daughter saw you pass by this morning; and since on Monday I absolutely must return to my surgery and my patients, I thought we could meet up tonight in our garden, weather and insects permitting. Don't expect anything too grand: it'll be bread with tomato and ham, Spanish omelette and not much else." When they arrived, however, they had been offered prawns and mussels in a wine sauce, tuna pasties, and rolled beef stuffed with vegetables.

"I didn't know you were coming until late this afternoon, so I had to make do with what I could find," Marichuli said. "If anything turned out all right, it's thanks to her; if it didn't, it's my fault," the doctor joked. "Don't listen to him, Marichuli, you're a wonderful cook," Martita said, to settle the issue.

"That was a truly magnificent meal," Prullàs added, staring fixedly at their hostess, who met his gaze. The light from a lantern hanging in among the flowers lent her skin a coppery sheen and gave her dark-ringed eyes a wild gleam. Yet during the meal she had hardly taken part in the conversation, as if her obligations as a hostess were more important than whatever was being discussed at table.

"What an odd couple!" Prullàs commented, finding himself alone with Martita after the others had gone to fetch the champagne and the glasses. "They're new to the village, and they want people to like them and to make friends," Martita replied. "That doesn't mean they aren't odd," he said. "You've hardly met them." "That's true," Prullàs quickly admitted, seeing Marichuli on her way back, accompanied by a maid carrying four champagne glasses on a tray. "I know it's not done to leave guests on their own, but it's so difficult to find anything in this house," she said. "The previous tenants had a very strange sense of order: they kept some of their glasses in the pantry, and the rest in a cupboard on the first floor, would you believe?"

Doctor Mercadal reappeared, brandishing a bottle of Veuve Clicquot. "That's a fine gift!" Prullàs commented. "Oh yes, and he was a fine patient too: I took some large polyps out of his rectum," the surgeon explained. "Did you have to go into details?" his wife moaned.

The surgeon uncorked the bottle with a loud bang. "O.K., now go on telling us about the theatre," he said; "we're all ears for more." Prullàs gave a dismissive shrug. He was always surprised at the interest people not involved in the theatre had in it, even those who wouldn't dream of setting foot inside one. His gesture did not escape Marichuli. "Don't give yourself such airs," she said in a tone of friendly reproach. "Anyone would think you don't like the theatre!"

"You're right there!" Prullàs replied. "I sometimes find it amusing to write comedies, and I enjoy the backstage theatre world. But theatre as a spectacle, the theatre that entertains people and receives their applause, that kind of theatre leaves me cold. And it's not just a personal opinion or a matter of taste," he went on; "still less a pose: as I see it, and I mean it in all seriousness, real theatre has ceased to exist."

"And what in your view would this real theatre be?" Doctor Mercadal wanted to know. "Oh, cloak-and-dagger dramas," Prullàs said, "with cardboard-cutout sets. I can still remember from my childhood," he went on, "seeing some of those melodramas where the final curtain always fell on a stage heaped with bodies, while makeshift kings with beards tied round their ears fulminated at heaven and hell. There was something for everyone: plots, assassinations, usurpers, impossible loves, instantaneous conversions, suicides; the stage teemed with generous bandits, satanic monks, victims and executioners, all of them side-by-side and in perfect harmony; and the plays demonstrated the virtues of every conceivable way of killing someone: pistol, dagger, poison, and sometimes as a real treat burning at the stake, the guillotine, or defenestration. In other words, the kind of theatre that took the sublime Enrique Rambal to the top."

"There's a lot of truth in what you say," the surgeon replied, "and it reminds me of a marvellous anecdote. Once when I was a little boy my father took me for All Saints' Day to see a performance of 'Don Juan' by a third-rate company. It was the sacrilegious dinner scene, when the statue of the Commander comes on stage, preceded for greater effect by a huge electrical display: lightning, thunder and hellfire. Unfortunately, this time the fire proved only too real and took hold of the Commander's cape. The actor didn't realise this and came on with his cape in flames. When he saw what was happening, Don Juan's face took on a terrified expression that exactly fitted the plot of the play, and was probably the only sincere and appropriate bit of acting he'd ever done. The commander, seeing the other man's face, must have thought: it's really going well tonight, and began to deliver his speech with gusto. It might all have ended in a real tragedy if Captain Centellas, waiting in the wings for his fateful duel, had not thrown himself on the Commander and stifled the blaze with his own cape. The Commander was running about like someone possessed, wreathed in smoke and having completely forgotten his immortal status; Don Juan looked on bemused, his legs caught up in his sword. The audience was hooting with laughter and applauding. And best of all, in the midst of all this confusion, the poor actors kept on reciting their lines, in the most melodramatic way."

"How cruel!" Marichuli cried; "I don't know how you can find something like that funny."

"It's perfectly normal," Prullàs retorted; "and as far as I can see, there's nothing cruel about it. To the audience that evening, your husband included, there was no difference between the absurd plot of the play, with its apparitions from beyond the grave, and the disaster of its staging: all of it was theatre. I'm sure it was a great performance, a version of 'Don Juan' that would have pleased Zorrilla himself. And I can recall having seen something similar, although quite the opposite, in the María Guerrero theatre in Madrid, in front of all the capital's smart set. The great Ernesto Vilches was playing Ibsen's 'An Enemy of the People'. In the third act, during the moving monologue by Doctor Stockman, or whatever his name is, the chair he was sitting on came unstuck and collapsed without warning. The actor immediately got up with great dignity, dusted off his frockcoat, gazed out at the audience which was waiting with bated breath, opened his mouth wide . . . and said not a word. The shock of what had happened had made his mind go blank: he couldn't remember a single word of his role. He couldn't even think what play he was in. They had to bring down the curtain." "And how did the public react?" Doctor Mercadal asked. "In the only possible way," Prullàs replied; "they applauded politely with the curtain down and left the theatre in an orderly fashion. That kind of thing would be impossible today," he said with a hint of nostalgia. "Audiences nowadays would find it unbelievable, because they've all been spoilt by films and all their mushiness . . . "

"Don't start attacking the cinema," Martita said, "you're always at it! Marichuli and I both love films. And deep down, you know you do too." "Not true," Prullàs objected; "I only like Westerns." "Well, you'll have to get used to it, because cinema is the coming thing," Doctor Mercadal said, "and nothing can stand in the way of progress. And anyway," he added, "if the kind of theatre you're defending were no longer marginal, or a simple curiosity – if that kind of play really was all there was to see, and if performances were always like the ones we've just described, the theatre would be finished in no time at all. Oddities like those can only be the exception to the rule. I'll explain it to you with an example from my own experience. In his personal library, my father had quite a few picaresque or 'suggestive' French novels as he called them. He had of course forbidden me to read them, and of course I read them behind his back, in snatches, whenever I could, understanding almost nothing of what they said, but with huge excitement. Reading became a clandestine pleasure and, to some extent, an initiation ceremony to the mysteries of life. But if my father had given me those books, and encouraged me to read them; and if I had studied them as if they were set texts at school, then reading them would have ceased to be a harmless, even useful pastime, and would have become a perversion, a sure sign of degradation."

"Is it true that stage actresses are always fickle and cruel?" asked Marichuli, obviously exasperated by her husband's musings. "No, of course not," Prullàs replied; "some of them are, but they don't get very far. To succeed in the theatre, you have to be both disciplined and sensible, to be able to get on with others and to work in a team. And you also have to have that indefinable thing we call class. Oh and by the way, going back to what we were talking about, the other day in one of those magazines you women like to waste your time reading, I saw something ghastly: a celebrated Hollywood star was showing off her home. As far as I could make out, that's the latest bit of vulgarity to become fashionable: to show off the luxurious and horrendous mansions of the stars for the delight and scorn of the poor. No theatre actress would do that: firstly, because she has more dignity, and secondly because she wouldn't have anything like a decent house to show off."

"What about the play you're going to put on?" Doctor Mercadal asked. "What's it called, what's it about? If you want to tell us, that is." "'Arrivederci, pollo!'" Prullàs said, "and like all my plays, it's a police thriller played for laughs. And if you want to find out any more, you'll have to buy a ticket," he concluded.

"Oh, that's not fair," the doctor protested; "if I'd known, I wouldn't have wasted the champagne." "Don't insist," Martita said; "he's quite likely not even to know how it ends. Once he only decided the end of a play a couple of days before the opening, didn't you, Carlos?" Prullàs denied his wife's claims with a weary gesture. "What torture that must be for the actors," Marichuli exclaimed.

Prullàs shrugged. "Bah," he said, "actors are nothing more than vain parrots; don't waste your pity on them." "Just a moment ago you were defending them tooth and nail, and now listen to you: how can you be so contradictory?" Doctor Mercadal cried out. "Two-faced, more like," his wife chimed in. "Actors," Prullàs insisted, "have always been looked down on by society, because they are marginal, nocturnal beings, who live for pretence and deception. In olden days, the Church would not allow them to be buried in cemeteries; the fact that they were actors meant they weren't worthy of lying in hallowed ground." "That doesn't seem right to me, even if the Church said so," Marichuli remarked. "I've read that even today in India, cinema stars are treated like plague-bearers; they can't go into people's homes, and can only marry among themselves," Martita said. "Serves them right for getting mixed up in films!" Prullàs laughed. "India," Doctor Mercadal solemnly pronounced, "is a society of castes; if you don't belong to one, you're nobody. As for actors being mere parrots," the surgeon went on, "I don't agree at all: if actors weren't sensitive people, they couldn't move us in the way they do." "Who do they move?" Prullàs asked; "I've never been moved in a theatre." "You're just a cynic," Marichuli replied, in the same teasing tone as the whole conversation. "But I can remember having soaked more than one handkerchief over a play: none of yours, though, I must admit." "Don't listen to him, Marichuli," Martita said: "he's showing off with his cynicism now, but I've seen him in tears sometimes even before they raise the curtain." "Come on, let's finish the champagne and not fight," Doctor Mercadal said. "Hear, hear!" Prullàs agreed. "It's delicious champagne, you must thank your patient on our behalf." "Oh, he's been pushing up daisies for a while now," the surgeon laughed. "I'll go and prepare the coffee," their hostess said. "I'll go with you," said Martita. "Bring a bottle of whisky too for the gentlemen, and a couple of glasses," Doctor Mercadal shouted after them.

"D'you know, I've only been in this house at night?" Prullàs said when the two men were alone. He was merely trying to break an awkward silence, but the association of ideas sparked by this trivial phrase suddenly brought the blood to his cheeks.

Fortunately, Doctor Mercadal was not listening to him; the jovial good humour he had been in at dinner had vanished, and he seemed pensive. He cleared his throat and said: "I'd like to thank you and Martita for coming to dinner with us tonight . . . and more generally, for being so kind to us." Prullàs tried to cut short this embarrassing formality, but the other man went on: "We're new here, and it's not easy settling in to a place where you don't know anyone; because of my profession, I don't meet many people, and when I see my patients they're always under anaesthetic . . . but it's not just that I'm referring to. The other night at the club, I was telling you how worried I was. That worry hasn't in any way diminished since – in fact, quite the opposite. I can see Marichuli withdrawing into herself more and more, as if she were being consumed by something . . . I don't know, it's hard for me, I find it almost impossible to reach all her hidden parts: if a woman doesn't want to, there's no way medical knowledge can help. But you two have a good influence on her, that's obvious straightaway. When she's with you, she's another person. I've been observing her . . . Sshh! here they come."

"Marichuli, you shouldn't drink coffee; it keeps you awake," Doctor Mercadal said in a concerned tone. "I know what I should or shouldn't do, Rafael, don't go on at me so!" his wife replied with a sharpness that surprised Prullàs and Martita, but had no apparent effect on the person it was aimed at, as he smiled calmly and went on to explain to them: "Marichuli's body reacts badly to stimulants like coffee or tea, but she insists on consuming them in great quantities. Then, later, in bed, she starts sighing and sobbing and shudders so violently she makes the springs creak like a soul in torment. I tell her smoking would do her good, but she won't listen. I've also said she shouldn't eat starch, because it irritates the bowels." "Starch and films," Prullàs put in, "especially American ones; dining on starch and then going to the cinema is a sure way to give you a sleepless night."

"You never talk about the theatre: you never tell me stories or discuss your opinions; I don't understand why tonight was such an exception," Martita said on their way back home. "After such a splendid banquet, I felt I couldn't refuse," Prullàs said. "Look at all the stars tonight!" he added, coming to a halt on the street corner.

At that late hour, there was no-one about in the village, and although the sea was calm, they could clearly hear the waves unfurling on the beach, and the murmur of the water as it drew back from the sand. "Tomorrow will be another fine day," Martita said. She couldn't help sighing as she did so. Prullàs asked her what she was thinking about, and she replied Marichuli Mercadal and her husband, Doctor Mercadal. "What's so special about them?" Prullàs asked. "They're a strange couple, don't you think?" "Ah, when I said a while ago how odd they were, you wouldn't hear of it, and now here you are agreeing with me: who can understand you?" "I was talking about another kind of strangeness," Martita said; "not in their behaviour, but in their relationship, if you know what I mean."

Prullàs gave his wife a sidelong look. " 'If you know what I mean,' " he repeated. "You mean that between the good doctor and his wife there's no . . . if you know what I mean?" Martita grunted: "Don't be so vulgar, Carlos!" "Hypocrite! Isn't that what you were insinuating?" he said. "Not at all!" she protested. Prullàs hugged her. "Not everyone is lucky enough to have a husband like yours," he said.

From beneath a wide-brimmed straw hat that protected her whole body from the sun, Marichuli Mercadal was carefully studying the progress of a small dinghy steered by such inexpert hands that it was cutting through the calm sea a few yards beyond the breakwater as if it were fighting a Force 9 gale out in the ocean. The sharp slap of waves against the boat's hull, and of the sail flapping in the wind, could be heard above the children's shrieks. Prullàs came hopping over the burning sand and knelt down in the shade of the tent. Marichuli gave a start. "I didn't see you coming!" she said.

She searched around in her holdall until she found her sunglasses. "Thank you for the flowers and the card," she whispered. Prullàs dismissed the importance of the gift with a gesture. "It was a splendid meal from every point of view: the food and the company," he said. "Does that mean you find my company splendid, Señor Prullàs?" Prullàs tried to make out her eyes as she said this, but could not see them through the dark lenses. "Don't get nervous, there's no ulterior motive to what I'm saying. It's never been my style, and I've never caused a scene, whatever my feelings; even when I was an adolescent no-one could tell when I liked someone, even if I liked them a lot; even if I thought I'd die of heartbreak if they didn't notice me. Perhaps that's why no-one would come near me; they must have thought I was an iceberg and they didn't want to risk getting scalded; so in the end I had to marry the first man who asked me, and doubtless he was under the influence of whisky."

Before Prullàs could respond to this tirade, Marichuli Mercadal lifted her hand to her mouth and stifled a cry. "What's the matter?" "Nothing," she replied. As he tried to tack, the dinghy skipper had been on the point of capsizing the boat altogether. "Is the shipwreck apprentice your husband?" She nodded. "Oh, and Alicia's with him," Prullàs said. "Alicia and your children," she replied. "Martita can't have imagined that such an eminent surgeon could also be so eminently clueless in a boat, and let them go with him." Prullàs shrugged: they didn't seem to be in any great danger. "What did you come to tell me?" Prullàs left his bathrobe inside the tent so that he could get some sun. "Nothing: just hello." After a while, he added: "I'm going in, are you coming?" Marichuli shook her head. "Not now," she said, and quickly went on: "Carlos, I don't owe you anything, and you owe me nothing either, not even an explanation; there's no unfinished business between us." "Fine," he said. Outside the tent, he could feel the heat of the sun beating down. If I stay here a minute longer, my skin will start coming off in strips, and I'll look like one of those "atomical" bomb victims, he thought; but he did not dare leave her. "D'you think I'm off my head too?" she asked. "We all are a bit," Prullàs replied.

"Señora, would you be so kind as to check that this handbag I'm passing you is a perfectly normal bag, with a single opening, and no pockets or folds where anything could be hidden? Go on, take it, turn it inside out if you like, put your hand inside and show it to your friends around you. Meanwhile, could you, dear sir, tell me the time? Oh, what a splendid wristwatch! Would you be so kind as to lend it me a moment to carry out a small experiment? Thank you, sir, and don't worry about your watch, it's in very good hands. Señora, have you finished examining the bag? Are you satisfied? Is it exactly as I described it to you? Good! May I have it back then? Thank you.

"And now, ladies and gentlemen, boys and girls, and everyone in this wonderful audience, here we have a cloth handbag and here, a magnificent wristwatch, the property of this gentleman. Look carefully as I place the watch inside the bag. And now that the watch is safely in the bag, let's tie a tight knot with the strings, so that the watch won't fall out. That's it: as you can all see, the bag is now tightly shut, and inside it is the wristwatch that this gentleman was good enough to lend me. And now, ladies and gentlemen, to carry out this harmless experiment of mine, I need the assistance of someone from the audience. Is there a volunteer? Come on, don't be afraid! Is no-one willing to take the risk? Ah, here's a volunteer! Thank you, young man. Come on up onto the platform. Careful, mind you don't trip. Are you nervous? Slightly? Not at all! He's says he's not at all nervous, ladies and gentlemen, so we'll have to believe him, won't we? Tell us, what's your name? Say it out loud, so that everyone in the audience can hear. What was that? Roquet el de los Fems? Well then, a round of applause for this brave young gentleman.

"Well now, Roquet, tell me truthfully: are you a strong, determined sort? You are? We'll soon find out. Here, take this mallet. It's heavy, isn't it? Yes, of course it is. Now, listen carefully to what I'm going to ask you to do: I'm going to ask you the following. D'you see that closed bag containing, as we've all seen, the magnificent wristwatch belonging to that gentleman in the second row? I'm going to place the bag on this table, and I'm going to ask you to hit it as hard as you can with your mallet. Yes, yes, that's right. Goodness gracious me! I didn't have to ask twice, did I, ladies and gentlemen? I can see you really are a strong, determined kind of fellow: you almost split the table and the platform in two. Go on, hit it again, as hard as you can, my friend. Put your back into it! Thank you, thank you, that's quite enough. Give me the mallet back, please, but don't go away. Since you did all the work, it's only fair you get your share of the glory. Let's open the bag and see what's happened."

The magician loosened the strings and poured the contents of the bag onto the table: springs, screws and metal shavings fell out. "Goodness, Don Roquet, I'm afraid it looks as though my trick hasn't worked this time!" he said, with a wry grimace. The village idiot was roaring with laughter: the fact that he'd smashed a watch like this seemed to him hilarious. His laughter infected the audience: only the owner of the watch did not appear to be enjoying things so much. Oblivious to the performance, Joaquín and his two sons were circulating among the customers with drinks trays held high above their heads.

"Can I serve you another whisky, doctor?" "Don't trouble yourself, Joaquín, just leave the bottle and I'll serve myself as and when," Doctor Mercadal told him. "You shouldn't drink so much in the state you're in," his wife protested in vain. That morning's maritime adventure had left the novice sailor with a bad sunburn: parts of his skin were inflamed and red, and in general he was a glowing mottled aubergine colour. Marichuli shrugged at her husband's annoyance. Fortunately the children, who were more accustomed to the sun, had emerged unscathed from their escapade. They were now staring open-mouthed and enchanted at the age-old tricks performed by the insipid conjurer. His appearance on the makeshift stage had been greeted by catcalls from the audience, a hostility to a large extent of his own making, as the reality he demonstrated was a far cry from the image shown on the posters he had put up in all the strategic points of the village.

Standing there before them, this person who called himself the Diabolical Doctor Corbeau turned out to be a bony old man with effeminate airs, hair badly dyed a jet-black colour, thick eyeliner plastered on his eyelashes, bright lipstick smeared round his mouth, and spots of red on both cheeks; he walked with small, mincing steps, spoke in a high, reedy voice, and moved his hands like a puppet on a string. The public's reaction did not appear to affect him in the slightest, however; he greeted the sarcastic compliments, the jeers, and the anonymous shouts of "fairy" and "faggot" that punctuated his performance with conspiratorial winks that seemed to be saying: I know my tricks are worthless, but the fun you're having laughing at me makes it worth your while being here.

"This is disgraceful," Martita said as soon as she saw the conjurer, "let's go." But Prullàs would have none of it. "Calm down, the children don't even notice these things." Deep down he found himself admiring a man who every evening confronted such a torrent of abuse, and yet refused to renounce the pathetic coquettishness that provoked it. In Prullàs' eyes, the man's ridiculous stubbornness was the sign of a desperate kind of nobility.

"And now, ladies and gentlemen, boys and girls," the magician went on, the watch having reappeared intact in a small chest at the opposite end of the stage, "there will be a short break of 20 minutes before we come to the most dangerous, difficult and spectacular part of tonight's unforgettable entertainment. I would beg you most earnestly not to leave your seats, not only to avoid someone else stealing them, but also and most importantly because I, the Diabolical Doctor Corbeau, will be taking advantage of the break to pass among you with my magic hat in order to receive whatever generous contributions you care to make. As you know, we artists live off the public's applause, but from time to time even we need to eat! I know you have paid extra for your drinks, but that only covers the expense of hiring the room, and in no way involves any payment to this humble artistic servant of yours. So please, don't leave! I count on your generosity. Thank you."

While those members of the audience who found themselves presented with the magician's top hat tossed in coins or banknotes, the more daring and mischievous among them surreptitiously pinched his bottom; the conjurer responded by wiggling his hips outrageously and trying to convert his grimaces of pain into louche, silly giggles. When he reached their table, Prullàs gave each of the children a five-peseta piece to drop in the hat. "Thank you, sweethearts." Martita rose in her chair. "Leave those children alone, you shameless old man." Prullàs slipped a fifty-peseta note into the magician's hand as he was quickly withdrawing it from one of the children's cheeks. "You're more than kind, Señor," the performer said incredulously after he had glanced out of the corner of his eye and seen how large a note he had been given. "I'm in the same line of business," Prullàs said. Doctor Corbeau gave a sly smile. "I mean the theatre business," Prullàs hastened to explain.

"There was no need for such a performance!" Martita said when the magician had left their table. "He's just a poor devil," Marichuli said in a conciliatory tone. "Some people have to choose between eating and dignity," Doctor Mercadal pronounced thickly. Martita continued to scowl. "We already have our hands full with that sainted Gaudet of yours," she grumbled. The argument passed over the heads of the children, who were falling asleep on their folding chairs. "I'm taking the children home," Martita announced. "We're leaving too," Doctor Mercadal said; "it's not good for Alicia to stay up late, and my back's raw from the sun."

Marichuli said she was staying for the second half; she wasn't sleepy and anyway, now came the best bit. "You're not staying on your own in all this crowd," her husband said. "They won't eat me," she replied, in a firm voice that was almost defiant. "In that case, I'll stay as well," Prullàs said; "there's nothing more painful for an actor than to see his audience disappear in droves. It's something no-one can escape," he added, "from the most famous star to the newest understudy." "As you see, I'll be well protected," Marichuli said to Martita. "Or would be if strength were measured in words," Martita replied. But she didn't say this unpleasantly: she wanted to get out of there herself, and to remove her children from this ambiguous atmosphere which all the people, the heat, and the cigarette smoke only served to heighten. If she could do that, she was not concerned about anything else. It was plain she felt at ease with Doctor Mercadal, to whose drunken state she was completely oblivious, and that she saw nothing untoward in leaving her husband in charge of her friend. "Alone at last!" Marichuli exclaimed sarcastically.

"Ladies and gentlemen, girls and boys, thank you, thank you for being so patient. I can promise you, you won't be disappointed by the second part of this evening of magic offered to you by the mysterious, the disturbing, the extraordinary, the Diabolical Doctor Corbeau. And I beg you to pay attention, close attention, because tonight is a very special night, and this is a very special audience, and that is why I am going to present to you, ladies and gentlemen, an extraordinary experiment never before attempted in Spain, for fear of its possible consequences. It involves, ladies and gentlemen, the use of deep hypnosis of the kind practised by a few secret sects in Hindustan, the techniques of which are revealed only to the most dedicated initiates. It's an experiment, as you well know, that carries with it great risks for the hypnotist and the person hypnotised, since both of them reach such a profound level of concentration that the slightest interruption can cause deep and permanent character changes, including on occasion madness and death, as happened only last year in a famous – and now sadly infamous – theatre in Buenos Aires, Argentina: a tragic event you doubtless recall, as newspapers the world over took up the story. It is no coincidence therefore that this kind of experiment has been banned in many countries throughout Europe and America. And yet tonight, in this very room, in a few moments you, ladies and gentlemen, will have the honour and perhaps the terror of witnessing such an event. It is my duty to warn you of the extreme danger inherent in this experiment, and I would therefore urge anyone in the audience – particularly any young lady – who feels they are of a nervous or timid disposition, to leave the room before the magic commences. Once the preparations have begun, no-one will be able to leave, or even to stir in their seats, make a noise or speak to their neighbour, because as I said, even the slightest disturbance could cause irreparable damage."

This speech had its effect on the audience; the chattering and fidgeting stopped, and everyone fell silent. The magician removed the table from the stage and replaced it with a chair. Then he signalled to Joaquín's eldest son and the boy carried out his instructions, dimming the lights in the room. "Please," Joaquín's voice rang out, "don't let the children up onto the billiard tables, they'll rip the cloth!" Doctor Corbeau stood stock still next to the chair, chin down on his chest and the fingers of both hands pressed against his temples in an effort to recreate the idealised image of himself that his fraudulent poster had spread throughout the village. When he lifted his face to look out at the audience, his eyes blazed and his features had taken on a scrawny priest–like quality that recalled Bela Lugosi, but were suddenly and unexpectedly genuinely solemn.

"Ladies and gentlemen, the experiment is about to begin. Don't be alarmed if during the course of it you hear strange noises or even if you think you see some nebulous shape materialise in the room: these are not hallucinations, but para-psychological phenomena that have been studied and accepted by medical science. And now, ladies and gentlemen, I will again need a volunteer to come up and take part with me in this unique, sensational experiment. No, Don Roquet, you've already had your turn, with the watch. Let's see, who will accept the challenge? I need someone with steady nerves and who is in perfect mental and physical health. You, Madam? Are you sure? A big round of applause please for this young lady!"

A stocky young woman with a rustic air who, to judge by the whispers among the audience, was unknown to any of them, climbed onto the stage, sat on the chair and was trying bashfully to pull her skirt down over her knees. Marichuli's fingers dug into Prullàs' arm. "Let's go," she said, "this man scares me." "Are you crazy? It's no more than child's play," he hissed. "I don't care, I'm frightened and I want to leave; if you won't come with me, I'll go on my own." "Stop talking nonsense and wait till the show has finished, everyone's looking at us."

"Ladies and gentlemen, I'd like you to concentrate now; we have here a young lady who until this moment I have never had the pleasure of meeting. Tell me Señora or Señorita, have you and I ever seen each other before?" The woman shook her head, although nobody could help noticing the knowing look she gave the magician. "Both on my behalf and on that of all those present here tonight, I'd like to thank you for agreeing to take part. If you will permit me, I'm going to ask you to follow my instructions to the letter. Above all, don't be afraid, relax and cast everything from your mind, forget all your worries for a few minutes. Relax . . . relax . . . you're too tired to think, too tired, you cannot control your muscles, your eyelids are getting heavy, you're trying to keep your eyes open, but you can't, you can feel all your body going to sleep, your body is becoming weightless, you can feel it floating in the air, floating, floating . . . let it float, Señora, go to sleep . . . to sleep . . . And now, while you're still asleep, raise your head and open your eyes, slowly open them."

The woman opened her eyes and stared blindly at the back of the room. A murmur of real admiration ran through the audience: this simple hoax, performed in the clumsiest manner, had succeeded in winning over a hostile public. Prullàs noted a satisfied grin flick across the conjurer's effeminate face.

"Ladies and gentlemen, you can all see that this person, who was completely unknown to me before tonight, is in a deep sleep thanks to the hypnotic passes of my mesmeric art. She is in a state where her consciousness and her willpower have been suspended; she will obey everything that I tell her to do. To demonstrate this, I am going to put her to a small test. Here in my hand I have a glass: note that it is empty, clean and dry. Now look closely!"

Without realising what was happening, out of the corner of his eye, Prullàs saw and then heard a body crashing to the floor next to him; with an absurd, instinctive gesture he grabbed hold of the chair and managed to prevent it falling over as well. The uproar the incident provoked spread around him in concentric circles through the room. Forgotten by a public which had now completely lost interest in the spectacle, the diabolic Doctor Corbeau and his sly assistant openly signalled their bewilderment and impotence to each other. Prullàs had lifted Marichuli's inert body from the floor and was vainly trying to push his way towards the door. Joaquín's son turned all the lights on, and the sudden glare brought expressions of panic to many faces. As the man in charge of the club, Joaquín elbowed his way through the crowd, shouting advice: "Don't crush each other, let some air in, open the windows, call a doctor!" Nobody paid him the slightest attention. Now that the light allowed everyone to see who had been involved in the incident, comments and exclamations flew thick and fast. To the summer residents, naturally inclined to gossip and suspicion, this strikingly attractive woman, who dressed so provocatively and adopted an attitude that was both haughty and unsociable, had been this year's main topic of conversation;

now there she was, lifeless in the arms of a man who was not her husband! "It's that woman who lives in the foreigners' house!" Prullàs heard people whispering behind his back, "the surgeon's wife!" Joaquín struggled over to them. "What happened?" he asked. "Señora Mercadal has fainted, help me get her out of here." Joaquín raised his eyebrows. "I reckon she's in a trance," he pronounced, but then he shrugged and said: "Lay her on the billiard table and I'll clear the room."

"Where am I? What happened to me? Who's taken all my clothes off?" Prullàs grasped her by the shoulders to prevent her from sitting up too quickly. "You're at the club, you passed out, and you're wearing all the clothes you came in, except for your shoes, which Joaquín took off so you wouldn't tear the green baize with your heels." Joaquín nodded gravely, and offered Marichuli Mercadal a glass of brandy. "Drink this bit of brandy, Señora, it'll do you good, you'll see." She refused it, sat up on the billiard table, and looked around her: the club-room had been evacuated thanks to Joaquín's persistent efforts, and the lights had been turned down once more. All that was left on the platform was the empty chair. "What about that man?" she asked. "He must be fast asleep by now, it's past midnight," Prullàs said. "I'm afraid you ruined his performance, but don't worry about him: he'd already made sure he got payment; how are you feeling?" "Better, take me home." Joaquín asked them to wait a minute: he'd get his van out of the garage and go with them, but Marichuli declined his offer. "I've already caused you more than enough trouble," she said, "and besides, it will do me good to walk for a while, if Señor Prullàs would be so kind as to accompany me, and you could give me back my shoes." Joaquín did not insist; he stole a furtive glance at her inviting neckline and the secrets fleetingly revealed to him as she clambered unsteadily down from the table. When things as serious as that are involved, best not get mixed up in them, his discreet attitude seemed to suggest. "Put the cognac on my bill," Prullàs said. "Oh please," Joaquín protested, "it's on the house!"

"What must people have thought!" Marichuli burst out once she and Prullàs were safely away from the club. "Do you really care?" he asked. "I don't want to be the source of any scandal," Marichuli replied. "Did I do or say anything embarrassing?" "No; when you fell to the floor, you showed your legs a bit, and that was very well received; then you and I looked like a still from *Gone With the Wind* for a moment, but I don't think we'll be getting any calls from Hollywood." "Oh shut up, that's nasty and uncalled for!" "I was only trying to see the funny side." "Well don't, and don't hug me in front of everyone." "I'm not hugging you; I'm holding you up so you don't fall down again; and anyway, at this time of night there's no-one in the street." "I bet they're spying on us from behind their shutters!" Prullàs looked up and down the street; there was no sign that anyone was watching. "You've nothing to be afraid of: you fainted due to the heat and the crush of people; it happens all the time." Marichuli walked on ahead of Prullàs. She tottered on her high heels and had to lean against a tree; Prullàs caught up with her and could see tears coursing down her cheeks. "I didn't faint, Carlos," she said in a hoarse voice. "When that man began his cabbalistic passes, my mind clouded over, and I lost all notion of time and space, but I didn't lose consciousness." She fell quiet for a moment as if she were out of breath. "And then I had a horrible vision: everything was in darkness, and beneath my feet a deep, dreadful hole opened up, it was like a tomb and an abyss; both of them were reserved for me; I understood that it was my soul's eyes I was seeing with. We're in a state of sin, Carlos, you and I are in mortal sin, and if we were to die at this moment, we would go headlong down to hell for all eternity." Her body was wracked with deep sobs, and Prullàs could see her terror was real. At a loss, he looked up at the sky, and saw a shooting star crossing the firmament; just at that moment, by a strange coincidence, a train whistle blew. "You can go to confession first thing tomorrow morning," he said tentatively. "God's mercy is infinite: I heard Father Laburu say so recently, and he seemed well-informed on the subject." Marichuli shook her head despairingly. "That would be no use," she said, "because I haven't truly repented. D'you know that from thinking of you I've been on the verge of losing my reason more than once?" she added, more in sorrow than in anger. Prullàs did not know what to reply: he felt a profound sadness for this woman. He gave her his hand-kerchief and she dried her tears. Poor thing, he thought; it's as though nature endowed her with all she needs to succeed and be happy, and yet her personality and her strange mental disposition have made it impossible for her to carry anything through; her life seems to have been one long succession of mistakes; and even her physical attractions, instead of opening all the doors for her, have worked against her, driving all worth-while and sincere men from her side, and in the end only serving to create a harmful notoriety. On impulse, he bent over and kissed her; as he did so, he realised her lips were freezing and her teeth were chattering. "What are you doing?" she cried, "you're out of your mind!" "Yes, and you're ill: I'll take you home and your husband can look after you as is fit and proper," Prullàs replied.

On summer Sundays the ten o'clock Mass was by far the most popular. Prullàs and his father-in-law abandoned hope of get-ting inside the church and stayed on the steps, while Martita and her mother pushed their way through the throng. When Mass was over, Prullàs looked carefully at the stream of worshippers coming out to see if he could spot Marichuli; he was not surprised that she did not seem to have come. Martita was having a lively conversation with several women. "Why didn't you tell me what happened at the club after we left?" she scolded him when she came over to join him; "it's the talk of the village, and I hadn't the faintest idea!" She was so flustered she had forgotten to remove her mantilla. "How could I tell you? By the time I got back you were fast asleep, and this morning we all ran out of the house to avoid being late for Mass; I was going to tell you afterwards – although it looked more spectacular than it really was." "I'll go on ahead to the cake shop," his father-in-law said, "we don't want them to run out of iced cakes, do we?"

A few hours later the maid interrupted the family drinks: there was someone who wished to speak to Señor Prullàs, she said. Through the reed curtain they could see a silhouette under the canopy on the house terrace. Who can it be? In broad daylight he had trouble recognising the shrunken figure as that of Doctor Corbeau, perhaps because he was not an old man, as all his make-up the previous night had suggested; but someone in his middle years, with an unhealthy and poorly-fed look about him. "Joaquín told me where I could find you," the magician said after a lengthy preamble aimed at excusing such an unexpected visit. "I only came to enquire after your wife's health following the unfortunate incident during my performance. Believe me, nothing could have been further from my intentions; to tell you the truth, no-one was more surprised than me. As you yourself saw, I'm nothing more than a charlatan who earns his living amusing adults and children with his magic tricks." The hypnosis number was a fake, he willingly admitted, he had never hypnotised anyone in his life, and had never even tried to, and it went without saying that there had never been an occurrence like the one that had happened the previous evening. This could ruin his career, he went on;

143

he was not a member of the artists' union, and did not have an official permit. "As you can see, I'm not trying to hide the truth from you," he added; "if you report me, it's the end for Doctor Corbeau." Prullàs set his mind at rest: not for one moment had he considered reporting the incident to the authorities; after all, it was simply an accidental case of mesmerism for which no-one was responsible. The conjurer again repeated how sorry and grateful he was, and then handed Prullàs an envelope. On opening it, he found it contained the fifty-peseta note he had contributed during the previous night's show. Before he could say anything, the conjurer had quickly descended the steps, reached the street, and gone over to a car parked on the far side opposite the house. A woman's face appeared at the front car window. Prullàs recognised her as the supposed volunteer for the hypnotic experiment. Doctor Corbeau whispered something in her ear, and she closed her eyes and sighed as though to say: Thank God for that! Then she gave the magician a small bouquet of flowers, and he came back up to Prullàs. "I've taken the liberty of bringing this small token of respect for your wife, although I know it has little value," he said. Prullàs saw no point in correcting the poor fellow's misapprehension. "Thank you," he said, "my wife adores flowers." The conjurer stood there hesitating, as if he wanted to add something else on a totally different matter. "Last night," he eventually said, "you told me you were in the same line of business. At the time, I took it as a joke; it's usual for the public to make fun of me, and this healthy banter is part and parcel of the show; but this morning Joaquín informed me that you are a famous playwright; I beg you to excuse my ignorance; from now on, I'll make a point of seeing all your plays. For my part, I'm just a comedian, a harmless cheat who doesn't try to fool anyone." He fell silent, then added: "Sometimes, though, there are people who can't tell the difference; but what fault is it of mine if those people expect something from me I can't give? As a man of the theatre, you'll understand what I'm saying." Prullàs slapped the magician's bony shoulder: "We're playing with fire, Corbeau my friend, playing with fire!"

CHAPTER THREE

I

"I've heard so much about you, it's as if I'd known you all my life," Brusquets said. With these words, a bald man of around 50 whose glittering, light-blue eyes seemed at odds with his rough-hewn features greeted his guests. "I'm delighted you were able to come to this little gathering," he added. "Fontcuberta told me he had invited you as I asked him to, but that he didn't know whether you were free to come. You can't imagine how delighted I am to see you here." His Castilian was perfect, if a little slow and full of circumlocutions. "On the contrary," Prullàs replied, "it is I who thanks you for the invitation."

Loud voices reached the entrance hall from the living-room. "If my ears don't deceive me, the place is full of men," Mariquita Pons said. "It seems I've come to a stag party . . . if only I'd known beforehand . . . " Brusquets was taken aback. "Yes, it's true, almost all the men have come on their own . . . it's the time of year, you know; it would probably have been better to put this off until the autumn, but I promised myself I'd have a get-together with my friends as soon as the last workman left, and that had to happen just in the middle of summer . . . Would you care to see the apartment?" Prullàs and the Fontcubertas nodded, trying to show an enthusiasm they were far from feeling. Their host's enthusiasm, however, was obviously sincere, a touch naïve.

A short while earlier, on their way there, Fontcuberta had told Prullàs something of Brusquets' background. The only child of an extremely rich family, Brusquets combined an exquisite education, a complete lack of culture, and a blissful ignorance of the ways of the world. He had never had to work, and every business venture he had embarked on ended up losing large sums of money. There was a story that he had once been swindled into paying a high price for a piece of land or a house of little value, on the pretext that a buried treasure was hidden there. After the purchase, Brusquets had proceeded to excavate the terrain or to demolish the house, depending which version you believed, but to no avail. "It was the same in everything he got involved with," Fontcuberta said. Ten years earlier, Brusquets had married a woman, not a bad sort, but who turned into a complete despot, although he loved her dearly in spite of everything. This woman apparently came from an almost penniless immigrant family with little or no education and she – perhaps for this reason, perhaps without even consciously realising it – wanted to take out on Brusquets all the humiliation and unpleasantness she had suffered in her childhood – although she also professed great affection for him. And now, after his wife had died following a long and painful illness during which she became even more bitter, Brusquets could not get used to the void this shrew had left behind. Brusquets himself had been distraught when he told all this to Fontcuberta, as the latter informed Prullàs; whenever he was left on his own, he didn't know what to do with himself, and spent hours wandering around his apartment like a lost soul: he would sit down, get up, stare out of the window, sigh endlessly, and finally throw himself down on the verge of tears. "In short, he needs to be entertained constantly," Fontcuberta concluded.

"It's a splendid place," Prullàs said, glancing to right and left;

"I congratulate you on your good taste." Their host's eyes gleamed with delight, and his face puffed with pride at this compliment. The apartment was in fact decorated with simple elegance, in line with the spirit of those days. Only a few years earlier, all of them had witnessed how dangerous it could be to make any great show of wealth in turbulent times. It was also true that those events had to some extent seen the end of the great hereditary fortunes, and those who had now taken over from the traditional families in positions of power and wealth were little disposed to enjoy their riches ostentatiously, not so much from a sense of austerity as from a lack of imagination. If they spent money, it was in a haphazard fashion. It did not occur to them to collect works of art, become patrons, taste exquisite delicacies or wear fine clothes, as their predecessors had done. In their ignorance, they merely flaunted their wealth in a way designed to create servile flattery. This ridiculous waste, more a form of boasting than a real enjoyment of privilege, only succeeded in arousing criticism and mockery. Now among the highest levels of Barcelona society into which Brusquets was born, people with illustrious family names went out of their way to appear modest in lifestyle and behaviour, although this did not apply to their aims and desires, where, as ever, envy and greed were the order of the day.

"It's the decorator who deserves your praise," Brusquets replied modestly, "he didn't let me take many decisions. In fact, all I saw of these blasted works were the problems . . . and the costs, as you can well imagine. There's nothing worse than trying to redesign an apartment, but I couldn't see any other solution: it didn't fit in at all with my new life the way it was before. Of course, I could have stayed where I was, but when my wife died I decided to move, because I couldn't stand the idea of going on living in the place where I had spent so many happy years with her, may she rest in peace. So I rented this apartment. It's no palace, but it more than meets my needs, and it's a quiet neighbourhood. Perhaps later on you'd like to take a look at the library: my books are the only thing I'm really proud of. My books and the grand piano you can see over there, a magnificent Steinway I bought my beloved wife for our tenth wedding anniversary. She loved music, the poor dear, especially Chopin. The only thing that consoles me about her death is that in heaven she may have met up with Chopin himself."

Their tour ended at a spacious roof terrace. Brusquets' apartment occupied the top floor and penthouse of a new eight-storey building in Paseo de San Gervasio. It was by far the tallest building in an area dotted with small palaces and mansions that the new bourgeoisie had built for itself in the first decades of the century. The theatrical outlines of their battlements and cupolas stood out among pine trees, cypresses, acacias and palms, in the silver metallic light of a full moon. Now the neighbourhood was undergoing a rapid transformation: several of the luxury homes had been demolished and replaced by the skeletons of new buildings. That evening, however, everything was calm and a scent of spikenard hung in the air; it was an oriental night, full of enchantment. And I have to spend it with these bores because I accepted a stupid invitation, thought Prullàs, whose mind had suddenly been filled, perhaps because of the fragrance of the night, with an image of Lilí Villalba.

As they were going back into the living-room, a waiter came by with a tray of sandwiches. "Would you care for something to drink?" "A whisky on the rocks," Prullàs said. A middle-aged man came over and shook hands effusively. "A wonderful evening!" he exclaimed. "Oh, Tomeu, are you leaving already?" Brusquets asked. "Yes, yes," the other man replied. "I can't stay any longer; thanks for everything and may I wish you all the best in this new home of yours." He went out and Brusquets explained to Prullàs that the fellow was in the habit of turning up at all the receptions in Barcelona, greeting everyone, and then leaving at once, without any explanation. This strange behaviour had given rise to all kinds of speculation, none of which had ever been confirmed.

As he was saying this, Brusquets led Prullàs over to a group of four men standing in the centre of the room. Prullàs did not know any of them, but his host introduced them with extravagant words of praise. "As for Señor Prullàs, he needs no introduction: his fame is well-known." "I feel like a fairground attraction," Prullàs said, genuinely embarrassed. He need not have worried: the four men were considerably older than him, and of higher social standing, and so felt not the slightest compunction in ignoring him completely and carrying on listening to the speech being given by a tall florid man whom the other called Doctor Sanjuanete and who, Prullàs gathered, was Professor of Procedural Law at Barcelona University. He was barrel-chested, with a stentorian voice, and had a patrician air that was spoilt by the nervous tics of his mouth and eyebrows. He was giving a heated description of every last detail of a learned argument he had delivered – to judge by what he was saying – in the most brilliant manner, and on which the courts would soon give their decision. "I referred to a Supreme Court verdict from '89 which left not a shadow of doubt," he exclaimed. "A real broadside!" At this point he fell silent, lost in the contemplation of his own importance, and Prullàs took advantage of the pause to leave the group and join another one made up of three men he vaguely knew and whose conversation appeared to be following more normal lines. "A little bird told me your daughter has an official boyfriend, is that right?" "Official?" the other man replied, "no, not at all; she has been going out with a boy for a few months now, but that doesn't mean a thing; you know what young people are like these days: there's nothing they feel strongly about, and no ideals." "Yes, yes," the third man said, "a chip off the old block." This comment astounded all the others, because the mother of the girl mentioned had been involved in a notorious scandal a few years earlier. When he realised from the shocked silence how inappropriate his quip had been, the unfortunate author of the faux pas burst out laughing. He was from a high-society family, someone who frequently attended this kind of social event, where he almost invariably committed the worst indelicacy, which did not upset him in the least, but rather caused him great merriment. Everyone considered him a half-wit.

Prullàs continued his tour. The waiter brought him his glass of whisky. "D'you know how much it costs me to keep the house open?" someone next to him complained. "Two hundred pesos a week! Close to twenty pesos a day, not counting Saturdays and Sundays, of course." "I know what you mean," Prullàs said. "So what?" the other man said, "I wasn't talking to you." "Well, I'm on your side anyway," Prullàs answered, moving on again. Round the corner in a corridor, several more men were conversing in hushed tones; to judge by the serious expressions on their faces, Prullàs guessed they were discussing delicate matters, and refrained from joining them. From the few words he did manage to catch, he surmised they were talking about a scandal that had been widely discussed in the last few months, concerning a large shipment of Argentine wheat meant to help feed the poorer sectors of society, but which had vanished from under the authorities' noses and had been sold on the black market. Prullàs did not usually pay much attention to this kind of gossip, which appeared suddenly one day for no apparent reason, spread like wildfire, and then vanished again in an equally mysterious fashion. The stories were fragmentary and confused, based on guesses and hints, and generally referred to flagrant cases of waste and corruption by the powers-that-be, grave irregularities in appointments, tenders, or contracts, shady business deals and Swiss bank accounts. Nor was there any lack of people with feverish imaginations who described wild orgies in public ministries, which immediately became in the popular mind extraordinary dens of iniquity from a picturesque and depraved version of the *Thousand and One Nights*.

Prullàs passed through all the rooms in the apartment, until he found himself back once again with Fontcuberta, who was talking to some people he did not know. One of them was extremely agitated. "This time it really is the giddy limit; there has to be an armed intervention in Russia," he was bellowing as Prullàs joined the group. Then immediately, seeing that no-one was contradicting him, he went on ferociously: "And if that means the Third World War, then so be it!" The other man shook his head sceptically and said that, for good or ill, Russia was an impregnable country, invincible within its own borders, as first Napoleon Bonaparte and now recently Hitler himself had discovered to their cost. "Apparently," he went on, "it's fiendishly cold in Russia." He knew this for a fact, he said, because his wife's cousin had fought at Stalingrad. He had been lucky enough to be slightly wounded only a few weeks after being posted there with his regiment, but even so he had had more than enough time to see some horrific things: any soldier foolish enough to poke his head outside ther shelter had his ears ripped off by the Siberian wind, and sentries often had to have their frozen feet chopped off in order to save their lives. This was what his brother-in-law had told him. "The freezing temperatures did more damage than any enemy shells," he said, "and anyway, what was the use of it all in the end?" These arguments did not seem to convince the man he was talking to. "Well, I for one will not rest until I see our flag flying in the centre of Moscow!" he roared.

Prullàs could hear Mariquita Pons' voice in the entrance hall and went out to find her. "How do you manage to look younger and more beautiful each day?" a rasping, singsong voice was asking her. "Ah, if only they'd said things like that to me when I really was young and beautiful!"

The person speaking to the actress was Father Emilio Porras S. J., a gaunt, smartly dressed clergyman whom Prullàs had met some years before at a literary event. It was said that when Father Porras was a young man his intellectual leanings had led him to frequent the famous Students' Residence in Madrid, where he had become close friends with Federico García Lorca, with whom he maintained a sporadic correspondence right up to the poet's tragic death. Even now, according to the rumours, Father Emilio Porras S. J. kept these letters a closely-guarded secret and would not tell anyone what was in them. He even remained completely silent as to whether or not they really existed, refusing to confirm or deny all reports about them. Later on, after being victimised and imprisoned, not so much for what he had done as for his ideas and friendships, he discovered religion in his cell, renounced his turbulent past, and entered the Society of Jesus once he was at liberty again. A lector in theology, he had written and published several lives of saints based on modern historical methodology, explaining miracles in the light of the latest scientific discoveries. As a permanent member of a prestigious commission of hagiographers, he travelled regularly to Brussels and Rome.

"Father, I hear you've proposed Antonio Bienvenida for canonisation, is that so?" The question came from Fontcuberta, who had succeeded in escaping from his previous conversation and had joined their group. "He must certainly have his devotees," Father Emilio replied, laughing, then turning to Prullàs, added: "Fontcuberta here is such a joker!" "Look who's talking," the other retorted. "I've just heard you paying my wife all kinds of compliments." "The privileges of celibacy," the Jesuit responded urbanely, "and of age."

"What can I offer you, Father?" the waiter asked. "I'd love a nice cold beer, if it's not too much trouble." Prullàs put his empty glass on the tray and ordered another whisky. Mariquita clung to his arm. "Take me out onto the roof terrace," she said; "I'm roasting alive in here, and I need to talk to you before you get too tipsy." "Weren't we rude to the priest?" Prullàs wondered as they made for the terrace. "I hope he chokes on an olive," was the actress's irreverent retort.

Guests continued to arrive, pushing those already there back out of the hall and living-room; the interior doors of the apartment had been opened, and knots of people gradually took over all the rooms. Prullàs and Mariquita found the terrace full to overflowing. "What did you want to tell me?" Prullàs asked. "D'you think there'll be any dancing?" "With these stiffs? No, I don't think so. Was that what you wanted to say to me, Kiki?" Mariquita shook her head; there was a smile on her lips, but her eyes betrayed a hint of worry. "No," she said, "it was something else."

Brusquets came up, flustered and out of breath. "I beg your pardon, Doña Mariquita, but if you don't mind, I'd like to introduce you to some people . . . when they heard you were here, you can't imagine how excited they were! If you'll excuse us, Prullàs my friend."

Prullàs returned to the living-room, where he found the waiter struggling to force his way through the crush of people; he took his glass of whisky and asked for another one. "By the time you're back, I'll have finished this one," he told the waiter. "Stay close to the kitchen," the waiter advised him. Prullàs thought about rewarding this advice with a tip, then decided against it.

At the far end of the room, he could see Fontcuberta deep in conversation with a man he did not know but who looked friendly and interesting. He tried to make his way over to them but somehow found himself once more within the orbit of Father Emilio.

Someone was recounting that on the cinema news they had seen jet planes being refuelled in mid-flight. To do so, he explained, other huge planes, full of fuel and very aptly called the mother aircraft, let out enormously long tubes tipped with a kind of funnel. The jet planes connect their nose cone to these funnels, and are refuelled. This enables them to stay in the air indefinitely, without ever having to land. Day and night, these aircraft loaded with atomic bombs patrol the skies over Russia, ready at an order from the Pentagon to destroy that country totally, literally to wipe it from the map. It must be terrible to be one of the crew on a plane like that, stuck in a fuselage somewhere between heaven and earth, with only a bomb-load of destruction for company. "Really and truly," he concluded, "it's a miracle that there is still life on earth."

"It's true," the Jesuit replied, "that we cannot know what lies in store for the future of Humanity, but it is always worthwhile to remember the value of prayer in times of uncertainty. It's easy to say, as many do: there's nothing I can do, so I'll pretend the conflict has nothing to do with me! But people who think like that," Father Emilio went on, "forget that their prayers might help God enlighten the leaders of the Great Powers and get them to see the path of wisdom and understanding." "No, what I want to see is war!" a third man replied, and Prullàs recognised him as the person who a short while earlier had been so patriotically keen to see the colours of the Spanish flag flying over the centre of Moscow. "Someone has to put a stop to

Communism in the world, just as we did here in our own land!" he asserted. "Perhaps," the Jesuit said, "but don't let's forget that the Bible tells us to seek peace and harmony, even with our enemies, and to forgive their sins just as Christ forgives ours."

The other man stood there fuming silently for a few moments and then, recovering his calm as quickly as he had lost it, said goodbye to everyone and left. "What a warmonger Gallifa's become!" another of the guests said as soon as he had left their group. "He always used to be a peaceable sort, who wanted nothing to do with international politics, and now all of a sudden . . . " He left the phrase unfinished, then added: "They say he bought a machine-gun and keeps it loaded in his wardrobe; and there's a really silly reason for this sudden change of heart. I was having lunch with Porcar in the club last Wednesday, and he told me the oddest story, but one which explains the secret behind Gallifa's transformation."

He was about to launch into the story, when he was interrupted by someone who said he had seen in another newsreel, or perhaps in the same one, some planes which could travel faster than the speed of sound. When they broke the sound barrier, he said, there was a dreadful explosion, after which the aircraft entered a zone of absolute silence. It was like something out of science-fiction, he said. Apparently what couldn't be done was to travel faster than the speed of light, at least for the moment. But if one day it did prove possible, and there was no reason to think this wouldn't happen, then the door would be open for journeys through space. At last we would know whether there was life on other planets.

"Yes," the man who had been speaking before replied, "I haven't the slightest doubt that we'll soon be in contact with civilisations from other worlds, and that they'll be far superior to ours. They'll teach us a lot, that's for sure," he said. "Yet there's one question that bothers me," he went on, turning to the Jesuit; "that is, if there really are other inhabited planets, will Jesus Christ have appeared there too? Of course, it's odd to imagine Our Lord as a Martian, with a trumpet for a nose and with webbed fingers, but if he didn't become one of them too, how could he carry out his mission of redemption?"

"Well," the Jesuit replied with a hint of impatience in his voice, "the truth is I'm not sure what you're getting at. I personally feel we don't need to worry about that kind of thing for now." "Quite right," agreed a third member of the group; "as you yourself said, before we get to that point, first we have to reach the speed of light, and then, thanks to the law of relativity, we would also be crossing the time barrier. The pilot of a spaceship could leave Earth today and land tomorrow at a completely different moment in history, coming face-to-face with Nero or Nefertiti, or goodness knows who else."

Brusquets appeared out of nowhere once again, looking anxiously for Prullàs, which meant he never got to know the conclusion of this fascinating debate mixing science, philosophy and religion. "Come with me, Señor Prullàs, please; there's a female admirer of yours who is desperate to make your acquaintance . . . she's burning with the desire to meet you." "Well, we can't have her burning with desire, can we?" Prullàs replied. "Is she pretty?" Brusquets cleared his throat embarrassedly. "It's my mother-in-law," he said at length.

Five older women were squeezed onto a sofa. They were all talking at once, and fanning themselves so vigorously that the charms on their bracelets were clinking noisily. Prullàs kissed their hands athletically. "I so much wanted to meet you, Señor Prullàs," Brusquets' mother-in-law said. "I've seen some of your plays and was delighted. Don't ask me which: I've got a dreadful memory for names. I see a play and as soon as I leave the theatre you can ask me its title, the author, who was in it, the plot even, and I couldn't tell you a thing. As though they'd dragged one of those things you use in the bath right through my head. But I do remember yours very well, the plays. Especially one . . . oh, what was it called? My husband will know. Gordi, come over here!" she said, waving her fan. "What was the name of that evening we went to I can't remember when and I liked a lot?" The man she had been waving to came up, keen to please. "I don't know whichever you mean, my love." "Yes you do, stupid, the one we went to see in Madrid last year." "*He Died Laughing*, you mean?" Gordi said. "That's the one," Brusquets' mother-in-law shouted triumphantly, raising a finger with a diamond sparkling on it. "How could I forget, when I laughed so much? And there was that actor in it, who was so good, what was his name, Gordi?" "Pepe Alfayate, my sweet." "Oh, yes, Pepe whatsisname . . . " She turned to the other ladies who were following all this from their sofa, and said: "The plays this gentleman writes are those simple, unpretentious ones, for people like me now. Those that people in general don't think much of these days," she concluded. The other ladies smiled indulgently at Prullàs. Prullàs waited for them to finish scrutinising him, and went off again in search of the waiter.

But instead of the waiter, he found himself face-to-face with a Latin American poet who lived in Madrid. A baggy olive-green suit only partly concealed his ungainly bulk. Long locks of shiny black hair framed sagging cheeks that gave his doughy face a deceptively placid air.

"Carlitos Prullàs, my old friend, good to see you!" "José Felipe Clasiciano, *muchacho*, more impressive by the day!" "And you, more elegant!" The two men slapped each other on the back. "So you're just as much the pet poodle as ever, Carlitos," the poet said. "I saw you just now surrounded by a fabulous flock of parakeets, like a sultan with his harem." "Yes," Prullàs said, "and to make matters worse they thought one of my plays was by Adolfo Torrado. And you? I didn't know you were in Barcelona." José Felipe Clasiciano smiled a smug smile. I'm just back from a long trip. I went to the hotel because I was worn out. I intended to knock off a short nap, and set the alarm clock before I went to sleep, but the blasted thing didn't work. And an English alarm clock too! I bought it in London at the start of my journey, trusting to the proverbial English punctuality, but it's been hopeless. The British Empire is crumbling before our astonished eyes, Carlitos." In England, he went on, he had visited a world-renowned, aged poet, who lived as a recluse in a ruined castle. He was the last of an ancient family of degenerates, Clasiciano continued. He was so lazy that it was said he only got to his feet to play golf. The rest of the time he spent slumped in an armchair wreathed in opium and alcohol, surrounded by half a dozen bloodhounds who calmly relieved themselves all over the carpets. "He took me to his library and showed me handwritten letters by Coleridge. While I was looking at them he tried to stroke my buttocks. My, what things are coming to, Carlitos!" He broke off when he caught sight of Brusquets. His fleshy lips stretched into a fawning smile. "Ah, Brusquets, what a truly lovely little place! And who are all these wonderful people I don't know?" "Oh, I should be performing my duty as a host and introducing you to some good friends of mine," Brusquets said; "I see you already know Señor Prullàs. Of course, who doesn't? But please, come with me, make yourself at home!" Before following their host, Clasiciano said to Prullàs: "I'll be in Barcelona for ten more days, there's so much to see in this little port of yours! Why don't you give me a call so we can have lunch together, Carlitos?"

Freed from the mellifluous poet and his obsequious host, Prullàs succeeded in reaching the study, where Fontcuberta and the unknown friend he had been talking to had found refuge. "What d'you make of it?" Fontcuberta asked.

"It's a real bind," Prullàs replied. "How come you got me into something like this? I don't know anyone, and those I do know are people I'd prefer to avoid." "I couldn't help it," Fontcuberta apologised. "Brusquets insisted as if his life depended on it. "Well now, after parading me round like a circus animal, he couldn't care less," Prullàs said. "Thank your lucky stars for that", the stranger said; "Brusquets is a thorough bore." "It's true he's a bit dull," Fontcuberta admitted, "but deep down he's a good sort." "Not a bit of it: he's a deceiver," the other man insisted. "When it suits him, he's the most help-less and unhappy of creatures, but as soon as he's got what he wants, it's so long, been good to know you!" "Don't be so harsh," Fontcuberta said; "the poor man has had a hard time with the death of his wife." "Come off it!" the stranger laughed; "while she was alive, he used to beat her black and blue, and the day she kicked the bucket he was jumping for joy: beneath that harmless exterior of his lurks a real Bluebeard. I wouldn't be at all surprised if it wasn't Brusquets himself who dispatched her to the other side."

Prullàs looked at the stranger with interest: he didn't know whether he was joking or talking seriously. "D'you mean Brusquets' wife didn't die a natural death?" Fontcuberta asked with amusement. The other man raised an eyebrow. His face had a jovial but sly expression, as if he knew the answer to every question in the world and had nothing better to do in life than convince everyone else of it. This attitude, together with certain facial characteristics, made him look very like Bing Crosby, Prullàs thought. "I can't prove it," the man went on, "but I've read lots of thrillers and I'm convinced that Brusquets killed his wife for the insurance money, and now he's got together with the cook." Fontcuberta burst out laughing.

"Things like that only happen in Prullàs' plays," he said. "But his plays are always based on true stories, aren't they?" the stranger asked. "Of course!" Prullàs said, to keep the joke going.

"O.K.," the other man went on, addressing Fontcuberta this time, "I bet you a seafood dinner at Can Costa that Brusquets marries the cook before the year is out." "Done!" Fontcuberta exclaimed. "Prullàs here is witness to the bet; that way, whoever wins, you're invited to dinner as well," he said. "And I willingly accept," Prullàs said, "but I'm afraid I interrupted your conversation. I'll be off."

"No, no, stay," Fontcuberta said; "I was just saying that the last time I was in Madrid, in the lobby of the Hotel Palace where I was staying I saw a test screening of television. It was fabulous! The set is no bigger than a table, and the screen is about the size of that painting on the wall over there; you could fit it into any room. The image is almost as clear as in the cinema, and the sound is just as good. If you can have a gadget like that at home, I'd like to see who'll be fool enough to go out to the cinema, let alone the theatre!"

"So you'd better start preparing," the stranger said in his usual mocking tone. "And so should you," Prullàs retorted, speaking to Fontcuberta. "When Kiki is out of work, you'll see what kind of a mood she'll be in." "Speaking of Kiki, have you any idea where she's got to?" Fontcuberta asked; "I've lost all track of her." "As I was coming over I thought I saw her in the living-room, near the roof terrace and surrounded by admirers," Prullàs said. "In that case, I'll go and rescue her," Fontcuberta said, "if you'll both excuse me a moment."

With Fontcuberta's departure, Prullàs was left alone in the study with the stranger. "So," he said to break the awkward silence, "you're a great thriller reader?"

"Ah yes, I should say so," the stranger replied; "I count myself as having one of the most complete libraries in Barcelona on that score." "Who are your favourite authors?" "Favourites? All of them! Why, I even subscribe to that trashy Sexton Blake!" Prullàs was very favourably impressed by this reply. "I can see you're a real expert," he said. "I consider myself one," the other man said; "altogether, I must have read more than two thousand thrillers, and I've never once discovered who the murderer was: you can't deny that takes some doing."

Their pleasant exchange was interrupted by Brusquets' appearance in the study. "You shouldn't monopolise our guest of honour like that!" he admonished. "Am I the guest of honour?" Prullàs asked. "Of course, and I'd like to introduce you to someone else who has expressed a great desire to meet you," he said, stepping aside to make way for a middle-aged man with a military bearing and energetic gestures. "Yet again, there's no need for introductions," Brusquets said contentedly. "Of course not," Prullàs said, "it's an honour."

The line of the newcomer's pencil moustache lifted in a faint smile. "And for me," he said, "it's an honour and a pleasure; I knew of you by hearsay, and couldn't wait to shake you by the hand."

Prullàs muttered a few elaborately polite words, trying not to sound too abject. He felt abashed by this individual, whom everyone praised to the skies, but who was the subject of many surreptitious comments, half-finished phrases heavy with insinuations. "Don Lorenzo, who was so kind as to find a gap in all his commitments to honour this house, is a great theatre-goer," trilled Brusquets.

"More than that, I'm a great theatre-*lover*," the newcomer agreed, "if it's true theatre we're talking about, the sort worthy of the name, and not what passes for it these days, and which unfortunately seems ever to be gaining ground on our stages." "I couldn't agree more," Brusquets said. "I never go to the theatre, because quite frankly I have neither the time nor the inclination, but from what I've heard these modern writers seem determined to portray only what's filthy and despicable in man. And the less said about the language they use, the better!"

"True enough," Don Lorenzo acquiesced, with what appeared to Prullàs as a sarcastic smile. "But Señor Prullàs isn't one of those writers, are you, dear sir? I am sure you are someone who honours the noble tradition of our Golden Age."

"I'm neither one nor the other," Prullàs replied; "all I do is construct comic bagatelles: wholesome entertainment for middle-class couples."

"Oh, come now, don't be modest!" Don Lorenzo said; "I'm certain your works encompass values which rescue them from the sin of triviality. A few moments ago our friend Brusquets here was telling me that you're about to put on - might I ask you what the title of your work is?" "'Arrivederci, pollo!'" Prullàs said. "A very suggestive title," the other man replied after a thoughtful pause, "although I must admit I don't wholly understand it. What is it about?" "It's not about anything, as I've already told you: it's a comedy thriller: murders, suspects, clues . . . all the usual elements, but in fun." "Hmm, I'm sorry, but I'm afraid I can't say I approve of that kind of trifle," Don Lorenzo said with a frown; "unfortunately, my position brings me into close contact with the criminal world, and there's one thing I can guarantee you: there's nothing amusing about crime. To present it in a comic light seems to me to betoken a decadent and unhealthy attitude, and if I may say so without meaning to offend, it is offensive. Has this play of yours passed the censors?" "Yes, and been fully approved." "In that case, I have nothing more to add. I wish you every success, Señor Prullàs."

*

"I think I've just lost a customer," Prullàs commented as soon as the distinguished guest had left the study, hotly pursued by their host. "You can't please everyone," said the stranger, who had been following the cut-and-thrust of their conversation from a discreet distance. "That's true," Prullàs said, "but Don Lorenzo isn't the sort of person to get on the wrong side of. I didn't like the tone either of what he said or of what he implied. I just wish I'd never come to this blessed housewarming."

"I'm truly sorry for you," the other man said with a genuine feeling of emotion. "Yours is a wonderful profession which on occasion can also bring great success, but it has one singular disadvantage: everyone thinks they have the right to an opinion about it, even if it's the most arbitrary of personal judgments."

"Yes, you've put your finger on it," Prullàs said. "And, faced with that risk, the only solution is to make a run for it, which is what I intend to do right now. I hope I won't be shot in the back making my escape," he added, lowering his voice and shaking the stranger's hand. "I'm going to see if I can find the Fontcubertas and convince them to get me out of here."

His efforts were in vain: Brusquets himself told him the Fontcubertas had just left. So as not to interrupt everyone, they had not said goodbye all round, Brusquets explained. "Doña Mariquita confessed to me she was very tired," he went on; "apparently, the rehearsals for your next play are taking it out of her." What a liar, Prullàs thought; but if she can use that excuse, so can I. Brusquets put on a show of being sorry that he had to leave: "Just when we were having such a good time!" he protested. It was plain, though, that he did not really mean it; deep down he was pleased to be rid of a guest who Don Lorenzo Verdugones so plainly did not get on with. This rogue knows which side of his bread is buttered, Prullàs thought to himself when he realised how two-faced his host was being. Perhaps there was some truth in what the stranger had said, and Brusquets was basically mean-spirited.

He was lost in these gloomy thoughts when he reached the front door and bumped into the very same stranger once more. He said goodbye to him again with some annoyance. He had come with the Fontcubertas, he explained, and now due to their lack of consideration he was stuck without any means of transport in a lonely and isolated neighbourhood. "God knows where I'll find a taxi at this time of night."

"Today really isn't your day, is it?" the stranger laughed; "but at least I can solve your transport problem easily enough, if you'll allow me. I'm leaving myself, and my car is outside; I'd be more than pleased to take you wherever you like."

"You don't know how grateful I am!" Prullàs replied.

2

Outside in the street, the air was fresh and sweet; as they walked by, a pet dog behind a garden wall barked frenziedly at them; the city spread below them was shrouded in mist, like a badly focused telescope. "Where shall I take you?" the stranger asked.

Prullàs, who had recovered his spirits as soon as they left Brusquets' place, felt irritated and depressed again when he saw the bulky black shape of Don Lorenzo Verdugones' limousine parked on the street corner. A guard in uniform was dozing with his head on the wheel, while another, his round cap tilted back on his head, sat on a mudguard smoking a cigarette. "Wherever I can find a taxi," he said. "No, no, I wouldn't dream of it," the other man protested, "I'll take you to your front door, I insist; to your door, or wherever else you choose. Look, I've had an idea: why don't you come for a drink with me?" "No, don't trouble yourself." "It's no trouble, quite the opposite: we've escaped from a trap, your family is away on holiday, and I have nobody waiting for me at home either, so why not take advantage of the opportunity? Besides, it's plain to see you're not in good shape."

Prullàs accepted his offer, and the stranger started his car.

They drove down Calle Balmes without meeting a soul, apart from a half-empty trolleybus in Diagonal; they went on down Avenida de José Antonio and the Rambla de Cataluña, finally coming to a halt on the corner of Ronda Universidad. It took hardly any time at all; the car sped along the deserted streets, its headlights sweeping over sleeping houses and reflecting in shop windows hidden behind their grilles; stray cats arched their backs defiantly, and solitary passers-by, fearful of a police caution, dodged into dark doorways as they went past.

In the La Luna café, the last of the night-owls were trying to ignore the waiters' baleful stares. Their conversation moved smoothly and peaceably between football, politics and even literature, and though strong views were expressed, there were no shouts or theatrical gestures, out of consideration for the seriousness of the place and the late hour. In one corner, a bohemian poet was reading his manuscript to a friend, who was quite openly drifting off to sleep; nearby, two middle-aged foreigners, bloated from the heat and wine, were staring red-eyed up at the slow rotation of a ceiling fan. "We're about to close," the waiter warned the two newcomers. "We're dying of thirst, all we want is a quick beer and we'll be on our way," the stranger promised him.

An elusive shape appeared at their table. "Poveda!" both of them exclaimed in unison. The black-marketeer almost bent double in his fawning greetings. "Always at your honours' service!" he declaimed in unctuous tones, and immediately added, without being asked, that he was there for literary rather than business reasons. A group of young avant-garde poets met here regularly, he said, pointing to the far corner of the café, and he liked to help them with generous plaudits and thoughtful advice. "I try to guide them in these stormy seas," he added, with the rueful smile of a clown. "They're youngsters with more enthusiasm than skill, hotheads who haven't the faintest idea what a Phaleucian hendecasyllable is. Young people nowadays grow up without much knowledge, but they're healthy in body and spirit; and in accordance with the times there are also several young lady university students in this modest Parnassus of ours, all of them from good families, and all of them well-endowed by nature . . . for the art of verse-making, don't get the wrong idea, will you," he lisped with a pandering smile. Prullàs signalled to the waiter, and when he came over, said: "If the kitchen is still open, have them serve this gentleman a couple of fried eggs with sausage, and put it on my bill." "Don't trouble yourself, Señor Prullàs . . . ," Poveda said. "Just be quiet and eat, Poveda, you're all skin and bone from composing so many verses!" Poveda withdrew, bowing and scraping as before, and leaving behind him the ghastly smell of his musky brilliantine. Prullàs smiled indulgently. "He's a pain in the neck," he said, "but he's really a good sort." "Don't you believe it," the other man replied; "our friend Poveda is a snake." "Well, you seem to know a lot about a lot of people," Prullàs said. "More than you can imagine," the stranger said, lifting the frothing beer mug as he did so. "Your health!" "And yours!" Prullàs said, also raising his mug.

"I can see you're still a bit down," the other man went on. "Is it because of the nonsense Don Lorenzo Verdugones was spouting? Don't worry about it: by tomorrow morning that stuffed shirt will probably have forgotten who you are; and if he does remember, so what? Your play has been passed, and that's all that matters." "I appreciate your saying that," Prullàs replied, "but the fact is I can't get rid of the disagreeable sensation our meeting created; I know it was only a trifling contretemps, but something tells me it could have disastrous consequences for me."

The stranger could not help but concede he might be right. Prullàs' fears were well-founded, he said. When Don Lorenzo Verdugones had arrived in Barcelona some time earlier to take up his present post, his extraordinary fame had preceded him. Apparently, he was a true hero, a man who not very long ago had carried out amazing feats, defied the greatest dangers with unthinking boldness and emerged from them unscathed, as if he had really enjoyed the invisible protection of a superior force. In accomplishing these deeds – sometimes all alone, at others in command of a handful of brave men, whose will he had galvanised with his own intrepid example – he had not only faced dangers but also countless sufferings and hardship: he had walked almost barefoot for days and nights over harsh terrain without pausing for rest; almost naked, he had survived icy temperatures; had drunk foul water that was a mixture of mud and urine: had not shrunk from eating vermin such as cock-roaches, lizards or rats; had even, as could be gathered from hints he himself had dropped, been known to eat human flesh. For all these real or imaginary merits, he had received a whole panoply of medals and decorations, and had been promoted to the very top of his profession. And yet a little over a year ago, for some unknown reason, he had been transferred to Barcelona, where he was in a position which despite its heavy responsibilities and all the honours it entailed, as befitted his high rank, was nevertheless far removed from the real centres of power. Now this feared and admired man was carrying out duties that were doubtless very important, but which were, when all was said and done, those of an administrator. His privileges were limited in practice to gaining sackfuls of money by dubious means and to being the constant object of a base, hypocritical adulation: poor rewards for someone whose courage had only a short while before scaled the heights of gallantry. There were differing opinions about his achievements in Barcelona: many people praised his rectitude, the enormous interest he showed in his work and the boundless energy he displayed; he seemed to have the gift of being everywhere: not a day went by without his appearing at an inauguration, commemoration, or special event, always marking the occasion with a lengthy and uplifting speech, stuffed full of moral and political import. Others however, whilst not denying these qualities, saw in him a need for absolute command, which they considered detrimental to the role he was meant to play, as it led him to do everything himself, even down to the most trivial functions; if he did delegate something he went about it in an absurd way, without the slightest plan. That was why, in the opinion of some, despite his immense display of energy and activity, everything in Don Lorenzo's administration ended up topsy-turvy. When the stranger had finished his observations, Prullàs, who had already heard similar comments, said that faced with that singular figure he himself felt an unease bordering on apprehension. Of course, Prullàs was far from being a hero, as he openly admitted; he had always done whatever he could to avoid any extreme situation whose resolution might require a display of bravery or cowardice, and so far, thanks to this attitude and to the help of influential people, he had managed to avoid any threat of physical danger in even the most difficult predicament. That was why his idea of what it must be like to be a hero came from the least authoritative sources: adventure films, the books he had read long ago as a child and nowadays, the comics he bought for his children – *The Man in the Mask*, *The Masked Avenger*, and other such unreliable material. To him, he went on, a hero was an archetype, someone completely taken over by the rôle, for whom any activity that was not truly heroic was unthinkable. He could not conceive of a sedentary hero, someone reduced to passivity either through his own choice or by the force of events, someone stripped as it were of his heroic nature. Deep down, he wondered if this man whose hand he had just shaken and with whom it might be said he had had a verbal duel, did not feel oppressed by normal life, bordering on insanity, constantly on the lookout for an opportunity to unleash his heroic qualities; in short, a powder keg about to explode.

The stranger waved his hands airily as if to drive away these gloomy predictions. "Don't give it another thought," he insisted. "Your new play will be opening in a few weeks: the only thing worrying you now should be what the critics say about it, and even more, the audience's opinion. And anyway," he continued, "if I were you I shouldn't worry too much on that score; I'm sure it'll be a great success; the play is funny and quite original, except for the part of the stammerer, which seems to me a bit old hat. Oh, don't be surprised, I've already told you I know more than you could imagine," he added with a laugh, "but not through any magic arts. I'm Ignacio Vallsigorri; perhaps you've heard my name in relation to Señorita Lilí Villalba, a young actress who has a small part in "'Arrivederci, pollo!'"

"Well, I never," Prullàs exclaimed, "that's a good one!" "Don't think I meant to keep it from you on purpose," the other man said. "At first I thought our friend Miguel Fontcuberta must have told you who I was, and then, once I discovered my mistake, there has been no opportunity to . . . "

"Now we really must close; it's government regulations," the waiter said; "if you gentlemen would kindly settle the bill . . . " Prullàs reached for his wallet, but Ignacio Vallsigorri stopped him. "Allow me," he said; "it was my idea to come here, and besides, I owe you some reparation for having concealed my identity. Anyway, I was going to suggest we celebrate our meeting by going somewhere else. The night, as they say in these cases, is still young, and we won't lack things to talk about. I know a bar that's rather dingy but quite lively, and they serve an excellent sherry. I'm sure they'll manage to cheer you up there: you know what gypsies are like, they're as likely to lift a jinx as they are to put a curse on you." Prullàs got up and said: "I've never tried that remedy against official obloquy before, but I suppose it can't do any harm." "That settles it then," said Vallsigorri.

3

They walked down the Ramblas to enjoy the sea breeze, which gave the night a balmy air. Doubtless for the same reason, a crowd of people were walking up and down the avenue, singly or in groups, paying no attention to the clock on the Poliorama theatre which with official exactness showed a quarter past two in the morning. The doors of the theatre were shut for the summer break, but on the opposite pavement, a huge billboard outside the Capitolio cinema announced the madcap adventures of the Marx Brothers, while a smaller one advertised a comedy of intrigue starring Josita Hernán. By the Cañaletas fountain, a drunk was weaving a *pasodoble* rhythm and shouting: "Viva la Pilarica and Viva the Rock of Gibraltar!"

"Whatever they may say, there's no city in the world where you can live better than here," Ignacio Vallsigorri exclaimed, filling his lungs with the night air; "they talk nonsense about it abroad, saying people are dying of hunger in the streets, that no-one can leave home for fear of pickpockets, that they refuse to sell bread to anyone who doesn't go to Mass, and who knows what else! To listen to all the slanders, you'd think Spain was a waiting room for Hell; but just look how peaceful it is now, and how lively!" And all, he added, with a sarcastic mock serious-ness that appeared to be his hallmark, "Thanks to your good friend, Don Lorenzo Verdugones." As the two men walked by, several beggars held out their scrawny hands in search of alms, and they both distributed coins in a spirit of warm friendship.

By now they had reached Plaza del Teatro. At the foot of the statue to Pitarra, a student group was singing and playing their instruments. No-one was listening to them, but they were merely doing it for fun; when a nightwatchman tried with paternal sternness to silence them, the rowdy youths shouted back at him: "*Gaudeamus, gaudeamus igitur.*" Vallsigorri and Prullàs turned down Calle Escudillers. The bars there had their doors shut to comply with regulations, but the noise from inside betrayed the fact that there was plenty of life still. On the right-hand side before the end of the street, a dark and dank cul-de-sac appeared. Vallsigorri came to a halt in front of a door above which a sign blackened with grime and soot announced this was the Taberna de Mañuel, and knocked loudly. As they waited, they could hear drawn-out moans and groans coming from inside. Some moments later, a grille in the door slid open, and the dark-skinned, gaunt face of a woman like a vixen peered out. Examining the two men in the orange glow that filtered out of the bar, she eventually opened the door and let them in.

The bar consisted of a single long, oddly-shaped room, with a low ceiling. Old bull-fighting posters covered the worst of the flaking walls. A cloud of stale smoke hung around the heads of the drinkers. The woman pointed roughly at a table in the centre of the room. Prullàs and Vallsigorri sat down. At a nearby table, a man with a skinny body and an enormous head was singing doleful verses they had heard from the street, accompanied only by the drumming of his fingers on the tabletop.

A sizeable audience showed itself completely indifferent to the singer's sufferings. There were a few women, but most were weather-beaten men who appeared lost in thought: some of them were gypsies, the rest dockworkers or labourers, soldiers on leave, small traders. All of a sudden the singer halted, came over to their table, and asked them perfectly naturally what they wanted to drink.

"A bottle of your best manzanilla," Vallsigorri said. At the far end of the bar, a couple of women began to clap their hands in a desultory fashion; when no-one took up the rhythm, they gave up. The barman brought them a bottle of sherry, two glasses and a ceramic dish overflowing with black olives. "There doesn't seem to be much of an atmosphere tonight," Prullàs commented. "That's always how it is," Vallsigorri told him. "I'm a regular in this kind of place and I know from experience: every so often, for no apparent reason, someone gets started, the mood spreads, and before long the whole place is in uproar. But that only happens once in a blue moon. The rest of the time, nothing happens. In civilised countries, shows are planned from start to finish and work like clockwork, because that's what they are: shows. Here in Spain on the other hand, we leave everything to the inspiration of the moment. And it isn't just with shows, but it's the same with everything else; in fact, shows in their proper sense don't exist here, because we ourselves are the show. We Spaniards," he went on, including everyone in the room in a sweeping gesture, "are by nature a passive but temperamental race; all our energy is spent on singing and dancing, and if we have any left, we are quick to exhaust it in arguing and knife-fights at the slightest excuse; we avoid any sustained effort or commitment as if they were the plague;

rather than lift a pick or a shovel, we're happy to live an uncertain, lazy existence, to deceive or to steal to get by, or at the very most to settle for a comfortable, badly-paid job where we get our daily bread and give nothing in return. Yet we have a very special charm that saves us from being accused of baseness. As I said, I'm a regular in this kind of place, and I fit in well in these surroundings. What I can't stand are fancy nightclubs. Occasionally I'm obliged to go to Rigat's or somewhere similar, pretentious and trying so hard to be like Paris, and you can keep the lot of them, I tell you. The men there are a bunch of speculators who never stop trying to do business, and the girls are leeches whose only aim is to encourage them to waste money by appealing to their repulsive vanity. Everything in places like that is snobbish, self-promoting and fake. Here, on the other hand it may be vulgar and coarse, but at least it's authentic. Señorita Lilí Villalba," he immediately added, as if one idea naturally led to another, or as if he were trying to clear up any possible misunderstanding, "is by no means a vulgar person, and her intellectual capacity is far greater than her age or social status might suggest."

Prullàs stared at his companion to try to discern whether this was said with his usual irony, but when he could detect not the slightest hint of sarcasm, he tried to hide his confusion by taking a long sip of his manzanilla; it was obvious that Vallsigorri took the matter very seriously indeed.

"Don't get me wrong," he went on. "Whatever there may be between Señorita Lilí Villalba and myself has nothing to do with it. I imagine you must only have dealt with her on a superficial level, at rehearsal, with other people around. That being so, you've probably formed the wrong impression of what she's like: naïve and rough around the edges. Nothing could be further from the truth. Señorita Villalba has a very strong personality; a disturbing personality, I would say. I'm old enough to be her father, and yet, when I'm with her, I get the feeling that I am the innocent and needy one. You're probably thinking I'm talking like this because I am – not to mince words – obsessed by her; that Lilí Villalba's youth and charms have turned my head. But that's not so. I consider myself an expert in this kind of adventure, and yet, even so . . ." Suddenly he fell silent, as if emotion had made him lose his thread, and Prullàs, caught out by this silence in the midst of a rush of his own memories and vague ideas, felt something akin to panic. Perhaps this was because he recognised something of his sentiments in his companion's exaggerated outpourings. "But let's get to the point," Vallsigorri went on. "As I said, I've read your play. Don't be surprised: I like reading plays, whether they're classical or modern, Spanish or foreign. The theatre has always been my secret passion. If I'd only had a talent like yours, or that of Señorita Lilí Villalba . . . but I'm nothing more than a businessman, a materialist. Even my name gives the game away: my grandfather was a banker from the Basque country. He was sent to Barcelona, married a young Catalan girl, and settled down here. He even shortened his name and made it seem more Catalan. Over the years he became president or vice-president of the Real Club Deportivo Español; which is why all his descendants are firm supporters of the football club. But he could do nothing about the mercantile spirit he had inherited from his forefathers, and which he in his turn bequeathed to his father, who passed it on to me. It's pointless to fight against destiny."

At this juncture, their conversation was interrupted by the arrival of a man whom ill-fortune seemed to have pursued with a ruthless vengeance: he had only one arm, which was of little use to him because he had to employ it to wield the crutch he needed to make up for the lack of a leg; almost half of his face was covered in ghastly stitches, while livid scars showed the place where an eye and an ear should have been. This poor wretch struggled across the floor slippery with sawdust. He came to a halt in front of Vallsigorri, opened his crooked, toothless mouth and let out a prolonged groan. Vallsigorri stared at him in amazement. Try as he might, he could not prevent repugnance and horror from showing on his face. "Did you say something, my good man?"

Drawing breath, the cripple croaked out once more: "I bring you good luck . . . " Vallsigorri could not prevent himself laughing out loud. "Luck?" he shouted, thumping the table, "that's all I needed!" The cripple made the meaning of his words clearer by wagging his chin at the lottery tickets pinned to his coat lapel. "Tomorrow! The draw's tomorrow!" "Let's buy ten each," Prullàs said; "unless you've got something against games of chance, that is." "Oh no," Vallsigorri replied, "I'm a born gambler, and in this case we're not risking much, but I insist on buying the tickets." "No, that's not on," Prullàs said; "we should each buy our own. You know the superstition: a ticket you get as a gift never wins."

"Have it your own way," Vallsigorri replied. As they were going through the process of buying the tickets, the barman-singer came up waving his arms in the air. "Pretty Face, haven't I told you a thousand times not to bother my customers?" he shouted at the cripple. "And you two shouldn't be buying tickets from him; he's a good-for-nothing and a blot on the face of the earth: just look at him." "That's as may be," Prullàs replied, "but I do what I like with my own money." "I don't give a fig for that," the other man snorted. "I am the owner of this establishment and I have to think of its reputation! It's thanks to people like you that the word gets around and the place fills up with parasites!"

The legless man limped across to the door; when he was safely there he turned and pulled a long and furry tongue at the barman. "May you tread on the shadow of a black cat when you get home, and find a snake in your bed!" The barman spat several times on the floor to ward off the curse, then went about his business.

Ignacio Vallsigorri smiled at this picaresque interlude and returned to his theme. "As I was saying, I read your play several times, as carefully as possible. I wouldn't be so presumptuous as to offer you any advice. Apart from the man with the stammer, it seemed to me an excellent piece, as all yours are. And besides, any judgment is premature – I know plays can change a lot during rehearsal; what I read was merely a first version. And it was when I read 'Arrivederci, pollo!' that I thought it might be a good opportunity for Señorita Lilí Villalba, whom I had first met around that time."

"I'm sorry," Prullàs said, "but I thought it was Señorita Villalba who showed you the manuscript." "No, no: quite the opposite: reading 'Arrivederci, pollo!' it occurred to me the play could help launch her, as at our first meeting she had already mentioned her theatrical ambitions. At first of course I took them as nothing more than a whim; nowadays every bright young thing dreams of triumphing on stage or screen. But as I got to know her better, I became convinced Lilí Villalba had a true vocation for the theatre. She was kind enough to act out some scenes – in private, of course – and I must admit I was pleasantly surprised at her gifts. I thought that perhaps Providence, after having denied me the talent necessary to enter the theatre world by the front door, was now offering me, in the person of Lilí Villalba, the possibility of sneaking in through the back. I don't know if I'm making sense." "Perfect sense," Prullàs said.

Their dialogue was cut short once again by the hissing of people in the room calling for silence. An outlandish figure had appeared on the platform at the far end of the bar. A tightly-fitting frilly Andalusian dress accentuated the grotesque curves of the voluminous physique, while thickly applied make-up created the caricature of a brash matron. The public fell silent, and the weird apparition opened its mouth: "Top of th' evenin' to yous, my friends, top o' th' evenin' an' welcome to La Taberna de Mañuel, known to one an' all trough th' five continents." The public whistled and stamped, and the artiste went on in a guttural, hesitant voice: "People call me La Fresca, an' as you'll be seein', I'm an ahrtis' in th' Spanish song and dance. But before I get shtarted, I'd just like to shay how trilled I am to be appearin' for my beloved public here in Barcelona again now, me who loves you as much as you love me, on this my return from a triumphan' tour of all th' best variety theatres of Lon'on, Paree and Buenos Aire." The audience in the bar laughed rather forcedly: the performance always began with this stale joke. "Yes, ladies an' gennlemen, by rights I oughtna say this, but yours truly here has triumphed all over the worl'! No sooner had I pitched up in Paree, no mishtake, right there on the way into Paree, and there was a whole crow' of people shoutin' fit to bust theirselves: Viva La Fresca! Not the way I says it o' course, but in that there strange language o' theirs, that Frenchie way they have. And well now, I'm no stone statue, it left me blubberin' like a wee one. And as for Lonnon, what can I say? Even that tiny little princess they have there, such a charmin' woman, she came an' applauded me now, so she did! Ye don't believe me? Well then, I'll bring yous the photy from the papers!" The performer sighed deeply, and went on in a voice thick with sentiment: "But ladies and gennlemen, here I am back now, I'm back because I could never live far awa' from my beloved Spain, that I couldna! There's nothin' in the whole wide worl' like Spain! Spain is the beautifullest, most wonderful ting the Good Lor' ever invented, so 'tis, an' anyone who wasna lucky enogh to be born Spanish, has no idea jus' wha' they are missin'! An' dat's woy oim here tonite, all of you, tonite as every night. I'm La Fresca!"

Against all expectations, this harangue, with its cheap and sentimental jingoism, made a great impression on the simple, brutish minds of the bar's clientele. Although there was still some low laughter and sarcastic catcalls, others cheered and applauded La Fresca's speech, and tears brimmed in more than one pair of eyes. Prullàs found this whole spectacle nauseating. "How revolting!" he whispered to his companion. Vallsigorri turned to him: "What was that?" "No, nothing, this nonsense gets on my nerves, that's all," Prullàs said. "Yes," the other man agreed, "I feel the same, but what can you do? Anything to do with nation, mothers or girlfriends immediately appeals to simple minds, drunks or military personnel, so its only normal that a performer like this should make use of such a priceless trick to win over such a volatile audience." "Hey, hey, what are you two whispering about?" the barman butted in. "Nothing that concerns you," Prullàs said. "Just as well," the man replied, "because I may not be a supporter of this regime, but if I hear anyone criticising Spain, I get like a tiger, I do. Like a tiger!"

"You see what I mean?" Vallsigorri went on when the bartender had moved off, muttering imprecations under his breath. "That rogue would be capable of any skullduggery, the worst kind of treachery, but just touch his patriotic sensibility, and he leaps up as if a scorpion had stung him." "That's true," Prullàs conceded; "and I can't understand what could be the reason for this apparently honourable reaction, which seems to be inversely proportional to the moral qualities of the person feeling it. The more reprehensible the character, the greater the patriot. I've even wondered if it doesn't come from some kind of last remnant of a sense of honour buried beneath innumerable layers of wickedness."

"Not a bit of it," Vallsigorri retorted. "These honourable reactions, as you call them, are no more than the organism's instinctive response, like a sneeze; in other words, mere ways of getting rid of something. And yet, in some people, these outpourings can be incredibly intense and produce incalculable effects, as in the case of heroism, which we mentioned earlier when we were talking about Don Lorenzo Verdugones, or, in another order of things, can produce the miracles and visions of Lourdes or Fátima."

Prullàs agreed. A few months earlier, the statue of the Virgin of Fátima had left its sanctuary and been taken on pilgrimage through Portugal, Spain and France to the Dutch city of Maastricht, where a Marian congress was being held. The lengthy journey had caught the attention of the media, and not without reason: in every diocese where the statue had halted to be worshipped by the faithful, there had been cases of surprising cures and improbable conversions. On its way through Madrid, the procession had paid a visit to the Head of State, who, according to reports, had shut himself up alone with the statue and he had enjoyed a very interesting conversation, during which the Virgin had vouchsafed to him further details about the conversion of Russia, and other topics of equal, or even greater importance. According to the same sources, this had not been the first time the Head of State had spoken to the Virgin, although it was the first he had talked to the Virgin of Fátima in person.

All the while La Fresca had been singing her tuneless verses. "All the posters are showin' a name I'd rather not see: Francisco Alegre *ol'e*, Francisco Alegre *ola*."

Prullàs found the song over-long and tedious.

When it was finally over, someone in the public threw a crust of bread onto the stage, and this was quickly followed by several olives, two slices of mortadella, a piece of cheese and two cigarette butts. La Fresca scooped all this up from the floor, and thanked their audience for their gifts with a leery grin. This was the payment for her performance. Really, Prullàs thought, there's nothing sadder or more ghastly than the lower classes. Gaudet couldn't be more wrong in this respect: to identify oneself with the poor might show that one was good-hearted, but it was also undeniable proof of bad taste. Apparently guessing what was going through his mind, Vallsigorri said as soon as the room had calmed down again: "It seems you don't like this sort of entertainment."

"You're right," Prullàs replied; "this must be the only country where we value and even revel in the ugly and grotesque. That miserable specimen of a human being ought to be in an asylum or in jail, and yet we put her on here, for the amusement and delight of an audience."

"But a taste for the grotesque is very Spanish," Vallsigorri replied. "You can see it in Quevedo's verses or Goya's paintings. And I have to admit I have a soft spot for this kind of attraction, however unworthy it may be, just as I like boxing and wrestling, even though I detest the brutality involved. If I can, I never miss an evening at Price's or The Iris." "Now there's a coincidence," Prullàs said. "I love boxing and wrestling too; my wife naturally enough hates them, so I rarely have anyone to go with. If you agree, we could go together." "Of course, it would be a great pleasure," Vallsigorri said.

Prullàs' satisfaction at discovering this new shared interest, which further strengthened the basis for the burgeoning friendship between the two men, was suddenly clouded at the thought of Lilí Villalba. Could she have been so rash as to tell him what happened between us? was the question constantly on his mind. The proof that this could not have been came immediately when his companion went on, as if with the express desire to dispel his doubts: "Forgive me for insisting on a topic that for you quite naturally is neither here nor there, but before we were interrupted I was saying how interested I was in Lilí Villalba's career, and how concerned I was that a failure right at the start could shatter all her illusions."

"A failure at the start?" Prullàs exclaimed; "d'you mean 'Arrivederci, pollo!'?"

"No, no I'm not worried about the play," Vallsigorri said hurriedly; "I'm sure 'Arrivederci, pollo!' will be a huge success. But if you don't mind, I'd like to speak plainly to you." "Please do," Prullàs said. "I'm worried about the way rehearsals are progressing," Vallsigorri went on. "I'm no expert in theatrical matters, but I am a businessman and it's my job to know when things are going well and when they aren't, and believe me, Prullàs; there's something here that isn't working. D'you know what it is?"

"You tell me," Prullàs said. "Your director," Vallsigorri replied. "I must warn you, Gaudet is a friend of mine." "I know, and your loyalty does you credit, but don't worry, I'm not going to speak ill of Señor Gaudet. I know his reputation and respect it, and besides, I'm not in the habit of criticising people in their absence. But it seems to me Señor Gaudet is not at his best; if you are his friend, you'll have to agree with me. I suppose you've heard I went to visit him at the theatre a few days ago." "Yes, I have," Prullàs concurred. "And did you hear what we talked about?" "He did tell me something, but I prefer to hear it again from you."

"Quite right, because I've no idea what exactly Señor Gaudet can have said to you. In fact, I think we were talking at cross-purposes the whole time. You be the judge: my only intention in going to see him was to talk about Lilí Villalba. That was all, as I made clear to him from the start. I was trying to help Lilí Villalba's artistic career, I explained, since I had decided to sponsor her, adding that I was well aware of the decisive importance for her of starting out on such an uncertain path under the guidance of a good director and that, this being the case, I was delighted my protégée should be in such good hands as those of Señor Gaudet. However, I added immediately, in the course of the rehearsals I had been able to observe a change in Lilí Villalba's attitude: at the start, I told him, this had been one of great enthusiasm, but it had since changed dramatically, first to one of uncertainty and now to one of frank discouragement. At this point, Señor Gaudet reacted as if someone had thrust a burning firebrand at him. Out of the blue, he started viciously insulting me. What authority did I have to change his cast, he wanted to know. I tried to put a halt to his tirade, but it was to no avail. Then I realised I was dealing with someone at his wits' end, and decided to let him have his say. As far as I could gather from what was an almost incomprehensible torrent, he was a man of great talent, a real artist treated badly by life; a variety of circumstances had conspired to ruin his career. If he had been born elsewhere, things would have been very different, he said, but our country was barbarous and cruel. As a result of all of which, he now found himself obliged to direct mediocre comedies starring vulgar and pretentious actresses. If only he could, he insisted, he would throw it all up and form his own company of young actors and actresses, people like Señorita Villalba, and would put on really important plays like 'La Nausée' and others which were all the rage in Paris at the moment, he said, showing me some typewritten sheets. The only thing preventing him from doing so, he added, was a lack of means. He asked if I would give him my support for such a project. He meant of course my financial support. If I did, he told me, he could guarantee he could make Lilí Villalba a great dramatic actress of the calibre of Eleonora Duse or María Guerrero. By this time he was so worked up I really feared he might have a fit if I contradicted him, so I simply said yes to everything he proposed. That seemed to calm him down, so I took advantage of this change for the better and put an end to our conversation on the spot."

"So at no moment did you suggest that Lilí Villalba take over Mariquita Pons' role?" Prullàs asked.

"No, how ridiculous!" Vallsigorri protested. "The idea never even occurred to me. First of all, I haven't the slightest power to impose such a change, and even if I had, I wouldn't dream of doing so. I've known Kiki for years now, and not just as an actress, but as a friend, through her husband, Miguel Fontcuberta, with whom I've enjoyed a long-standing friendship, as you yourself know. I've seen Kiki act many times, and I admire her extraordinary talent, her comic skills and the sheer elegance with which she treads the boards. Lilí Villalba on the other hand is a mere beginner. To give her a more prominent role would be a disaster for both the play and for her. No, no, Lilí is a young woman just starting out, whereas Kiki is one of the great names in our theatre, a consummate actress and the person who keeps the play afloat; without her, 'Arrivederci, pollo!' would sink without a trace." "Does it seem so flimsy to you?" Prullàs asked.

"Hello, you handsome pair, would you like some fun?" a plump woman daubed with thick make-up asked them in a gruff voice, sidling up to their table. The two men waved her away. The whore insisted: "Come on, sweethearts, it's almost dawn, and my man will cut me to ribbons if I come back empty-handed; two for the price of one, all right?"

"No, get away," Vallsigorri said, but the whore clung to him in drunken desperation. "I'm as sweet as honey, darling." "You're as drunk as a lord, and all the ladies too," laughed Vallsigorri as he struggled to prevent the woman depositing her more than ample backside onto his lap.

Prullàs took a five-peseta coin out of his pocket, thrust it into the whore's hand and gently pushed her away. "Do as you're told," he advised her. The whore staggered off. "She's left my jacket soaked in perfume and sweat," Vallsigorri protested. "It'll all come out in the wash," Prullàs said, signalling to the bartender. "The bill, please!" The barman came over clutching a greasy bit of paper covered with scrawled figures.

"Don't even try!" Vallsigorri said. "I told you this was on me, and that was the agreement . . . " But he did not finish his sentence; first he went pale, then bright red, then shouted out: "Someone's stolen my wallet!"

The barman lifted his hand: "Not in my bar, they haven't, everyone 'ere is 'onest."

"Don't talk nonsense!" Vallsigorri protested; "a few moments ago I had the wallet in my pocket, and now it's not there; I can clearly remember putting the tickets I bought from the cripple in there. That was when I last saw it." "See what happens when you encourage that sort of person?" the bar owner said. "I warned you that man was a scoundrel." "No, it can't have been him," Vallsigorri said; "he'd already gone out by the time I put the tickets in my wallet. It must have been that fat queer who was just slobbering all over me." "I don't know what fat queer you're referring to," the bar owner said, "we don't allow that kind of customer in here."

"Arguing won't get us anywhere," Prullàs interjected; "just tell me how much we owe you." "Not a cent," the barman replied haughtily; "I'm not responsible for what happened, but I don't want you to leave with bad memories of the Taberna de Mañuel: it's on the house!"

Day was barely breaking, yet already the first bars and lunch counters were open for business; dockers and porters were making their way down to the port; watchful customs men disappeared under the arches of their offices. A street vendor was pushing a barrow heaped with coconuts, toy trumpets and paper windmills to the Golondrinas landing-stage. In the centre of the boulevard beneath the leafy tunnel of giant plane trees, a photographer was setting up his rudimentary props: a box camera and a faded cardboard rocking-horse. A team of six carthorses was leaving the San Beltran pier pulling a huge tree trunk from Guinea on a wagon up towards the Parallelo; the siren from a ship docked in the harbour drowned out the clatter of their hooves on the cobblestones. Prullàs and Vallsigorri walked back up the Ramblas in silence.

"D'you want us to go and report the robbery?" Prullàs suggested, seeing his companion's preoccupied look. "It's not worth it," the other man hastily replied; "there was nothing valuable in my wallet, only a bit of money, a couple of identity cards that are easy enough to replace, some stamps and a few photos. It's what happened that's annoying me, not what I've lost. Can I ask you a favour?" "Of course." "Don't tell anyone about it, as I say, it's not important, but I feel ridiculous. To let something like that happen to me!" Prullàs promised to forget the whole thing, and when they reached the car, said goodbye. "Are you sure you don't want me to take you home?" Vallsigorri asked him. "Thanks," Prullàs replied, "but I like walking in the city at this time of day, and the fact is, I don't often get the chance to do so. Just look: the air is clear, and everything is so quiet and peaceful . . . anyway, I won't go on with my ramblings. Let me lend you some money; it's not a good idea to be without cash in these parts." "No, there's really no need; I'm going straight home, and I have some spare cash there, unless of course I've been burgled as well," Vallsigorri joked. They exchanged cards and agreed to phone each other to go to a boxing match or the theatre together. They shook hands warmly and Vallsigorri said as they parted: "Get some rest, and don't forget what I told you about Señor Gaudet." "I won't," Prullàs said.

Unlike the port area, the streets of the Ensanche neighbourhood near Prullàs' flat were still empty; there were no lights in the apartment blocks, bars, shops or offices. This stillness suited Prullàs, who walked along absorbed in his thoughts, and submerged in a sea of doubts. The account of the meeting with Gaudet he had just heard from Ignacio Vallsigorri was so different from that given by the director himself that there could be no doubt one of them was lying; the problem was: who? His longstanding close friendship with Gaudet forced Prullàs to exonerate him from all suspicion. But, he wondered, why on earth would Vallsigorri want to lie about it? He was only interested in furthering Lilí Villalba's theatrical career, and surely by creating conflict between the two people who could help her in that respect, he would be damaging those prospects? On the other hand, Gaudet's eccentricities had been growing at an alarming rate in recent weeks. Could it be that his general physical decline, his aversion to work, his bad temper and his distancing from Prullàs were all really part of a desire to give his life a new direction? Was Pepe Gaudet in crisis? Prullàs turned the question over in his mind. I wonder if that rogue is preparing to betray me in the name of social realism and avant-garde theatre, he said to himself. What about Kiki? Was she part of the plot? What was she doing in Gaudet's place a few days ago, when I caught her out there on the telephone? Could they be rehearsing a Jean-Paul Sartre play in secret together?

Vallsigorri on the other hand had made a very favourable impression on him. Prullàs felt a friendship had sprung up between them that could only grow with time. But how could he accommodate that friendship with the question of Lilí

Villalba? That was what worried him most. It was obvious he could not continue his adventure behind the back of someone who, according to every rule in the book, had preferential rights over the young actress. As a gentleman, it was his duty to inform the other man of the situation; but if he did so, how would Vallsigorri react? Doubtless he would feel betrayed by Lilí and break with her, thus depriving her of his protection; and if that happened, wouldn't Prullàs feel morally obliged to take over the young woman's upkeep? That prospect alarmed him. Unlike Vallsigorri, who was not only a man of substance but also a bachelor, Prullàs was a married man with a family, and with no fortune of his own; even though he could dip into his wife's substantial means without any questions being asked, a large, regular payment of this kind would arouse suspicions, not in Martita, but in her sharp-eyed father, who, as Prullàs knew from reliable sources, had considerable experience in keeping mistresses. Moreover, to associate himself with an aspiring actress whose abilities he was among the first to question, and whom he had criticised vehemently in public on several occasions, would put him in an impossible position. No, no, he told himself, it was impossible even to consider such an eventuality. Before things come to that, I'll have to decide: either not to see Vallsigorri anymore, or to end my relationship with Lilí once and for all. It was a painful choice. Perhaps, he thought, I'm exaggerating things a bit. After all, Vallsigorri is a man of the world; in all likelihood he wouldn't be angry if he discovered what happened between her and me, Prullàs argued. In the end, why should he care? They could probably reach some agreement, he went on thinking, a sharing out of days and times that suited them both, and perhaps they could share the expenses too. That was the best solution for everyone concerned, he concluded. And at that very moment, he realised he could never accept it. He came to a halt on the pavement, as though a magnetic force was preventing him moving, and felt an immense sadness gnawing at his heart. He raised his hands to his head; his mind was whirled with conflicting emotions. What is happening to me? he wondered.

He was roused from this overwhelming paralysis by a loud, rhythmic noise that grew steadily in intensity as it approached him. The sound came from a horse and cart, driven by a man who sat swaying, half-asleep, on the driving seat. The cart was headed for the market with a load of spinach, onions, beans, aubergines, peppers, celery and leeks. The horse nodded as it zigzagged down the road, and the driver nodded in rhythm as he flicked the whip mechanically and aimlessly. On the seat beside him was a basket of fresh eggs; on the other lay two dead rabbits with slit throats; their glazed eyes and twisted mouths offering a dramatic, savage spectacle. To avoid walking along in such unpleasant company, Prullàs let the cart get some way in front of him before he started off again. The dark sky was giving way to the first shadows, heralding dawn. Prullàs followed in the wake of the vegetable cart, which took on an unreal, funereal air in this timid pre-dawn light of that blurred all outlines. As he walked past the ground floor apartments, Prullàs could hear snores, disturbed mutterings, coughing; occasionally through the shutters he caught fleeting glimpses of interiors: a piano, a trunk, a display of arms, a darkened room full of shadows.

As he passed the market, he caught up with the cart. The driver had just begun to unload his produce. There were other carts lined up beneath the iron canopy, and there was a never-ending movement of crates into the market stalls, where redoubtable women bathed in the exotic glow of the petrol lamps were busy scrubbing down their counters before they displayed their merchandise on them. Outside the canopy, the flower-sellers were also setting up their stalls: these were simple planks of wood on piles of bricks, where they piled bunches of hydrangea, carnations, pansies and camellias in sad tin buckets. Another woman was hanging calico aprons on a portable clothes rail. In a bar alongside the market, several cart drivers were sipping on their early-morning coffees with brandy. Outside, still hitched to their carts, horses chewed peacefully on the fodder in their nosebags. The ground was littered with cabbage, cauliflower, lettuce and beet leaves. Down an alleyway, a gas-powered truck loaded with oranges grunted and groaned. Coated in the early morning mist, its bodywork dimly reflected the dull orange glow of a gas-lamp. Birds had begun to sing in the tree tops; a donkey laden with earthenware jars brayed; in the improvised corral of a flat roof somewhere nearby, a cock crowed. Different kinds of vendors hurried by, some carrying blocks of ice on their backs, others crates full of beer, soft drinks or soda siphons. As if in an educational drawing for some schoolbook, a man with a whitened face carrying a sack of flour crossed the path of another, streaked with black, who was bent under the weight of a bag of coal. Little by little, the city was coming back to life, and Prullàs felt lifted by the huge surge of energy all around him. The first shops were opening their doors in a clatter of wood and metal. Some of them were very spacious, with mirrors lining the walls, two or more marble counters, tiled entrances and big display cases for cheeses, sausages, biscuits or preserves. Others were so narrow, they had room only for one small strip of dark wood, worn shiny by use; these premises, usually looked after by an old woman dressed in black, sold only one range of goods: powder for soup, sweets, or blocks of soap. Fishmongers gave off the deep-sea smell of salted fish; from ovens wafted the scent of freshly baked bread and buns. Prullàs took a deep breath: he was fascinated by this spectacle of a hidden Barcelona, a city of overalls and work aprons, where everything was well-ordered, tenacious, hard-working, so different from the other Barcelona of starched shirt-fronts and long gowns, the frivolous, callous, hypocritical, night-time world that life had led him to share, and in which he felt completely at ease. What's happening to me? he wondered again, what are these absurd thoughts? Bah, it's nothing serious: just the unusual hour and my tiredness. But watch out! A sudden impulse could lead me to make a disastrous mistake. And he ended by telling himself: I'll speak to her today, and make everything crystal clear: I'll tell her what's what politely but firmly. I'll give her a present so I'll not seem stingy. A really good present! The main thing is to clear up any misunderstanding; to get any false hopes out of her head, if she has them. I may still be young, but not so young as to let myself be bewitched by the siren's song.

CHAPTER FOUR

I

CECILIA: Aaaagh!

JULIO: Ooooh!

LUISITO: Eeeeeh!

JULIO: (*clips him around the ear*) Don't go on so!

CECILIA: Let him be, will you? After all, it's not every day a body turns up in the linen cupboard.

LUISITO: (*pointing to* TODOLIU'*s body*) Is he de. . de. . dead?

JULIO: As a dodo.

CECILIA: What the hell was he thinking of, dying like that just when we were going to kill him! Poor man, perhaps he had a weak heart, and he'd chased after the maid so much it just went pop! and he had a cardiogram or whatever they call it.

JULIO: Look, Cecilia, I know you never managed to finish secondary school, but even you should know that when someone has a heart attack, he doesn't tie his hands behind his back, gag himself, and last but not least, lock himself in a cupboard with the key on the outside.

CECILIA: Oh, yes! I hadn't noticed those little details . . . so . . . you think that . . .

JULIO: Yes, I'm convinced someone beat us to it and murdered Todoliu.

CECILIA: Well, that's one chore less for us.

JULIO: Fine, but what about our alibi?

CECILIA: Alibi? What alibi? But we don't need an alibi now.

JULIO: Precisely, my little numbskull! Don't you see? We'd carefully prepared our alibi so we could commit the murder at a certain time and place, and in a certain way. And now that Todoliu's dead, not only is our alibi irrelevant, but it'll attract all the suspicion onto us.

CECILIA: Suspicion! But we haven't killed anyone!

JULIO: And who'll believe us? We haven't got a cent, we're Todoliu's only heirs, we have more than enough motives to want him dead, and opportunities to kill him. Todoliu has been murdered in our house, and to top it all, we've organised a whole trail of false leads which, if they work as planned, will inevitably turn against us. The taxi-driver who's coming for the trunk, the call to San Sebastián, and above all the meeting with your dear boyfriend, who was meant to find out that Todoliu's fears were all unfounded, and who'll be here at any time now and will see with his own eyes now that those fears, which we invented and attributed to Todoliu, were not only well-founded, but have come true! Ah, Cecilia, we're done for! It's the rope for us!

CECILIA: Ugh, the rope! When I tell them at the club, no-one'll believe me!

"You can't complain about the rehearsal today," Mariquita Pons said; "the scene with the cupboard went perfectly." "Yes, just perfect, but if you're not more careful, poor Todoliu is going to break his neck falling out of the cupboard, he's not up to all these circus tricks these days," Gaudet grumbled. "Well, tell him not to fall forward like an ironing board: where on earth did he get that idea?" "From me," the director said:

"a corpse that appears when a cupboard door is opened has to be stiff and fall over quickly; if he just collapsed slowly to the floor it wouldn't be funny at all; you need to be ready to grab him before he hits the ground; that's why there's three of you." "Boy, there's no pleasing you, is there?" the actress muttered. "And what does our distinguished author have to say about it?" she added, addressing Prullàs this time.

"This distinguished author doesn't talk to traitors," he replied. "Last night they abandoned me in the back of beyond," he explained for Gaudet's benefit. "It was my fault," Mariquita said, laughing. "So many men and cigars suddenly gave me claustrophobia. Some evening, wasn't it? Did you stay late?" "No," Prullàs said, "as soon as I realised you'd gone, I looked for a charitable soul with a means of transport and went straight to bed." Mariquita walked off towards the dressing rooms but paused to say: "Miguel's got a meeting tonight and won't be back till late; take me to the cinema, will you, Carlos? I need some entertainment. They're showing a film with Cary Grant and Mirna Loy at the Savoy which I missed the first time around; apparently it's very funny. Afterwards, if you behave, you can take me to supper, and I can talk to you about a few little things." "All right," Prullàs said, "I'm not one to bear a grudge; I'll come and pick you up around nine."

The actress disappeared into the darkness of the wings, and Prullàs took advantage of this to say to Gaudet: "Last night, by complete chance, I had a long talk with Ignacio Vallsigorri, and he told me some incredible things. We need to talk as soon as possible." "O.K.," the director said, glancing at his watch; "I've said I'll meet the costume designer, but it won't take me much more than an hour; come to my place at eight. If you have to meet Kiki at nine, that gives us an hour to talk over whatever you like, unless you prefer to leave it until tomorrow." "No, no," Prullàs said; "the sooner we sort it out the better;

I'll be at your flat at eight o'clock sharp; put a beer in the icebox for me, if you have an icebox, that is." "I do," Gaudet said, "but I don't have any ice." "Then forget the beer."

As he was leaving the theatre he heard a voice behind him. "Señor Prullàs! Wait for me!" It was Lilí Villalba, rushing up out of breath. Bonifaci was in his box reading a newspaper. "Let's get out into the street," Prullàs growled at her. They walked along for a while in silence. "What can I do for you?" he asked. "I just wanted to say something to you," she said, "if that's not a problem?" "Of course it isn't, child." His meetings with Mariquita Pons and Gaudet had led him to forget his early-morning resolution. Remembering it now, he was suddenly inexplicably hesitant; he decided to put off what he thought was bound to be a violent confrontation until another time. He said: "But you seemed in such a hurry . . . " She came to a halt on the pavement, bathed in the orange glow of sunset and looked at him with a perplexed, hurt expression. "I didn't want you to escape me again, Carlos, I've been thinking a lot about you these past few days. After what happened that afternoon," she went on, "I thought you'd like to see me again; I'm not asking you for anything, and if I was a disappointment to you, you've every right not to want . . . "

"Come on, child, don't talk such nonsense," Prullàs cut in; "I've been very busy, that's all, but you didn't disappoint me in the least, far from it. To tell you the truth, I've been thinking a lot about you too; I could hardly wait to be with you again." These words came out spontaneously, without him being able to control them, and somehow made him feel so happy, he was almost giddy. To hell with everything! he said to himself. Out loud, he told her: "Lilí, I adore you." She lowered her gaze and seemed to doubt for a fraction of a second. When she lifted her eyes again, there was a determined gleam in them. "If you're not as busy today as you have been recently," she said, "we could meet in half an hour at the Hotel Gallardo." "Let's go together," Prullàs said; "let's not lose an instant; I've got the car right here." "No," she said, "I have to go home first, and I don't want you to see where I live. Go to the hotel and wait for me there."

She hurried off; Prullàs made no effort to retain her. I'll have to postpone my talk with Gaudet until tomorrow, he thought. Ah well, it's not that important; what Vallsigorri had to say can wait till then. As for Kiki, I hope to be free by nine. Anyway, he told himself, I'll phone both of them, and tell one that I'm cancelling our meeting, and the other that I may be a bit late.

He soon discovered there was no telephone in the hotel. "We asked for one more than a year ago, but you know what it's like if you've no contacts," the receptionist with the gardenia in his buttonhole said by way of an excuse. "If it's a really urgent call, try the bar on the corner." "D'you remember the person I was here with last time?" Prullàs asked. "No sir, a lot of people pass through here, and it's my duty not to remember a single one of them, if you get my drift." "I certainly do," Prullàs said, taking out his wallet. "I'll pay you in advance and go and telephone. If by chance the person I mentioned should arrive, and if by another chance you happen to recognise her, could you please tell her to wait for me in the room?"

The bar was empty. Inside, the atmosphere was hot and heavy with the smell of rancid food. The roof fan was immobile and had probably been out of action for a long while, to judge by the cobwebs between the blades. While Prullàs called out, a woman appeared; the first thing she did was to shake a wet cloth to drive off the flies that had settled all over the *tapas* displayed in clay dishes on the counter. "If you have a 'phone and it's working, I'll have a glass of stout," he said. The woman pointed to a telephone on the wall at the back of the bar. The earpiece was so sticky and grimy that Prullàs kept it well away from his ear while he dialled.

After some moments, he returned to the bar counter. "Did you get through?" the woman asked. "No, on one number there was no reply, and the other was busy; I'll try again in a few minutes." "Would you like something to eat meanwhile?" she suggested. Prullàs considered the snacks on display, to which several flies seemed to have become permanently attached. "Not just now, thank you," he said. He drank his beer slowly then tried Gaudet's number again, with no success; Mariquita Pons' was still busy. He was too impatient to be with Lilí Villalba again to wait any further, so he paid for his drink and went back to the hotel. "Has she come?" The receptionist seemed to be busy sniffing his gardenia; he replied in the negative without raising his eyes from his buttonhole. "I'll wait upstairs," Prullàs said; "if she comes, send her straight up."

Alone in the room, he stared at the building opposite; the goldfinch was still hopping about in its cage, while in another room an old grandfather was snoozing, sitting in a rocking chair in his pyjamas and a felt hat. What does that little tart think she's playing at? Prullàs muttered to himself in a bad mood; I'll give her what for when she gets here. He drew the curtain, stretched out on the bed, and without meaning to, fell fast asleep. He woke up in a daze, bathed in sweat and overwhelmed by a tremendous feeling of menace; it took him some time to realise where he was. It had gone dark, and the curtain let in only a little light from outside. He switched on the lamp and looked at his watch: it was five past nine. With his head throbbing and a queasy stomach he walked down the stairs to confront the receptionist. "Don't blame me," the man said, "nobody came for you. If the person you mentioned had come, I'd have sent her up as you told me."

Feeling like death, Prullàs staggered out into the street. That damned beer must have been poisoned, he thought. No, more likely the glass hadn't been washed in months, and the last person to use it left all kinds of bacteria in there. And Lilí, why didn't she show up? Can something have happened to her? Huh, I bet she was annoyed at me and wanted to get her own back. That's it, she set up this false rendezvous to get her revenge for my lack of interest. Damned women, he thought, they're all the same!

He stumbled to his car and with great difficulty managed to drive to his apartment avoiding an accident and without knocking anyone down. His reflection in the hall mirror justified Sebastiana's shocked reaction: "Oh, my God, sir, you look dreadful!" "I'm just feeling a bit sick, Sebastiana, it'll soon pass." "You must have eaten some rubbish that's made you ill; goodness gracious, it's impossible to leave you men on your own, isn't it?"

In the bathroom, Prullàs was sick and immediately felt a great relief. "Has anyone phoned?" he asked. "No, sir." "Señor Gaudet? Doña Mariquita? Anybody else?" "No sir, no-one." He called Mariquita Pons and the maid said her mistress had gone out some time earlier without saying where she was going or when she would be back. There was still no reply from Gaudet.

Sebastiana brought him a camomile tea. "You should call a doctor," she told him. "Thanks for the advice!" Prullàs retorted; "at this time of year there isn't even a miserable quack left in Barcelona." "Well, then at least get into bed," the maid insisted. "Not a chance, I'm too much on edge and I wouldn't get a wink of sleep; that would only make me more nervous and the cure would be far worse than the illness," he said. Ignoring the pleas from his faithful servant, he went on: "I'm going out; if anyone asks for me, I've gone to Masnou." "You're driving off at night and in the state you're in? Holy Mother of God! How foolish can you get!"

Sebastiana was right. As he was driving down the stretch of

road through the evil-smelling industrial zone of San Adrián, Prullàs felt dizzy and had to pull over at the roadside to be sick again and rest for a while. He could hear the distant rumble of the sea, and close by him could see the ghostly flames from the bonfires lit all along the beach by the inhabitants of this sprawling area of poor shacks. He fell asleep again, only to be awakened by the touch of something hot and sticky on his cheek. His startled jump made four tiny figures, and especially the one who had been poking his face through the open window, flee from the car. "You see? Didn't I tell ya he wasna dead?" the boy hissed. His companions conceded he was right. There were three boys and a girl, all of them filthy, bleary-eyed, and with unkempt hair. The four were barefoot, and the only clothes they wore were ragged T-shirts. Prullàs instinctively reached for his wallet and was relieved to feel its bulk in his pocket. The children stared at him fascinated. The girl said: "Hey mister, is your car a Mercedes?" "No," Prullàs stuttered, "it's a Studebaker." "A Studiobacon?" "No, a Studebaker." "Ah."

He switched on the engine and the headlights. As the beams of light shot out, the four children disappeared into the contrasting darkness. "Go and sleep," Prullàs shouted at them, "get back to your homes: it's far too late for kids like you to be out and about." "Hey mister," the little girl shouted above the engine noise, "what did you say the make of the car was?" Prullàs didn't reply, pulled back onto the highway and set off with no idea of how long he had slept or where he was headed, unconsciously following the car's dictates. As he left Barcelona behind, he thought he saw some vague white shapes like phosphorescent skeletons waving about among the reedbeds; then on the Montgat promontory he caught a glimpse of the shadow of a bloodthirsty giant. If he tried to avoid these visions by concentrating on the road, he saw the highway splitting into two in front of him; while he was wondering which of these he should follow, the split dissolved in the distance, and he eventually realised he was experiencing some kind of optical illusion. And when he wrenched the wheel from side to side to try to avoid imaginary obstacles that were nothing more than the wavering shadows of the roadside trees, he nearly turned the car over completely. But at no point, not even confronted by these horrendous scares, did it occur to him to give up. The house-warming at Brusquets', his uneasy encounter with Don Lorenzo Verdugones, Mariquita Pons' veiled insinuations, Vallsigorri's puzzling revelations, and Gaudet's probable treachery, plus the failure to meet up with Lilí Villalba, had all combined to create a mysterious web of deceit, conflict and disappointment in his intoxicated mind. It seemed to him that this suicide journey was his only hope of salvation: that to get away would put distance between himself and danger, and free him from corruption. Only in the bosom of his family and conventional order would he be safe from all lures. Fortunately for him, at that time of night there were no other vehicles on the road, and no militia patrol intercepted him.

The dining-room clock was showing a quarter to four. Martita had gone to bed early and hardly even woke up when he pulled open the mosquito net with a feverish hand and slid between the sheets alongside her. "Please, Carlos, let me be, I'm exhausted," she murmured. Lacking the energy to insist, Prullàs went to his own bed and fell asleep at once.

"I tried to embrace you last night and you didn't even open your eyes," Prullàs complained to her the next morning, "how did you know it was me and nobody else?" Martita shrugged her shoulders. "Who else could it be at that time of night?" "I don't know, anyone, an admirer, perhaps." "In our bedroom? Why?" Martita replied, "how would he have got in?" "Through the window," Prullàs suggested. "Carlos, things like that only happen in Bob Hope films; I knew it was you, and that's all there is to it."

2

Marichuli Mercadal was walking with her head down, trying not to catch her straw sandals in the uneven bed of the dried-up mountain stream that wound its way down from La Merced chapel to the larger river on the outskirts of the village. From time to time she lifted her gaze from the ground to supervise her daughter, who was running around her. Alicia, come here, don't go so far! Don't climb on that rock! Be careful of those nettles! Don't touch that bush, there may be a wasp's nest in there! But the little girl paid no attention to any of this advice, which anyway showed more concern than annoyance.

Marichuli was preoccupied and depressed: in recent days, morning Mass had become a torture. If it had been up to her, she would not have gone, but she didn't dare do that for fear of incurring divine wrath. A few years earlier, when the specialists had diagnosed her daughter's illness, she had made a solemn promise to attend Mass every day without fail as long as the Almighty preserved her daughter's health. Her husband had criticised this promise: as a surgeon and a man of science, he was a disbeliever, and was against mixing religion with medical matters. "What your priests call the soul is in fact the psyche," he told his wife, going on to tell her the well-known, impious story of a colleague of his who always said he had performed a huge number of operations without finding a trace of the soul in any of the nooks and crannies of the body. In return, his wife wanted to know if that surgeon or any other had found the psyche either, to which the doctor responded by saying that the psyche was no more than the sum of the brain's molecular reactions to stimuli from the nervous system. In order to clarify this and make it more comprehensible to his wife, who knew little of these things, he compared the human brain to a radio set, which receives Hertzian waves and transforms them into all kinds of programmes: competitions, news, record requests and so on, although there are no human beings inside the apparatus, only a few valves and some electromagnetic coils. Marichuli accepted this explanation, but deep down continued to be convinced that there was an almighty God who held the life and death of her daughter in his hands.

Now she felt guilty. Ever since passion had led her to fling herself into Prullàs' arms, and stubborn desire had meant she had been incapable of confessing her mistake, she had not taken Communion. When the priest began to distribute the sacraments, she had joined the line of communicants, but when she reached the altar steps, she would kneel down, bend her head, and then get up again before she had received the bread or wine. After that she returned to her seat and spent several minutes kneeling in prayer; she hoped that this would help conceal the fact that she had abandoned the sacraments. Yet she was more than aware that God would not be deceived by this comedy. While the rest of the congregation prayed, she trembled in fear lest her deception be discovered either by another of the faithful or by the Lord singling her out with a sign of her disgrace. Born out of her sense of remorse, these fears sometimes acquired the dimensions of true visions: as she prostrated herself on the prie-dieu, she imagined that an arm from the figure of Christ which hung above the main altar freed itself from the cross and pointed at her, while a voice cried out: "Woe unto you, scribe and pharisee, hypocrite! For you are like a whited sepulchre, which indeed appears beautiful outward, but is within full of dead men's bones, and of all uncleanness." At other moments, when the priest was giving his homily, she waited with aching heart to see whether the Holy Ghost descended on him and inspired him to pronounce a dreadful anathema against her.

Nothing remotely like any of this ever happened. None of the holy images came to life, nor did the aged assistant priest who officiated at the tiny La Merced chapel for the summer visitors seem to have any wish to be a scourge of sinners; instead his sermons were usually about divine mercy, Christian charity and how it was appropriate for those favoured by fortune to be generous when it came to helping their less fortunate brethren. Touched by these considerations, and grateful for the postponement of punishment for her infamy, Marichuli deposited extravagant amounts in the basket the sacristan passed round the congregation. This constant state of torture was not reflected in either her face or her demeanour; her expression was always so tranquil that she gave an impression of calm bordering on the oblivious, and the smile on her lips was such that it might have been thought sarcastic if it had been directed at anyone, but as it was seemed merely enigmatic; not one of the men who turned around to more or less openly admire her voluptuous figure or her swaying hips as she passed by could have imagined the torment raging inside her. "Now there's a real woman," they said, "just look at the way she walks!"

In the porch of her house she saw Prullàs talking to her husband; her heart leapt into her mouth. "I fell ill yesterday in Barcelona," he explained to her, "and when I couldn't find a doctor, I decided to come and bother your husband." "Nothing serious, I hope," she managed to say. "Oh no, just a summer bug," Doctor Mercadal said cheerfully; "nothing more than an inflamed gut and the vomiting and diarrhoea that go with it." Turning back to Prullàs, he went on: "As I said, two or three days eating only boiled vegetables and chicken breast, and check your faeces for tapeworm."

Prullàs said goodbye to the doctor and Marichuli left with him, saying she wanted to see where Alicia had got to. "Isn't that typical of you men!" she exclaimed. "If you're feeling fine you stay in Barcelona to enjoy yourselves, but as soon as your temperature rises, you rush home so your wife can look after you." She was still carrying her missal and wearing her mantilla. "I was at death's door," Prullàs said. "I wish you'd shut it behind you," Marichuli sighed. "Because of you, I'm the one not living."

After that they walked on in silence until they almost bumped into Martita's father and the children. "Marichuli, how on earth d'you manage to look more beautiful each day?" Martita's father said. "It's you who see me better every day," she replied. "Where are you going in this heat?" Prullàs asked his father-in-law. "To buy glue, sandpaper and brushes, those children of yours have wheedled me into making a scale model of the battleship *Missouri*, so here I am, at my age, turned into a shipbuilder." "Don't say that, Don Luis," Marichuli protested, "why, you're barely a spring chicken." "No, no, sweetheart, don't tease me, let me be old in peace; go on tell me, how old d'you think I am?" "Sixty-five," she said gallantly. "I only wish I were! All that and ten more besides," Martita's father said, "but it doesn't worry me in the least. Listen, I'm going to tell you something: every morning I go out to stretch my legs before breakfast; not for any special reason, just for the exercise; well, at first I used to say to my grandchildren: 'Would you like to go for a walk with your grandfather?' And they always replied: 'No thanks, granddad.' Then one day it occurred to me to say to them: 'I'm going to the kiosk for some tobacco, do any of you want to go with me?' And they all said yes please straight-away, because they knew we were going somewhere, and also that when we got there they would persuade me to buy them some sweets or other. Ever since then, if I feel like company, I make up something I need. It never fails. D'you know why? Because it's part of human nature to want everything, even what we most enjoy, to have some purpose. Yes, my dear," he went on, "human beings need a reason for doing things; we need one even to carry on living. And mine, as you can see, are these little devils; to watch them grow; to make them happy as long as I'm around; to keep an eye on their education and, when the Good Lord calls me, to make sure they want for nothing. Thanks to that philosophy, I can live with harmony with myself, and laugh at the passing years."

When the old man and his grandchildren moved on, Marichuli's eyes were moist with tears. "Don't listen to him, it's just the old fox's way of flirting with you," Prullàs said; "he was just trying to set his cap to you."

"But you're a happy family, Carlos; I'd never do anything to put your happiness in danger." She fell silent for a moment, sighed deeply, and then added: "And yet I'm sure you're in great danger." "What d'you mean?" he said dryly. "Did you have a revelation at this morning's Mass?" "Everyday I expect and fear a revelation," she murmured; "but this time it's not that, it's simply a premonition. I'm not superstitious, Carlos, but today at Mass the altar server dropped his bell during the elevation of the host, and at that same moment, I had a premonition that something truly evil was about to befall you. Be very careful," she begged him.

3

He spent the rest of the morning dozing in his deckchair in the shade of the pine trees, reading a thriller without much conviction; from time to time he fell asleep despite himself, and then his dreams became mixed up with the images his reading conjured up, and vice versa; whenever he woke up again he found himself obliged to go back and read the last couple of pages he had already read in order to get the plot straight in his mind. The house was quiet: Martita and the children had gone down to the beach, and their grandfather had made an exception and accompanied them, even though he loathed the sun and the sea; the maids were rushing to and fro cleaning the rooms, doing the washing, ironing and cooking.

As it struck twelve, his mother-in-law came to offer him a piece of toast and some stewed apple. "It will help settle your stomach," she said in a sad, timid voice, as if excusing herself for her boldness; "it's a godsend for diarrhoea and indigestion pains." She was a good-natured, silly woman of few words. Her mistakes, blunders and tactlessness were a source of great amusement in the circle of her family and friends; she didn't understand a thing, knew even less, and got it all confused anyway. A few days earlier, when the talk had been of Stalin's ghastly deeds, she had thought they were talking about some-one called José Antolín, the dressmaker's husband, and openly expressed her amazement that such a weak and not very bright man should have the great powers by the throat. This and other similar misunderstandings had confirmed her reputation as an amusing person, which could not be further from the truth. Yet, as often happens, her extreme simple-mindedness was taken for common sense. Her own husband, who was the first to laugh at his wife in front of everyone, never took a decision without first consulting her, even though he was well aware that all he would receive by way of advice would be some vague platitude.

Prullàs could not stand his mother-in-law; he never suffered fools gladly, and her doll-like helplessness exasperated him.

Occasionally he wondered if she was aware of the sad figure she cut, and whether perhaps she accepted the rôle willingly in exchange for the right to survive alongside the innocent and incapable in a ruthless world; whenever he felt like this, she awoke in him a fleeting compassion. The rest of the time, he treated her with respect, but tried his best to keep away from her. The poor booby is delighted I'm ill, he thought, as he ate the piece of toast and compote, that way she can give all her sickly concern free rein. Yet even so, as he slowly swallowed the simple food, almost despite himself, he felt a tremendous sense of happiness. His mother-in-law was scouring his face anxiously, as if hoping to see some miraculous sign that her home-made remedy had had instantaneous results. After a while, as no such miracle cure had become evident, she withdrew, and Prullàs resumed his reading and snoozing.

At exactly two o'clock, the bathers reappeared. The children were protesting at having to leave the beach earlier than usual. "Papa is ill, so he shouldn't eat too late," their mother scolded them; "and anyone who complains will stay at home this afternoon and not go out again."

Martita's father came to enquire after the health of his son-in-law. He was in shirtsleeves, revealing a dreadful pair of flesh-coloured braces, and had a straw boater on his head. "You look like someone from a zarzuela musical," Prullàs said. His father-in-law smiled, then became serious. "Stay for a few days, Carlos; it would make Martita happy, and the children need their father around: this place is full of women, and I can't get about as much as I used to; they need the masculine touch." Prullàs agreed with a vague gesture. "How's that little play of yours coming along?" his father-in-law asked. "Fine," Prullàs said. "Wonderful, wonderful; I'm sure it'll be a success," his father-in-law replied, "and if it isn't, there's no problem, you can soon write another one. You're young, you have your whole life in front of you, what's the point in being successful too early on? You couldn't ask for a better life, could you?" he added, pointing to the garden, the house and the blue sky, as if they were all part of a precious inheritance passed down to Prullàs alone. "Come on," he said, "let's go in. That smell of lamb chops has been tempting me for some time now." Prullàs got up and followed his father-in-law, unable to understand what had prompted this sudden speech.

When he awoke from his siesta, he looked down at Martita asleep beside him. He stared at her for some time, not daring to wake her. He tiptoed out of the room, and then out of the house, and walked round the garden breathing in the perfume of the flowers. He sat down again in the deckchair under the pines, intending to finish the novel, but soon felt drowsy again, and allowed himself to drift off once more into a deep sleep.

"Carlos, wake up! You have a visitor!" It wasn't so much what Martita said as the edge of anxiety in her voice that roused Prullàs from his lethargy. He looked around distractedly, but rose quickly to his feet when he recognised the visitor. "Don Lorenzo Verdugones!" he exclaimed with the shock of someone who can hardly believe his eyes. "What a surprise!"

The eminent personage smiled, pleased at the effect his presence had created. "I'm sorry to disturb your reverie," he said in a jovial way that contrasted sharply with his elegant civilian suit and his severe expression, "but your charming wife was so good as to treat me as a friend, so I took advantage of the privilege to come out here and disturb you." Martita looked taken aback by this contrived flattery, but Prullàs came to her aid. "My wife was being perfectly sincere, you can be sure of that," he said; "you're very welcome here."

"Why don't you both come up to the terrace?" Martita interrupted him, "you'll be more comfortable there; I can serve you a cold drink . . . or whatever you'd prefer." "Oh, I don't want to put you to any trouble, Señora," Don Lorenzo Verdugones said. "In fact, I was just passing through this delightful seaside spot and it occurred to me I might come and say hello to you and have a little talk with your husband, if you have no objection." Martita understood what he was trying to say. "I'll go and see what the children are up to," she stammered; "if you'll excuse me." Don Lorenzo bent down and picked up the novel that had fallen from Prullàs' lap. "*The Murderers of the Red Widow!*" he exclaimed. "Not even in this earthly paradise do you let your thirst for blood rest, my dear Prullàs," he said slyly. "My thirst for ideas more like," Prullàs replied, adopting the same jocular tone. "I find it harder every day to invent new situations for my comedies, so I have to borrow where I can, and sometimes even have to resort to straight plagiarism."

"Is that so? I thought it was all a question of mastering a technique," the official said, gently dropping the book onto the armchair; "combining and repeating the same old formula with a few small variations. After all, in my humble opinion you and your colleagues who write crime fiction have a great advantage: the murderer, the victim and the detective are all willing from the start to obey the conventions of the genre, to behave themselves without the slightest selfishness, to co-operate with each other and to be as intelligent or as stupid as the plot demands." He gave a weary smile, and added: "God knows what would happen if things were like that in reality! Thankfully for us, real murderers are dumb, impetuous and disorganised people; they show their crimes on their faces, and give themselves away by their stupidity or even by boasting about them. Because I can assure you, if criminals behaved with the foresight and skill they're credited with in the novels you read and the plays you write, their crimes would go unpunished. Shall we take a walk round the garden?" Prullàs nodded. "Yes, no-one will disturb us there," he said.

"Your wife really is charming," Don Lorenzo commented à propos of nothing, "and so is your father-in-law: he's what I call a perfect gentleman." "I didn't realise my father-in-law and you knew each other," Prullàs said. "Oh, of course, we've met on several occasions," the other said, "and I said hello to him again just now. He showed me the model of a warship his grandchildren had insisted he make. A fine man, an exemplary family, a household, in fact, where one imbibes such typical Catalan serenity!" he concluded.

Roused by the recent watering, snails had left trails of their laborious crawling along the garden wall, while two dragonflies, one red and one blue, criss-crossed the hot air. A stone wall ran along one side of the vegetable patch; it had been built before the house, and though at first sight it looked very rough and ready, a closer examination showed it had been made by an expert hand: stones of all shapes and sizes had been integrated into it. It now formed a discreet, harmonious part of the landscape. Prullàs, for whom this humble construction represented the fruit of a long tradition and an ancestral love of the earth, and of work felt a special affection for the wall. "Take care where you're stepping, Don Lorenzo, you don't want to get your shoes muddy!" "Bah, it doesn't matter, the shoeshine will make sure they're as good as new," replied the other. "But how well one breathes here! The sea breeze, the watered earth, the vegetables in season, the air is like a balm! I'm not surprised you take advantage of the slightest gap in your schedule to escape here to this haven of peace. What time did you leave Barcelona yesterday?"

"I couldn't tell you precisely," Prullàs replied, somewhat taken aback by this abrupt change of tack; "I felt ill all of a sudden and decided to come here without looking at my watch. It must have been after half past nine, perhaps ten. I do remember, though, that I took a long time to get here because I felt so bad and had to drive very carefully. I stopped for a rest halfway on a bit of level ground, where there were a lot of shacks." "Did anyone see you?" "Only some children." "D'you remember their names?" "No! They were only kids; I didn't even see their faces properly. When I eventually got here, everyone was asleep. I recall looking at the living room clock, and it was past three in the morning, almost four. I got undressed in the dark so as not to disturb my wife, and fell straight asleep." "Someone must have seen you in Barcelona before you left," Don Lorenzo insisted. "Where did you have dinner?" "Nowhere; as I've just told you, I felt ill all of a sudden. According to Doctor Mercadal, who attended me this morning, I had a typical summer stomach complaint. At any rate, I stopped off at my apartment before I came. My maid saw me. Perhaps she remembers what time I set off: why are you so interested?" "For no reason, mere curiosity; I like to know how people live. A professional weakness, I suppose. What did you do yesterday afternoon after the rehearsal?" Prullàs thought it better not to tell him of the hours he had spent at the Hotel Gallardo waiting for Lilí Villalba. "I walked around town," was all he said; "strolling about, looking in shop windows." "For several hours? With this hot weather and feeling ill?" "I wanted to be alone to think over some scenes from the play. I do that sometimes after I've been to rehearsal. Things look very different up on the stage than they did on paper."

"Yes, that's certainly true! But I thought the rehearsals were going ahead splendidly: at least that's what you said at Brusquets'." "Well, there are always loose ends, tiny details . . ." "That's right, loose ends," Verdugones exclaimed. "But nothing that you're not equipped to deal with . . . to properly confuse your poor audience. But you can see I was right: in novels, everyone has an alibi, including the murderer; and yet, in prosaic reality, no-one can know what you did yesterday afternoon once the rehearsal had finished soon after seven, until the time you left Barcelona; or between half past nine in the evening and four o'clock in the morning, if you really did arrive then, as not even your wife heard you come to bed. Oh my! Just look how big those aubergines are," he went on without a pause. "I spent all my childhood in a dry region, and I'm still astonished when I see what can be grown in vegetable gardens. Yes, yes, I was born and brought up in a dry scrubland, full of brambles and bushes; there were no butterflies or swallows like there are here, only scorpions, kestrels and snakes. To me, nature means a struggle; a struggle and the survival of the fittest! For you, on the other hand, nature is a source of pleasure and ease, it's like a showcase of produce that seems to be saying: come and eat me! Oh, I know!" he said hoarsely, as if giving account of his thoughts to an invisible presence, "it's not other people who have to try and understand me, but me who has to try to understand them: that's why I've been sent." For an instant, his eyes lost all their gleam and life, as if a foreign body, passing across the orbit of his thought had momentarily eclipsed his use of reason; but he quickly recovered his composure, cleared his throat, and said: "Forgive me this digression. In fact, I didn't come here by chance; I came for a reason, but I find it hard to bring it up; that's why I've been avoiding it. Oh well, better take the bull by the horns. My dear friend Prullàs, I've some bad news for you: this morning Ignacio Vallsigorri was found dead at his home."

Prullàs stopped short in the middle of the path. A petrol engine used to raise water from the well throbbed noisily. A little further on lay the remains of an old water wheel, its broken buckets covered in rust. "Vallsigorri? Impossible!" he shouted, "I was with him the night before last and . . . !" He thought about what he had said, and quickly added: "Of course that doesn't mean a thing; excuse me for being so stupid." "Nothing of the kind," Don Lorenzo said. "We all tend to react with disbelief when we hear such an unexpected piece of news. I should ask you to excuse me: I'm afraid my style is very undiplomatic, I speak my mind frankly, like a soldier, and have little tact in these matters." He paused for a moment, before going on: "You are an intelligent man, so I hardly need to tell you that the death of our friend was not from natural causes, or I would not be here. Someone killed him. Of course we do not know who or why. He died from a deep wound to the chest at heart level produced by a sharp instrument; this would appear, at first sight, to have been the cause of death, a dreadful and instantaneous one; but that will only be confirmed once we have the forensic report. Nor can we be certain at what time the crime took place: his body was discovered shortly after eight o'clock by the cleaning lady at his home." He paused again for a longer time, then asked: "Were you close friends with Ignacio Vallsigorri?" "No," Prullàs replied. "In fact I only saw him once in my life, during the party at Brusquets'." "But you hit it off straightaway," the official said; "I saw you chatting like old acquaintances, and you left together." "That's true. The Fontcubertas left, so I had no transport to get home, and Vallsigorri very kindly offered to take me in his car, in spite of the fact that, as I said, we had only just met," Prullàs explained.

A swift swooped down from the sky, wheeled round only a

few inches from the ground, then soared up again without for an instant slowing its incredible speed. This prowess reminded Prullàs of the stupid conversation at Brusquets' about advances in aviation and the possibility of breaking the barriers of sound and light. All that silly gossip seemed so distant now.

"But he didn't take you straight home, did he?" he heard Don Lorenzo say at his side. "How d'you know?" he asked. "Bah, it's not difficult," the other said; "someone called Poveda who knows both of you – who, in fact, supplies you both with black-market goods – saw you in the La Luna café just before it closed. You bought him a plate of fried eggs; he told me so himself. Good old Poveda knows half of Barcelona, and naturally, I know good old Poveda," the governor explained; "it's my duty to be well informed. Where were we? Ah, yes; when the café shut, Vallsigorri suggested you continue the fun in a disreputable late-night bar; and you accepted the idea without much enthusiasm – all this according to Poveda, of course – who has sharp ears and whose powers of observation are far from negligible. That was when he lost track of you, so at some point I'm going to have to ask you to give a detailed account of your little spree. It's understood, isn't it, that I'm not asking you to account for your acts. This is a free country. However, there has been a murder, and I need to verify carefully all those who last saw the victim alive, what he got up to, in order to shed light on the case and catch the murderer. You are probably one of the last people Vallsigorri talked to. Anything you can tell us is of the utmost importance."

The governor fell silent for a while, as if giving himself a breathing space, or offering one to his companion. He glanced around the end of the vegetable garden they had reached, and exclaimed: "Oh my, such big red tomatoes, and they're ripe too! A real gift from mother earth. D'you mind if I pick one?" "As many as you wish," Prullàs replied, "and if you like, I'll have a basket of vegetables made up for you as a reminder of your visit to a house whose doors are always open to you." "That would be delightful," Don Lorenzo said. "I live alone, and I'm not the sort to enjoy either variety or refinement; to tell you the truth, my diet at home is rather monotonous. But to return to our business: for a number of reasons which I'll explain to you later, I've decided to take on this case personally. By that I don't mean supervising the investigation, which is part and parcel of my position anyway, but personally to take charge of the proceedings. I shall of course be able to count on the invaluable assistance of the police, but I'm new around here, if you'll pardon me the expression, and I have the distinct impression that we are up against a difficult case, one which doesn't fit into the ordinary scheme of things I mentioned earlier: we're dealing with an intelligent, cold criminal who knows exactly what he's doing – if not with regard to the murder itself, then certainly the way he has covered it up – someone, in fact who is much closer to the characters in your plays than to the crooks of our underworld. So you see, my friend, for once life and literature have come together, and they do so, however much we might regret it, to perform a vile murder. And this," he went on, "brings me to the real motive for my visit. To put it bluntly, I've come to ask for your help."

"My help! You mean you'd like me to help you solve the case?" Prullàs said and, faced with the other man's tacit agreement, he exploded: "This must be some kind of joke! I know less than you think about this kind of thing – what am I saying? I know less than anyone. Listen, Don Lorenzo, as I told you the other day at Brusquets' house, I spend my time writing plays for the theatre; I write innocent and ridiculous farces, which have nothing whatsoever to do with reality, and are copied mostly from English or French comedies . . . "

"Prullàs, my friend," the governor said, stretching out both arms in a gesture that the tomatoes in his hand made look comical, "you can't really be refusing me your assistance!" "No, of course not," Prullàs stammered, "I am at your service."

Martita watched them coming back from the terrace. "Good Heavens, how hot and bothered you two look! You're just like children. And you Carlos, what are you doing out in the heat after you felt so ill? How pale you look!" "Señora, in this delicious spot, one loses track not only of time but of heat," Don Lorenzo said gallantly. "You mean my husband is an inveterate talker and you're a too-polite listener," Martita replied. "On the contrary, Señora, this time it was me who did all the talking, and it was your husband who listened closely and politely. But don't worry, we weren't discussing any-thing important: we were talking about my home region, so different from this beautiful part of the world." "Where are you from, Don Lorenzo?" "From a small village lost somewhere in Spain's vast geography; I'm sure you won't even have heard of it. It's a wild and tough place, but it has its own charm. Nothing could please me more than to show it to you, should the occasion arise." He sighed to express his regret that there was little likelihood of being able to fulfil that desire in the near future, and concluded rapidly: "I'm terribly sorry, but I have to leave. With your permission, I'm taking your husband with me. Don't worry, I'll return him safe and sound." "You're leaving?" Martita asked, casting a perplexed glance in Prullàs' direction. "But I thought . . . "

"It's nothing," Prullàs said, trying to sound natural. "I left a few loose ends in Barcelona, and since I feel fine now, I'll take advantage of Don Lorenzo's transport to see to them. I'll return in a couple of days. Say goodbye to your parents for me, and tell the children that when I come back I'll bring them all a present."

Don Lorenzo was passenger in Prullàs' Studebaker. Two uniformed motorcyclists went ahead of them, and his car was followed so closely by the governor's black limousine that even in his small rear-view mirror Prullàs could make out the silhouettes of the driver and beside him a guard with his round helmet tipped back on his head. The sight of them disturbed him so much he was unable to string together more than a few words in the whole journey. Prullàs' prolonged silences did not seem to bother Don Lorenzo; casting aside his usual reserve, he had taken off his jacket, rolled up his shirtsleeves, and loosened his tie; he sat back and let the warm breeze ruffle his hair while he contemplated the sparkling surface of the sea.

Raising his voice so that Prullàs could hear him, he recalled how, many years before, when he was still a student in Valladolid, he had seen the actor Enrique Borras in the play *Tierra Baja* on tour; his performance had been so convincing, he said, that for a long time he had thought all Catalans were like the irascible character in Guimerá's play. It was thanks to fate bringing him to Barcelona that he had discovered how different reality was from his prejudices, he concluded. Prullàs agreed without taking his eyes off the road.

When they arrived, the two men walked into the imposing governor's palace arm-in-arm. The driver followed them, carrying the basket of vegetables. The guards saluted respectfully as the governor passed by but cast inquisitive and threatening glances at Prullàs. Don Lorenzo responded to their salutes with a curt nod. "Every time I come in here and see so many moustaches and scowling faces my heart sinks," he whispered in Prullàs' ear; "you can't imagine how much I envy you in your profession, where you're always surrounded by gay, pretty women. But perhaps it's better this way; I'm a weak man, and doubtless I'd end up yielding to temptation. Not that I mean to suggest that you do, far from it; I'm sure you don't even notice when a pretty girl walks by, swinging her hips." "It depends," Prullàs replied, in such a faint voice he had to repeat his words for his companion to hear them. After a short pause for thought, Don Lorenzo said: "Of course, of course."

In Don Lorenzo's office they found a pale, gaunt young man whose thick glasses gave his face a perplexed, startled look. He seemed to have been waiting for hours in the same place and with the same pose, clasping a thick file of papers. When he saw the governor come in, he bent forward without losing any of his rigidity or poise; then, as soon as his superior had sat down, he crossed to the desk and laid the file open in front of him. "Your papers," he said briefly. Verdugones sighed wearily.

"Put me through to the Ministry," he said; "and you," he added, casting a withering glance at the driver who had followed the two men into the office, "what the devil are you doing in here with a basketful of vegetables? Take them away, will you, and get rid of them. This isn't a souk, you dunderhead!" Then turning to Prullàs, who was still hesitating on the threshold, he added in a friendlier voice: "You must excuse me, Señor Prullàs, but as you can see other important matters are claiming my attention; as soon as I've finished I'll join you again and we can go on talking about our business. Sigüenza here," he said, pointing to the sickly-looking young man by way of introduction, "will go with you. Sigüenza, accompany Señor Prullàs, will you?"

The obsequious official left the file on his desk, went out into the corridor, and signalled to Prullàs to follow him. Prullàs was quick to do so, thinking he was being shown out of the building. Sigüenza, however, came to a halt outside a tall, narrow door, stood to one side, and as soon as Prullàs had stepped inside, closed the door behind him.

Prullàs found himself in a square room with a very high ceiling; the furniture consisted of a three-piece leather suite blackened by use, a low table and a standard lamp. The walls were covered in a dark wallpaper, hung with antique engravings of pastoral themes. He tried to open the door that had been closed behind him, and succeeded with no difficulty; he was not locked in, but the official was standing guard outside next to a coat-rack. "If you need the bathroom," he said, "it's at the end of the corridor."

Prullàs declined Sigüenza's offer and shut the door to the room once more. On the opposite side of the room there was a balcony with an iron balustrade. Three flagpoles projected outwards, each of them with a large flag attached. Prullàs went out onto the balcony and spent some time watching the people strolling up and down the street. All the shops were shutting, and both clients and shopkeepers were making their way home. As they walked by the building, several of the passers-by raised their eyes to the three flags. Worried that he was being observed in such a compromising place, Prullàs slipped back into the room: the last thing he wanted to do was to draw attention to himself.

There were no newspapers or magazines in the room to make the wait more bearable, and trying to organise his thoughts only depressed him still further. Some time later, two men in uniform came into the room; Prullàs jumped up, but they walked straight past him without speaking or even looking in his direction, went out onto the balcony, hauled down the flags, folded them up like sheets and left the room again without so much as acknowledging his presence. Prullàs, who had thought it best to observe their ceremony in respectful silence, sat down again. He watched the sun go down through the balcony window, but the heat did not diminish with the sunset, and the humidity increased.

It was gone half past nine when Don Lorenzo himself came into the room, in a hurry and sweating profusely. Prullàs stood up again, once more at a loss as to what was going on: the governor was now dressed in a striking uniform, with high boots, leather belt and straps, and a white cap with a crimson tassel dangling from it. "I'm sorry for keeping you waiting," he said; "you know how difficult it can be to get a decent telephone line; either you are cut off in mid-conversation, or you find you're interrupted by the most extraordinary and unexpected voices. And to cap it all, I have to be at an opening ceremony in a few minutes; just imagine, at this time of night and with this heat! And I'm afraid that afterwards there will be a gala dinner. Sigüenza! Where can that idiot have got? Sigüenza, you numbskull, where are my decorations?"

The official came gliding in. He was clutching a small, gleaming wooden box lined with velvet in both hands. He proffered it to Don Lorenzo, who chose a gaudy medal and handed it to Prullàs. "Could you pin it on for me, Prullàs? Would you do me the favour? I always put my medals on crooked; I'm all thumbs. As for Sigüenza, the less said the better, isn't that right, Sigüenza?"

Prullàs did as he was asked, and Don Lorenzo said: "I can't take you with me, I'm afraid; but you're not missing a lot – four speeches, four toasts, and not much else. Sigüenza will show you out and have your car returned to you. Don't be surprised if you find something odd in it: they'll have to carry out a routine search. Just routine, I assure you. Better safe than sorry, as you Catalans say. Oh, it's really late; I should have been there by now, and the ceremony can't start without me. Once again, please forgive me for keeping you here for nothing. What with one thing and another, it's nearly night-time now, and you must want to get out of here and have a rest: go home, have dinner and go to bed; we've a lot to do tomorrow.

I'll come and pick you up at half past nine, if that's all right: we have to visit the apartment where the incident took place, or as you literary people say, the scene of the crime. The criminal always returns to the scene of the crime, isn't it? The scene of the crime! What a curious expression. Crime as a stage scene, what a romantic notion! It conjures up dramas of passion, doesn't it, Sigüenza? Tempestuous stories of rivalries and jealousy . . . Bah . . . ridiculous fantasies, I'm sure the reality will be far more prosaic. Well, time will tell."

6

"Here you are at last, sir!" Sebastiana's voice betrayed her great concern; her dry, lifeless eyes showed she had been crying. "The authorities have been here," she whispered, as if trying to prevent any neighbours hearing.

"Drat it!" Prullàs replied, out of breath; most of the neighbourhood had no electricity, and so he had been obliged to climb the stairs on foot, feeling his way up the wall and counting the steps. "Did they do anything to you?" "No, sir, on the contrary, they were very friendly, they asked me where I was from and when I told them, it turned out they knew someone from my village. But it gave me a fright all the same," she added. "Thankfully the light was still on when they were here."

To demonstrate her state of mind she rolled her eyes and threw up her arms in a clumsy melodramatic gesture, which the flickering candlelight only served to exaggerate. "What were they like?" Prullàs wanted to know; "an older, well-dressed man, with a fine moustache, and a younger, rather sickly-looking man called Sigüenza?" "Ah, sir, I was so nervous I didn't notice any details like that," Sebastiana replied. All she could tell him was that two agents of the law had come, one of whom was obviously in charge, because during the interview it was he who had always taken the lead, while the other one just cast sideways glances at her and took notes with a pencil in his notebook. When the first pencil got blunt, he took another identical but sharpened pencil out of his pocket. Sebastiana had seen this as convincing proof of his professionalism.

Prullàs headed for the living-room, followed by Sebastiana, who was carrying the candelabra. He collapsed into an arm-chair. "What did they ask you?" "About you," Sebastiana said, carefully depositing the candelabra on a sideboard and then standing in the centre of the room, hands folded across her lap and her head tilted to one side. "All sorts of things. There was nothing strange about their questions," she said, "but I could see what they were after: it was as though they wanted to get a secret out of me, just like you were a criminal or something."

"A criminal?" Prullàs shouted; "you don't know what you're saying, you're an old fool. A criminal! Did they say anything to suggest that?" "They didn't say anything of the kind, sir, they didn't even mention the word: that was my idea; but it was easy enough to see what their intention was by the questions they asked and the way they looked at each other. Just like in gangster films." But despite the shock, Sebastiana had lost none of her usual common sense, and when Prullàs pressed her, she unhesitatingly gave him a precise account of all that had happened.

Early that morning, she said, she was in the laundry room when she heard the doorbell ringing loudly. She had opened it, and found two men out on the landing who showed her their identity papers. She could tell straightaway they were representatives of the law. At no point had the two policemen expressed any desire to search the apartment: the questioning had all taken place in the hall. They had started by asking her routine questions: her surname and Christian names, place of birth, the name, age and profession of her father and mother, the year she had come to Barcelona, how many households she had worked in, how long she had been in her current employment, and so on. And then, Sebastiana went on, they had asked her about her master's habits: if he worked at home, if he followed a regular routine, if he went out often and for long periods, if he went out at night on his own or with his wife, if he had many visitors. Sebastiana had replied to these questions by informing them that, as far as she had been able to tell, her master worked at home, where he had a study specifically for that purpose, whenever he was writing a play; if that were the case, he spent many hours shut up in there every day, except for Sundays; if, on the other hand, there was a rehearsal of one of his plays, he would go out almost every day; he would leave home after lunch and not return until it was time for dinner, or later still. But this only happened in the weeks leading up to the first night of a new play. In general, her master was a man of regular habits. He and his wife went out quite often, to the theatre or to variety shows, to bullfights, to the Liceo opera house and to the cinema, as well as to dinners and to go dancing, or to weddings, baptisms, parties and banquets. Naturally, neither of them specifically told her what they were doing, but nor did they deliberately try to hide anything; they spoke of their plans in front of her and more often than not, as they were leaving they would say goodbye, saying: see you later, we're going to the cinema, or we're going to such and such a place. All her replies had been warmly welcomed by the two policemen, as if the information she gave more than met their expectations. After that, Sebastiana went on, the more senior of the two had asked what her master had done the previous evening, and she had told the strict truth: the master had only appeared briefly at home around nine o'clock, had washed and changed his clothes and then left again. Had he said where he was going? Yes, sir, to Masnou. Had he said he felt unwell? Yes, the master had said he did not feel well, and to prove the point, he had brought up everything he'd eaten that day.

When they had reached this point, the one in charge had broken off his questions to thank her for being so accurate in her replies, and had asked the other man if he had taken down everything exactly as she had given them. The younger man said yes, and read them out again: everything was correct. Sebastiana couldn't understand how he had managed to write down so many words as she spoke them without once making a mistake or getting nervous. It seemed as though they had finished their questions and were about to leave when the senior figure, apparently suddenly remembering something, had taken a photograph out of his coat pocket and showed it to Sebastiana. "Does this face mean anything to you?" he had asked. It was of a man Sebastiana had never seen, and that was what she told him.

"What did he look like?" Prullàs wanted to know, and when Sebastiana shrugged her shoulders, he added: "Did he look a bit like Bing Crosby?" "Well, now you come to mention it, and depending on how you look at it, yes, he did have a similarity to Bing Crosby." "What then?" Then the policeman in charge had put that photo back in his pocket, and pulled out another one. "What about this girl, have you ever seen her?" Sebastiana had easily recognised Señorita Lilí Villalba, but almost without thinking, purely by instinct, she had said no, she didn't know her. "Are you sure, Sebastiana?" the older man had insisted. "Yes, sir," she had replied, "quite sure." The policeman had put away Lilí Villalba's photo with the other one, had looked at his watch and said: "It's getting late, thank you for everything, and the next time we come, try to remember." "Remember, sir? What should I remember?" "Everything," the one in charge had replied.

"Hmm," Prullàs said, "congratulations, you came out of it very well; but why did you say you had never seen Señorita Lilí Villalba?" "Because that girl is trouble, sir; all she'll bring you are headaches and complications. I may not know much, but there are some things that don't escape me. A few days ago, that young hussy turns up here, and now it's the law: what could be clearer?" "I think," Prullàs said, "that what I need is an aspirin and a whisky and soda."

7

He could not sleep, and staying in bed only made him feel more on edge, so Gaudet got up and began to prowl through his flat without switching any lights on. He had been born in this huge gloomy apartment and had lived there all his life, first with his mother and then on his own; he had no need to see to know where everything was, the shape and weight of every piece of furniture. He moved quickly and unconsciously through the most distant rooms, as if he might find some peace of mind in one or another of them. But it was no use: whenever he came to a halt, he was overwhelmed by old, distasteful memories, obsolete ghosts; the water gurgling through the worn-out pipes sounded to him like faint voices chanting an incomprehensible, painful litany. As he passed a balcony, he decided to go out onto it; all the lights of the neighbourhood were out, and there was no noise from the street below. Gaudet wondered how people could sleep, how all they had to do was to get into bed to fall asleep night after night. And yet until recently I myself enjoyed that privilege, although now it seems like a miracle, he said to himself. He was thirsty but couldn't face drinking: he knew he wouldn't be able to swallow a single drop of water; the mere thought of it made him retch. He felt so weak he decided to stretch out again on the bed. He tried to smooth out the sheets, wrinkled from his earlier tossing and turning, but he did it so badly he could still feel the creases in the small of his back. That and the heat from the woollen mattress made him think of a naïve print he had seen of Saint Laurence being roasted alive. The ticking of the living-room clock made him even more tense, but a superstitious fear prevented him from stopping the pendulum. He tried to focus his mind on something concrete, but to no avail; the most unlikely thoughts kept assaulting his mind; his brain was a whirlwind he could not escape. When his mother finally died after an interminable illness, he had been forced to reconsider his life, now that he did not have the excuse of having to look after her as he had done for several years. His work no longer interested him, and there was nothing about his present or past private life that gave him any pleasure. Whichever way I look, I can only see reasons to be ashamed, he told himself. All of a sudden something happened to jolt him out of his deranged soliloquy. Through the wide-open door of his bedroom he saw a strange figure cautiously advancing: it could not be real, but he was not asleep, so it couldn't be a dream either. Wide-awake, Gaudet could clearly make out the apparition's features: it was a Chinaman with lemony-coloured skin, slant eyes and straight moustaches that hung down to his waist. It was dressed like a mandarin, and was slowly fanning itself with a silk fan. Gaudet struggled to escape from its grotesque presence, but neither his limbs nor his brain responded: he was inexorably caught by this Chinese phantom. Sweat began to course down his forehead, neck and chest. The Chinaman walked on, wafting himself with his fan; although his mien was friendly, he instilled fear, as if his hieratic gait was aimed solely at concealing a vague but terrible threat. Gaudet could hear once more the voice of the water from the corner of the room: bad boy, bad boy.

The sound of a ringing bell finally dissolved this vision; it took Gaudet some time to realise it was the telephone. He got up to answer it, annoyed that he had been rescued from this exhausting phantasm. His life had become a hell, but to be dragged out of it was not so much a relief as an exile from an interior world where despite himself he now felt completely at home. His whole being was concentrated in this internal cell full of suffering and misery. "Hello, Pepe, it's me. I'm sorry to wake you, but I'm in a spot of bother and I need your help. No, for the moment it's nothing serious, but I can't say anything more about it . . . not on the 'phone, if you follow me. I'm coming to see you." "Carlos, couldn't it wait until tomorrow? I'm not feeling too good, and it's rather late."

"I know that," Prullàs replied; "I've got a watch as well; and I wouldn't disturb you if it wasn't really important. Go on, get dressed and come down and open up for me in ten minutes . . . no, I can't call the night porter, no-one should see me. If I'm a few minutes late, don't worry: it means someone is following me and I've had to shake him off . . . Yes, of course it'd be better not to use my car, but at this time of night and with this heat I probably wouldn't find a taxi."

Grumbling, Gaudet did as his friend had asked, and soon after he had gone down to the front door, he caught sight of Prullàs' unmistakeable silhouette, creeping along the walls and theatrically attempting to go unnoticed. Fortunately there was no-one around to see what a ridiculous figure he cut. "I've left the Studebaker round the corner as a precaution," he whispered. "I think that's very wise," the director said with a sarcasm that fell wide of the mark.

They went up to Gaudet's apartment, where Prullàs flopped into a decrepit armchair in the living-room, lit a cigarette, and told his friend what had happened to him over the previous few days. The news of Vallsigorri's death didn't seem to disturb Gaudet unduly. When Prullàs pointed this out, his friend said that although naturally he was surprised, for some time now he had come to look on death as something natural and to be expected.

"Don't go all macabre on me, Pepe; if that's the kind of mood you're in, you'll be no help to me," Prullàs said. Then he gazed around the room and raised his arms in a gesture of disgust. "You can't go on like this! You have to make an effort to snap out of your unhealthy melancholy. Just look at your place: it's a real pigsty – filthy, untidy, and it stinks. And you don't look much better yourself. Take my advice, get a maid; you've got more than enough money, so there's no reason for you to live like a jailbird."

Gaudet protested: it wasn't because he was stingy that he had no help, as Prullàs knew only too well. For many years, Gaudet had employed an ideal maid: clean, hard-working, honest and discreet. But in the end age had got the better of her, and she had finally decided to go back to her village and spend the rest of her life in peace and quiet. Gaudet, who was genuinely fond of her and was extremely grateful for the nights she had spent watching over his mother during her long drawn-out final illness, had given her a large sum of money and reluctantly let her go. When he tried to replace her, he had been through a couple of unfortunate experiences, after which, although he had not completely given up hope of finding someone, he had gradually let himself slip into apathy. A few weeks earlier though, he said, Mariquita Pons had sent him a young woman who looked promising and seemed very willing to work. "She made a very good impression on me, and we agreed she should start as soon as she could," he went on, "but the days have gone by and I haven't seen any sign of her. You know how irresponsible these people can be," the director concluded. Prullàs groaned. "Pepe, I'm caught up in a murder, and all you can say is how hard it is to find a maid these days. For Heaven's sake!"

Gaudet burst out laughing. Prullàs frowned, but then almost immediately roared with laughter too. The sound of their laughing spread to the darkest corners of the apartment, dispelling the last remaining phantoms of Gaudet's morbid thoughts.

"You really are in a mess," Gaudet admitted once they had recovered their composure, "but I don't see why you have to act so furtively. If I understood correctly, all you have to do is go with this Don Facundo or whatever his name is on his investigations, and if you have an idea, tell him it. There's nothing complicated about that."

"Ah, Pepe," Prullàs replied, pointing to the books piled on the floor, "if only you read less Sartre and more Agatha Christie, you wouldn't talk such nonsense! You don't have to be an eagle to spot that Don Lorenzo doesn't want me at his side to take advantage of my abilities as a detective, but for a much more sinister reason. Before they set off to find me at Masnou, Verdugones and his henchman, who goes by the name of Sigüenza – who's like something out of the *Cabinet of Doctor Caligari* – went to my apartment and put Sebastiana through a thorough grilling; they showed her two photos which more or less link me directly to the crime, asked her about my habits, tried to trip her up, and get a full confession out of her. Then they kept me shut up in that office, cut off from the world, simply in order to intimidate me and make me lose my head, while they were busy searching my car for traces of blood or God knows what else . . . it was torture, Pepe, a real psychological torture! And that's not all: tomorrow they intend to take me to the scene of the crime to see how I react, or contradict myself – in other words, to see if I give myself away. There's no doubt about it, Pepe, Verdugones has me on his list of suspects, and possibly at the very top."

"You're crazy," Gaudet exclaimed, amused rather than alarmed at his friend's predicament. "How could anyone think such rubbish? You're a respectable person, an exemplary citizen, almost a national treasure. Why on earth would you kill someone you had no links to? Who ever heard of a motive-less crime?"

"Pepe, I haven't told you everything," Prullàs said, "and I wouldn't burden you with this kind of admission if it weren't really serious. The fact is," he said after a moment's hesitation, "that without meaning to, I've had a fling with Lilí Villalba. Please, don't say anything! I know what you're thinking, and it's not what you imagine . . . or perhaps it is, but that doesn't make any difference. She appeared at my place one day; she said she was worried about how she was getting on in rehearsals – she must have realised she wasn't up to your standards, and she has a really high opinion of you, Pepe, I assure you, and her dedication to the theatre is genuine. All I can say is that in the middle of our conversation, when she thought I wasn't taking her seriously, she started to cry and said some things that were . . . really profound. Well, to cut a long story short, that same evening we met in a small hotel. We haven't seen each other again since then outside the theatre. What I mean is, we were supposed to meet up again a couple of days ago, but she didn't show up, then I felt ill and went off to Masnou. So as you see, I'm in a difficult situation. What d'you think?"

"Two things," Gaudet said: "First, you're a fool; second, I still can't see any reason for linking you with the death of Vallsigorri. Just because you took advantage of Lilí Villalba."

"What! You don't think that's motive enough to kill

someone?" Prullàs shouted angrily. "It's unbelievable that you've dedicated your whole life to the theatre and yet you know so little about human nature! Even Sebastiana, who doesn't know how to read or write, has a clearer idea of things: she kept quiet about Lilí Villalba's visit because she instinctively realised that she was central to the whole thing."

"Nonsense!" the director retorted with a scornful sweep of his arm. "Lilí has nothing to do with the murder, and this Don Segismundo or whatever he's called is perfectly well aware of it. Look, Carlos, I've known dozens of girls like her, they're passed on from one to another, they change protectors like you change shirts; and Lilí Villalba is no exception. She must have realised Vallsigorri was growing tired of her, saw her way of life was threatened, and quick as a flash presented herself at your apartment to demonstrate her wares; and that's all there is to it: no crime, nothing."

"But that's not true!" Prullàs protested, "it's not true! Vallsigorri wasn't getting bored with Lilí; on the contrary, he himself told me he considered her an exceptional person in every way. Didn't he go and see you to show how interested he was in her progress? No, no. Both Vallsigorri and I have . . . or rather, I mean had . . . well, anyway, if he had so much as suspected that Lilí was betraying him with someone else, in other words me, by now I would be the person killed, and he would be the murderer. But then you don't understand these things, do you, Pepe? You don't understand the passion a woman can arouse, or to what extremes of violence and despair it can lead a man to, because you're a . . . a . . . Marxist! That's what you are."

Gaudet burst out laughing again. "Well, how can I help you?" he eventually asked. "So you will help me then?" "Of course, you know I could never deny you anything," the other man said resignedly. "I'll help you just this once, but not beyond that."

"I need to find Lilí Villalba as soon as possible, it has to be tonight," Prullàs explained. "Don Lorenzo knows about her relationship with Vallsigorri and he's bound to go and find her; she's young, and I'm sure they can get her to say whatever they want. But I don't think either the police or Don Lorenzo has questioned her yet. In that case, I'll go and ask her not to mention her visit to my apartment, and still less our rendezvous in the hotel. I'll warn her to keep quiet."

"I think that's very rash, Carlos," Gaudet objected; "sooner or later your affair will come to light, and when they discover you've tried to cover it up, it really will look suspicious. Concealing evidence is in itself a crime; at least, that's what they always say in courtroom dramas."

"But I'm not trying to hide any evidence, Pepe," Prullàs argued; "I'm only trying to gloss over a tiny fact, which has nothing to do with the enquiry, as you yourself said a moment ago, but which, if it became public knowledge, could cause me enormous personal problems. In other words, I'm trying to hide a slip I committed from the eyes of my wife, my children and my in-laws. That's not a crime, nor should it be: our most fundamental laws expressly protect the family, and I'm doing the same. And besides," he went on, "as I understand it, the Spanish police are extremely efficient, among the best in the world: so in a few days they'll have found the true culprit and then what will it matter what Lilí and I might have done one summer's evening? I only want to gain some time, Pepe."

Gaudet clapped his hands effusively: the conspiratorial air of their meeting, their conversation, and in general the unexpected novelty this absurd event had brought to his life had entirely dissipated his gloomy hypochondria. "Well then, let's not waste any more time in futile talk!" he exclaimed. "What d'you want from me?" "Lilí Villalba's address."

"I haven't got it," the theatre director replied; "you're the one who should have it, seeing how close you two are."

"Pepe, existentialism has rotted your brain," Prullàs said; "neither you nor I have got her address, but it must be at the theatre. We've got to go there right away: you go in, find it, and then give it me. I'll be waiting outside for you. If the doorkeeper saw me going in at this time of night, he'd suspect something. But you can give him a hundred excuses: you can say you were preparing for tomorrow's rehearsal and realised you hadn't got all your notes, or something of the sort . . . anything will do: everyone at the theatre reckons you have a screw loose anyway."

Three quarters of an hour later, Gaudet emerged from the theatre with a bundle of papers in his hand; he got into the Studebaker and explained he'd taken them all so as not to rouse the doorkeeper's suspicions, although in fact the watchman had been more put out than curious at the director's sudden appearance at the theatre, and eventually confessed he'd been working his way through a quart bottle of Valdepeñas and had felt a little queasy as a result.

"But have you got Lilí Villalba's address or not?" Prullàs asked impatiently. "Of course, what d'you think I am, an idiot or something?" his friend protested, holding out a piece of paper with wobbly handwriting on it. "I hope you can read my writing, I'm feeling out of sorts, as I told you, and my hand isn't very steady." "Must be because you're scared," Prullàs said, starting up the car. "Drop me off at home, Carlos, I'm very sleepy and I really don't feel well," Gaudet begged him. "Don't make me lose any more time!" Prullàs protested. "Come with me, and I'll drop you off afterwards; it won't take me more than ten minutes to talk with the girl. Look at the address: where can it be?" "In Barrio Chino," Gaudet said with a sigh;

"drive down the Ramblas and I'll show you." "Oh, and how do you know where it is?" Prullàs wanted to know. "I'll tell you some other day," Gaudet replied.

8

The place they were looking for turned out to be a sordid cul-de-sac that led off a dismal square and ended a hundred metres further on in a patch of waste land whose edges disappeared into the darkness. In one corner of the square stood the charred timbers and bullet-riddled walls of the Buen Jesus chapel; a few metres away was a gaslight with four arms, and a cast-iron fountain; the rest of the square was nothing more than a rectangular space added to the street due to the collapse of a block of apartments. This had happened several years earlier, and now the heaps of rubble that no-one had bothered to remove, and the remains of rooms that could be seen on the only remaining façade of the building, gave the place a harsh, ghostly aspect. In the darkest corner of the square, beyond the reach of the feeble gaslight, a clan of gypsies had set up camp. They lay wrapped in brightly-coloured blankets around the ashes of a bonfire; a few caravans and some unsaddled mules dozing beside bundles of their loads completed the squalid picture. Prullàs stopped the car under the gas lamp, switched off the lights and engine, and opened the door. "Wait here for me," he told Gaudet; "I'll only be a moment." Gaudet replied that the last thing he wanted was to stay in a place like that, but Prullàs pointed out it was better for him to do so: that way, if he didn't come back in a few minutes, Gaudet could go for help, he said. "What if it's me who needs help? How do I get in touch with you?" the director asked with quavering voice. Prullàs told him not to be so ridiculous. There wasn't the slightest risk, he reassured him and anyway, if the worst came to the worst, he could ask the gypsies to help him. Before Gaudet could respond that it was precisely the presence of the gypsies that worried him most, Prullàs had slammed the car door and walked off hesitantly along the dark street.

As he walked down it, the increasing darkness made it seem narrower and narrower, as if its walls were being squeezed inwards by a pair of pliers. When he reached number six, he pushed at the door, which creaked loudly but opened without any problem, either because the people living in the building felt there was nothing inside worth protecting from possible robberies, or because they had decided to entrust the security of their belongings and themselves to more extreme measures than the broken, rusty lock that could still be seen hanging from the doorframe. Stepping inside, Prullàs found himself at the foot of what the flame from his cigarette lighter showed to be a steep staircase with narrow steps. The flame flickered, and Prullàs was suddenly afraid that the choking acrid smell that hit him might be a lethal gas. He was relieved to realise it was nothing more than the inoffensive stench from several centuries of urine and fried food.

He walked up the stairs nervously, and when he reached the second floor knocked on a door, at first gently but soon with rather more force when it appeared nobody was responding to his call; from inside he heard the noise of footsteps and whispering; then the door opened and in the yellow halo of light from an oil lamp he could make out an apparently naked man, with a broad face and flattened nose, as hairy and massive as a gorilla. Looking more closely, Prullàs saw that in fact, underneath the rolls of stomach fat, he was wearing a filthy, ragged piece of cloth as a pair of underpants. The contrast between this caveman figure and Prullàs' elegant attire was so great that the pair of them stood silent and immobile for an instant, staring at each other in disbelief. At last the burly giant reacted and, fixing eyes reddened from sleep and anger on his unexpected visitor, growled at him: "What the devil?" His curse echoed down the staircase and a scrawny pigeon perched in a crack in the wall flapped its wings and squawked at them.

"Good evening," Prullàs said, contriving a firm, clear voice. "I have to speak to Señorita Lilí Villalba, if she is in." The brute scratched his belly with great pleasure, sinking his fingers into the mat of hair, then lifted the lamp and pushed his face up close to Prullàs; there was still a ferocious gleam deep in his glassy eyes, and his breath was like a volcano, but his attitude betrayed more curiosity than hostility. "There ain't no-one here," he said flatly. Then he sighed and his eyes clouded over, as if this affirmation had plunged him into the deepest melancholy. A moment later his face became belligerent once more, and he said: "And who are you anyway? This ain't no time to go botherin' decent folk. They need sleep; not like you high an' mighty lot who sleep all day and go out at night an' spend all the money others have earned fer you while you're asleep . . ." At this point, he lost the thread of his argument and paused, frowning. "Load o' shite," he growled in conclusion.

"I'm sorry to have woken you; don't think I don't know I've disturbed you," Prullàs insisted, "but I must talk to Señorita Lilí Villalba at once: it's a matter of life and death. If she's not here, tell me where I can find her. I promise you'll get your reward," he added, putting his hand in the inside pocket of his linen jacket. All at once he realised how foolish this gesture was, and dropped it quickly to his side.

"This is a decent house," the burly ogre replied; "there are no young women here who have anything to do with men at this time of night. No young women or anything of the sort." As he said this, he scratched himself even more frantically. By the lamplight, Prullàs could see fleas leaping in among the hair on the man's shoulders, and took a step back. Somewhere in the building a baby started to cry, and the man's eyes glowed again with anger: "See what you've done? Go on, get out of here," he said, and when he saw Prullàs was not following his advice, he added: "So you want me to punch yer face in, do yer, you runt?"

Prullàs reacted to this threat in such a strange way it took both the other man and himself by surprise: he raised his fists, flexed his knees, jumped backwards, lost his balance and would have fallen head over heels down the stairwell if the brute hadn't caught him just in time. The baby's bawling rose to a new pitch, the man was swearing and shouting, and Prullàs was shrieking out loud: "Let go of me and fight, you coward, on guard, on guard!" All the neighbours, doubtless used to this kind of thing and fearful of the consequences, kept a discreet silence. Then in the midst of all the confusion a voice could be heard: "Let him go, papa."

The brute immediately released him from his grip, and Prullàs fumbled to straighten his crumpled jacket and smooth his hair. Lilí Villalba appeared out of the darkness and stared at them both sternly. "Forgive me all this noise, Lilí, but I had to talk to you at all costs," Prullàs said, his voice trembling from all the excitement and scuffling. The man raised an eyebrow. "Lilí?" he asked quizzically. His daughter tried to put him straight: "This gentleman is from the theatre," she explained, "not *the* gentleman from the theatre, but *also* from the theatre." The man's features softened. "Why didn't you say so from the start? Come in, come in. This is a humble house, I'm afraid, we're not used to visitors. Come on, child, don't stand there like a broomstick, offer the gennelman a seat. You don't receive people standing up, d'you, dammit! What can we offer you? There's still a bit of sausage they sent us from our village." "Thanks, but I never eat between meals," Prullàs said.

He had entered a tiny room separated from the rest of the house by a curtain made of sacking. The infant was still howling behind the curtain, and a rough voice shouted at it: "Why don't you shut up, you little blighter!" The man looked for somewhere to rest the oil lamp, and when he couldn't find anywhere, put it on the floor. "I'll go and get the chairs from the other room," he said. As soon as she was left alone with Prullàs, Lilí lifted her hands to her face and broke into sobs. Beneath the translucent folds of her nightdress, her whole body was shaking, and the light thrown up by the lamp from the floor made her gigantic shadow on the wall look even younger and more shapely. "What's the matter, Lilí? Why are you crying?" Prullàs asked. "I'd rather have died a thousand times than have you see me in this hovel," she said . . . "I feel so ashamed!" "I had a bit of an argument with your father, but I'm entirely to blame for that: this really is no time to come hammering at anyone's door." "We sublet this place," she said, paying no attention to what Prullàs had said, or the conde-scending tone in which he had said it. "It's our landlady's baby who is crying. My father is a greedy pig, and this place . . . My God, how embarrassing!" Prullàs pulled her towards him. "Everything will be all right," he whispered in her ear. "I'll take care of this and of everything else, you don't have to worry about a thing. But listen, there's something important I have to tell you. Have the police been to see you?"

The young actress's body, which seemed to have relaxed against Prullàs' chest, suddenly stiffened again. "The police?" she hissed, breaking away from his embrace and crouching against the wall. As she did so, her shadow shrank as if by magic until it was nothing more than a fine line around her frail figure. "Why should the police want to see me? We haven't done anything wrong," she added uncertainly. It was plain that when she spoke of "us" she was referring not to

Prullàs but to her father. "I know, my love," Prullàs said, "but something dreadful has happened: Vallsigorri has died. I know you truly cared for him, and I'm really sorry. I thought a lot of him as well, although I hardly knew him. But what's done is done. As for the rest," he went on hurriedly, before she had time to take in the magnitude of what had happened and its consequences, "you've no need to worry; as I said, I'll take care of everything. All you have to concern yourself with is this: the police will come here, perhaps tomorrow morning or perhaps later, but they will be here, and they'll ask you about Vallsigorri and about me. It's always best to tell the truth in these situations, but it doesn't have to be the whole truth. For example, don't tell them what happened between us: it has nothing to do with what they're after, and would only complicate things. D'you understand?" "Carlos, I don't want any trouble, I can't *allow* myself any problems with the police." Prullàs took her in his embrace once more. "Don't worry; nothing will happen, this doesn't involve either you or your father. In a few days, everything will be back to normal, and then nothing and nobody can keep us apart. I never forget a favour, Lilí, and besides, I can't live without you, I think of you all the time, I'm crazy about you."

The young actress struggled to free herself. "Let me go, what are you doing? My father could come back at any moment; don't paw me *here,* I'm not your plaything. Just look, now you've gone and torn my nightdress," she groaned, without daring to raise her voice. The brat started howling again in the next room and in their exasperation someone kicked a washbasin. Lilí shook her head in what seemed like a sign of surrender, and wiped away a tear with the back of her hand. "Please go now, my love," she begged him. "I can count on your silence then?" Prullàs asked, already out on the landing, and when she nodded her agreement, he went on. "At the theatre we have to go on pretending we don't know each other; especially at the theatre. Only Gaudet knows about us, nobody else. But don't fret: we'll soon be together again." "That's *all* that matters to me," she said.

The kiss she gave him made Prullàs forget the brouhaha coming from the far side of the curtain. It was only as he was feeling his way down the stairs that he realised he had forgotten to ask her why she had failed to come to their rendezvous the previous afternoon at the Hotel Gallardo, but it wasn't the moment to go back up, so he decided to leave it for another time. Gaudet was curled up asleep in the car. When he heard the door opening, he woke up bathed in sweat and shivering uncontrollably. "You've been ages," he moaned, "now take me home, for the love of God."

CHAPTER FIVE

I

"I trust you slept well, Prullàs, my friend, we have a day full of emotion and discoveries ahead of us." These were the words with which Don Lorenzo Verdugones greeted Prullàs; they were spoken in a neutral tone but with a hint of irony. For his part, Prullàs could barely stand up after all he had been through the night before. Out in the street, the slanting early-morning rays of the sun were already burning like hot coals. "It's going to be a hell of a day," the governor said, stepping into his car and lowering the window. "I trust the body hasn't started to decompose too much," he added; "you of course will have seen many autopsies." "Never!" Prullàs gasped faintly; "not a single one!" The governor's early arrival had prevented him from enjoying his usual breakfast and leisurely read of the day's papers. This inconvenience had produced a sense of physical discomfort that only added to his dismay. The possibility of having to watch an autopsy was enough to plunge him into complete despair.

"In that case, we must make sure you don't miss this one," Don Lorenzo boomed cheerfully. "And afterwards, the bar of the Police Forensic Institute serves the best rolls and sandwiches you've ever eaten; sheer delight! But all that will come later," he went on. "First, we have to visit the dead man's home."

*

Vallsigorri's apartment was on the top floor of an elegant building on Avenida Generalísimo Franco, near Calle Aribau. A uniformed guard stood outside the front door, and curious onlookers filled the balconies of the neighbouring flats. The arrival of the governor preceded by two motorcycle outriders provoked a buzz of comment; two women dressed in black waved white handkerchiefs when the governor descended from his car.

"You've been here before, I suppose," Don Lorenzo said as they were riding up in the lift. When Prullàs said he hadn't, the governor showed his disappointment: "Oh, and there I was hoping you could help point out anything unusual in the household: you know, an ashtray out of place, or something of that sort."

There was another plainclothes policeman posted outside the apartment. He had brought a chair out onto the landing and was trying to stave off boredom by reading *Marca*. When he saw the governor getting out of the lift, he stood up and saluted by raising his magazine to his head. "Nothing to report," he said. He took a key out of his pocket, opened the apartment door, and shut it behind them again once the two men were inside. Prullàs noted a sharp smell of sweat and stale tobacco. The floor of the flat was strewn with cigarette butts.

Seeing his companion's surprise, Verdugones quickly explained: "A lot of people have been here since the dead man's body was found: the forensic people, the police, the medics . . . it's amazing how many people live off crime! It won't be easy to discover any clues after all this trampling," he said with a hopeless gesture, "but we'll do what we can. Luckily, the living-room where the murder occurred is still untouched," he added, pointing to a glass door. "Those were my orders. D'you think a criminal always returns to the scene of the crime, as they say? It sounds fishy to me; if I committed a murder I'd make sure I didn't come within miles of the scene of the crime, although, who knows, there may be some kind of morbid fascination. Have you read *Crime and Punishment*? It's heavy going, and has an amoral tone I disapprove of, but it is interesting. I can recommend it to you, although I know it's not your style."

The living-room was furnished with Louis-Quinze-style furniture and several paintings in large golden frames hung on walls decorated with paper showing an indistinct love scene on a light-green background. The windows were closed, but a slanting, diffuse light filtered through the half-open shutters. It was stiflingly hot, and a sweet, sickly smell hung in the air, or at least so it seemed to Prullàs' heightened nerves. The contrast between the decadent refinement of the room and the bloody event that had happened there made him shudder.

"You can feel a strange sensation, can't you?" Don Lorenzo said. "That often happens: wherever there's been a violent death, the atmosphere is charged with electricity. They say that at the moment a murder is committed, both the victim and the murderer feel a tremendous emotional release, and that this freed energy stays in the same spot for many years, centuries even. That might be the origin of apparitions, the scientific explanation for phantoms: some sensitive people could perceive this energy as whispers, things glowing in the dark, or other similar occurrences. Looked at in that way, it doesn't seem so unreasonable, or to be in any way contrary to the teachings of the Church, don't you agree?"

"Where was the body found?" Prullàs asked, keen to fulfil his part of the bargain quickly and get out of this sinister room as soon as possible. The governor pointed to a small armchair. "I thought Vallsigorri had been stabbed," Prullàs murmured.

"So it seems, although we'll have to wait for the autopsy results," Don Lorenzo replied. "But I can understand your hesitation: if someone was stabbed to death in this chair, why aren't there any bloodstains on the upholstery? That's simple: Vallsigorri wasn't killed in this chair, but in an identical one which has been taken away, together with other items of furniture, for laboratory tests. I myself had another chair placed here so that we could reconstruct what had happened, if necessary. But do sit down," he added, pointing to the chair. "You don't look well."

"It's nothing," Prullàs said; "just the heat and this room . . . I've never had any personal contact with a real case and I'm a bit – how shall I put it? – affected by it. I'd love to have a drink of water, if that's possible; my throat is dry as dust."

"Of course, of course," Don Lorenzo replied; "I think I saw that the guard outside had a jug of water; we'll ask him if we can have a drink on the way out. Where were we? Ah yes, the blood! Well, the fact is there wasn't that much of it: one cushion was soaked, and there was a small pool on the floor, but there was none splashed on the walls or anything like that. Look for yourself at the paper: it's as good as new. Everything suggests the victim received his murderer unsuspectingly, as if he had no idea whatsoever of his intentions. The murderer was someone he knew: Vallsigorri was dressed in a suit and tie, on a summer evening and in his own home; that suggests he dressed up specially to receive someone, or perhaps he was about to go out, or had just come in. We don't know whether or not he was expecting a visit: someone he chose to meet here in his living-room." He paused for a moment before continuing: "The attack must have been very sudden. He didn't have time to react; he didn't even have the time to protect himself instinctively with his arms: he was stabbed once and died immediately. But all this is mere speculation, and I leave all that kind of thing to you. I have to stick to the facts, plain and simple."

He took a case from his pocket and offered Prullàs a rustic-looking cigar. "Here, try one of these," he said; "let's see if the smoke helps dispel the ghosts in here." Prullàs did not dare refuse the invitation, so the two of them began to smoke a cigar in the lugubrious room. The coarse tobacco combined with his lack of breakfast made Prullàs feel nauseous. Verdugones on the other hand seemed in his element. He puffed contentedly on the stinking cigar, shook the ash onto the floor, consulted his notebook and read out:

"The lifeless body of Ignacio Vallsigorri was discovered yesterday morning, that is Wednesday, at six minutes past eight, by one Sancha García Fernández, aged thirty-six, a married woman born in Pizarrón del Rey in Badajoz province, presently a resident of the Hospitalet district, and a cleaner by profession. In her current position for the past twenty months in the household of the deceased, for whom she carried out the task of housekeeper or charlady, as it is known in Catalonia. Before working for Vallsigorri, had been employed in two other households: from which she presents impeccable references. Prior to her, there had been two live-in maids, one Tiberia Cabestro, aged fifty, a native of Burgos province, the second, Araceli Sepelio, twenty years old, born in a hamlet close to Andújar in Jaén province. According to our information, one fine day the older maid began to cough at all hours of the day and night, and Vallsigorri, worried that this might be a symptom of tuberculosis, got rid of her. A short while later, the younger maid confessed she had got into trouble with her latest boyfriend; Vallsigorri turfed her out on the spot. Ever since then, he relied on someone coming in every day to clean, make the beds, and so on; all the washing was sent out to the local laundry; the deceased usually had lunch with a friend or acquaintance in the Riding Club, or the Liceo Club, the Polo Club or the Barcelona Tennis Club, in all of which places he was a member; in the evening he almost always ate alone in a restaurant close to his apartment. All this must have been rather awkward, but you know how difficult it is these days to find a clean, honest and hard-working maid. And in addition, as Vallsigorri was a rich bachelor, this arrangement gave him more independence to come and go as he pleased, and to receive whoever he liked at home without fear of any indiscretions from his staff. Apparently he was quite a womaniser, God forgive him, and perhaps he was mixed up in an affair that might have compromised him. Yesterday afternoon, the cleaner left his place at her usual hour of five o'clock. Her employer, as she herself told the police this morning, was at home then; he had lunched out as he always did, and returned to his apart-ment around four. A few minutes before the cleaner left, she remembers that a woman called on the telephone, asking for Vallsigorri, and he had a short conversation with her in private. Nothing strange happened that day, or at least, that's what the cleaner thinks: she's a simple woman, who's still suffering from shock. She'll probably remember more tomorrow or the next day. The porter didn't let anyone into this apartment or any other. He goes off duty at nine in the evening. This suggests that the murderer arrived after then, and that it was Vallsigorri himself who let him in. This however is a very hasty deduc-tion: there are a thousand other possibilities, so we must proceed with caution.

"To go back to where we started," the governor went on, "the cleaner Sancha García arrived at the apartment yesterday at five past eight. She remembers the time very clearly," he added, consulting his notes, "because the tram she takes to get here every day was later than usual that day and she was worried her employer would say something to her. When asked if her master often scolded her, she said he didn't, but that 'every now and then he gave her a good tongue-lashing.' She opened the door with her own key. She can't remember whether the door was locked or simply shut: 'She didn't notice one way or the other.' Sancha García has a key to the apartment and to the main door to the building; it was Vallsigorri himself who gave them to her a few months after she had been working for him and he had been able to verify she was trustworthy. At first it had been the porter who let her in, but that arrangement didn't suit anyone, since at eight in the morning the porter had not yet shaved or washed, and was in pyjamas and slippers, which meant he was letting down the tone of the building.

"As soon as she came into the apartment, Sancha García noticed that the living-room door was wide open. She remembers having shut it the previous day 'so the furniture wouldn't get dusty.' When she looked inside the room, she saw the lifeless body of her employer in the chair. She immediately understood he was dead 'because of the way he looked'. The first person to respond to her cries for help was the downstairs neighbour, one Arsenio Cascante, a public notary, and therefore an exceptionally valuable witness. Don Arsenio 'corroborates *in toto*' what the maid says. It was he who telephoned the police. There were no signs of a struggle in the room. In fact, it was exactly as you saw it, except for the body and the chair. The cleaner says there is nothing missing. In a drawer of that chest," the governor said finally, pointing to an inlaid piece of furniture, "there were more than two thousand pesetas in silver five-peseta pieces. The victim had a gold watch on him, and there are statuettes, vases and other very valuable antiques in the room. At first sight, it seems nothing has been taken."

"I understand," Prullàs said, after closely following all these explanations while he let the cigar burn itself down; "it seems then that robbery was not the motive for the crime."

"Don't worry about that," Don Lorenzo said with a laugh; "there are more than enough motives. As many as there are hidden folds in the human soul: honour, jealousy, spite, a deadly rivalry, some long-standing vengeance . . . our unfortunate friend was a businessman. *Cherchez la femme* as the Frenchies say, but *cherchez* as well his accounts."

"And the murder weapon?" Prullàs asked. "It hasn't been found yet," the other man replied. Then he added hurriedly: "Let's get on with our inspection."

They examined the rest of the apartment without turning up anything of interest; everything that might shed some light on the murder had already been removed by the police experts. The library shelves were filled with soberly-bound volumes, which must have been closely and pleasurably read by someone who had died more than a hundred years earlier. The dried and stuffed figure of a small animal stood on a pedestal: it was a small black-haired monkey, with a self-absorbed expression on its tiny face. A tin label gave the details of when and where it had been shot: Guinea, 19-5-1942. Prullàs noticed that one of the walls was lined with shelves stuffed with dirty, torn cheap novels, many of them bought in second-hand bookshops. "Vallsigorri boasted to me about his wonderful collection of thrillers," he said sadly; "and he wasn't exaggerating; here it is, just as he described it. I wonder who's going to inherit it, and what they'll do with it."

"The question of the inheritance has yet to be resolved," Don Lorenzo replied, consulting his notes once more. "Vallsigorri was a bachelor, but I'm sure he made a will; I know we'll learn a lot when it's read. And as for those thrillers, you know my opinion: I'd pile them all up, sprinkle petrol on them, and set a torch to them." "I'm not going to be their defence lawyer," Prullàs said; "they're the sort of books whose only worth is the pleasure they give when they're read. But some of them do have a certain literary value." "I wouldn't save any from the flames, even if Cervantes himself had written it," the governor replied; "and anyway, reading them didn't do much for Vallsigorri: it's as if instead of sharpening his wits, all these pulp novels only softened him up, because in the end he died like one of their most unsuspecting victims. At the very least he could have left us a coded message written in his own blood, a hieroglyph on the floor or another clue that would have helped us identify his murderer."

A sliding door led on from the library to the bedroom. This was a smaller room, filled almost entirely by a huge carved wooden bed. The heat inside was unbearable; Prullàs wondered how on earth anyone could possibly sleep in there. He immediately realised how ridiculous this thought was and was annoyed at himself: of necessity, he began to make a great effort to memorise all the details of the room and to draw some conclusion from them, but this only led him to dismiss everything as superfluous and to see his observations as worthless.

The bed was made. Don Lorenzo went over and pressed it with both hands: the springs creaked, and the imprint of his fingers stayed for a few moments on the bedspread. "A feather bed!" he exclaimed, straightening up. "A bachelor who chooses a double bed like this is making a declaration of principles, don't you think?" "Perhaps it was his parents'," Prullàs said, put out by the jokey way the other man referred to the dead man. "If that's so, he only kept one bedside table," Don Lorenzo pointed out. "And as you can see from that, it seems our friend had the habit of sleeping on the right-hand side of the bed. I wonder who slept on the left? They say he was a bit of a rogue. Of course, as a man and a bachelor to boot, he wasn't doing anybody any harm, was he?" "No, that's true," Prullàs agreed lamely.

"If he had been married, I would have thought differently about his conduct," the governor said gravely. "I'm no prude, but I do not approve of adultery: it symbolises the laxity of morals and undermines the institution of the family, which is the mainstay of the State. But none of that applies to our dead friend: he chose the path of bachelordom, and what he did on his own is between him and God. Ah, if only sheets could talk, what amazing tales they would have to tell! And while we're on the theme," Don Lorenzo went on as if a random thought had just struck him, "I've heard that Vallsigorri had . . . how shall we put it? . . . a flirtation, with a young actress who had a neat pair of legs and few scruples. I've also heard she forms part of the cast of your next play. I imagine you have also heard the same rumours." "No, the truth is I haven't heard anything of the kind," Prullàs replied.

"Oh, come now, my friend, who are you trying to protect?" Verdugones responded. "No amount of rumours can affect poor Vallsigorri now, and the girl in question can't be too worried about her reputation if she did what she was doing. She must be one of those . . . well, you know, one of those youngsters crazy about films. They dream about becoming stars, and men encourage them, getting what they can out of it along the way. After that, it's not easy for them to return to where they started out from. They imagine the whole world is Hollywood; the Mecca of cinema! But Spain isn't Hollywood, my friend. Not Hollywood nor anything remotely like it."

"If it's Señorita Lilí Villalba you're referring to," Prullàs replied drily, "of course I know her, but only by sight. Of course as the rehearsals have progressed, I've had the opportunity to study how she looks and how she acts. But I haven't had any contact with her outside the theatre, and know nothing of her private life."

Verdugones smiled at him with a knowing air. "I thought as much," he mused. Then, without explaining the meaning of this ambiguous statement, he looked at his watch and said: "It's just gone twelve, and our appointment with the forensic surgeon is at one. We've completed our inspection more quickly than I expected. To tell the truth, I was hoping you'd take a magnifying glass out of your pocket and peer into every nook and cranny, find a button on the floor somewhere and shout 'Eureka!', solving the case at a stroke. What are you staring at?" "Nothing," Prullàs replied. He'd opened the drawer of the bedside table and found some typewritten sheets of paper inside. He had only needed to give them a cursory glance to see they were from 'La Nausée' by Jean-Paul Sartre. But Don Lorenzo didn't give him time to go on searching. "Come on," he said, "let's forget about that jug of water; we've got time to have a glass of beer in the bar downstairs. It's on you."

While they were drinking their beers, the gaunt, pallid young man Prullàs had met the previous afternoon in Don Lorenzo Verdugones' office came into the bar. "Have a beer with us, Sigüenza," the governor said in a friendly manner. "Thank you, Don Lorenzo, but you know I mustn't," Sigüenza replied, pointing to his side to show the reason for this prohibition; the mere reminder of his condition led him to pale still further, and his bloodless lips twisted in a grimace of pain. "I'm sorry to disturb you, sir, but the policeman told me I'd find you here, and if you don't mind I wanted to show you the photos and the inventory. They've just arrived," he announced, placing a leather briefcase on the bar and taking a long envelope and several typed sheets out if it. Don Lorenzo opened the envelope and looked through the photos with evident satisfaction. "They came out very well," he said thoughtfully. He passed them to Prullàs. All of them showed Vallsigorri sprawled on a chair identical to the one he had seen in the room. Despite the fact that the photographs were not of the highest quality, and the contrast between light and shade was very marked, the dark stain on the victim's shirt and jacket, the dislocated pose of the body, and above all the frozen gaze of his rigid face, indifferent to the presence of the photographer and the camera flashes, left no doubt as to their macabre meaning. Prullàs laid them face down on the bar, and quickly swallowed the rest of his beer. "How ghastly!" he said.

"Now you see how little reality has to do with those cheap novels you're so fond of!" Don Lorenzo said disdainfully. He handed Prullàs one of the typewritten sheets. "Here's the inventory of all the personal effects found on the victim or in the room. Everything's here: his shoe laces, the stiffeners from his shirt collar, his garters, it's all there. The copy's a bit blurred, because we're short even of carbon paper, but it is legible." Prullàs scanned the list of items and noticed that a calfskin wallet was among them. He remembered the robbery in the Taberna de Mañuel and wondered if the inclusion of a wallet in the list was meaningful. Perhaps Vallsigorri had recovered it between their night-time adventure and his murder, or perhaps he had lied and it had never been stolen. In all likelihood, however, Vallsigorri had several wallets, or had bought another one straightaway to replace the one he had lost. The inventory made no mention of the contents of the wallet, found in the dead man's pocket.

Verdugones snapped him out of his thoughts. "You can keep that blessed sheet of paper and read it at home. We have to hurry now: we mustn't keep the forensic expert waiting."

"Do I really have to attend the autopsy?" Prullàs begged him, glancing at the backs of the photographs. The governor laughed out loud, and even Sigüenza's lips parted in a wan smile. "No, no, that was only my little joke! The autopsy was carried out yesterday, and the body received a Christian burial this morning in Sarría cemetery."

The courts stood vacant in the torrid summer months; without its usual troop of litigants, lawyers, magistrates, barristers and officials, the Palace of Justice was plunged in a sombre, timorous silence. In the endless corridors, protected from the noonday sun by narrow shutters, the light was so dim that only vague outlines of the few people inextricably caught up in the morass of the law could be made out. They seemed to have as little place there as in the world outside. Occasionally a lawyer appeared among these silent figures, trying to give the impression of studious diligence. They wore brand-new togas with lace ruffs, and birettas tilted down over one eye as they strode forward, chins sunk in the soft velvet of their cravats, trying in vain to bypass the poor unfortunates continually leaping out to intercept them to find out how their cases were going. Any lawyer detained in this way would gaze sternly at the brief he was carrying, then envelop the plaintiff in a warm, beatific smile and murmur: "Patience, patience, everything is going just fine, but we mustn't rush things, the judge has already given a ruling and called on the two sides to appear before him, *ipso jure*, it would be counter-productive for us to proceed in any other manner."

Closely-guarded prisoners shuffled wearily up and down the wide main staircase and the darker, narrow side ones. For the most part, they were cheap swindlers who had been caught *in flagrante*; their eyes cast down or raised to the heavens in supplication, they were destined for the magistrate's court to give their statements, or heading for the cells after doing so, where they were to wait for transfer to prison. And once there, forgotten by the outside world, they risked waiting forever, until their case was finally heard. Some of them had bruises and cuts on their faces, and pieces of filthy plaster covered their foreheads or cheeks, the visible consequence of having stubbornly refused to admit their guilt. That could soon be me if things don't work out, Prullàs thought.

They were received in the offices of the Anatomical Forensic Institute on the second floor of this imposing building by a clerk they found snoozing behind a pile of documents which protected him from any curious gazes. On his desk, oil was oozing out of a bread roll onto several sheets of officially-headed paper covered in neat handwriting. Don Lorenzo Verdugones picked the roll up and carefully dropped it into the wastepaper basket, without saying a word. The clerk raised his head, blinked in disbelief, then got up silently and quickly disappeared through a frosted-glass door. The governor took advantage of his absence to explain to Prullàs that although the autopsies were carried out in the Clinical Hospital, the forensic surgeons had these offices in the Palace of Justice because they needed to consult with lawyers, public prosecutors, and judges. Prullàs felt relieved when he heard this, as he had feared being confronted by a display of limbs in formaldehyde jars. A few moments later, the clerk returned to inform them that Doctor Capdevila would see them in his office.

Doctor Capdevila was a cordial, good-natured man in his mid-forties. He was short, but with a large head, short bristling hair, and thick lips. He was smartly dressed, with a bow tie, and smelt of hair lotion. He was effusive in his greeting of Don Lorenzo, who introduced him to Prullàs who had – the governor explained – been so kind as to interrupt his summer vacation to give him a hand in solving the case. "Oh, that's very good of you," Doctor Capdevila said, "very good; and where do you spend your vacation, Señor Prullàs? In Masnou? What a lovely spot! An old acquaintance and colleague of mine has rented a house there this summer, Doctor Mercadal: perhaps you've heard the name." "Yes, of course," Prullàs said, "and I've also had the opportunity to meet him personally. He's a charming fellow, with a wide range of interests."

"He was always like that," Doctor Capdevila agreed; "when we were at university together he used to write poetry: it wasn't particularly good, but it was poetry all the same. A very lively man, though somewhat pessimistic – although that didn't stop him marrying a gorgeous woman. A real expert, that's for sure," the forensic surgeon said, winking, "that's the only word for it, an expert. As for yourself, Señor Prullàs, I must admit I'm delighted to meet you, even in such a cheerless place; your comedies have given me some unforgettable moments, truly unforgettable. But I have to tell you," he added, "that in here we often see cases that would be perfect for your plays, if not pure farces! Stories which, if they were put on the stage, would be considered as completely unbelievable by the public but which, I can assure you, are as true as life itself. Ah, if only I had your talent for writing," he concluded with a sigh. Then he rubbed his hands together and sighed: "Well, so be it!" A moment later he went on in a more neutral tone: "But you two have come here for a specific purpose, and here I am chattering on: let's get down to business, shall we?"

Doctor Capdevila put on a pair of half-moon glasses, picked up some sheets of paper from his desk, and began to read out loud: "In Barcelona, on the so and so of the year nineteen hundred and such and such, in the presence of the judge and the undersigned, the forensic surgeon blah blah blah who by virtue of the oath he has sworn to carry out his duties faithfully to the best of his abilities, etc., etc., etc., does solemnly swear that in pursuance of said task and blah blah blah, he has carried out the autopsy on the body of Vallsigorri y Fadri, and that a first external examination revealed no bruising or other signs of violence, and that on examining the cranial cavity there was no evidence of any cerebral haemorrhage . . . The next part doesn't interest us . . . Let's see, let's see . . . Ah, here's the good bit! There are signs of physical aggression with a sharp instrument (a knife or similar) that penetrated five centimetres into the fifth left intercostal space at some eight centimetres from the sternum, which affected the precordial mass as well as the right auricle of the heart, causing the severing of the aortic arch and the upper *vena cava* . . . at the very first blow then," the doctor said, glancing up from his report, "some people are born lucky!" Then he returned to his reading: "On proceeding to the dissection of the abdominal cavity, everything was found to be normal; the mucous membrane at the mouth of the stomach showed nothing unusual; the contents of the same contained remains of cauliflower cheese, pheasant in a vinaigrette sauce, cheese, bread, wine and coffee. All of which gives rise to the conclusion that death was due to the wound caused by the aforementioned sharp instrument, etc., etc., etc."

He dropped the sheets of paper onto his desk, took off his glasses, put them away in his jacket pocket, rubbed his hands again, and summed up by saying: "If you wish, I can give you a copy of the full legal report, but what I've just told you is a resumé of the most important findings. Any questions?" "Yes, doctor, at what time, in your view, did the death occur?" Verdugones asked. "It's very difficult to be precise, but I would estimate that, within the margin of error possible in cases such as this, that the attack took place between twenty-one hundred hours on Tuesday evening and zero hour on Wednesday: that's to say, between nine and twelve at night; or perhaps as late as one or one-thirty in the morning, if we take into account how hot and humid that particular night was. I myself spent most of the night unable to sleep, until I decided to get up, fill the bidet with cold water, and soak my feet in it."

Don Lorenzo Verdugones put another question: "What sort of person could have delivered a blow such as the one you described to us? Does it require any special skill?"

Doctor Capdevila cleared his throat. "From a strictly physical point of view," he said, "anyone could have done it. By that I mean that no special skill was required, nor any particular build. It would have been different if the victim had been strangled, or there had been a struggle; in that case, since the victim was athletic, things would have been more complicated; but our examination has ruled out either of these hypotheses. In short," he concluded, "I would say that the murderer acted with premeditation, intending to produce a fatal wound in the victim, and that luck, if you pardon the expression, was with him or her. It is obvious that the attack took the victim by surprise. I would say that the person who carried it out was known to the dead man. But that is no more than a hypothesis." "However that may be," Don Lorenzo said, leaning forward, "the crime could have been committed by a young or an old person." "That's true," the forensic expert agreed, "and by a man or a woman." He gave a sharp, enigmatic laugh and burst out: "You know what they're like!"

"It's a shame," Don Lorenzo commented when he and Prullàs had left the Palace of Justice under a burning sun, and climbed back again into the official car, "that we haven't found the murder weapon: I'm sure that would clear up a lot of things. By the way, in that little play of yours there's a murder as well, isn't there? Of course, of course, seeing it's a thriller there's bound to be that ingredient, isn't there? And what's the murder weapon there?"

"A dagger," Prullàs reluctantly admitted; "the character dies from a blow to the heart, just like poor Vallsigorri. It's true, it's a most unfortunate coincidence," he went on hastily.

"I'd love to change the script, but I can't see how to do so without altering the whole plot." "Bah, I don't think anyone will link the two things," the governor said; "they'd have to be very evil-minded. If I were you, I wouldn't change a thing: it must have been more than enough work writing it in the first place. By the way, is the knife you use in the play real?"

"No, no: not at all," Prullàs replied; "it's a special theatre knife: not one that pushes in when you stab someone, but one that's blunt and has the tip rounded off to make sure nobody is harmed by accident." "Or by design," Don Lorenzo quipped.

3

"The mistress phoned asking after you; I told her the master wasn't home, but didn't say where you had gone. The mistress asked if the master was all right, and if everything was as it should be, and I said yes it was." "Quite right, Sebastiana; there's absolutely no reason to be worried, still less to worry other people," Prullàs replied. "Is there anything for lunch?" "There's nothing prepared, sir; as you don't normally eat at home, I didn't think of it. But if you like, I can prepare something right away. There's a cauliflower . . . " "No, no, anything but that. The truth is, I'm not in the slightest bit hungry. This heat is so dreadful!" "Well then, try to cool off, and I'll make you a potato salad with tuna and boiled egg, followed by meat and fried peppers and a tomato with dressing, then fruit and cream for dessert. You'll see, it'll be great."

Sebastiana bustled off to shut herself in the kitchen and Prullàs went into his study. He picked up the telephone, dialed 09 and asked to be put through to the Social Club in Masnou; then he had a shower, put clean clothes on, and sat by the balcony to read *La Vanguardia*. Among its news items was a report on a tram accident in Zaragoza. The vehicle had come off the rails while turning a corner on a steep descent, and had careered out of control until it smashed into a shop window. There had been considerable material damage, but fortunately nobody had been hurt in the incident. There was however no mention of Vallsigorri's murder, even though there was a half-page death notice. This said that Vallsigorri had died a Christian death "comforted by the holy sacraments and a final blessing", and that the burial had taken place in the strictest intimacy "at the deceased's express request"; the announcement ended with his family and friends called for a prayer for the dead man's soul to seek eternal rest, without saying who these family members were, or their relation to the deceased. Don Lorenzo Verdugones had not mentioned any relative, and until now there had been no sign of any.

The ringing of the telephone interrupted Prullàs' thoughts. He answered and could hear Joaquín's voice at the far end of the line. Prullàs said who he was, and asked Joaquín to pass on the message that he was fine. "Everything is splendid," he added; "I'll be coming up there as soon as I can. Tell her not to bother to phone me; I'm hardly ever at home. Yes, the weather's good here as well, but it's far too hot. No, I'll call again when I have a moment." Joaquín repeated the message to show he had understood, and promised he would have it delivered there and then. Prullàs hung up and then, ignoring Sebastiana gesticulating at him from the doorway to come and eat, he dialled Mariquita Pons' number. He told the young woman who answered that he'd like to speak to Señor Fontcuberta. "I'll go and see if he's here," the young girl said evasively.

"Carlos! How're things?" "I hope I'm not disturbing you," Prullàs said. "No, of course not, you caught me between lunch and my siesta," Fontcuberta replied, "and I'm very pleased you

259

phoned: I wanted to talk to you – you've heard about poor Ignacio, of course? I couldn't believe it when I was told, it just goes to show, doesn't it, you never can tell." "That's precisely what I wanted to talk to you about," Prullàs said; "you had business dealings with Vallsigorri, didn't you?"

"Yes and no," Fontcuberta replied after a pause. Prullàs wondered if he was aware of the circumstances of Vallsigorri's death; nothing in what he said gave that impression, but it was unlikely he hadn't heard; what was more probable was that Fontcuberta was also trying to work out how much Prullàs knew."Vallsigorri and I were partners some time ago, but since then our activities have diverged. Of course, on a more general level we were interested in similar areas: sometimes we joined forces, and at others we were loyal rivals. Why do you ask?" "Well, knowing you were a friend and a business colleague of his, I thought you could help me clear up some obscure points about him. Don't think this is mere curiosity on my part . . . in fact, as I'm sure you're already aware, Vallsigorri did not die a natural death. I mean . . . " "No need to go on," the other man interrupted him, sounding relieved; "I know everything! Don Lorenzo Verdugones telephoned me yesterday afternoon to inform me of what had happened, and to get information about poor Ignacio." "Really? Don Lorenzo Verdugones himself phoned you?" Prullàs exclaimed with surprise; while to himself he muttered: How did that busybody find the time to talk to so many people? "What did he want to know?" he asked out loud. "Don't push me, Carlos, they were confidential financial matters. Strictly speaking, I'm not supposed to tell you what we talked about, especially on the 'phone. But it was you who called me to ask something." "Not something, several things," Prullàs replied. "Did he have any relatives? Vallsigorri, I mean." "He had an elder brother, who's been living in Argentina for years, and a sister, who lives in Madrid and has business links with Fernando Po. She's expected here today. Both of them are married with children. And there are other more or less close blood relatives: cousins, second cousins, and so on."

"Who's going to inherit his fortune?"

"Whoever's mentioned in the will, naturally, except for the tax and the corresponding legal fees. I have no idea what's in the will or whether it has already been communicated to his heirs and legatees. I don't even know if a will exists, although I'd be very surprised if such a meticulous man like poor Ignacio – may he rest in peace – had not drawn one up. Anyway, as far as I can tell from a conversation we once had when the topic came up obliquely, Vallsigorri did not have close ties with his family, even though he hadn't exactly quarrelled with them either. It's quite likely even that he left the bulk of his wealth to a charitable institution. I once heard him say he intended to leave everything to the San Rafael old people's home or the San Juan de Dios hospital. But I've no idea whether he was being serious or was just saying that: you know what he was like. But now it's me who has a question for you: Why are you so interested? You hardly knew him."

"That's a very good question, Miguel, but I don't want to answer by telephone either. If you like, we could meet up later and talk about it just between us. After rehearsal I could call in at the Oro del Rhin; if it suits you, I could see you there and tell you everything." "How mysterious," Foncuberta said; "you sound like Smith the Silent One."

CECILIA: (*pointing to* TODOLIU*'s body*) You and your stupid ideas! What are we going to do now?

JULIO: I don't know, let me think. Don't badger me.

CECILIA: Fine, you think all you like, I'm off. (CECILIA *heads for the door stage right. Just as she is about to open it, there are loud knocks.* CECILIA *steps back, terrified. She turns to* JULIO, *who gestures to her to act normally and answer)*

CECILIA: (*in a syrupy voice*) Who's there?

ENRIQUE: (*outside*) It's me, sweetheart, Enrique.

CECILIA: Good heavens, it's my fiancé.

JULIO: What the devil is he doing here at this time of day?

CECILIA: Don't you remember? You told me to ask him to come at noon so he could see Todoliu was alive.

ENRIQUE: (*offstage*) Can I come in?

(CECILIA *runs to the door and locks it*)

CECILIA: No, my love, you can't! I'm getting dressed . . . I've almost nothing on!

ENRIQUE: (*offstage*) In your living-room?

CECILIA: Yes, yes . . . of course . . . I've just been brought a new dress and I couldn't resist the temptation to try it on straightaway.

ENRIQUE: (*offstage*) All right, I'll wait. In the meantime I'll have a word with Todoliu, apparently he had something important to tell me.

CECILIA: No! I mean . . . it's better if you don't see Todoliu at the moment.

ENRIQUE: Why can't I see him?

CECILIA: Because Todoliu . . . Todoliu . . .

ENRIQUE: (*offstage*) Is something wrong with Todoliu?

CECILIA: No, no, on the contrary, he's never better, never better.

(*As* CECILIA *is speaking,* JULIO *tries to hide* TODOLIU's *body under the sofa, but an arm or a leg keeps popping out*) The thing is . . . Todoliu's in here with me.

ENRIQUE: (*offstage*) With you? While you get dressed and undressed?

CECILIA: Well . . . yes . . . you see, when the package

from the dressmaker's arrived he was in the living-room
with me, and it didn't seem polite to ask him to leave.
But don't worry, Enriquito: he can't see me . . . I mean
that while I get undressed he's doing the *ABC* crossword. If only you could see how absorbed he is, trying
to find a tributary of the River Tagus, five letters!

"How's the rehearsal going?" Prullàs asked.

"As you can imagine," the stage director said. "The news
spread like wildfire, and everyone's in a panic. You know how
superstitious theatre people are. And as if that weren't enough,
someone's had the bright idea of saying there's a madman
hiding somewhere in the theatre who's going to murder us all
one by one. I've told them not to worry, because if the play's
as bad on our opening night as it has been in rehearsal, the
public will make sure none of us are left alive anyway. Even
poor old Bonifaci is striding round the corridors like a caveman
with a fireman's axe. What about you? Have you been up to
any more nonsense since I last saw you?"

"I've been at the scene of the crime and then in the morgue
or something very like it," Prullàs complained. "You can't
imagine what a hard time they've given me, Pepe. And it's still
as deep a mystery as ever: there are no clues, no motives, no
suspects. Nothing at all. At lunchtime I was asking about his
heirs, but everywhere I look it's a dead end. Has the girl said
anything?" "Who, Lilí Villalba?" Gaudet said. "No, on the
contrary; today she was more subdued than ever: she didn't go
flashing her thighs at the stall seats or winking at the assistant;
a real nun she was. Something's changed in her: I think it must
be love." "I'm not in the mood for jokes," Prullàs growled. "I
wasn't joking," Gaudet said slyly; "she herself gave me this
billet-doux for you. Apparently she's worried your eyes will
burn a hole in her nylon skirt if she comes anywhere near you.

Here," he said, handing him a piece of folded paper, "and think carefully, because tonight, Don Juan, is all we have to find our resting place." Paying no attention to his friend's repartee, Prullàs unfolded the paper and read: "The polise came to arsk me questions, I told em nothin but I nead to see you imediately, I love you, Lilí." He folded the paper again and put it in his pocket. "I'll take care of it," he said.

At the end of the rehearsal, he headed straight for the dressing-rooms, without worrying that the stagehands might see him. What the heck, he thought, there's nothing strange about an author sharing impressions with the members of the company, and when all's said and done, anything has to be better than this web of suspicion and pretence which is going to end with us in prison, if we're not in the asylum first.

As he was pondering these things and groping along the dark corridor in search of Lilí Villalba's dressing-room, he suddenly heard the strangest of noises coming from Mariquita Pons' room. He went up to the door and again heard the sound, which now seemed to him like the howl of a mortally wounded wild beast. He recalled what Gaudet had said about a madman loose in the theatre and, convinced the actress must be under attack from this deranged person, he flung himself into the room.

He was confronted by Mariquita Pons' lifeless body stretched on the floor. He peered fruitlessly into every corner for the assassin: there was nobody there. The howling, brutish attacker must have escaped by a secret door, Prullàs deduced. But no sooner had this idea taken shape in his mind than he heard the terrible groaning again, right by his side. It was then he realised it must be coming from the celebrated actress herself. She's gone mad! he thought. He crouched down, shook her shoulder and cautiously called her name: "Kiki, Kiki my dear, are you all right?" The actress lifted her face from the floor and gazed wildly up at him, her eyes unfocused. "Who let you in?" she groaned. "Kiki, for the love of God, are you feeling all right?"

Mariquita Pons made a great effort to recover her control; she struggled to her feet, and pulled her open bathrobe around her. She staggered drunkenly across to her stool and sat down. The mirror reflected back her contorted features, red eyes, her bloated, twisted mouth. Her hands shook as she put a cigarette into her mother-of-pearl holder, lit it and avidly inhaled the tobacco smoke. "It's over now," she said gruffly. "I'm sorry if I startled you."

Prullàs had also got to his feet and was staring uncomfortably at the image of desolation the mirror gave back to him. "Close the door," Mariquita said. "D'you want me to go?" Prullàs asked. "Shall I call the dresser?" "No, stay with me; pull up a chair and keep me company while I put on some make-up."

Prullàs did as she suggested. Mariquita Pons meanwhile opened a drawer in her dressing-table, took out a thermos, poured out a glass of amber-coloured liquid and drank it at one gulp. "Don't look at me like that, it's only cold tea," she said sarcastically when she saw a worried look on Prullàs' face. "I bring a flask into the theatre every day. The water here is undrinkable, cold tea quenches your thirst, and it's not as sweet as bottled soft drinks." All this, she explained in the most natural manner imaginable, as if she had already wiped what had just happened from her mind, had been taught her many years earlier by Catalina Bárcena when Mariquita was living and working in Madrid, and the two actresses were topping the bill in the re-run of A Necklace of Stars.

"If you want to tell me something, I'm all ears," Prullàs said, when she had finished this brief digression, "but if you prefer to say nothing, I'll pretend I didn't see a thing."

Mariquita Pons wiped her face with water from the dressing-table. "There's nothing to tell you, Carlos," she said in a flat voice; "it was just a moment's weakness. It happens to me now and then; the doctors say it's nothing to worry about. It's the heat, my nerves: the usual things." She waved a hand in the air and went on, wearily: "Sometimes I get the feeling that my whole life is falling apart. Perhaps it's only a momentary weakness, perhaps it's a flash of lucidity, who knows? Afterwards everything returns to normal." Prullàs had the feeling it wasn't Mariquita talking to him, but the hideous mask that lived in the lifeless world of the mirror. "The years go by," she said, "and instead of adding to our lives, they steal what little we thought we had; it's always the same: for a long time we want something with all our heart, and when we finally get it, it's either too late, or it's not as good as we had imagined, or we discover that deep down we didn't really want it all that much anyway. All our dreams are petty when they come true. And yet, if we miss out on something, we're inconsolable. That's life. I always knew it, but what I didn't suspect was how quickly everything happened. When I look into the past, there's nothing." She paused for a moment, then said: "I don't want you to write any more young women's roles for me, Carlos; promise me you won't."

"Don't talk nonsense," Carlos replied, "you're the least old of all Europe's leading ladies, and the most attractive." The actress dabbed rouge on her cheeks and pencilled in eyeliner. "You're right," she said, studying the result of her repair work with her head on one side. "I'm just in low spirits. It'll pass."

She stubbed out her cigarette, got up, and went behind her screen. Prullàs remained at the dressing-table, fiddling with the lipstick holder: as he raised and dropped the little lever in the side of the tin tube, the greasy, obscene red bar of lipstick appeared and disappeared. "Why don't you take me to the pictures?" the actress said from behind her screen. "My husband is a tyrant who refuses to leave his apartment, and besides, you owe me a film." "I can't; the fact is, I have to see your tyrant husband in a short while in the Oro del Rhin," Prullàs replied. "Aha," Mariquita said, "so you came in here to ask my permission, did you?"

Prullàs didn't know what to say: he didn't want to tell her that in fact he had been looking for Lilí when her howls of despair had led him away from his initial intention. "Who's to say I didn't come to peep on you through the keyhole?" For the first time, this brought a smile to Mariquita's face. "You're a dreadful liar, but don't stop flattering me: after we reach a certain age, it's only our monstrous vanity that convinces us we're doing something important."

She emerged from behind the screen, dressed in a summer frock that restored her graceful look. She pouted coquettishly. "My husband is a monster: can you believe he reckons he's off to Madrid again in a couple of days? Just when I most need him!" "When have you ever needed your husband?" Prullàs said with a laugh. Mariquita sprayed perfume onto her neck. "You men will never understand women," she said. "Nor women, men," Prullàs retorted. "That's because there's nothing to understand," the actress replied.

4

At this warm and peaceful hour of the evening, there were no free tables on the terrace of the Oro del Rhin for even the most regular and generous of customers. The waiters were in despair about it, unable to satisfy people who had won their friendship by coming here often and giving lavish tips. A steady stream of cars and trams made Avenida José Antonio quite busy, while on the shady Rambla de Cataluña, now the working day was over, office girls and shop assistants strolled arm-in-arm in groups of four, zigzagging along and filling the air with the bright and shrill laughter of young, unattached women. The sumptuous façade of the Coliseum cinema was partially covered in the figures of Loretta Young and Henry Wilcoxon, splendidly decked out in their famous characters' costumes. A few beggars were trying sneak past the waiters and get close to the restaurant tables.

Inside the venerable café, the ceiling fans were ensuring that the smoke from roll-up cigarettes, cigars, pipes and the luxurious smell of real coffee were all spread throughout the room. Serious-looking men in dark suits were pontificating on banal topics in lengthy swathes of rhetoric that they rounded off with a final stab of irrefutable, sententious wisdom. Scurrying between the tables to offer their services were several pale, shifty-looking men, with greasy skins and furtive expressions on their faces, dressed in sweaty, striped suits and lumpy shoes, straw boaters and briefcases. These were people who liked to go by the undeserved name of mediators. They would spend each morning in the City Hall or the central government headquarters, the tax office or the economics and development departments, or anywhere else that might be a strategic point for state bureaucracy, or they had a relative or a friend who worked in one of them or had some other channel that allowed them access to these vital organs of civil society. Thanks to them, prior knowledge could be gained of what the authorities were intending to do, or other information essential to the success of a deal, speeding up official permission, the granting of a licence or a contract, learning of a change in fixed prices, making it easier to obtain identity papers and other documents, and in general oiling the complicated wheels of bureaucracy by arranging personal contact with middle-ranking officials. These men's briefcases always contained a ream of headed paper, stamps and official seals, as well as several copies of the Official Bulletin, whose minuscule type they read with myopic eyes, their tongues sticking out as they followed each line with nicotine-stained, long-nailed fingers. There were all sorts among them: inoffensive charlatans, seeking a fleeting moment of imaginary power, and dyed-in-the wool swindlers, who thrived on innocent or stupid victims, on those blinded by greed, or drowning in despair. Miguel Fontcuberta nodded a discreet greeting to them all.

Resigned to the fact that they would have to settle for a table far from the windows, Prullàs and Fontcuberta sat in a corner next to a white-bearded man with thick glasses whose eyebrows and lips moved in time to his reading of *La Prensa*.

Foncuberta was dumbfounded as Prullàs finished telling him about all his recent adventures. "The truth is," he said, lowering his voice as he did so, "it's not looking good! It goes without saying, I have no doubt about your innocence; more than that, I'm willing to state it on oath to whoever might ask. Yet it seems to me there's nothing strange in the fact that the police or even Don Lorenzo Verdugones should suspect you. I'd do the same in their place. You're a self-made man, married to a rich woman, you spend your time writing thrillers, lead a bohemian life, hang about with theatre people, and have a justified reputation as a bit of a Romeo: what more do you need? Just look at me; I'm a businessman who's known and respected all over Spain, I am completely at home in all circles in Madrid, and yet, simply because I'm married to an actress, God knows what nonsense is said about me! Because I know what it's like, I'm telling you straight. Then look at the circumstances: Verdugones himself saw you talking to Vallsigorri at Brusquets' the night before the murder, he saw you leave together, and knows you were out on the tiles in the seedy part of town. Nobody knows or can possibly know what went on between the two of you; we only have your version, and that of course has little value in this case. In fact, Verdugones only needs to find a motive for the whole jigsaw puzzle to fall into place. So now, tell me the truth: might there have been a motive? You can trust me like a brother."

"Well . . . let's see . . . yes, there might have been what you could call a motive. Don't force me to give you the details, but there's a woman involved."

"Aha, well then, things are far worse than I had imagined," Fontcuberta said, lowering his voice still further. "Any false move could mean disaster. The first thing to do, Carlos, is put the matter in the hands of a good lawyer; it's best to be prepared for any eventuality. Look, here's what we'll do," he went on to say, as if he'd suddenly had a flash of inspiration. "We'll go straightaway and see Don Marcelino Sanjuanete. He's the most prestigious lawyer in Barcelona, and in a case like this there's no sense in beating about the bush."

"Prestige did you say? Sanjuanete has a reputation for being a crook," Prullàs said. "Up to a point!" Fontcuberta replied. "D'you think he'd see us?" Prullàs asked doubtfully. "Of course," Fontcuberta reassured him, "he knows me well, and he knows you too − I saw the pair of you talking together at Brusquets' the other night." "Bah, we only exchanged a few pleasantries, I doubt whether he'll even remember me," Prullàs said.

They walked down to the corner of Paseo de Gracia and Diputación, where the famous legal expert had his chambers. After telling a uniformed and forbidding porter where they were headed, they climbed to the first floor up a marble staircase and rang the bell beside a colossal door. A short while later, a clerk appeared, and Fontcuberta scrawled a few words on the back of his card and handed it to him, requesting he take it to the lawyer. The clerk showed them into an indescribably sordid office, where five clients sat in a stupor brought on by endless hours of waiting. "D'you have an appointment?" the clerk asked the new arrivals. "No, but our business is so important it can't wait," Fontcuberta said. "And in fact, it's just a short consultation. These gentlemen," he added in an inaudible whisper, "are in less of a hurry than we are, if you follow my drift? Please tell your learned friend that, and keep this cigar for yourself, to smoke at the bullfight on Sunday in our honour."

The other clients wailed like souls in Purgatory when they saw this manoeuvre, which was bound to prolong their boring wait still further, but none of them complained. They were of more humble origins, and knew that by coming to this prestigious office they would have to give way to certain privileges of rank; if they had gone to a less well-known lawyer, they would have been better treated but would have stood less chance of success.

The clerk returned to the waiting-room almost immediately, and begged Fontcuberta and Prullàs to follow him. He led them on a long walk: one corridor led onto another, which in turn gave onto a third. The building was a dark, ugly maze. Every now and then off these corridors were rooms that had been turned into soulless offices, lit only by the dim grey light of fluorescent tubes. In them, an army of assistants of all ages were working at spacious tables heaped high with papers, surrounded by metal shelving stuffed with folders and concertina files overflowing with case notes. Some of the assistants had taken their jackets off and were wearing rat-coloured coats; the older ones amongst them wore black cotton oversleeves. Pale-faced women with lifeless expressions were typing out endless documents on antiquated machines at a snail's pace. All the windows were firmly shut to avoid any distractions: only the occasional screeching of trams on their rails gave any notion that the outside world still existed. A few filthy black fans perched precariously on top of the ledgers piled on the filing cabinets stirred the fetid air.

"My dear friend!" Sanjuanete exclaimed as he smiled broadly and flung open his arms to greet Fontcuberta on the threshold of the double doors that the clerk had opened wide for them, "this is indeed an honour! How are you? And that charming and beautiful wife of yours? And what about you, Señor Pallarés? Do come in, and make yourselves at home; it's a great pleasure for me to receive you here and to be of service to you."

This pompous rhetoric was in stark contrast to the dirty, unkempt image the illustrious lawyer presented: he was in shirt-sleeves, his tie loosened, and as he stood up to greet them his trousers were stained, and their buttons undone. His office was in semi-darkness, but that could not hide how untidy it was: the columns of legal briefs piled on tables and chairs had toppled over in successive disasters, carpeting the floor with layers of torn, trodden papers in complete disorder; there were books open or with their backs torn off in the shelves, and between a pair of legal analects stood a tray with a dirty glass and an empty soda siphon. It seemed impossible that in the midst of such chaos any matter could be dealt with methodically or sensibly. It was common knowledge in the city's legal circles that in these prestigious chambers legal briefs got lost, the most vital papers were mixed up, dates and time limits were ignored, facts were made up and cases were conducted in the most careless manner, and yet, despite this, they were all won.

"Let's see what we have before us," Sanjuanete said, sitting down once more and spreading his podgy hands on the desk. A beaming smile spread across his face, as broad and pouched as that of an ancient French king. Prullàs hesitated. "It's rather complicated to explain," he stammered. "That doesn't matter, take all the time you need; we're in no hurry." "I saw you had several people in the waiting-room . . . " Prullàs noted. "Oh, don't worry about them," the lawyer said. He rang a bell; the clerk appeared. "Is there something you require, Your Honour?" the clerk said. "Are there still people waiting?" the lawyer asked. "Yes, sir, five of them." "Tell them to come back tomorrow."

The clerk left the room and Prullàs began to explain the situation he found himself in. The lawyer interrupted him: "No, no, before that, before that! Go back to how everything started," he said, "and don't keep anything from me." "As far it concerns me, I shall," Prullàs said, "but there's a young woman involved, and I wouldn't want to see her name or situation compromised." "Oh, you can compromise her as much as you like!" Sanjuanete insisted. "The information won't leave this room, and one never knows when something might be useful." "Well then, it's a young woman with whom the deceased had close relations and whom I . . . recently . . . made the object of my attentions."

Fontcuberta interrupted his story to ask: "Do I know her?" "No," Prullàs said flatly; "and don't you breathe a word of this to your wife." "Were the deceased Ignacio Vallsigorri and you pursuing her affections at the same time?" "I'm afraid so." "Hmmm. Are there any eye-witnesses to your . . . dalliance, apart from the young lady in question?" "I don't think so," Prullàs said. "In that case," the lawyer determined, "we'll take it that there weren't; kindly go on."

Prullàs finished his story in as clear and orderly a way as possible. When he fell silent, the lawyer leaned back in his chair, crossed his plump fingers over his stomach, closed his eyes and appeared to fall asleep. After a while, he opened his eyes again, but still said nothing. "Well," Prullàs finally asked, "what d'you make of the case?" "Me?" the illustrious legal expert said in a tone of great surprise, as if the question had taken him completely unawares; "it's not good, not good." "Tell me why, for goodness sake!"

The lawyer shrugged. "Well, it seems to me they already consider you guilty," he said; "that much is clear. And there's little that can be done to counter other people's opinions. They'll put you in jail, Pallarés my friend: take note of what I'm saying: in jail." "That's impossible," Prullàs shouted, "I haven't done anything!" "Oh yes, that's what they all shout on their way to Modelo prison," Sanjuanete laughed, "and even on their way to the gallows! It's a poor tactic, believe me, a poor tactic; don't ever go proclaiming your innocence again: it's a bad mistake and, from the conceptual point of view, it has no validity in law."

For a minute, Prullàs kept a brooding silence. Then he said: "What about the police investigation? That must produce some results. The police are busy with that, surely they'll find something that will exonerate me completely." The lawyer gave a beatific smile. "It's possible," he agreed, "although I have to say that in all my professional life I've never known anyone reach a conclusion that didn't confirm his first suspicions. Nor have I ever met anyone who didn't believe he was perfectly in the right. That is why I have chosen to stick scrupulously to the letter of the law. Far better to trust to procedure than to put one's faith in people being honest, or in justice. Subjectivity is a plague, my dear Pallarés."

The illustrious lawyer fell silent for a long while, then returned to his deliberations: "From what I hear, this Ignacio Vallsigorri was a good fellow, honest and hard-working; but a bit of a madcap, wasn't he? When he wasn't at his club, he could be found at some bar or other. A good sort though, despite that; everybody thought very highly of him, poor fellow; or at least, everybody spoke very highly of him. Never was a client of mine, although I had dealings with him once, over a problem concerning a long lease, I can't remember what exactly . . . but there was no problem when it came to settling up, that I do remember. Chased after skirts, so they say. Bad for the health, for the pocket, and for peace of mind. There's all kinds of women: some of them are good, others are real heartbreakers; the trouble is, there's no way of telling the difference. Ah well, there's no point giving advice to a dead man: it's far too late. And as for you, Pallarés my friend," he went on without looking at the other man, "you say you swear you did not kill him. But the circumstantial evidence is not in your favour. You are someone who is . . . how shall I put it? rather unconventional: what with the theatre and all that . . . if you follow me."

"That's exactly what I was telling our friend Prullàs here just now," Fontcuberta put in; "and I gave myself as an example. Just imagine: I've been married for years to one of the most respected and outstanding actresses in the Spanish theatre; we're a model couple in all respects and yet God knows what malicious gossip is spread about us everywhere." "Oh please, my dear Fontcuberta, your wife is a great actress, and all that is ever said of her is praise," the lawyer protested, "only praise! And to return to your case, Pallarés my friend, in my humble opinion what you have to avoid is being charged. If it were to get that far, there would be grave consequences for your professional life, your social circle, your position with the authorities; you would be permanently under suspicion. Years could go by before the case was heard, and in the meantime, how would you live? As I understand it, you write comedies; but if you are charged with murder, you will never be allowed to put on another play. Even if you are not put in prison on remand . . . and in the end are acquitted. That would be too late: the harm would have been done. Everybody learns when someone has been charged with a crime, the news spreads like wildfire; but who bothers what the final outcome is?"

The legal expert spread his palms to show how powerless he was, and added in a plaintive voice: "Unfortunately, there is nothing I can do to avoid them pressing charges. You must try to do that on your own behalf. My intervention would only be counter-productive. If I were to become involved, everyone would immediately consider you guilty. They'd say: look at him, using his father-in-law's money to get someone to keep him out of jail."

"But if *you* can't do anything, what on earth can *I* do?" Prullàs said. "Oh, you must have influential friends," the lawyer said, "citizens above reproach. Talk to them. Sometimes a personal approach can achieve more than a thousand legal manoeuvres. Bad lawyers always want to take matters to court, as if they liked putting on their robes and making a speech. Sheer vanity, and the need to show off! A good lawyer will always prefer to arrange things quietly, between gentlemen. If you talk, people can reach agreement, and if to get that agreement you have to pay out along the way, then so be it! Peace is well worth a few pence. Mark you, I'm not saying that the due process of law should be subverted. No. But if, as you say, you had nothing to do with this case, as soon as the investigation produces results, there's nothing to worry about; and if, for argument's sake we say you were guilty, we still need to gain time. Of course, I'm not giving you this little piece of advice in my legal capacity, but as a friend. If you choose not to follow it, all well and good, and if you do choose to follow it and it doesn't work out, then come back and see me and we'll rethink our strategy. Forgive me if I don't show you out," he said rising from his chair, "but I have to study a claim that I should have settled weeks ago. Goodbye, Pallarés my friend. And as for you, my dear Fontcuberta, don't forget to convey my very best wishes to your wife: a wonderful lady!"

After this brief but intense introduction to Sanjuanete's chambers, Prullàs felt extremely relieved to find himself out on the leafy Paseo de Gracia with its everyday bustle of cars and passers-by. This was not enough, though, to dissipate his anger. "That fellow is an arrogant, unscrupulous rogue," he exclaimed. "He couldn't give a damn what happens to me."

"Don't say that," Fontcuberta chided him. "Sanjuanete is a strange sort, a real genius, with his corresponding dose of eccentricity. After all," he went on, "lawyers are like doctors: hidden behind every legal dispute, or legal circumlocution, there's usually a painful human drama. If lawyers had to take the suffering of all their clients to heart, their lives would be unbearable; precisely in order to be able to help others, they have to keep a cool head. You were looking for sympathy, and he offered practical solutions: you'll have to make do with that. But don't make the mistake of discarding his advice: perhaps it's the answer to your problem."

"In what way? Finding someone to guarantee my innocence? I don't know what use that would be: Don Lorenzo won't let go of his prey so easily." "That depends on who's asking him to," Fontcuberta replied. "You need to find someone who carries real moral weight: a high-ranking military officer would be ideal. Do you know any?"

"No," Prullàs said, "I don't know anyone of that ilk. When I come to think of it, the most influential person I know is my father-in-law, but that would mean getting my family mixed up in this mess; and after him, you yourself are next in line."

"Well," Fontcuberta said after a few moments' hesitation, "as I told you before, you can rely on me for anything; but

277

everybody knows we're friends, and so my word would count for little."

"You're right, but if the support of one's friends is useless, who can I turn to?"

"I don't know, we'll have to give it some more thought. Right now, in the middle of the street, and surrounded by all these pretty girls, we're not going to get anywhere. By the way," he said, pointing to a group of girls strolling down the opposite pavement followed by a couple of soldiers, "did you see that one over there? Just look at the way she walks! Of course, it seems you're well covered on that score, you old devil!"

5

"Pleased to see you so bright-eyed and bushy-tailed," the governor said. "To tell you the truth, I half expected to find you still in your pyjamas. I was forgetting that as well as being an artist, you're a Catalan: which by definition means hard-working. What about this case of ours? Have you made any interesting discovery? Any great deductions?" "Oh, no," Prullàs replied, "the more time goes by, the more confused my ideas become." "In that case," Don Lorenzo replied, "we'll have to try to find new evidence; as they say in my village, he who has no head has to have good legs, or something like that: which I take to mean that if ideas don't come to you, you have to go and look for them, wherever they may be hiding, the blaggards! Anyway, don't be despondent: you'll enjoy the place we're visiting today, you'll see."

In Don Lorenzo's limousine they went down Calle Muntaner, avoided the trams at the San Antonio roundabout; when they reached Calle Floridablanca the car stopped and Don

Lorenzo invited Prullàs to get out. "Here we are," the governor said, indicating the glass doors of a luxury establishment.

"But this is a beauty clinic!" Prullàs said.

"Exactly right," said Verdugones. "I told you you'd like the place. But don't be fooled by its frivolous appearance; this building holds the most modern chemical laboratories in Spain. And yet you can imagine," he said with pain in his voice, "how demeaning it is for an agency of the state to have to resort to clinics like this just to have a few simple tests carried out. The lack of facilities we suffer from in our country is a crying shame. And then abroad, all those who see it as in their interest to do us down have no hesitation in calling Spain a police state. Yet see for yourself what our police has to turn to in order to carry out its noble work efficiently."

As diligent and painstaking as ever, Sigüenza came out to meet them, notebook and pencil in hand. The reception area was soothingly quiet. "I've informed the director," Sigüenza whispered, as if worried his masculine tones would disrupt the airy femininity of the atmosphere. "If she doesn't show up, she'll have me to deal with, the vixen," the governor growled. But even as he was uttering this warning, the sound of high heels could be heard on the clinic floor and a slender, attractive woman appeared, dressed in a dazzlingly white coat.

"Good morning, Don Lorenzo," she said sweetly; then turning to Prullàs and smiling to reveal two rows of perfect teeth, she added: "I'm Doctor Maribel. Please come with me, would you?"

The corridor was painted in an off-white shade, and lined on either side by closed doors behind which they could hear the muffled hum of machines and running water. The air was heavy with the scent of cosmetics, occasionally complemented by the acrid smell of singed hair. "If you'd be so kind as to wait for me here while I go and get the laboratory report,"

Doctor Maribel said after showing them into a small, austere but brightly-lit office. The three men remained standing, as if inhibited by an atmosphere in which they felt like intruders.

"Listen to this," Prullàs said, picking up a clinic brochure: "Unfading beauty that lasts throughout time, and an attractive, alluring personality – we can turn a woman's dreams into reality!" "Good Lord," Don Lorenzo laughed, "so you can come in here looking like a hobo and leave like Lana Turner, can you not, Sigüenza?" Sigüenza confirmed this quip gravely, as if he had verified it with his own eyes.

Doctor Maribel came back into the room carrying a folder, sat at her desk, placed a cigarette between her cherry-red lips, waited for Prullàs to light it for her, thanked him with a fluttering of her eyelids, and said: "The analyses carried out in our laboratory confirm, as we had suspected, that both the blood samples taken from the clothes of the victim and on the chair upholstery are from the same group as those of the deceased. However, the hair found on the lapel of the jacket is undoubtedly that of a woman: it's slightly wavy, and has been dyed with a common dark chestnut dye. This discovery does not get us very far: most women, not to say all, dye their hair, either to disguise the appearance of a few indiscreet grey hairs, or to make its colour more suited to their skin or their features. Call it coquettishness, passing fancy, or vanity; I prefer to think of it as a natural female desire to offer the man she loves an image that is forever fresh and seductive." After this observation, the doctor cleared her throat and went on: "As I was saying, the presence of this hair on the lapel could have something to do with the murder, but equally it might not. Perhaps the said hair had been stuck to that particular item of clothing for several hours, even days. Some hairs are very persistent, and can only be removed by a vigorous brushing, as any self-respecting housewife could tell you. We also looked on the lapel and surrounding areas for any traces of lipstick or other similar products, to determine whether the hair was present as a result of a tender embrace, although it's true a hair may become stuck to cloth in a crowd, in any means of transport, public place, or in a thousand other accidents of everyday life which have no romantic significance whatsoever. Be that as it may, in this case the coat lapels showed traces of several cosmetic products: powders, eyeliner, rouge: in short, all kinds of make-up. It's also possible to detect the faint trace of a perfume. At the moment, we are trying to separate out the products, to identify them and, if possible, to determine which brand each of them is. This takes time, as it has to be done by contrasting each product with similar ones on the market; it could take us hours, days or weeks, depending whether fortune smiles on us or not. Considering the social status of the victim, I've ordered them to start the comparisons with the most expensive, high-quality products available, but we can't rule out the possibility that the deceased had close relations with women of a lower rank, as we might say."

"So, for the moment at least," said Verdugones, "we can affirm that the victim embraced or was embraced by a woman shortly before his death." "If by the phrase 'shortly before' we mean a period of two or three hours, that is so," Doctor Maribel agreed; and Sigüenza noted this down in his book. "Neither on the carpet, nor on the upholstery of the other chair, was any sign of another person found. When the bedsheets were examined, they were found to contain several body hairs from the thorax as well as the front and back pelvic regions, and from the upper and lower extremities. These were compared to those supplied by the Forensic Institute and it was established that they all came from the aforementioned regions of the deceased's body; their presence on the sheets possibly arising from the fact that the person in question scratched himself, or was produced simply by rubbing against the material. From all of which, we can conclude that no-one shared the deceased's bed in the last three days and nights, always supposing that the bed linen was changed on Monday, as the cleaner Sanchez García has testified. That's all I can tell you for now, gentlemen."

"In that case, that will be all for today, Doctor Maribel," the governor said. "As soon as you obtain any positive results from your tests on the products, be so kind as to inform me."

"Have no fear on that score, Don Lorenzo," the doctor said. "You know what an honour and a satisfaction it is for me and for the institute to be of service to you. Are you married, Señor Prullàs?" she asked, turning to him. When he nodded, she opened a drawer and handed him several pamphlets: "Here, give these to your wife from me; perhaps our treatments would interest her. Our skin requires constant care, but never more so than over the summer months. The sun can be treacherous: a suntanned skin is a skin in danger. For now, take her this cucumber milk sample and tell her to call me for a first appointment: here's my card. She can find me at the clinic every day, at any time."

6

The building in which the Reverend Father Emilio Porras, S. J., lived and worked, carrying out his somewhat vague duties surrounded by scholars and saints, and where Prullàs had arrived to fulfil the appointment made for him the previous evening by Miguel Fontcuberta, stood on the northern corner of the intersection of Calle Rosellón and Calle Balmes. It was an austere construction of grey stone, free of any sign of ostentation apart from a colossal main gateway, whose size reflected the universal teaching vocation the institution professed, conceived as it was to spread its beneficial influence over the widest possible sectors of society. Now, however, as if deliberately to express the painful contradiction between the ideals of the spirit and the practical necessities imposed by reality, this ecumenical gateway was completely closed to the outside world by a huge door in several sections, which was only opened on special occasions, and in which a small, low panel allowed the visitor access, once his or her identity had been checked through a narrow spy hole. In this way, after being put through a lengthy examination by a sort of secular messenger who was short in stature, in sight, and in intelligence, Prullàs finally gained entrance to a dark hallway, dominated by an immense wooden Constantine cross. A virtuous smell of convent floated in the air, composed of incense, caustic soda and soup. The messenger told him how to find the study of the Reverend Father Emilio Porras S.J., and then slid back into his lodge.

"Forgive me for receiving you in my study like this, with all this mess of papers and thick books," the reverend father began, immediately adopting a tone of familiar intimacy, "but these summer weeks are when I can get most work done. Our boys have gone on camp, thank Heavens, which frees us for a while from our pastoral labours. Did you notice the heavenly calm here? If you came back after classes had begun again, you wouldn't believe your eyes! Nor your ears!" "In that case, I feel guilty twice over," Prullàs said, "because not only am I disturbing you, but I've come at an inopportune moment. In fact, it was our mutual friend Miguel Fontcuberta who insisted on arranging this meeting with you."

"Oh, there's no reason for you to feel guilty, and please, don't stand on ceremony; after all, we are colleagues: the pen is our common bond, laying aside whatever other possible spiritual links we may share. I have always said that creative people like you, even though you deal with profane subject matter, are closer to God, without knowing it, than those of us who draw our knowledge from our studies. What is born of the spirit is spirit, it says in the Gospel according to Saint John; although Saint Luke reminds that those who have been given many talents will have much demanded of them."

After the short pause which followed these words, Prullàs said: "I don't know if Miguel Fontcuberta gave you any indication of the kind of problem I'm facing." "He simply told me you would be coming to see me and would tell me what it was about," the Jesuit said; "and so much the better: it's always preferable to hear the person involved give their version of events without any preconceived ideas. Do you smoke?" he added, taking a leather pouch and a packet of cigarette papers out of his pocket. Prullàs declined the offer and, reining in his impatience at the other man's forced friendliness and repeated attempts to see things in a positive light, as if he were determined always to look on the bright side, he proceeded to tell his story as succinctly as he could, without forgetting to add at the end his plea for the priest to intervene in his favour with Don Lorenzo Verdugones, or whoever had influence over him.

Father Porras, who had listened intently to the whole speech, now and again smiling faintly or nodding his head, as if to imply that the events he was hearing about all formed part of a harmonious whole that was entirely in accordance with his view of the world, stubbed out the cigarette in a bakelite ashtray and rubbed his hands briskly, as though he were winding up some inner mechanism. Eventually he spoke: "Carlos, the story you have just told me, despite its simple appearance, has a great lesson to offer us. Yet you haven't come here in search of advice, but practical help, so I'll spare you the sermon. To put it briefly and bluntly, my dear friend, there is little I can do for you, and in any case, not in the way you wish. I'll explain it to you, and you'll soon understand. You see, as a priest I have the authority to administer the sacrament of penance, instituted by our Lord Jesus Christ to save our souls. But this also means that it is my bounden duty, my bounden duty, I repeat, to keep everything I hear in confession as a sworn secret, even if it costs me my life. If you tell me something in confession, even the most revolting of crimes, not a word will pass my lips. However, you are not asking me to do that, but the opposite: in other words, to hear your declaration of innocence and make that public. It is self-evident that this would be going contrary to my duties as a priest. And even if I did do as you ask, my intervention would be useless, because it would lie outside my prerogatives. Render unto Caesar the things that are Caesar's, as Jesus Christ himself said. If that is the kind of help you are looking for, then go and find a good lawyer." Father Porras sneaked a look at his wristwatch, then added: "All this doesn't mean, however, that I cannot or will not help you. Rather the opposite: you came in search of help and I will offer you help, but on my own terms. Carlos, you have committed, as you yourself have said, several reprehensible acts: you have sinned, you have led others into sin, and you have created several clear occasions for scandal. Woe unto him who provokes a scandal! It would be better for him if a millstone were hanged about his neck and he cast into the sea. You are corrupted, and worse still, you have corrupted others. To kill someone is a dreadful crime, but even more horrendous is to cause a soul's eternal damnation. That is what should really be on your conscience, not the rest of it. What is the point of escaping from prison here on earth if it only means you end up in the prison of hell, where there are no amnesties or remissions? You are a criminal, Carlos, in human law or beyond it. How can you be surprised then that the finger of suspicion points at you? Why shouldn't someone who is willing to break one of God's ten commandments be capable of breaking the other nine too? I'm not going to insist on this point. God works in mysterious ways: perhaps this mess, this distressing situation you find yourself in, are simply further opportunities He is offering for you to come to terms with your conscience. Don't shut your ears to his voice. He himself told us: Watch and pray, because you know not the day nor the hour. You might object: Why this preaching now? and think: Far more urgent matters are pressing in on me, there'll be time enough to worry about my soul afterwards. We cannot build a house on shifting sands, or polish a chest without first cleaning out all the filth inside. Do as I suggest: cleanse yourself inside, confess; in short, return to the narrow path that leads to eternal life. Only then will your innocence shine out, and I myself will be glad to bear witness to the change that has come about within you. It is written: ask and it shall be given you; seek and ye shall find; knock and it shall be opened unto you; for everyone that asks receives, and he that seeks shall find, and to him who knocks it shall be opened."

At this, Father Porras fell silent, and Prullàs got up and started walking around the room to calm his nerves. He would have dearly loved to have slapped the Jesuit's colourless grey cheeks or at least, to have given a sarcastic dismissal of all he had heard, but he controlled himself, realising that to do so would only increase the distrust that he seemed to inspire in everyone he had dealings with at the moment. Nothing like this had ever happened to him before, he thought: never had he imagined he could be taken for a monster. And yet now it seemed as though everyone considered him guilty. Where did I go wrong, he wondered, I've always behaved like a gentleman!

"Well?" Father Porras asked him. "You're perfectly right," Prullàs replied, coming to a halt and adopting a contrite attitude: "I'll never be able to thank you enough for speaking so sincerely to me. Your words moved me, and your advice will not go unheeded, I can assure you. It's just that at this moment I don't yet feel prepared to confront the change you're asking of me. I need time to think. The path of repentance is long, and I need to start in my own time."

"Don't think for a minute," Father Porras said, "that I don't understand you. I was like you once. What am I saying? I was worse, far worse! But one night, when I was in jail, I had a dream or, if you prefer, a vision. I saw before me a disturbing, most beautiful image, a being which gave off a blinding light. I realised I was in the presence of the Holy Virgin, and from that moment on my life changed completely. The same could happen to you." Putting an end to the interview, he stood up and said in a business-like manner: "You know where you can find me, day or night. The doors of repentance are always open. What woman who, having ten drachmas and losing one of them, does not light a lamp, sweep the house clean, and search everywhere until she finds it? And when she has found it, she summons her friends and neighbours and tells them: Rejoice with me, for I have found the drachma I had lost. So there is greater rejoicing in Heaven for one sinner who repents than for ninety-nine righteous men who have no need of repentance."

7

It was lunchtime when Prullàs emerged from his fruitless interview with the Reverend Father Emilio Porras, S.J. All the shops were shut and the streets looked desolate beneath the noonday sun. On the pavement, oblivious to the heat, a young boy dressed in rags and with cropped hair and broken sandals was throwing and catching a small rubber ball tied to his wrist by an elastic band, repeatedly ignoring a stern voice shouting at him from the darkness of a porter's lodge: "Antonio, come in, your mother's calling for you!" A tram went by with a single passenger on board and a car sounded its horn needlessly. The sunlight was so blinding that the boy was no more than a blurred outline. Prullàs mopped the sweat from his brow with a handkerchief and cursed his luck. I can't take any more, he thought; I'd be only too happy to get on a boat and emigrate to America. But once I got there, what would I do?

When he arrived at his apartment, he phoned Fontcuberta. "Ah, Carlos, how did you get on with our good friend the Jesuit?" "Dreadfully! I told him all about my situation and he said yes he would help me, but only if I jump through the hoop; you know – Confession, Communion, procession and everything that goes with it. Priests never give anything for nothing. And you can't imagine how he left me feeling! On the way out I looked in the hall mirror to check I didn't have horns and a tail. But dammit," he went on, raising his voice, "they're the ones; they're the real devils. Didn't he try to buy my soul in return for favours? Anyone would think this is a city full of saints, and I'm the only reprobate. It's such hypocrisy, Miguel! Hypocrisy, arrogance, and nothing more! And the worst of this is, even though I'm getting nowhere, I'm making a fool of myself talking about that young woman. Of course, I've named no names . . . "

After this there was a pause. Fontcuberta was thinking. Finally he said: "Don't give up so easily. Rome wasn't built in a day. Listen, I've just had another idea: why don't you see if the writers can help you? You know who I mean: the ones who used to meet in the Ateneo; now, if I'm not mistaken, they meet up once a week somewhere else." "No, Miguel, that's not on," Prullàs replied. "We're not on good terms. In the best of cases, they reckon I've sold out; in the worst, they think I'm a police informer. They're very suspicious people."

"Don't underestimate their *esprit de corps*," Fontcuberta

replied, "nor traditional Catalan solidarity. When things look black, they stand together. Look for someone who might support you. At Brusquets' I saw you talking to José Felipe Clasiciano. He thinks a lot of you, and he gets about. If he's still in Barcelona, I'm sure he'll help you. Call him, tell him you're in a fix, tell him whatever you like without compromising me or anyone else. If you think you can win him over with money, offer him the moon; although I don't reckon that'll be necessary." Prullàs hesitated. "D 'you think it'll be of some use?" "Of course! In recent months, the authorities have become very careful not to upset them; if you get their backing, you can be sure Verdugones won't turn a blind eye. Anyway, what do you lose by giving it a try? Things can't be worse than now."

Prullàs hung up, lit a cigarette, and paced nervously up and down the long corridor. Sebastiana stuck her head out of the kitchen, and when she saw him, crossed herself, muttered Holy Mother of God, and quickly hid herself again, as though there was a wild beast in the apartment. The telephone rang again, and Prullàs rushed to pick it up. "Hello?" he said. At the other end of the line, it was Marichuli's voice. "Carlos, are you all right?" "Oh, it's you." "Is that a problem?" "No, where are you calling from?" "From a bar in Calle Provenza." "The dentist again? No, today I used my dressmaker as the excuse. I've only got a couple of hours: I promised I'd be back before dinner. Where can we meet?" "Nowhere!" Prullàs erupted, "this is no time for emotions." "That's not why I came," she said calmly; "I know you're in trouble and I want to help, that's all." "Trouble? Wherever did you get an idea like that?" "From your phone call," she said. "Yesterday afternoon I was chatting with Martita in your house as usual, when Joaquín came with your message that everything was fine and normal; I knew at once there must be something very wrong, and to judge from your tone now, I wasn't far from the mark."

"Hmm," he said, "and what about Martita? Does she suspect something as well?" "Ha, Martita is so used to your fibs she'd believe anything. But I know you better," she added. "Tell me everything." "All right," said Prullàs after a moment's hesitation, "but not on the phone, or in an apartment or a public place, I could be being watched. Listen, and do as I tell you: take a taxi and wait for me at the corner of my place without getting out: I don't want anyone to see you. I'll be down in about ten minutes: is that clear?" "Perfectly," she replied.

When she found herself outside the revolving door of the Hotel Gallardo half an hour later, Marichuli Mercadal shrieked in protest. "Carlos, you've brought me to the house of assignment. Aren't you ashamed of yourself?" "No, it's a simple, quiet hotel where we can talk without being interrupted and where nobody will ask us for our papers. Surely in our situation you don't expect to go to the Ritz, do you? And anyway, what of it? Nobody here knows you," Prullàs argued as he paid the taxi-driver. "It's nothing to do with other people, Carlos, it's about me, and my own sense of dignity. I'm an honest woman – a sinner, but still honest; and honest women don't set foot in hotels like this." "You'd be amazed if you knew how many decent women have crossed this threshold," he retorted, "but that's something you never will know, because this place is the soul of discretion. Besides, you don't have to come in if you don't want to: you can catch the coach and before you know where you are, you'll be back home, with your dignity intact." Marichuli heaved a sigh. "All right," she said, "just this once; but you have to promise you won't treat me like a loose woman." "I give you my word of honour," Prullàs said.

Marichuli let herself be led docilely to the room. But as soon as they had entered, and the receptionist with the gardenia in his buttonhole had bowed profusely and withdrawn, she sat on the edge of the bed and broke into sobs again. "How terrible, my God, how terrible! Coloured sheets and lewd engravings on the walls, what on earth am I going to tell my confessor? Oh Virgin of the Forsaken, please ensure my daughter never learns what a disgrace her mother was!"

Prullàs stood looking out of the window, waiting for her complaints to subside: in the house opposite the bird was still captive in its cage, and the old man in the cap was again fast asleep in his rocking-chair, his face tilted up to the ceiling and his mouth wide open. Through the partition wall he could hear the muffled sound of voices from the next room; after a while, the noise ceased and someone began to cheerily whistle a popular song. Marichuli recovered her composure and Prullàs, still standing at the window, told her what had happened. She listened with such exaggerated attention, hanging on his every word, that Prullàs doubted whether she had in fact taken anything in. "Did you understand?" he asked once he had finished. "More or less," she said; "I understood what you told me, but not why anyone should suspect you: you don't seem like a bad man." Prullàs smiled indulgently. "There are a few details I didn't mention, out of consideration for you." "Don't be ridiculous, Carlos: you bring me to a place like this and I'm not supposed to know what details you're talking about? You must have had an adventure with some trollop you shared with that Ignacio Vallsigorri, or am I wrong? But that's no motive to kill anyone; or at least, not for you; not that or anything else – you're someone who could never kill, and this Señor Lechugones must know that. No, Carlos," she said in a sombre tone that took Prullàs by surprise, "there's something more to this."

"Something more?" he said, "such as what?" "I don't know, my love, but I'll tell you what I think: someone is making sure the investigation points in your direction; someone wants you to be held responsible for the crime; and what's more, I reckon that it's someone you know and trust. I once saw a film where something similar happened: Ray Milland was in it, and that dark-haired girl whose name I can't remember," she said, as if this clinched her argument.

Prullàs shrugged: deep down, he didn't think much of Marichuli's opinions; he even agreed with Doctor Mercadal that she might be on the brink of insanity, so what she said now seemed unimportant to him. As if reading his mind, Marichuli sighed again and said: "I can see you don't believe me. I don't seem worthy of your attention, and perhaps I'm the one to blame for that: I've always behaved like an idiot where you're concerned. But that's not me: my passion may be idiotic, but there's nothing I can do about that. How could you take me seriously when I give in time and again to my impulses and your whims? Who could respect a married woman, a mother and a practising Catholic, who willingly allows herself to be dragged to a house of ill repute like this? But don't be fooled by appearances: what I said was true: someone close to you is trying to harm you. All I can do is warn you. Warn you and pray for you. Here, I've brought you something."

She opened her bag, rummaged inside and eventually brought out a rectangular card. "Are you going to give me a photo?" Prullàs asked. "That wouldn't be a bad idea," she retorted. But it wasn't a photograph, rather a coloured print of the Virgin of Fatima, the very same statue which had undertaken its miraculous pilgrimage through Spain and France before reaching Maastricht, where his Holiness Pope Pius XII was waiting. "She'll protect you," she murmured, lowering her gaze, "even if you mock." Prullàs rushed over to her and took the print. Marichuli stood up quickly. "Please, take me to the coach stop," she begged him. Without a word, Prullàs left the room and returned a few moments later. "They've gone to call a taxi," he said; "they'll tell us when it arrives."

By now it was Marichuli who had gone cautiously over to the window and was staring up at the sky. Prullàs felt a wave of tenderness for this beautiful, unhappy and bewildered woman. "Before we part," he said, "there's something I'd like to ask you." She passed her hand over her face and turned to him. "What's that?" Prullàs cleared his throat. "D'you dye your hair?" he said finally, then, seeing her surprised reaction, hastily added: "It's not just a frivolous question; when they examined the murder victim's clothing, they found a dyed hair. The day we met, you said that this was your hair's natural colour; now I'd like to know if it's true."

"Well, it wasn't me who killed him, if that's what you're asking," Marichuli said. "And no, I wasn't lying to you that wild night; neither then nor at any other time have I lied to you; I wouldn't know how to even if I wanted to. I'm a natural red-head. Yet as I'm sure you know, all of us women, to a greater or lesser degree, do things to our hair: young and old, pretty or ugly, honest or flighty; even Martita has highlights put in, not that you've ever noticed. The police are bound to know that."

"This is nothing to do with the police. The analyses were done in a beauty clinic run by someone called Doctor Maribel; have you heard of her?" "Yes, of course, and above all I've *heard* her: Doctor Maribel is a real celebrity in Barcelona. Every morning she has a programme on the radio; she gives advice about personal problems, recipes, and hints on how for example to prevent your shoes going damp in the wardrobe. I listen to her when I'm at home with nothing to do; in other words, almost always. She has a very pleasant voice, and what she says is full of good sense. Perhaps you should confide in her, since you won't do so with me. One thing, though: don't bring her here." "I'll suggest it to her, and we'll see if she's as full of good sense as you say," Prullàs joked. At that moment, the receptionist with the gardenia in his buttonhole came in and said their taxi was outside.

8

José Felipe Clasiciano, the mellifluous modernist poet, usually put up in a modest hotel close to the Puerta del Angel that was frequented by secondary figures from the world of bullfighting: picadors, ring assistants, matadors' attendants and others, who were always surrounded by apprentices looking for work. The walls of the hotel foyer boasted photographs signed by famous matadors, and in the bar, above an oblong mirror, there was a stuffed bull's head. Lola Montes was on the radio singing *La zarzamora*, while at the bar the poet was deep in conversation with a smooth-cheeked youth. "What a pleasure to see you, Carlos, a real pleasure!" He gave Prullàs an ostentatious hug, and sent the youngster on his way. "Run along with you, dear boy; I'll come and find you later." The youth left them, practising cape movements as he went. "Oh, Carlitos," the poet sighed, "I just love chatting to these little urchins, I love it! They're so sweet! They believe every word you say, and get so excited about everything. They see whatever their fantasy suggests. That little angel thought I was a bullfight impresario from overseas. As for me, Carlitos, I just want to be loved a little, that's all. It never does us any harm, does it? Such a fine young colt! So different from the pair of us, men of the world and so blasé. What about you? What's going on? What was all that crap you mentioned on the 'phone?"

"You know I have a bit of a difficult relationship to those writers, José Felipe," Prullàs said.

The poet gave a self-deprecating shrug. "Happy to be of

service to you, Carlitos. That's what friends are for, dammit!"
And to the barman: "*Sommelier*, two finos!" Then, in a whisper:
"I've asked Montcusi to meet us in the Central in half an hour.
I took the liberty of inviting him to lunch in your name, and
he was delighted. The food in that place is nothing out of the
ordinary, but the Ateneo writers meet there every Thursday
and I thought that as it was their territory, they might feel less
intimidated."

"Your arrangements are perfect, José Felipe, and I thank
you for them with all my heart, but in any case, I'm the one
who should feel intimidated," Prullàs replied. "I don't see
why," Clasiciano retorted. "Whether you like it or not, you're
the successful one, Carlitos. That's why, though there's no
personal animosity, there'll always be a great gulf between
you. It's painful for us Spaniards from outside the country, with
our love of Spain and its culture, to see the sad state it's been
reduced to simply by force of circumstance."

"That's true," Prullàs admitted; "there was a time, years ago,
when we could all have sat down together round a table and
looked each other in the eye. But the opportunity was wasted,
if it ever really existed, and now it's too late. Although there's
no difference between us on matters of principle, they feel bitter
and mistrustful towards me."

"Don't judge them too harshly, Carlitos. Just think how
badly life has treated them. To find yourself torn from the
security of your job and home, cast into an exile full of
upheavals, hardships and humiliation, to have to rely on many
occasions on other people's compassion: that must be terrible,
dammit! And then, thanks to another twist of fate, finding you
have to return to Spain to save your skin."

"But nobody bothers them here," Prullàs said. "Of course,"
Clasiciano countered, "because they're no longer a threat to
anyone. But even so, they're still absent, Carlitos, their eyes

and thoughts are fixed on a distant spot, a homeland that for them has ceased to exist."

"Don't be so melodramatic, José Felipe; things here will soon be back to normal." The mellifluous poet let a faint smile wander across his mulatto features. "That's what some of them think," he agreed. "They're convinced everything will have a happy ending in the not-too-distant future; and then, they imagine, not only will their lifelong qualities finally be recognised, but they'll also be compensated for all they've suffered during the long years of oppression and fear. In the meantime, they wait for the slightest snippet of news that might confirm their hopes, falling for every rumour, every promise they hear, however ridiculous or fantastic. Others," he went on, "have resigned themselves, deep down inside, to go on living forever in this hapless state. Both sides, it seems to me, are condemned: History has moved on, and for that there's no remedy. When it comes down to it, Carlitos, we're all the playthings of fate: so there's no reason for you to feel defensive." "But will they help me?" Prullàs asked. "That remains to be seen."

They paid their bill and left the hotel bar. Out in the street, the bullring assistants were practising their art.

The *maître* led them to the table, where Montcusi was already waiting for them. "Are we late?" the mellifluous poet wailed. "No, no, not at all," the other man replied. "I came early, hoping to meet up with Santamans; it seems he's looking for me." These words came from a tall, strong-looking man with an enormous head and severe features that looked as if they were chiselled in stone. Behind his back it was said that his character was on a par with his looks, and the story went that once, when he was going through a particularly tough period, blinded either by despair or for some other reason, he had shot his wife with a revolver, seriously wounding her. He had travelled all over the world, and had a very broad culture. He was especially well up on German philosophy, having apparently studied under Heidegger at Freiburg. It was further said that some time earlier he had inherited a considerable fortune, which he had quickly squandered. "Our friend Prullàs here," the mellifluous poet trilled, "would like to explain his troubles and, as far as it's possible, to call on the support of his fellow-writers." "It was very kind of you to accept our invitation," Prullàs added. "It's for me to thank you for the opportunity to meet again," Montcusi replied. "We haven't seen each other for a long while; perhaps not since that performance of *La Nausée* last year," he said thoughtfully. This play, which had enjoyed an overwhelming success in Paris, had been given official permission for a single evening performance, properly censored, by an amateur company in a tiny theatre. Prullàs had been at pains not to go to this performance, which had made a great impression on all those who saw it, but he preferred not to correct Montcusi, and simply waved his hand vaguely.

The *maître* reappeared, and they began to discuss more general topics. Montcusi, who was a good talker and had a seemingly inexhaustible stream of sparkling anecdotes, told them how a few months before he had been invited to a university in New York and had been asked to a grand banquet without really knowing why, nor indeed knowing any of the other guests; he had felt at a great disadvantage because he did not speak a word of English. Imagine his surprise then, he said, when he found himself seated at table next to Marlene Dietrich, with whom he kept up a lively conversation in French throughout the evening, the famous film star showing great interest in the history of Catalonia and the pecularities of its language and culture.

Conscious of his role as mediator, Clasiciano led the conversation back towards the topic which had brought them all there, before he started in on his ham *panaché*. "Our friend

Prullàs here was very keen to talk to you," he said; "but I'd better leave it to him to explain what it's all about." Prullàs cleared his throat. "In fact," he muttered vaguely, "it's all a bit symbolic. I've recently had a slight problem with the authorities, the consequences of which are still unclear, and I thought that if I could count on the moral support of some prestigious intellectuals, that might perhaps deter these same authorities from taking certain legal measures which you might say, erm, affect me personally." Having got this far in his explanation, he suddenly stopped. What he was trying to do suddenly seemed to him a crass mistake. It was obvious that Montcusi was well aware of Vallsigorri's death, and of Prullàs' involvement in the case, but the fact that he himself was collaborating with Don Lorenzo Verdugones put him in a delicate position. He could see in Montcusi's eyes the question he was asking himself: Who's side is he on?

Their embarrassment was cut short by the arrival of a slight, fragile-looking man with a face like a hare. "There you are, Santamans! I heard you were looking for me." Beads of sweat stood out on the newcomer's brow, and he was very excited at the news he had brought. "*El pobre Arnalot és mort,*" he panted, "*a Mexic!*" He was about to go on when he realised who Prullàs was, and quickly interrupted himself: "Oh, I'm sorry, I didn't see you there . . . " "That doesn't matter, really," Prullàs said. "Please, do go on; I can understand you perfectly." But Santamans kept a careful silence. "Come and sit with us," Montcusi said to relieve the tension. "You're still in time to join us; as you can see, we've only just begun." "Yes please, do join us," Prullàs said.

Santamans thanked them but declined their offer. He suffered from a strange blood disorder that forced him to follow a strict diet and to rest nearly all the time. He stayed at home, translating classical texts, and only went out once a week to meet the other writers or to go to the cinema, he explained in a laboured voice. "Don't be so awkward," Montcusi insisted. "Sit down even if you don't want to eat, and join in our chat." Santamans submitted meekly, and sat on the fourth chair at the table. He asked for a glass of water and a spoonful of bicarbonate. Prullàs, who hardly knew him and had never exchanged more than a couple of words with him, didn't know what to say. Santamans was famous for his timidity and shyness, but not for his lack of courage; when faced with a real danger, as had happened more than once during the dreadful years of the Civil War, he would moan and lament, but in the end behave far more honourably than many who at similar moments struck a heroic pose but acted in an undignified and disloyal fashion. Many people saw in this silent heroism the start of his crippling illness. Now his presence at the table, as the bearer of bad news, made their communication more difficult and the situation all the more tense. "I'm sorry for what happened," Prullàs murmured. Montcusi merely shrugged. It was obvious that the death of his friend in a far-off land had affected him greatly, but Prullàs realised he would never express sorrow in his presence. Prullàs had once publicly made sardonic reference to the works of the dead man, which were as impenetrable as they were learned. Now his unkind judgment hung in the heavy atmosphere of the restaurant. "Our friend Prullàs here is in difficulty and is asking for our help," Montcusi said.

Santamans stopped stirring his bicarbonate and looked at Prullàs with feigned innocence. "Naturally, naturally," he exclaimed with just a trace of irony. "We're always ready to do our bit in the fight for the republic . . . oh, the republic of letters, I mean!" This jibe incurred Montcusi's silent censure. Scarcely a month before, another of the regulars at the meeting of Ateneo writers had been arrested and tried for slander after composing a satirical poem for the imagined funeral of a certain public figure and reading it aloud in the course of an intimate dinner. Thanks to the intervention of several influential people, the sentence had been set aside and the affair ended as nothing more than a scare, but the incident had shown that even in such a small and apparently homogeneous group, there was an informer. As a consequence, the biting wit and mockery that was so characteristic of their meetings had been toned down considerably.

"Let's stop beating about the bush, shall we?" Montcusi said; "the matter is obviously serious and for our part we'd be very glad to help you. But what help could we give anyone, when we are the ones who need it most? On the other hand," he went on, "things are slowly getting better; in recent months, several things have been permitted . . . what we were saying earlier about 'La Nausée' is one example. There are some signs of an opening, there's a bit less pressure, which is something! Yet they still keep a close watch on us. Our friend Clasiciano here, who can judge these things impartially, will correct me if I'm wrong."

"Impartial, yes, but that doesn't mean I don't feel for you," the mellifluous poet agreed. Then, in a sudden change of tone, he added: "And any ill-considered move could be counter-productive, dammit."

Santamans lit the pipe he had been ceremoniously stuffing and murmured from behind the smokescreen: "You better than anyone can testify to our affliction." Once again, Prullàs noted a hint of irony in his words. Everyone present was aware of the fact that the mellifluous poet was a hypocrite who enjoyed the favour of official institutions because of his abject professions of devotion to the motherland and of admiration and loyalty towards those who ruled its destiny. Despite his duplicity he was tolerated among the Ateneo writers and other groups because he had a passport which allowed him to travel unhindered throughout Europe and North America, and he was constantly on the move, forever leaving a trail of debts and unpaid bills behind him, but during his frequent visits to Barcelona bringing books, magazines and news from the outside world which, for a few brief moments, at least managed to satisfy the local writers' cosmopolitan thirst.

Clasiciano thanked him for the compliment and added: "It's a prerogative of those who have no country or home like your humble servant here to become the recipients of all the trials and tribulations there are in the world. For example, I've just been to Vienna, where my wandering footsteps took me for the very first time. I was left speechless when I saw that my image of this city which, after all I'd read and all the exquisite music I'd heard, had always seemed to me the pinnacle of elegance and culture, was so far removed from the harsh reality. The vast majority of its buildings are still just ruins, and the opera house is a pile of bricks; there's no light or gas, and barely any water; food is scarce and even the most basic goods can only be found on the black market, at exorbitant prices and by dint of all kinds of subterfuge. It's dangerous to be out on the streets, especially after dark: gangs of louts set on passers-by, honest women have to put up with outrages by a drunken and unruly soldiery, and every night people are kidnapped and never heard from again. In this Vienna in tatters, with its soul torn out, I went to a musical evening. It was nothing more than a tourist trap. In a rat-infested castle, some lackeys in patched-up coats and holes in their stockings served us a snack of rye bread, cheese and onion. While we were desperately chewing on this indigestible grub, the lady of the house sang a few Schubert lieder: *Auf dem Wasser zu singen* and other similar pieces. As soon as this musical interlude was over, with the sounds of the pianoforte still echoing through the ancient salon, she came to beg money from us without the slightest scruple. She told me she still did not know her husband's whereabouts, and that all her wealth had remained over the border in Hungary. It was disgusting what was happening in Hungary while the world looked on impassively, she said, disgusting! She went on plaintively to describe all the crimes the army of occupation were committing, the abuses of the Bolshevik regime, and Cardinal Mindszenty's heroic resistance. Do something, for God's sake, all of you who still enjoy freedom of action and of speech; do something, she implored us. *Et elle avait des mamelles grosses comme ça!"*

The rest of the group greeted this probably apocryphal story with murmurs of approval. Prullàs hated this kind of anecdote, whose only object seemed to be to convert the misfortunes and weaknesses of others into a source of amusement, if not ridicule. I'd never do anything like that, he thought. At this point, Montcusi broke in: "Let's not forget the main aim of this meeting, that is, Prullàs' request." "There's nothing more to add," Prullàs said. "Talk to the others, weigh up the pros and cons carefully, and then do as you think fit. I want you to know," he immediately went on, "that whatever your final decision is, I thank you beforehand for the interest you've shown, and I hope one day to be able to respond in the same way, as far as I am able."

"Ah no, we're not two-faced!" Montcusi roared, banging his fist on the table. "You're welcome to hear everything we have to say, of course you are!" "I didn't mean to offend you," Prullàs replied hastily, thinking to himself: Things are going from bad to worse. Fortunately, at that precise moment a well-known voice captured all their attention. "Well, this is a surprise! Señores Montcusi and Santamans with Don Carlos Prullàs and Don José Felipe Clasiciano! The Great Bear, the Pole Star and the Southern Cross!"

"Poveda!" Prullàs cried. The blackmarketeer unctuously

bowed and scraped. "Always at the service of such illustrious company!" He shook them all by the hand, except for the mellifluous poet, whose hand he kissed in a rapid, furtive gesture. "This moment will stay forever in my memory," he gushed. Then he wiped the sweat from his brow with a hand-kerchief, made some room on the table, put his bulky bag on it, and quite openly began to take out cartons of American cigarettes. "Leave your baubles till later and have something to eat, Poveda," Prullàs said; "it's on me."

Poveda shut his bag and straightened up. "No, Don Carlos, I don't mean to upset you, but I'm not hungry, if you don't mind. To tell you the truth, I've already eaten; I live with my aged mother and we have lunch very early; in that sense we're very prudish." As he was blurting out these words, he took his money for the cigarettes, and then rushed out of the restaurant, leaving behind only the scent of his hair lotion. "How strange!" Montcusi commented, apparently calmer now, "Poveda gener-ally stays for a while, getting up to his tricks and reciting those bawdy lyrics of his. Something must have happened to him today." Prullàs, realising that it was his presence which had led the blackmarketeer to take to his heels, felt extremely depressed and throughout the rest of the meal responded to the conversation only with a few monosyllables.

9

The next day, the telephone rang while Prullàs was finishing his breakfast and was pleasurably immersed in reading *La Vanguardia*. For the second time that month, a flying saucer had appeared over a small town in Arkansas. Many people bore witness to the sighting, as well as to the huge circle of burnt grass left by the spacecraft's engines. The Head of State meanwhile had gone to his mansion in Meirás for a well-earned rest: he was spending his leisure hours fishing, painting landscapes, or strolling in his garden with his granddaughter Carmencita: all of which was recorded in rather fuzzy photographs. The legal routine of the case against Alfried Krupp had been dramatically interrupted with the appearance on the stand of the accused's mother. Doña Bertha Krupp was a lady of advanced age but still lively and imposing. In the early years of the century, following the tragic death of her father – an insidious press campaign had accused him of having illicit relations with his butler, leading him to commit suicide – she had taken control of the family business. A short while later, her husband, Baron Gustav von Bohlen, who on his marriage to her had not only acquired the company but assumed the illustrious name of the Krupps, baptised a powerful mobile 420mm gun in her honour. It weighed one hundred tons, fired shells that were a metre long and weighed eighty kilos, and needed a gun crew of two hundred men. This extraordinary creation, a real feat of engineering skill, became known as "Big Bertha" and was used by the Kaiser's army to successfully bombard England from the coast of France during the Great War. Now this renowned figure, whose name was forever engraved in the annals of artillery warfare, was appearing before the judges in her twin roles as wife and mother. Her heart torn with sorrow, she was defending the honour of her line and begging for mercy for her son.

"Señor Prullàs?" "Speaking, who is that?" "Sigüenza, at your service. Don Lorenzo Verdugones would like to have a word with you. Please hold, I'll put him on."

Prullàs waited for several minutes. By the time he finally heard the governor's voice at the other end of the line, the earpiece was stuck to his ear with the heat. "Hello there, Prullàs, how are things?" "As ever, Don Lorenzo, nothing to report." "Don't get disheartened, young man! Remember the Samaniego fable: a monkey climbed up a walnut tree . . . What plans do you have for this weekend?" "None," Prullàs replied. "But I'd like to go to Masnou, if I have your permission, of course. If I don't go, my family will be worried." "You don't need my permission, Prullàs, you're a free citizen in a free country: you can go wherever you wish. Unfortunately, I can't say the same for myself: this afternoon I have to close the International Conference on Apologetics that's being going on all week in Vich as part of the Balmes Centenary, and tomorrow I have to go to Reus to preside over a charity bullfight with Pepe Calabuch. That's why I was calling: to see if you wanted to go to Reus with me. First we could eat some seafood, and then – to the bullring! But family comes first, of course," he immediately said in the same jovial tone. "Go to Masnou, relax, think things over . . . and don't forget to say hello to your father-in-law from me, and send my very best wishes to that charming wife of yours." After he hung up, Prullàs felt like a boy with a day off from school.

He called Mariquita. "I'm off to Masnou," he told her. "I can't leave my family abandoned for so long, and besides, I deserve a rest: you can't imagine how busy I've been these last few days, what with the police investigation and everything else." "I can see you're having a great time," the actress said on the other end of the line. "It's no joke, this is very serious," Prullàs protested; "if you don't believe me, ask your husband, he's really pessimistic about it." "Bah, my husband's packed his bag again and gone off to Madrid," she said in an offhand way that betrayed a bitter undercurrent; "he must be chasing some skirt or other there." "Don't be so nasty-minded," Prullàs said. "I'm not nasty-minded, Carlos, but I am annoyed; all of you are gadding about, having fun, gallivanting around and enjoying yourselves royally; while here I am, a faithful wife and wage slave, having to spend my whole summer shut up at home or in a dark, unhealthy fleapit of a theatre, disgusted with my work and paler than Saint Teresa." "Didn't Saint Teresa ever go to the beach?" Prullàs asked. "She only went once, and someone stole her towel while she was levitating," said Mariquita. "As soon as I get back, I'll take you out to dinner and to the cinema, I promise," Prullàs said. "Have you heard anything from Poveda recently?" "No." "I'd like to see him and ask him a couple of questions; if you get the chance, tell him to call me, would you?" "Yes, sir, certainly sir."

That's women for you! Prullàs thought after his conversation with Mariquita Pons: they're convinced they're all victims and that we men, simply because we are men, have got it easy. Right! It's true we like a bit of a flirt if we have the chance, but don't women do all they can precisely to give us that chance? Don't they dress up and groom themselves, go on diets and exercise and put themselves through real Chinese tortures just to drive us crazy? Just look at that Doctor Maribel and that secret police operation she runs! And as for being honest, you'd have to look at the statistics: we men may not be saints, but they can be pretty dreadful too; the only difference is they know how to hide it better.

These thoughts cheered Prullàs up so much he even considered for a moment going to see Lilí Villalba. It was still early: he could spend a couple of hours with her in the Hotel Gallardo and arrive in Masnou in time for dinner. Then he remembered she worked all day in the packing factory and reluctantly had to give up this attractive idea.

He went down to the street and asked the porter to clean the windows of his Studebaker; then he went to the kiosk on the street corner, bought *Triunfo* and *El hogar y la moda* for Martita and his mother-in-law and several surprise packets for his children; he went into the bookshop and bought an SS van

Dine novel for himself, hoping he hadn't already read it. The bookshop owner was busy reading a novel by Concha Linares Becerra. "What's it like?" he asked her. "Not up to much," she replied, "but yesterday I read *Jamaica Inn* by Daphne du Maurier, and I liked that; take it for your wife." "How is your husband?" "*Malament*," she said, pointing to her side, "*el fetge.*" Prullàs went back up to his apartment, changed, told Sebastiana he was off to Masnou, and left again. As he was getting into his car, he was intercepted by a haggard-looking young woman. "Hey, 'andsome, spare me a few coppers, you've got a lot an' others ain't got nothin'."

The sun was setting as he started out; the black smoke from the Barcelona factories blended into the livid sky, giving the dusk a gloomy, unpleasant feel. Soon after he pulled onto the highway, a train crammed with passengers passed him on the nearby tracks; the ground shook as if there'd been an earthquake, and the rush of air almost blew the car off course. As the train disappeared into the distance, the hum of the carriages on the rails and the piercing engine whistle lingered in the twilight.

A few minutes later, however, once Prullàs had rounded the Montgat promontory and left behind the acrid stench of sulphur from the factories, the panorama changed completely. In the hills to his west, dark pines stood out against the crimson streaks of sunset, the clear air brought the smell of burning leaves, and on the other side, the calm blue sea was as magnificent and serene as it had been through the ages. It's as though I've crossed the threshold into a totally different world, Prullàs thought. Yet the welcome he received at Masnou was disappointing. For his family, lulled by the monotonous, pleasurable routine of summer days, time had gone quickly by, leaving no trace. For him, on the other hand, the week of rushing around and of such unpleasant surprises had seemed an eternity. He felt he was returning home from a dangerous journey or a war, only to discover to his chagrin and annoyance that nobody appeared to have noticed he was gone. While I was going through hell, he said to himself, nobody missed me in the slightest. After a short while, though, the peace of that safe, closed world, untouched by anything that wasn't easy pleasure and family intimacy, lifted his spirits; he regained his good humour, dined with a hearty appetite and later, when his children and his in-laws had retired to bed, suggested to Martita they go for a walk. "Aren't you exhausted?" she asked; "when you arrived you looked dog-tired."

"That was because I was still feeling all the pressure from Barcelona," he said, "and from my work; now it's as though a stone's been lifted. Let's walk to the club: a bit of a stroll and a brandy will relax me completely."

Martita agreed without much enthusiasm. "I'll go and put something on, I'm a real mess like this." It was obvious she would have preferred to stay at home, but this fresh demonstration of her lack of interest didn't upset Prullàs this time; in Masnou, Martita lived in an atmosphere in which by now he was an intruder; although her love for her husband was as strong as ever, his arrival meant an awkward change to her routine, which she would have to get used to bit by bit. Prullàs lay back in a deckchair and breathed in the perfumed night air. Through the leaves of the magnolia tree he could see the waning moon. He smoked a cigarette to stay awake until Martita returned, her hair freshly combed, scented with perfume, and wearing a flimsy sleeveless red dress.

Prullàs got up and she clung to his arm. I must be crazy to get mixed up with anyone else when I've got all I need and more right here, Prullàs thought. As soon as this ridiculous case is cleared up, I'll send the theatre to the devil and take Martita on a trip. We've never been to Venice. They say that in summer the canals stink to high heaven, but they can't be that bad.

That's it, he went on fantasising, we'll go to Venice; that could inspire me to write another comedy. What with one thing and another, it's been ages since I put pen to paper. In the evenings in Venice, in a café or at the hotel, I can take notes. Then once we're back, I can write the play and we can open on Easter Saturday. This time though it'll be different, something new: no more hilarious crimes, no bodies falling out of wardrobes; no more stammerers or *double entendres* or stock characters in their underpants. It'll be a romantic comedy, with some tears along the way, but a happy ending. A beautiful love story! "Are you talking to yourself?" Martita said with a laugh. "I might be, did I say anything in particular?" "No; you were just moving your lips and your eyebrows as if you were trying to convince someone of an idea you felt strongly about," she replied. "In fact, I was thinking about us; about you and me and Venice." "Why were you talking under your breath then?" "I don't know; in Barcelona I lost the habit of talking," he said. "Where are you going?"

They had reached the street and Martita, still clutching her husband's arm, had headed off away from the club. "To the club, but the long way round," she replied. "You said you felt like a walk, and this way we pass by the Mercadals' house – if the light's on, we could invite them." "Do we have to?" Prullàs asked, not very happy at the thought of meeting Marichuli again at that moment. "If you don't mind," Martita said, with a pleading look on her face, immediately adding in a confidential voice: "Marichuli's not well; I don't know if it's her health, but in general. She worries me: she doesn't eat, she doesn't sleep, she's always depressed. Her husband hardly dares leave her on her own."

Prullàs tapped his temple. "It must come from here," he said. "A lot of illnesses are from here," Martita agreed, "but they are just as real, and even more difficult to cure than the rest. The other evening," she continued in a whisper so as not to be overheard by the old women of the village, who sat out in their wicker chairs to enjoy the cool of the night, dressed in black from head to toe, "Marichuli came to see me. We spent a couple of hours chatting away quite happily, when all of a sudden out of the blue she burst into heart-rending tears; there was no way to console her, so I had to give her camomile tea and smelling salts. When she finally calmed down, I asked her why she'd broken down like that, but she couldn't explain it. She did though half-tell me some things from her life. The poor woman has had terrible bad luck. No, bad luck isn't the word: her life's been a real tragedy."

By now they had reached the house and peered in through the railings: at the far end of the garden they could see the pointed roof and its lightning conductors standing out against the night sky above the treetops; but the windows were obscured by vegetation. Martita could not decide whether to go in or to leave, so she sat with Prullàs on the pavement kerb, waiting for something to happen. Although no-one was out and about, and the only sound was the chirping of the crickets, Martita whispered as she described what her friend had told her. Apparently, Marichuli's parents had died in dreadful circumstances; their death had been very tragic and much talked-about. This had happened many years earlier, when Marichuli herself was still a little girl. The event had been crushing for her, not only because of the repercussion of something of this enormity on a child's mind, and the fact of suddenly becoming an orphan, with all that entailed, but also because at that time nobody had wanted, doubtless with good reason, to tell her the truth about what had happened. As a result of this, the death of her father and mother had always been shrouded in an air of complete mystery, and when later on she had tried to discover the truth, she couldn't find any convincing explanation of something which had been confusing when it occurred and had become distorted by the passage of time, by being kept a secret, and by gossip. All her efforts to discover the real facts surrounding the death of the two people closest to her, Marichuli had told Martita, had foundered in the troubled waters of ignorance, compassion or slander. In the end, she had given up trying. But giving up in this way led her to a terrible conclusion: in Marichuli Mercadal's eyes, there could be no possible reason to justify her parents' abandoning her in such a way. All that was clear, she ended up thinking, was that they had not loved her enough: this was what she told Martita, and what Martita finished conveying to Prullàs.

A train whistle added a mournful echo. It was probably a long, slow freight train. As silence returned to the street, Martita shuddered. "Let's go," she said, getting up, "I'm cold, it must be the damp." Prullàs said nothing. When they had first met, Doctor Mercadal had led him to believe something similar to what he had just heard from Martita. But on that occasion, he recalled, the doctor had explicitly spoken of suicide.

Walking briskly, they soon arrived at the club. The bar was dimly lit and there were only a few people inside. Three men in shirtsleeves were playing billiards, and Doctor Mercadal himself was at the bar counter talking to Joaquín. By common consent, Martita and Prullàs came to a halt in the doorway, hoping to be able to turn around and go home, but just at that moment Joaquín saw them, and doubtless seeing this as a good opportunity to free himself from the doctor's small talk greeted them with exaggerated enthusiasm. Now they had been sighted, they had no choice but to go in and join Doctor Mercadal.

The surgeon had been drinking heavily: his eyes were bloodshot, his speech was slurred and his bottom lip quivered.

Prullàs enquired after his wife's health. "Martita tells me Marichuli's a bit off-colour." It took Doctor Mercadal a few seconds to understand what Prullàs meant; then he merely shrugged his shoulders. He was unshaven and his clothes were crumpled; he looked unkempt and slovenly. "The chief characteristic of the human mind," he said, "resides precisely in its constantly changing condition, as I was saying to Joaquín here when you arrived: everything changes constantly according to experience; each new experience is added to the sum of our previous ones, and thus forces us to a re-accommodation of all the elements in the system. This re-accommodation, as I was just telling Joaquín, will be greater or smaller depending on the size or importance of the new experience, but each and every new experience, however slight, is bound to produce a change in the entire system."

Joaquín gestured to Prullàs as if to disclaim any responsibility for such a theory, and therefore also to deny any responsibility for whatever it led to.

"In exactly the same way," the surgeon went on, "the destruction of a single atom produces a chain reaction and a holocaust: a nuclear holocaust! Boom!" In order to emphasise this assertion with a dramatic flourish, he took both his elbows off the bar, flung out his arms, and would have fallen flat on the floor had he not collided with Martita, whom he almost dragged down with him. There was a moment of complete chaos and confusion, which attracted the attention of the billiard-players. The click of the balls gave way to an uncomfortable silence.

"I'm leaving!" Martita growled. One of her shoulder straps had been torn in the struggle. "I'm so sorry, sweetheart," Doctor Mercadal spluttered.

Prullàs grabbed the doctor under his arms and yanked him upright again. Joaquín shrugged powerlessly. "This is a disgrace;

you should never have allowed it to happen," Martita spat at him. "Just to earn a few miserable pesetas you permit dreadful scenes like this in your bar. Let's go this minute, Carlos," she added to her husband. "Señora, I have a business to run, and that's to serve my customers," Joaquín replied.

Prullàs considered the situation. "Let's take him home," he said; "we can't leave him like this." "He'll sober up," Martita said; "he's an adult and ought to know by now what he's doing; or at least face up to the consequences. But if you want to link arms with him and march off singing *Asturias patria querida*, that's up to you. I'll wait for you at home."

Prullàs lost his patience. "You be quiet and do as you're told," he muttered without raising his voice, but in a tone that brooked no argument.

It was not as difficult as they had thought to prise Doctor Mercadal from the counter and help him walk slowly but relatively surely out of the bar. The billiard-players looked on with great amusement as the three of them made their way out of the club. "You're good people," Doctor Mercadal said; "you're my best friends, and I love you both! I've never had such good friends as you two." As he spoke, he made strenuous efforts to take steady steps forward. "The problem is the impossibility of including the emotions in our scientific concept of the world," he added. "How revolting!" Martita said, walking on a few yards and keeping a safe distance between herself and the two men.

When they reached their destination, Prullàs left the doctor leaning against the garden wall and tried to open the gate. Fortunately it was on the latch, and soon he and his drunken companion went in, negotiated the gravel path, and got to the front door of the house. At this point, the doctor recovered a semblance of common sense: "Don't call anyone," he said. "I've got a key, and there's no need to wake anybody."

Prullàs waited patiently while the other man found his bunch of keys, chose the right one, managed to insert it in the keyhole after several failed attempts, and at last succeeded in opening the door. Before being swallowed up by the darkness of the hall, Doctor Mercadal stuck his head out of the door and whispered: "Thanks, Carlitos . . . I'm sorry for what happened, but really, atomic fission is a disgrace. Mother Nature should never have done this to us." With that, he closed the door, and the sound of his footsteps, accompanied by the occasional crash as he bumped into something, gradually faded away inside the mansion.

Prullàs began his walk back. Before the first bend in the lane, he turned round and studied the house; when he saw no lights on, he continued on his way. He'd done all he could, he told himself. Martita was furious when he arrived. He tried to calm her down. "He's a sensitive man, and he's under great pressure; you yourself told me what Marichuli is like, which must affect him a lot, and then there's their daughter's situation as well. And don't forget the work he does. Just think of it, being a surgeon. To have every day the life or death of a human being hanging in the balance."

"Don't talk rubbish!" Martita said; "that man's behaviour was disgraceful, and so was ours. What will those people who saw us think?" "I couldn't care less," Prullàs replied with growing irritation. "Let them think whatever their tiny minds can come up with!" Martita burst into tears.

At mid-day on Sunday, shortly after the whole family had come back from Mass and was busy preparing to go down to the beach, the Mercadal family maid appeared with a huge box of sweets for Martita from the doctor. Martita did not even deign to read the card that came with the gift; she dismissed the maid curtly, telling her to take the sweets with her while she was about it. "Take them back where they came from," she said. The young girl's face turned bright crimson; she was dressed in a black uniform with starched cap, collar and cuffs, hardly suitable attire to go running around Masnou in under the scorching noonday sun. She looked to be on the verge of collapse.

When she had left, Prullàs spoke up. "After all," he said, "it's no great sin if a man drinks." "A man maybe not," Martita retorted, "but he's a doctor: he should set an example, instead of making himself look ridiculous in front of a waiter."

That afternoon Marichuli Mercadal appeared with the same box of sweets. Martita received her coldly, but at least listened to her excuses. The two women talked for a long while on their own under the magnolia tree. Finally, Martita gave in to her friend's entreaties, accepted the sweets, and even read the card. This brought tears to Marichuli's eyes, and Martita's face showed she herself was on the point of crying.

Prullàs passed close by them on several occasions, pretending it was by accident, as if their talk was none of his business. But he was afraid that Marichuli, out of her apparent need to experience drama in whatever situation, would confess her extramarital affair to his wife. More than once he was tempted to butt in on their conversation, but did not dare: stepping in like that would upset them and, anyway, Martita's expression was of comprehension, not anger.

When Marichuli finally got up to leave, just before dinner-time, Prullàs took advantage of the opportunity to have a quick word with her. "We've hardly seen each other this weekend," he said, bending to kiss her hand; "Martita's kidnapped you." "That's so typical of you men!" she replied lightly, winking at Martita in a friendly fashion. "You don't have the slightest scruple about leaving us alone all week, and then you expect us to be completely available for you. We have to put up with you when you're small, when you're old and when you're ill; but when you're well, all you have time for is work, your chums, and who knows what else besides."

"Won't you stay to dinner?" Martita said. "No, thanks," Marichuli replied; "I haven't been home all afternoon." "I'll walk you to the gate," Prullàs said. "Only as far as the gate," Martita laughed; "why, on that first evening you took her all the way home like a proper gentleman, and now . . . Goodness gracious, that's where becoming friends gets us! Marichuli is quite right: you men are impossible."

Prullàs and Marichuli stood by the garden gate for a while in silence. The sun had set behind the mountains, but the sky was still blue and it was a clear, warm evening. "It looks as though things aren't going too well with you," Prullàs eventually said. "That's right," she admitted; "my husband has gone off the rails, I'm crazy, and our poor daughter, who's done nothing to deserve it, is paying the price. I'm lucky to have Martita: it's only talking to her that does me any good: she's a saint." "I hope you haven't mentioned what happened between us," Prullàs said. "Don't worry, I may be crazy, but I don't go looking for trouble, as I've told you before. Are you staying a few days?" "I can't; I have to leave tonight or tomorrow morning; the business you know about is waiting for me in Barcelona and besides, it's better if I go, don't you think?"

Marichuli Mercadal sighed despairingly. "Do whatever you think best," she said. "I suffer if I see you, and I suffer if I don't see you, but of the two, not seeing you is worse."

She was so troubled at this thought that she fell silent for a few moments, but then she quickly composed herself once more, brought her face close to his, and whispered loudly to him: "Something strange is going on." "In what way?" he asked. "I don't know," Marichuli said. "On Thursday, a neurologist from Valencia appeared at the house, a friend or acquaintance of my husband's. He had come on some urgent and important business. My husband and he were pacing up and down the garden, talking to each other with their heads down and gesticulating a lot. Then the visitor disappeared as abruptly as he had arrived, and my husband was left thoughtful and silent. Later that evening, when the servants had retired for the night and Alicia was asleep and he had drunk several whiskies, he began to talk more openly. He was more talkative than lucid, but from what I understood, that same day or the evening before, the Civil Guard had searched several yachts here."

"Yachts?" Prullàs repeated. "That's what my drunk of a husband said," Marichuli asserted. "And what's that got to do with my case?" "I told you at the start, I don't know," Marichuli hissed; "perhaps there isn't any link, and I've got it all wrong; but just in case, try to find out if your dead friend had a yacht, and what the Civil Guard is looking for. A yacht is a yacht, and they wouldn't take such important measures unless the order came from Don Lorenzo Lechugones or from someone even higher up," she concluded, pointing up at the red evening sky.

CHAPTER SIX

I

On Monday he got up late, had breakfast, and read *La Vanguardia* at his leisure. The *Queen Mary* had sailed from the port of New York for Europe in a trail of streamers and jazz. Among its passengers were the famous actress Ingrid Bergman and the illustrious Spanish philospher José Ortega y Gasset, who was returning from giving a series of lectures in American universities on his favourite subjects. For her part, the famous Swedish actress was headed for Italy to star in a film directed by the prestigious director Roberto Rossellini. Both the philosopher and the actress intended, they said, to take advantage of the cruise on the luxury liner in their own different ways. Alfried Krupp's trial had reached the summing-up stage. The previous day, the prosecuting counsel had made his final plea, and the defence had once again called for the dismissal of all charges against their client in an impassioned speech. The defence lawyer had reminded the court, whose authority he simultaneously rejected, that they were not there to judge a specific social group, of which the accused was undoubtedly an outstanding member, but the actions of a single individual, whose behaviour had at all times been based on practical considerations that concerned the smooth running of his business, and the strict fulfilment of his obligations, and had never broken any of the laws in place at the time. It was true, the defence admitted, that the accused had expressed open support for a political party, in this case the National Socialist Party, of which he had even become a member; but he had done so at a period when this party was officially approved by the constitutional regime of the so-called Weimar Republic. In fact, the defence counsel added, when the National Socialist Party came to power, Germany had continued to be a fully-fledged member of the League of Nations, and until the start of hostilities in September 1939, all other states, and in particular those the judges themselves belonged to, had continued to enjoy normal relations with the German state. What in reality was on trial, the defence went on to allege, was not one man's criminal acts, but the meaning of a historical event, which with hindsight was easy to judge as its results were obvious, but which before it had fully developed was impossible to evaluate. Of course, if one of the accused's talents had been the ability to see into the future, not only would he have behaved differently but undoubtedly would have placed his extraordinary personal prestige in the service of another cause; but since he, like every other human being, was denied the gift of prophecy, when faced with a historical dilemma, he had made a choice that implied a great risk but which in no way could be said to be criminal or blameworthy. If Hitler had made good his promise to create a wealthy state based on justice, the champion and beacon of a new Europe freed from the boundaries and quarrels of its past, then Alfried Krupp's participation in this noble enterprise would have received the unanimous applause of all nations. However, as matters had turned out differently, Alfried Krupp was facing this iniquitous trial, as if he were a hardened criminal. Was this justice? the defence wondered, or were we seeing the arbitrary result of a game of chance played on a global scale, with incalculable consequences for the future of Humanity?

Prullàs had a shower, shaved, and then phoned Gaudet to invite him to lunch. The director replied that he would prefer to stay at home working and that he intended to have a bite to eat on his way to the theatre; we could meet there, after the rehearsal. "No chance!" Prullàs retorted. "I need to tell you all that's been happening to me in the past few days, and you need to look after yourself. I'll see you at half-past two in the Suizo."

"I know how to look after myself," Gaudet said curtly, "and as for what you've got to tell me, couldn't you do it on the phone?"

Prullàs was rather taken aback. "I'd prefer to do it face-to-face, but if you insist . . . " and he went on to give him a summary of the interviews he had been involved in so far.

When he had finished, the director said disdainfully: "That's what you get for mixing with people like that. Lawyers are all swindlers and cheats, and what else could you expect from priests? Why will you never accept what they're really like, what evil they conceal beneath their fine manners and pompous phrases? Or don't you remember what it was like when we were at school?"

"Pepe, that was about a hundred years ago, why are you bringing it up now?" Prullàs said. But Gaudet wasn't listening. "Don't you remember those big bullies who got their fun hitting the weak and the fainthearted, who used fear and violence to impose their will on others? And do you really think the priests didn't know what was going on? Of course they did! Anyone could have seen it, and they more than anybody else. So why didn't they stop it? Because that savagery was not only part of their plan, it was the very essence of their teaching method: power in the hands of the strong, justice in the service of power, and the weak left powerless and submissive. That was how we were brought up, Carlos, that was the education we got. And, as a result, to defend ourselves or simply to survive from one day to the next, those of us who were weak had to resort to what was worst in us: flattery, hypocrisy, silence and abasement, all of Spain's historic ills. And who's to blame for this? The priests. Priests have made us what we are, and they've made this country what it was, is, and will continue to be until the day we put them all in a sack, fill it with stones, and throw it in the sea."

"Pepe, you're a bit over-excited," Prullàs said when his friend's outburst had finished; "wouldn't it be better to talk all this over calmly as I suggested?"

He got dressed and went to the barber's. While the boot-black was shining his shoes and the manicurist was seeing to his nails, the barber trimmed his beard and hair, and, before Prullàs could prevent him, rubbed his scalp with oil. Prullàs was treated to several jokes, and there was a heated debate about bullfight-ers in which other customers became involved. Some supported Luis Miguel Domínguín, others El Litri, while there were also those who said neither of them could compare with Don Juan Belmonte.

Gaudet stumbled as he entered the restaurant, apologised for being late, and sat at Prullàs' table. At the other tables, men on their own were eating with mechanical gestures, dividing their interest between their plates and their newspapers. "I've taken the liberty of ordering for both of us," Prullàs said: "a light summer menu." "Fine," Gaudet said, getting his breath back, and adding: "You look well, and you stink." "Oh, yes," Prullàs laughed, "that's thanks to the barber; it also did me a world of good going to Mansou for a couple of days, after being driven into the ground all last week. You could do with a break too, to judge by the way you look." Gaudet snorted. "I didn't sleep a wink last night either," he complained; "I'm tired out, but I find it impossible to sleep. The chemist sold me some sleeping pills he said would do the trick, but when I tried them they gave me a dreadful stomach ache, but didn't help at all; I even started counting sheep, I was so desperate." "It's the heat," Prullàs said; "as soon as it gets cooler, you'll sleep like an angel." "May God hear your prayer," Gaudet muttered.

"Well," Prullàs said impatiently, "we'll worry about your health some other time. But right now there's a more pressing matter to consider. My situation looks grim: as I told you, the finger of suspicion points my way, all the evidence seems to be against me, and wherever I turn for help they slam the door in my face. I'm beginning to think I'm not going to get out of this unscathed. There's nothing else for it but for us to carry out our own investigation. We have to discover who on earth killed Ignacio Vallsigorri. It's the only way I can see to avoid being arrested and quite possibly spending the rest of my life in jail. I've been thinking a lot these last few days, and I have a plan. You play an important part in it, but there are no risks. D'you remember Franchot Tone in . . . ?"

"Carlos," Gaudet said, cutting off his friend's speech with a gesture, "there's something important I have to tell you." His serious tone and almost desperate expression disconcerted Prullàs. Gaudet hesitated; the effort he was making to get out each word was painfully obvious. "I wanted to say," he finally managed to stutter, "that as far as this case goes, I mean Ignacio Vallsigorri's death and everything to do with it . . . well, you shouldn't count on me. Don't interrupt, first hear me out, and then you can say whatever you wish. I was thinking about it after your phone call," he went on, still gazing down at the table, "and I came to the conclusion that this affair is a hornet's nest, and I've no intention of sticking my hand in. I know that by doing this," he rushed on, "I'm being completely disloyal, but I have no alternative. When it comes down to it," he pursued in the same weak, whining voice, as if he were the one who had in fact been betrayed, "nothing's going to happen to you, you've got people to look after you, you're

322

one of the untouchables; they'll make life difficult for you for a while, then they'll leave you in peace; but as for me . . . you know how precarious my situation is."

As Gaudet was speaking, Prullàs had quickly dispatched his bowl of gazpacho. He dabbed his lips with his napkin and drank a sip of wine before replying. "I don't understand a thing, Pepe, I'm lost," he said. "I reckon those pills the chemist gave you didn't just affect your stomach, they got to your brain as well. Your reasoning is incoherent, and your attitude is ridiculous. Why this sudden fear? Has something new happened? Is there something you know but don't want to tell me? Or have you had another of your ominous dreams? Tell me the truth . . . and drink your gazpacho, for goodness' sake! If on top of not sleeping you don't eat, you'll end up pushing up daisies: that's what you should be worrying about, not your night-time fantasies."

"Either you don't want to listen, or you don't want to understand," Gaudet replied; "when something like this is being investigated, it throws up things that are best left dead and buried: that's not so hard to grasp, is it? What those secrets might be, I have no idea. All I know is that when the lid is lifted, I don't want to be around. That's why I'm asking you to keep me out of it: I don't want to know what you're doing, where you're going, or who you're talking to. I don't want to know anything. And I don't like gazpacho: it's got garlic, cucumber and vinegar in it: just thinking about it makes me want to retch. Waiter, take this bowl away immediately!"

When the waiter had removed both their bowls, Prullàs said: "That's easy enough to say when you aren't directly involved, but I can't simply go and get my hat and walk out the door. You're my best friend, Pepe; earlier today you reminded me of when we were at school, when everybody used to attack you and I defended you. Don't all our years of friendship count for anything?"

The waiter brought them the next course. "When it comes down to it," Gaudet said, "everyone tries to save their skin, come what may, and if by doing so they ruin their neighbour, nobody's conscience gets in the way: their scruples go out of the window." "But you too?" Prullàs asked, staring at him. "You're my best friend: would you sacrifice me to save yourself too? Wouldn't you have any scruples either?"

The theatre director poked at the vol-au-vent case on his plate and replied: "Me? You know I'm bound hand and foot, Carlos. I'm trapped! As long as I dedicate myself to providing entertainment for a middle-class public with comedy thrillers, there's no problem; but woe unto me if I step out of line! I haven't done anything to deserve their hatred. By the way," he went on, "since it was you who brought up our years of friendship, there's something I want to say: the time has come for you and I to go our separate ways. I'm not talking about ending our friendship, or about my feelings: I've always cared for you, and I always will, Carlos, perhaps more than anybody else ever has; all I'm saying is that we should go our own way professionally. We've reached the end of the road."

Prullàs was busily tucking into his vol-au-vent. The director stared vaguely up at the ceiling, then continued: "We began our theatre adventure together when we were students, still almost kids, when it was little more than a game. We were successful, and success blinded us. What we have to do now is call a halt, think about where we are while there's still time, and then give our lives a fresh direction."

"Right now you mean? Just at the moment when the police are accusing me of murder?" Gaudet smiled. "Nobody's accusing you of anything, Carlos," he said patiently. "As I told you before, no-one's going to touch a hair on your head. But it's now, when everything is topsy-turvy, when nothing makes sense, that you have to face up to change; before everything gets back to normal and inertia and routine paralyse us again."

"I can see what you're aiming at, Pepe," Prullàs said; "you're trying to take advantage of my weakness to get me on your side. But don't count on me, Pepe, I don't want to look like Sartre: he's a dwarf and that wife of his scares me to death."

"I didn't expect to convince you," Gaudet said, "but I had to try. A moment ago," he went on, "you mentioned our school. I haven't forgotten it, Carlos: even if I wanted to, I could never forget those years of torment. D'you remember that time when some boys from the fifth year tried to push my head down the lavatory? And you said to me: 'Stand up to them, Pepe, don't let them crush you.' I knew you were right and that in fact in my situation there was nothing to lose by fighting back. But I didn't revolt; I couldn't do it, I was trapped by my mother, by her false, vain, pretentious idea that by sending me to that cursed school she was saving my life. Anyway, Carlos, now it's me saying it to you: Don't let them crush you; leave behind the fantasies trapping you; you've got no obligations to meet; take the risk, and become what you have it in you to be."

"Come down from the clouds, Pepe," Prullàs replied; "all this is nothing more than cheap and inappropriate psycho-analysis. Just tell me what you intend to do, and let's say no more about it."

Gaudet hesitated for a few moments. "What I thought," he said slowly and emphatically, "was that after the opening of 'Arrivederci, pollo!' I might go to Argentina. There's a more open atmosphere there, and despite everything there's more freedom, and in many ways the theatre is more alive. Others have done it and been successful. I'm sure it won't be too hard for me to carve myself a niche. It may even be that there are people who remember my mother . . . "

"Your mother!" Prullàs roared, "if you think anyone remembers her these days, you really are off your head, Pepe. Your mother never was a famous actress; it may be she never even acted, or so much as set foot in a theatre; it may be that in America she earned her living as a waitress in a restaurant, or as a maid in some rich house, or even – I don't mean to offend you – as a streetwalker in Havana, who knows! She made up everything she used to tell us, Pepe; it was innocent enough, but it was all made up."

"Perhaps," Gaudet replied, "but it helped her, and it can help me too. And anyway, don't you think the world we've created is make-believe too? Look, while I was going through my mother's things last night, I found this photo," the director said, pulling an old sepia photograph with gilt edges from his jacket pocket. He handed it to Prullàs, who saw with surprise that it was the portrait of an old military man in dress uniform, with leather straps and a kepi; a sabre hung from his swordbelt, and his jacket was a display case of medals, crosses, rosettes and other insignia testifying to his courage. "He's my maternal great-grandfather," Gaudet explained; "he was a colonel in the infantry, and fought at Tetuán under General Prim; he was in Cuba with Weyler and in the Philippines with Polavieja. He twice fought duels either to defend his own honour or that of a lady, which to him was the same: he was a man of honour and courage, a patriot."

Gaudet fell silent as abruptly as he had started, and sat staring belligerently at his friend. It took Prullàs a few moments to react, then he threw the photo onto the table. "You're driving me mad, Pepe!" he shouted; "I've put up with all your nonsense until now because I can see you're not quite right in the head, but this photo rubbish is the last straw. What could I care if this dummy is your great-grandfather? A photo! How do I know you didn't just buy it from a stall at the San Antonio market? And anyway, what have your ancestors got to do with anything? I couldn't give a damn if your father was Gunga Din. The only thing that matters to me, Pepe, is that you're being a coward."

Gaudet raised his hands then let them drop by his sides with the fierce, exasperated gesture of someone who realises his efforts are in vain. "You didn't understand me, Carlos," he complained. "What I was trying to show you was how much easier it was to be courageous in the past." He got up and left the restaurant without bothering to pick up his ancestor's photo. Prullàs shrugged, muttered something under his breath, and asked the waiter for his next course with studied indifference. The truth was that Gaudet's unexpected behaviour, and the fact that his friend had deserted him in such difficult circumstances, had left him bewildered and hurt. He took little pleasure in the steak and the vanilla ice-cream that completed his meal, and then set off back home annoyed and sullen.

2

"Here you are, Bonifaci, I went into two ironmongers' on my way here, but neither of them had a candlestick: apparently with all the power cuts at the moment, there's been a run on them. In the end I decided to buy this nightlight; it should be just as good if you need it." The doorkeeper unwrapped the parcel and admired the gadget. "You shouldn't have done it, Don Carlos, it's lovely, but it must have been expensive." "Yes, it's a bit expensive, like everything that's imported," Prullàs said, pretending to be serious, "but safety and efficiency are worth paying for." "You're right there!" Bonifaci agreed, putting the light into his coat pocket, and adding: "I'll only use it in an emergency."

Before they reached the stage, the doorkeeper stopped and tugged at Prullàs' sleeve. When he bent towards him, Bonifaci whispered in his ear: "Doña Mariquita gave me a note for you; she asked me to give it you as soon as I saw you, but with the light and everything I forgot." As he said this, he handed Prullàs a folded piece of paper. Prullàs took it, unfolded it and read: "I absolutely must talk to you today. Come to my dressing-room after the rehearsal, and try to make sure no-one sees you. Especially Gaudet." The note wasn't signed, but Prullàs immediately recognised the actress's handwriting. Prullàs waved thank you, and Bonifaci let go of his sleeve, gave a solemn bow, and backed his way along the dark corridor.

ENRIQUE: Cecilia, why are you behaving so oddly? I'm asking you for the last time: let me see what's in that wardrobe.

CECILIA: (*standing in front of the wardrobe*) Don't insist, Enrique; I said no, and I mean no. You mustn't see what's in here.

ENRIQUE: Why not?

CECILIA: Because they're . . . family secrets!

ENRIQUE: So what? I'm your fiancé, Cecilia, but first and foremost I'm a police inspector, and I'm going to find out what's in that blessed wardrobe even if it means I have to use my service weapon.

(ENRIQUE *strides towards the wardrobe, but before he can open it,* CECILIA *clings to him*)

CECILIA: Enrique, my love, listen to me. When you open the wardrobe, you're in for a big surprise. It's Julio's fault, but I can't deny I was his accomplice. We all are. It's family business and you . . . well, you're almost part of the family. Try to understand! The situation had become unbearable . . . the creditors, the debts,

the dishonour, the lobsters . . . just imagine . . . to us
it seemed the only way out, even if it wasn't perhaps
the most honest. Enrique, my little dove, in the name
of all you hold dear, try to understand!
(ENRIQUE *hesitates when he hears this plea, but in the end his
sense of duty proves stronger, and he pulls out his revolver and
flings open the wardrobe door*)
ENRIQUE: Heavens above! What's this I see?
CECILIA: (*covering her face in her hands*) Forgive us,
Enrique! It wasn't my idea!
(*Terrified,* LUISITO *and* THE MAID *come out of the wardrobe,
their hands in the air. They are in their underwear*)
LUISITO: Don't shoo . . . shoo . . . shoot!

Gaudet raised his arm and shouted: "That's fine for today,
thank you!" This signified the end of rehearsals and Prullàs,
who had remained hidden in the wings, took advantage of the
momentary confusion, when the floodlights were going down
and the actors were gathering at the front of the stage to listen
to the director's comments, to cross behind the backdrop
and hide again in the darkness of the corridor leading to the
dressing-rooms. Taking refuge behind dusty and faded flats
from past productions, he saw all the members of the company
go by, tired and silent. Nobody noticed him. I'm like an outcast
who has to hide from his own people, he thought. This unpleasant thought was made still worse when he saw Lilí Villalba.
Oblivious to his presence, she was busy buttoning up the dress
she had taken off for the farcical scene in the wardrobe. Despite
the fact that to comply with the moral norms required of a
theatre she had been wrapped in something more like a house-
coat than lingerie, and despite the comic effect of the scene, the
sight of her had made his head spin. He was constantly longing
to be alone with her again, but for the moment other, more

urgent matters required his attention. For her sake as well as mine, at all costs I have to avoid anyone being able to link the two of us, he told himself; but as soon as this nightmare is over, I'll take her to Palma de Mallorca for a few days, whatever the consequences.

Once the actors had disappeared into their dressing-rooms and the stage-hands had gone, Prullàs came out of his hiding-place and went to Mariquita Pons' room. He knocked gently: "Who's there?" she asked, and when he replied, "Come in," she said, "and lock the door."

The actress was getting changed behind a screen. Prullàs pulled a chair up to the dressing-table and waited. It wasn't long before Mariquita came out from behind the screen, wearing an organdie peignoir with lacy frills. She ignored Prullàs and sat at the dressing-table. She picked up a pot and began to smother a thick white cream on her face. "Bonifaci gave me your message, and here I am," he said.

"Bonifaci is an angel," Mariquita said, finishing her task with measured, careful strokes. "I asked you to come without anyone seeing you because I'd prefer no-one to know what we say." "What's all this about?" Prullàs asked. "About Gaudet," she replied. "I'd rather talk about something else," Prullàs said.

The actress turned towards him on her stool and as she leaned towards him, her face was a rigid mask in which only the anxious eyes seemed to have any life. "Light me a cigarette, would you?" she said. Her mouth was a horizontal gash in the lower half of the mask. Prullàs put a cigarette in the mother-of-pearl holder, placed it in the slit of her mouth, and lit it. "I know you two had a difficult meeting in the Suizo yesterday," she went on. When Prullàs remained stubbornly silent, she blew a stream of smoke up at the ceiling, and added: "The night before last, the police picked him up at his apartment. He was already in bed, but they wouldn't let him get dressed: they

330

frogmarched him in his pyjamas to their headquarters in Via Layetana, and questioned him for more than two hours; they weren't violent, but they didn't beat about the bush either; then they let him go. He had to wander about for quite a while in his pyjamas before he came across a taxi-driver who would risk picking him up looking like that. When he got home, he woke up the porter and asked him to pay the taxi. He didn't have his keys either, but fortunately the porter had a spare set."

"Why didn't he tell me all this instead of showing me a ridiculous photo of a moth-eaten old campaigner?" Prullàs exploded.

Mariquita brought her immobile face close to Prullàs again, and stared at him with round, wide eyes like a snake's. "He didn't say anything in order not to worry you," she said; "he's scared, for himself and for you; he's worried something awful is going to happen to you. I tried to tell him not to worry, but he wouldn't have it. He can't eat or sleep for thinking of you: you know how much he cares for you." "Tell me what the interrogation was like," Prullàs said.

Mariquita turned back to the mirror and began to remove the face cream with a hand towel. "It was nothing," she said indifferently, as if she were no longer interested in the story. "I've told you; they asked him a thousand things about you, your habits, your friends, what you liked, what your vices were . . . things like that. Of course, he played dumb and only gave them vague answers."

"It doesn't matter," Prullàs said, "they must already know everything he could possibly tell them. All that does matter is why they're doing all this. They're trying to scare me, but why?" Mariquita shrugged. "Well anyway," he said, "thanks for the information. And then he asked, apparently à propos of nothing: "Why d'you put so much make-up on just for a rehearsal?"

Mariquita smiled ruefully at her own reflection. "Carlitos

my love, at my age if I didn't make up, I'd look like a chestnut seller," she replied; "that's why I put all the make-up on, and these frills, and spend half my day at the hairdresser's. Also I do it so your little chum Gaudet can get some idea of how I'll look when we open: after all, for now I'm still the leading lady."

"For now?" Prullàs asked. "What d'you mean by that? Have you had a better offer?" "No, and I'm not expecting one either, but there's nothing certain in this world: Gaudet might pack his bags, and you could end up in jail." "You get better every day, Kiki," Prullàs said; "in my next play I'll make you cross-eyed and with a moustache: that way, you won't need any make-up at all."

3

Worried about the ever more confused turn events were taking, but relieved at the actress's revelations about the real motives behind Gaudet's change of heart, Prullàs was on his way home, hoping to relax from all the cares of his day, when suddenly out of the dark near the front door he found himself face to face with the massive brute he had almost come to blows with a few nights earlier at Lilí Villalba's place. All he knew was that the man was a rough, quarrelsome, drunken individual who apparently also happened to be the father of the object of his ardent desires. This last attribute was not, however, sufficient to make Prullàs feel well-disposed or trusting towards him. "What are you doing here," he asked him curtly, "and who gave you my address?"

The brute was wearing a pair of corduroy trousers and a filthy, torn shirt that revealed his hairy body underneath. "Doan you worry yeself," he replied, "no-one gave me the address, and above all twasna the girl, yew doan wanna go thinkin' anythin' loik that about 'er: she's very careful o' things loik tha'. An' as fer me," he sighed, exhaling wine-sodden breath, "all I wanted to do was come 'ere an' present my respects loik, and to ask yer to forgive me wha' I said t'other night." "Good," Prullàs interrupted him, "well, now you've done so and you can be on your way; and I trust this will be the last time you ever set foot in my house." This took a while to sink in. "Don' take it loik tha', Jaysis, yours truly here didna do nothin' to cause yew offence, did he?" he said in a hurt voice.

"Sir," Prullàs cut in firmly, "the fact that I have dealings with your daughter for strictly professional reasons and nothing else does not give you any particular privileges. None! D'you understand? As far as Señorita Lilí Villalba herself is concerned, she knows where and when she can find me if she wishes to talk over anything related to her work. By this I'm trying to tell you, if I hadn't already made myself sufficiently clear, that you have no business being here; so if you do not remove yourself forthwith I'll have no choice but to call the police."

"Well now," Villalba said, obviously unimpressed by this threat, "yeh has to unnerstan, sir, tha' someone loik yours truly here doesna' know wha' to do or how he's meant to behave when he meets wit' fine folk loik yoursel'. I was so scaret before I come here that I went into a bar fer a little drink to gimme some courage loik, an' soon it were two or t'ree, I doan e'en remember, so yeh can see how weak I ham. Now all my best intenshuns have come to nothing, sweet Jaysis, so go on, call the polis; we're old friends, we are. I didna' have a father or a teacher or even a feckin' priest for to teach me the catenchism, oh no, but there was always a poli ready an' willin' to look out fer me, even if I didna' want one. Why just today the girl and meself spent the day in their headquarters, so we did, when we had done nothin' at all. They kept us there so long the poor child nearly missed her rehearsal, so she did, an' that was what

333

most upset her, sir: not all she had to hear, or the way they manhandles her; an' everything to protect you sir, because that girl o' mine has a heart of gold, so she does. An' all the time she would tell them: Oh my God, I mustn't miss my rehearsal! See how much to heart she's taken it." "The police took you in for questioning?" Prullàs said once this outpouring had finished. "Questioned?" the other man laughed. "The polis were tryin' to brainwash us loik a pair o'socks."

Prullàs looked anxiously around him. Luckily at that time of night the porter was no longer on duty, and there was no-one else about. "Let's go up to my apartment," he said, "we can talk more easily there. But try not to shout or swear; decent people live here." "I can tell that' just from lookin' at the furniture," the hairy brute said, casting an appreciative eye over the gilt fittings and the mahogany counter.

When they reached the hall of the apartment, Prullàs pointed to a chair for the other man to sit on. Villalba understood that this was as far as he was going to be allowed to get, and so sat down, not before he had carefully examined the room and nodded with satisfaction at each corner as a mark of respect. Prullàs watched this tomfoolery with a strange mixture of disgust, concern and curiosity. "Tell me how the questioning went," he said when the other's man little ritual was completed.

"Well, I'm sure yeh know what it's loik," he said, "early in the mornin' they comes an' takes us out of our house without so much as a by-your-leave, and as usual they didna' give any explanation of wha' they was up to or pay any attention to the fact that we needs to work, although in the case of yours truly that wasna' so bad, as fer the moment I'm between jobs as it twere, but the girl yes was upset because as yeh know she has her work over at the packagin' loik; they didna' even let her tell them, the bastards, an' of course there was no chance to complain! Yeh know, once I saw a filum wit' that Humprey

Boger and they was arrestin' a tief an' an' he says he does: I'll only talk with my lawyer presen', loik! If he tried that here, it'd be more loik: I'll only talk with my dentist presen', an' that's the truth, 'cos if yeh try any tricks like that yer likely to be eatin' your front teeth before yeh knows what's hit yeh. It's a fine thing in yer American filums, but 'twont work here for a jimmy nobody in this fine country of God an' the Holy Virgin." The man shook his head disconsolately, as if what he had just described was the ultimate failure of a life entirely devoted to the progress of humanity. "But here I am goin' on an' on loik a fuckin' eejit, an' all you wanna know is what they askt us. I'll tell yeh in just two words: they asks the girl if she knew someone by the name of Peliforri, and she sez yes; and did the said man help her out, an' she sez only very occasionally loik and just to be friendly; and if you sir were also helpin' her in the same way, and she says no not at all, (and then they slapped her a bit an' called her all the names under the sun, but she wouldna say anything more); that if she'd ever seen you sir and Peliforri together, and she sez no; that if Peliforri had talkt to her about yeh; if yeh had talkt to her about Peliforri, and so on and so on. And if she was with yeh on the night o' the crime; and she sez no."

Prullàs tried to assess the meaning of all this. "And what did they ask you?" "Yours truly? Nothin', what were they supposed to ask me, when this particular fight has nothin' to do with me? I don't even know wha' they took me in fer . . . if not to see wha' the girl was sayin'."

Prullàs saw a malicious gleam in the other man's eyes: it was obvious that by getting the Villalba father involved, Don Lorenzo Verdugones had something in mind, and that the former had realised as much. "Thank you," Prullàs said, trying to seem calm, "for your account of what happened, but I repeat that I have nothing to do with this case or with your daughter, and still less with you yourself. And now, if there's nothing more, I'd beg you to leave and from now on refrain from any contact with me either here, in the theatre, in the street or in any other place or circumstance. Good night to you."

The hairy brute clambered out of his chair and swayed for a moment until he was properly upright on his shapeless, lop-sided shoes. "I'll be off," he said resignedly, "it's plain that my presence in this house is not welcome. Don't think I don't unnerstand that; the presence of someone loik yours truly in this neighbourhood must be a scandal. An' yeh don't want a scandal, do yeh, Señor Prullàs? As fer me, I know I'm bound to bring scandal with me wherever I goes. I'm loik a wanderin' scandal ever since I come into this world; but not yeh, yeh has a reputation to think of, your own an' that of yer lady wife, yer two children, and for that father-in-law of yours, whose such a fine gennleman and respectred by everyone in society. An' as if that weren't enuff, now I imagine yeh's got to look after the reputation o' that lovely red-headed lady you spent Friday evenin' with in the Hotel Gallardo."

Having delivered this speech, the man looked casually up at the ceiling mouldings and started to whistle quietly to himself. "All right," Prullàs said, trying to keep his anger under control, "what d'you want?"

"Me? Nothin' at all!" the sponger said. "I wouldna dream of it! We're all friends here! I only comes here to tell you your secrets are safe with me, as safe as in the vaults of the Banco España." "Ah, and how much would it cost to keep those vaults shut?" Prullàs asked. "Next to nothin', Señor Prullàs, it's fer yeh to say." "And if I won't give you a penny, what will you do?"

The man smiled indulgently. "Well, I don't know," he admitted, "it's a possibility I hadna thought of, I'm not one to think much, as my poor father used to say, God bless his soul. If yours truly were a thinker loik, he'd go to that wireless and win all their compentitions, wouldn't he now? Come on, Señor Prullàs, don't make this hard: I'm only tryin' to help, I'm no stool pigeon, you can be sure o'that; just to think that your lady wife or your father-in-law or perhaps even the husband of that redhead could be mad with yeh for such a little thing drives me wild. Wild it makes me, just imaginin' it, Señor Prullàs!" "You haven't got any proof," Prullàs said, "you're just fishing in the dark."

The other man smiled again. "I like yeh, Jaysis, I like yeh a lot: you have what it takes, an' I appreciates that. An' it's true too, you're right: I don't have any proof, no photies, no witnesses, nothin' like that; I've only got my word, which isna' worth a fart 'n hell. But if I goes an' sez: we may be a black-mailer and a no-good, but we saw so-an'-so with such-an'-such in this hotel at this time, and you come along and say: no, this son of a bitch is makin' it all up, who're people goin' to believe? Better not put it to the test, wouldn't yeh say? People can be very nasty now, can't they? Especially all those posh types, 'cos they've nothin' better to do, now have they?"

This time it was Prullàs' turn to smile, in spite of himself. "What about Lilí?" he asked after a while; "with Ignacio Vallsigorri dead, she only has me to protect and help her. And if anything happens to me, if for example a scandal ruins my reputation,. what will happen to her career as an actress?"

The hairy brute moved his head from side to side like an ox under a yoke. "Nothin'," he said finally as if summing up his ruminations; "you wouldn't do something like that to the child; you like her a lot, don't you now? I could tell that from your eyes the other night, when you came to my place; the walls in poor people's homes are thinner than ciggie paper, and we can hear everythin', our neighbours' breathin' and every last word that's whispered, every bit of flattery. Let's leave the girl out o' this, Señor Prullàs, this business is between the two o' us, it's a gennleman's agreement. She doesna' even know I came here, and she'd be ashamed if she did know, because she's such a romantic is my girl, like they all is at her age, and she's really hot on yeh. She'd be heartbroken she would if she knew about that redhead, so we'd better make sure she doesna' find out, hadn't we? If yeh doesna' say anything, we won't either. We couldna' care less what yeh gets up to, less said, soonest mended loik. In yer place I'd have done the same, above all with that redhead, she's a real looker. But seein' as how goodlookers are not fer me, I have to find somewhere else to get it, as they say. And as fer the child, she's grown up a beauty an' no mistake, sweet Jaysis; why even yours truly here, who raised her at his own breast loik, why when I see her little arse wagglin' an' those melons o' hers, my prick stands up loik a howitzer." "You're a rogue!" Prullàs shouted.

At this, the hairy brute burst out laughing. "That's a good one!" he said, slapping his stomach. "You've got a young, rich wife, you do the dirty on her with the redhead, then you do the business with my girl as well, and it's me who's the rogue. What school did they teach yeh that catenchism then, Señor Prullàs?"

"O.K. O.K., don't take on so," Prullàs said, alarmed at the other man's shouts. "I'm not takin' anything, bollix, it's yeh who's makin' me mad! What d'you imagine? That the rest of us is here for yeh to trample on? That everythin' you've a mind to do should be free n'easy? Right, what else is a poor girl fer, if not to amuse the rich men's sons, isn't that so? Well no, it isn't right, sweet Jaysis, we're all equal here loik! When yours truly goes to the market and buys a pound o' spuds, he has to pay the price, doesna he? Well if your lordship likes that little spud o' mine, he's got to pay the same as me and keep his trap shut. And if he doesn't want to pay, he'll have to put up wit' the scandal. There's more scandal in the way we live, and nobody lifts a finger to help. There's eight of us at home, crowded into that one room with no windows, with rats, and everyone sick, no food to speak of, no baccy, no dough, nothin'. And seein' the way we're forced to live in suciety, you want us to be honest? Sweet bollixin' Jaysis, it's suciety to blame fer wha' we are. And we'll tell yeh that and anyone else who wants to know, even if the polis locks me up, because you can take away everythin' from a man, but not the right fer him to speak his mind. Down with Franco, long live the revolution!" "Be quiet, be quiet, that's all I need," Prullàs begged him.

Villalba calmed down, and a tense silence followed. "How much?" Prullàs asked. "Five thousand pesetas," the other man said. "You're out of your mind!" Prullàs shouted. Villalba was about to retort when they were interrupted by the ringing of the telephone. Who can it be at this time of night? Prullàs wondered.

They could hear the sound of footsteps on the other side of the thick hall curtain: it was Sebastiana going to answer the phone. Could his faithful maid have heard the denigrating talk with this blackmailer? Prullàs wondered. Out loud, he said: "Leave it, Sebastiana, I'll take it in my study!" Then, pointing to the seat, he said to the brute: "You stay here, nice and quiet," he warned him.

He ran to his study, closed the door and put the chain on it. He picked up the receiver and said: "Yes, who is it?" "Señor Prullàs?" a woman's voice asked. "Yes, it's me, who's calling?" "This is Doctor Maribel," the voice said. "I don't know if you remember me: we met yesterday morning at the Beauty Clinic."

"I remember perfectly, Doctor," Prullàs said, "and I've also learnt you're a radio celebrity." He heard a slight sigh at the far end of the line. "Don't pay any attention . . . and forgive me for ringing at such a late hour." "It isn't late at all," Prullàs replied. "I was just trying to get rid of an annoying visitor. What can

I do for you?"

There was another pause; then Doctor Maribel said firmly: "I've just been brought the test results from the laboratory. I'll hand them over to the police tomorrow morning . . . but I thought you might be interested in seeing them first." "Interested? Me? Yes, of course," Prullàs said, somewhat surprised by her offer. "In that case, if you're not busy, come and fetch me from the Clinic in half an hour. I'll be waiting for you."

Prullàs hung up, opened the study door, and shouted for Sebastiana. When she came up puffing and blowing as though she had just run a long way, he told her to iron his white jacket at once. "You're going out at this time of night?" the maid complained. "What's that to you? Do as I tell you and be quiet, there's a good woman." "Fine," Sebastiana said; "but when you leave, take that beggar in the hall with you." "So much for the chatterbox!" Prullàs said to himself.

He went out onto the balcony, lit a cigarette and smoked looking up at the stars. Then he went in again, stubbed out the cigarette in the ashtray, opened the wall safe, took out a bundle of notes, put it in his pocket and strode to the hall.

"You've taken yer time!" Villalba said; the wait seemed to have undermined his confidence.

"Yes, because this is my home," Prullàs replied disdainfully; "and besides," he added, "something has come up, so let's get our business settled right away, shall we? This is what we're going to do: I'm not going to give it all to you, for several reasons: firstly, because I don't have it, and I couldn't get it quickly without arousing suspicion; secondly, because if I gave it you, instead of spending it wisely, you would waste it all on wine, women and other such nonsense, and a few days later would be back again for more; and thirdly and most importantly, because I don't want to. What I'll do instead is give you three hundred pesetas a month, like a wage. Three hundred a month. But don't get me wrong: this money isn't to buy your silence; it's you I'm buying. From now on you're working for me; it's not a tiring job, in fact you'll hardly have anything to do, but from time to time I'm going to ask a favour of you, and then you'll have to prove your worth. Take it, or leave it."

While the hairy brute stared fixedly at the tip of his bulbous nose as if deep in meditation, Prullàs took the bundle of notes out of his pocket and began to count them out slowly. At the sight of the money, Villalba's last defences crumbled; he stopped pretending, shrugged his shoulders and exclaimed: "What you're doing is distortion, but a poor man can never choose, can he? Hand those notes over!"

"You've made a wise choice," Prullàs said, giving him some of the money. "I'll give you the same again next month, but don't come here for it: from this moment on, I forbid you to come to my home; at no time and for no reason, d'you understand? I'll have your wages delivered each month to your house by a third party."

The hairy brute cleared his throat. "There's a bar next to my place known as Uncle Ciruelo's; you'll find me there most days. If it's all the same to you, I'd prefer you to send the dough there; for no special reason, but if my family finds out . . . you know what I mean."

"I'll do as you say," Prullàs agreed; "and when I need your services, it'll be me who gets in touch with you. For the rest of the time, I don't want to see your ugly face. And remember: if you do anything unwise, or try to cheat me, or if anything happens to me for any reason whatsoever, the game's up for you, and your daughter will never appear in the theatre again. Is all that clear?"

Villalba gave grunts of agreement as he counted the notes

and put them away one by one in his trouser pocket; he took the last two, folded them, and put them in his socks. "You and I," Prullàs said before the other man disappeared down the stairs, "don't know each other, right? We've never met."

4

As Prullàs drew to a halt in front of the beauty clinic, he could make out the slender figure of Doctor Maribel waiting behind the glass door. The attendant removed his cap and held the door open for her to leave. Prullàs got out of the car, walked round it and opened the door. "I hope I didn't keep you waiting," he said.

"Not at all," Doctor Maribel replied, settling into her seat and smoothing down the simple blue-and-white summer dress with big pockets that had replaced her white coat. "I'd only just come down. What with the clinic and the radio advice programme my days seem endless: they could run into one another without time for me to sleep or eat." She spoke hurriedly, and despite her surface calm she could not avoid glancing around furtively in all directions, as if she feared being caught out doing something wrong.

Prullàs set off. "From what you say, I deduce you haven't eaten," he said. "Don't worry about that," she replied; "I normally just have a piece of fruit before I go to bed." "I haven't had dinner either," Prullàs said, "so I'll have to force you to change your diet, if that's all right." "Of course," she replied; "take me wherever you wish."

The garden of La Rosaleda was lit by hundreds of light bulbs strung between the trees. At the far end, in a bandstand decorated with red and yellow lights, a singer and a group of eight musicians in flowery shirts were playing a foxtrot. The *maître* came swerving through the groups of tables towards them. He bent low several times, apologised for not being able to offer them a table closer to the orchestra, then led them to one side, where the waiters were busy setting up a new table they had carried out. The scent of jasmine from the surrounding wall was overpowering. "We're very busy tonight," the *maître* said. "Don't worry, it's a wonderful spot," Prullàs said, slipping a note into the *maître's* hand; "we'll be fine here."

"Well," Doctor Maribel said when the waiters had gone and they could sit down, "if I'd known we were coming here, I'd have put something nicer on." "Don't worry," he said, "your dress is fine and it suits you perfectly." "Thank you. Are you a regular here? I saw they were very courteous to you." "I come from time to time," Prullàs said. "I prefer it to the Cortijo on summer evenings, there's more air. I hope you like it too." "Oh yes, I do," she replied with genuine enthusiasm; "it's a lovely spot; I'd heard of it, but I've never been here . . . D'you make so much from the theatre?" Prullàs smiled at this sudden impulsive question. "No," he replied, "not at all: it's my wife who's rich, not me." Doctor Maribel blushed. "I'm sorry," she murmured; "that was a very indiscreet question." "Not at all," he said; "I admire your frankness. You can ask me whatever you like, as long as I can find out what intrigues me about you." "About me?" she said in a whisper.

The *maître* came up to ask if they were ready to order; the kitchen was about to close because it was so late, he said. Prullàs glanced at the menu. "D'you feel like anything in particular?" he asked her. "No, you choose." Prullàs ordered asparagus salad and sole in white wine, and the *maître* went on his way. "It'll be a while before they serve us," Prullàs said. "Shall we dance?" "I haven't danced for years," she said; "I don't know if I'll remember how." "It's something you never forget;

343

wouldn't you like to?" "Yes, but I get the feeling everyone is looking at us," Doctor Maribel whispered. "That's natural, people come here to look at others and to be seen; but there's nothing wrong with that; don't tell me you're worried about gossip."

They walked across to the dance floor. At first Doctor Maribel danced very stiffly, her head down and her arms held out rigidly; her lack of confidence made her stumble and continually lose the rhythm. Bit by bit she relaxed, her dancing became more spontaneous and her limbs moved more freely. "You see how well you can dance?" Prullàs said.

She raised her face, smiled, then looked down again. "All the women are so smartly dressed," she muttered. "Don't talk nonsense: you run a prosperous business, you're a radio star, and on top of all that, you are an extremely attractive woman. All those snobbish, supercilious women would die if they knew the famous Doctor Maribel were watching them, and yet here you are behaving like a schoolgirl. Why d'you feel so intimidated?" "Don't make fun of me, Señor Prullàs." "I'm not; it's just that I can't make you out. You're very different outside the clinic; yesterday in your office I was almost scared of you." "It must have been the place," she said with a laugh, "or the white coat." "Or your attitude," Prullàs pointed out. "My attitude? Don't tell me that when I'm dressed as a doctor I look like a sergeant." "No, not a sergeant, more like one of those women professors in science fiction films, who are so cold and distant and are glued to their microscope until suddenly they're attacked by some slimy, evil Martian and then discover all their efforts were in vain. Besides," Prullàs said more seriously, "you are much more attractive outside your office." "There can't be much difference," Doctor Maribel protested, "I'm the same wherever I am; I don't follow any of the treatments I recommend, or any of the advice I give; but don't tell anyone."

The music finished and the dancers stopped and clapped half-heartedly. "Shall we go back to our table?" Prullàs asked. "I'd like to dance another one," she said unexpectedly, and when she saw Prullàs' look of surprise, quickly justified herself by adding: "I've been shut up for years in the dust and mud of that blessed clinic."

They danced again, and by the time they returned to their table the first course had been served. There was a bottle of champagne on ice in a bucket by the table, which the *maître* uncorked with a festive explosion; he wrapped the bottle in a white napkin, filled their glasses, put the bottle back on ice, and disappeared again. "I didn't hear you order champagne," the doctor said. "I didn't," Prullàs said; "the *maître* saw you and came to the right conclusion." Doctor Maribel blushed once more. "But I can't allow you to spend so much on me," she protested. "Don't let it upset you," Prullàs replied, "as I said, I'm in a comfortable position, and anyway, it's my business. Are you so keen on saving?" "I have to be," Doctor Maribel said curtly; "I earn enough, but I have a lot of expenses." She drank a sip of champagne, lay back in her chair, closed her eyes and let a feeling of pleasure spread through her body.

After a short while, she opened her eyes, pulled herself upright, looked directly at Prullàs and told him: "I'd better tell you everything: my husband's been in Burgos jail for nine years; I don't know when or if he'll ever get out. To make sure he doesn't go hungry or cold and gets some attention, I have to send him parcels of clothes, food and money all the time. I'm also trying to get his case reviewed in Madrid through lawyers and some influential people. All that costs me a fortune, which is why I'm so much against being spendthrift. But by that I'm not implying any criticism of you, nor any judgment about how you spend your money; on the contrary, I'm touched by your kindness and generosity."

She fell silent as abruptly as she had begun, and stared at Prullàs, trying to assess the effect of her revelations. "Please eat," Prullàs said; "I can't start until you do, and I'm starving."

Doctor Maribel speared a lettuce leaf and lifted it unenthusiastically to her mouth. Her eyes were brimming with tears. Prullàs attacked the salad with a will. "Why did you specialise in female beauty matters?" he asked after a while, hoping to turn the conversation in a less painful direction. "Is it another branch of medicine, like cardiology or pediatrics?"

Doctor Maribel wiped her eyes and smiled. "No," she said, "it isn't, and I'm not even a doctor really; I've no right to use the title. I'll tell you a great secret if you promise not to repeat it: I studied veterinary science, because I love animals; when I was a child, I dreamt of having a farm. Then I got married and abandoned my studies. My husband's family had a pharmacy, so I worked there. After a few years, when my father-in-law was getting old, and with his son – to whom he was going to leave the pharmacy – lost to him, he sold the business. I used the money to open the clinic. As you can see, I'm living on someone else's money too."

"It's not the same," Prullàs replied. "You work, and I'm just a good-for-nothing. But carry on telling me how you've been so successful; I already told you I find you very attractive, but now I'm discovering you're a very interesting person as well." "Thank you," she said, blushing lightly again, as if this praise had affected her more than the compliment paid to her physical attractions; "in fact, I owe my success more to luck than my own merits. You're quite right"; she went on, "female beauty is almost another branch of medicine: it's complicated and full of risks; it was very irresponsible of me to launch into it without any proper knowledge; but providence was kind to me and sent me Doctor Schumann. He's the one who really runs the clinic; I'm just its public face. He's an extraordinary man, a real fount of wisdom, he researches and works tirelessly, and as if all that weren't enough, he wears a monocle." "Doctor Schumann? And with a monocle?" Prullàs laughed. "Where on earth did you find him? In an Erich von Stroheim film? Or is he a Nazi refugee?" "My God, no, he's Jewish," Doctor Maribel replied, and without waiting for any sort of reply from Prullàs, she added in an almost defiant tone: "D'you have anything against the Jews?" "No," Prullàs retorted, "nor against the Nazis either." Disarmed by this unexpected reply, she became less indignant. The waiter cleared their plates, served champagne, and brought their fish.

"Is everything all the same to you, Señor Prullàs," Doctor Maribel asked when the two of them were alone again. "To a certain extent, yes," Prullàs replied after trying the sole, wiping his mouth and drinking a sip of champagne; "but not in the way you imagine. Look, I know it's the fashion nowadays in all civilised countries to blame the Nazis for everything. And of course, if what's said about them is true, they did many terrible, unforgivable things. But they didn't do them because they were Nazis, but because they were brutes. That's what I meant; I'm against the barbarism of what they did, but not against them as Nazis. I'm not against Christians either, even though I'm well aware that in their day they burnt thousands of poor people at the stake after accusing them of witchcraft and other equally unlikely crimes. What's more, if the Inquisition had been in possession of the technical advances of today, they would have killed as many people as they say the Nazis have done. Individual people are relatively good; but nations are without exception violent and bloodthirsty. In order to give free rein to their criminal instincts and at the same time assuage their consciences, they turn to any grandiloquent ideology, any commonplace, outlandish concoction, which they adorn with speeches, anthems and banners. What can we do about it?

Stupidity and brutality are part of human nature, and as such I have to accept them. When it comes down to it, I didn't invent human nature. I just detest theorising. Individuals interest me; ideologies seem to me to be all much of a muchness. Am I committing a great sin if that's how I think? And if I am, who has the authority to condemn or absolve me?"

A glint of curiosity shone briefly in Doctor Maribel's eyes. "I don't know if you're pulling my leg, Señor Prullàs," she said at length. "You're a genius at parody and ingenious puzzles, but I prefer to take you seriously, and so I'll take the risk of telling you what I think: your position wouldn't seem so bad to me if it were at all tenable; but in the world we live in, no-one will let you get away with it. No-one can spend their life swimming in midstream, not even you. I'm not saying that anyone will force you to change, just that the way things are, you'll be forced to choose between one ideology or another. You're mistaken if you think you're just an individual: nobody is. We are what we represent, what the past has made of us. Whether we like it or not, we have inherited hatred and injustice; we are the heirs of a history we did not make, but the fruits of which we have to pick." She paused for a moment, took a deep breath of the jasmine, and smiled. "I'm sorry," she said, "I got carried away without realising it; I never drink champagne." "Don't worry," Prullàs replied, "you didn't say anything ridiculous; but d'you really believe we can't live without adopting an ideology, even if we don't believe in any of them?" "Yes, Señor Prullàs, that's what I think," she said. "And does yours prevent you calling me Carlos?" he asked. "No, but my experience warns me against it," she replied.

Seeing their empty plates, the waiter came to clear them away, and the *maître* came over to ask if they would like a dessert. Prullàs ordered an ice-cream; Doctor Maribel, a slice of pineapple and cream. As soon as the *maître* had gone, she asked

Prullàs: "Let's dance again; I shouldn't be so forward, but I'm dying to try." And on the dance floor, à propos of nothing, as if she were suddenly and without thinking putting a silent soliloquy into words, she said: "No-one can live forever with open wounds." She fell silent, then asked: "Am I wrong?" "I don't know," Prullàs said, "I don't have an advice programme. To me, everything you do seems wonderful, but I'm a poor judge, as I've often found out." "My advice programme isn't a court," she replied; "I don't judge the people who ask my advice, I just try to understand them." "It's the same," Prullàs said; "understanding and judging are the same thing." "Then he changed his tone and asked: "By the way, where did the idea for the radio programme come from?"

"It was the radio station that suggested it. They were looking for someone to compete with a similar programme on another station, and somehow they got hold of my name. Now the two programmes co-exist just fine: mine is on in the morning, and the other at seven in the evening. Of course," she went on, "it was the money that led me to accept the idea, but I must say that by now I'm also rather proud of what I do. I'm saying that without boasting or false modesty. I don't think my advice has ever brought anyone happiness, but I do think it's saved a few of my listeners from unhappiness. I've quite often been able to sort out trivial problems that could have led to great trouble. Once a listener wrote to tell me that thanks to my tips on how to make a béchamel sauce without lumps in it, she had resolved a crisis in her marriage; my recipe, she said, had saved a relationship that had been on the point of collapse. I can see you're doubtful about it. Don't you believe me?"

"No," Prullàs admitted. "I don't believe you or that grateful listener. Unfortunately, things are more complicated than you're trying to suggest. Not even someone as superficial as I am would believe his emotional stability depended on a sauce.

I'd take advantage of a badly-made sauce to give vent to my feelings and my bad temper, but if anyone managed to correct that particular fault, I'd simply look for another trifling excuse. In the end, the result would be the same. You told me a few moments ago that my attitude seemed frivolous to you; well, now it's you who seem frivolous to me; frivolous and smug. Excuse me for my lack of tact, but I think you're far too intelligent to fall for that kind of thing. The explanation about money is less pretty, but it rings truer."

Doctor Maribel responded by dropping her head on his shoulder. At first Prullàs was worried he might have offended her with his straight-talking, but there seemed nothing false about her surrender to him, and so he decided to carry on dancing in silence.

After a while, Doctor Maribel suddenly clung more closely to him, raised her head, and whispered in his ear: "Is it true you killed Ignacio Vallsigorri?" Her question brought him up with a jolt. She laughed out loud. "Had you forgotten the real reason for us being here?" "I preferred the new direction we were taking," Prullàs said; "you're very vengeful." "I never said I was a saint," she replied, "and you haven't answered my question." "I didn't think it was serious," he said; "you're not the sort of person to dance with a murderer." "Perhaps I am, perhaps not," Doctor Maribel said. "D'you know who my favourite actors are? Basil Rathbone and Dan Duryea." "Doctor Maribel," Prullàs said, "at stake are my freedom, my honour, the chance to go on working, perhaps even my life itself, as well as the future prosperity or ruin of my family and other persons who depend on me to a greater or lesser degree; I can't believe that faced with such a difficult situation I am simply a spur to your fantasies or a game: is that how you treat your poor listeners?" Doctor Maribel pulled away from him, amused but slightly ashamed. "Let's go and sit down and make it up, shall we?" she said. She had completely regained her self-possession, and was once more the practical, independent-minded woman; but the secret pact established between them thanks to the spell of the music, the champagne and the scent of the flowers had been broken once and for all.

"Anyway," Doctor Maribel said when they had sat down again, "it doesn't matter what I think, because I have no authority. Don Lorenzo Verdugones does, though, and lots of it, and he thinks you're guilty. At least, that's what his assistant told me, a gloomy young fellow called Sigüenza. He's a sullen, timid, bachelor sort; he can't have much of a love life. He often comes to the beauty clinic on any kind of official excuse, and stays peeping about the place in case he's lucky enough to set his eyes on someone half-dressed. He's never seen a thing, but that doesn't stop him. The other day he turned up early, like he usually does, and while he was waiting for you and his boss, either to make himself appear important or simply to kill time, he told us all what had happened. Apparently there's evidence that you killed Ignacio Vallsigorri. Not enough to prove it, but enough to convince Don Lorenzo Verdugones that you're guilty. Since I didn't know you when Sigüenza told me all this, I didn't pay too much attention to what he was saying, and I didn't try to get any more details out of him. I don't know what the evidence is: perhaps there was an eye-witness, perhaps a letter or other compromising document; whatever it is, they seem to think it is crucial."

"Oh come now, Doctor Maribel," Prullàs cut in, "you must be joking! First, there can't be any such evidence, because I didn't kill anyone; I don't have any motive for doing so, nor would I do it if I had. Secondly, if Don Lorenzo has this crucial evidence, why hasn't he had me arrested?"

Doctor Maribel was enjoying both her slice of pineapple and her companion's discomfort. "I don't know," she replied, "but

I can think of several logical reasons. First of all, you're well-known and well-connected. Your arrest would cause a great commotion, and Don Lorenzo Verdugones' main function here is to promote peace and social harmony. He won't make a move until he's got cast-iron proof; and while he's waiting, he can use the excuse of your collaborating with him to keep you under close scrutiny at all times. It's a good plan. Yet I think that before we get into all these kinds of considerations, you should ask yourself why Don Lorenzo Verdugones has personally taken control of a simple murder case that he could just as well have left to the police detectives. Ignacio Vallsigorri was not such an important man and, without wishing to offend, neither are you."

"Go on," Prullàs said. "I don't know anything more," she replied; "but I don't need to turn to the wisdom of Doctor Maribel on the radio to guess that Don Lorenzo Verdugones suspects that Vallsigorri's murder forms part of a more complex affair in which more people are involved than the person who actually committed the crime; these could be important people from Barcelona; there could be endless ramifications, even a real plot perhaps. You know what the government high-ups think of the Catalans; no sooner do they arrive here than everyone closes ranks against them, and they interpret it as the symptom of a plot hatched specially against them or against what they think they represent or even incarnate: the political system, the motherland, an ideal, whatever."

"That really is the limit!" Prullàs exclaimed. "So now I'm a representative of treacherous Catalonia! It would have to be me, wouldn't it?" "Don't get so worked up," she said; "after all, I don't know if what I've just been telling you is true or not. They are only my conjectures based on more conjectures that Sigüenza was making, and all he has heard are rumours, and we don't know how intelligent he is anyway. But then again, if what I've just told you turns out to be true and isn't simply my error of judgment, then you really are in a tight spot, to put it mildly."

She had made short work of the pineapple, left her fork and spoon on her plate, wiped her lips with the napkin and stretched out her hand to reach for Prullàs' packet of cigarettes and his lighter, but at the last moment, she changed direction and covered his hand in hers. "Don't be angry with me," she murmured, turning to look at the garden as if she were trying to distance herself from the gesture she had made, or to attribute it to her hands rather than to any real decision on her part. "I'd like to help you, but I can't. My position as as weak as yours, if not more so. By calling you tonight, and by coming here with you, I've seriously compromised my husband's future and my own. Men like Don Lorenzo Verdugones can't bear to see a woman in my situation not only survive but prosper to a certain extent without debasing themselves. He loathes me, and wouldn't miss any chance to get me sacked from the radio or to have the beauty clinic closed down. I'm not saying this," she went on hastily, "to win your gratitude in any way; it was my idea to phone you; you didn't force me to come here, and in fact I'm very grateful to you: this evening has given me the only moments of happiness and pleasure I've experienced in many years." She drew her hand away, opened her hand-bag, took out her lipstick and started restoring the colour she had lost from her lips on the napkin throughout their meal. "It's very late," she added, "let's go."

Prullàs asked for the bill, paid it, and then the two of them left the restaurant, followed by the admiring gazes of the other diners. Doctor Maribel lived in a modern building in Calle Floridablanca not far from the beauty clinic. They did not speak during the lengthy journey but, contrary to Prullàs' expectations, she seemed in no hurry to leave the car when he pulled up outside her house. He switched off the lights and the engine and lit a cigarette. The church clock of Nuestra Señora del Carmen struck two. There was no-one about, and the sound of the bells echoed around the walls of the buildings for some time.

"The police," she suddenly said, "have discovered the restaurant where Vallsigorri dined on the night of the crime. He was on his own, and left shortly before ten. As for us, we still haven't identified most of the traces we found on the dead man's clothes, but the scent came from a French perfume called *Arpège.* If you can discover the woman who was wearing that perfume, you'll have taken an important step towards solving the mystery. I couldn't explain why, but that's my intuition." "D'you think a woman killed Ignacio Vallsigorri?" Prullàs asked. "It could be," she replied; "I'm no detective, and all my cases are far less serious; but if you want my opinion, I doubt it." "Why?" Prullàs asked again. "Because that fellow was a Don Juan, and they only attract stupid women. And stupid women don't kill," Doctor Maribel said in a low but resolute voice. "So you think that an intelligent woman could never fall for a Don Juan, Doctor Maribel?" Prullàs wanted to know.

"That's what I prefer to believe," she said; "I detest Don Juans. As you can imagine, in my situation I've had to deal with a lot of them, so I know them well; they're despicable creatures. They're only interested in conquest in the military sense of the term. To them, women are the enemy they have to defeat, by stealth, by force, or by whatever means they can. Their only aim is to humiliate and denigrate women. If they succeed, they boast about it in public; if they fail, they keep quiet and try to get revenge by the most underhanded and cruel methods. At first," she said after a pause and with obvious effort, "I thought you were a typical Don Juan. I was wrong, and I feel I should tell you so."

In the distance, they heard the nightwatchman striking the pavement with his staff. Doctor Maribel broke off and instinctively ducked down. Then she gave Prullàs a sad smile. "Please don't get out of the car," she said, "I don't want anyone to see me with a man at this time of night." She got out, ran to her front doorway, opened it with quick, precise movements and then disappeared into the dark passageway.

Prullàs finished his cigarette outside the closed door, and, when he realised it was not going to open again, started the car and went home. When he got to his apartment, he spent his time looking everywhere for the bottle of *Arpège* that Poveda had sold him, but even though he went through all his drawers, wardrobes, and coat pockets, he couldn't find it anywhere. He remembered buying it from the blackmarketeer at an exorbitant price and then taking it to Masnou with the intention of giving it to Martita; he also recalled he had lost it that same night in Marichuli Mercadal's garden: tiny details that now seemed to him remote and innocent. What then? She had found it and given it back to him the next day; he had tried to offer it to her as a gift, but she had refused – yet had she really returned it, or kept it in the end? He couldn't remember exactly. In all likelihood, he had got the perfume bottle back, yet he couldn't remember giving it to Martita afterwards, perhaps because he felt slightly guilty about it. What if he had offered it to Lilí Villalba during their one and only meeting at the Hotel Gallardo? The memory of that meeting still made his head spin: he couldn't recall the hours spent in the arms of that daring and accommodating young woman without getting hot and bothered.

Day was dawning by the time he gave up his search: the perfume bottle was nowhere to be found, and he was so tired his thoughts were completely confused. He went to bed, but sleep wouldn't come: he felt he was swept up in a maelstrom of strange ideas. Half asleep, he had a series of exhausting night-mares. In the end, he struggled out of bed, staggered off to the bathroom, stuck his head under the washbasin tap and let the water pour over his hair, face, neck and back; then, with it still streaming down him, he went out onto the balcony. The pale light of dawn crept over the flat roofs of the city, wisps of mist were rising from the damp streets, and the first house-martins had begun wheeling in the thin air. A lamplighter wearing rope sandals was going round extinguishing each gas jet. Prullàs went back to bed with little hope of finding any rest, but at once, without realising it, fell fast asleep.

5

When he awoke it was late afternoon. Sebastiana had not wanted to disturb him. "I heard you rummaging around in the early hours and thought it was better to let you rest," she said. "What shall I get you: breakfast, lunch, or tea?"

"I don't want anything," Prullàs said. "Don't even think it!" the maid said. "You're going to have some slices of bread with tomato and ham right now, and then we can talk." She sighed and added: "Oh, sir, it's always a bad sign when you don't want to eat. I reckon you work too much, and in this hot weather too! Why don't you spend a couple of weeks in the country with the mistress and the children? They must be dying to see you!"

Prullàs cut off Sebastiana's well-intentioned flow of words with a gesture. "Has anyone come to the door or phoned while I was asleep?" he asked. "In my dreams I thought I could hear the phone ringing." "I bet you did; it didn't stop all morning. First a man was calling to speak to you. I told him you weren't here, but he went on insisting. He called three times at least."

"Did he say who he was and what he wanted?" "No, sir; I did ask him, as you tell me to do, but he said he would only speak to you in person." "Was it Poveda?" "I couldn't rightly say, sir; if it was, it didn't sound like him; it sounded to me like someone who didn't want to be recognised and disguised his voice with a handkerchief." "You've been watching too many films," Prullàs groaned. "Was there anything else?"

"There was a parcel for you," Sebastiana said. "I'll go and fetch it."

A few moments later she came back with a small packet. "A messenger brought it around eleven," she said. Prullàs took it to his study, shut himself in, and eagerly unwrapped it, thinking it might contain something to shed light on his case. In novels, detectives often received very useful anonymous packages: things sent by reluctant witnesses who wanted to remain out of the spotlight to avoid reprisals. Until now everybody had been against him, he thought; it was about time he got some help. But the parcel only contained a used copy of *The Impatient Divine* by José María Pemán, together with a note: "Following on from yesterday morning's pleasant and instructive conversation, I am taking the liberty of sending you this work by our great poet and playwright, in the hope that by reading it you may feel drawn to consider a kind of theatre for which you could, and perhaps should, use the boundless gifts of imagination and talent given you by God before Whom, sooner or later, you will be called to account. Yours affectionately in Christ, Emilio Porras, S. J."

He put the book away in a drawer, wrote some words of thanks to the Reverend Father on a visiting card, slipped it into an envelope, put a stamp on it, and then dropped it into his jacket pocket. He asked Sebastiana to make him a milky coffee and some slices of toast with butter and jam. "I'm going out," he said. "If that fellow phones again, tell him I'll be back in late evening. You can also tell him from me that anyone who refuses to give their name is either an idiot or a rogue or both."

Then he phoned Mariquita Pons. "Kiki, did you get Poveda's details for me as I asked?" "I've tried, but had no success. He always calls or turns up without warning, so nobody has ever bothered to find out where he lives or whether he has a phone. In the afternoons, he goes round all the cafés: the Granja Royal, the Salon Rosa, the Gambrinus, and so on; you might find him there." "Kiki, that's like finding a needle in a haystack!"

He hung up and thought for a while. Then he dialled another number. Sigüenza answered. "Don Lorenzo is out and didn't say when he'll be back; is there anything I can do for you, Señor Prullàs?" "Well, yes, in fact, all I need is some information, and I'm sure you can give it me." The obsequious official hesitated, then said: "At your service as ever, Señor Prullàs." "I'd like to get in touch with Poveda as soon as possible." "The black-marketeer?" Sigüenza asked. "Is there another one?" Prullàs replied. "Hold on, I'll see if by any chance . . ."

It proved quite difficult for him to reach Poveda's apartment by car. It was in the lower part of Calle Aragón, which had been dug up in several sections. The City Council, in order to lessen the inconvenience, usually took advantage of the summer months when there was less traffic to carry out this work; but the work inevitably dragged on into the autumn and even well into the wet, unpleasant months of winter. A quick look at the workmen was enough to explain why things took so long: one was tying his shoelaces, another was rolling a cigarette sitting on the cement-mixer, and a third was eating a huge hunk of bread in the shade of their hut. Since the real aim of these repairs was to give work to the unemployed, and the pay they received was derisory, nobody cared how well they worked. So whole neighbourhoods were left to struggle on as best they could; for almost a year they were littered with piles of rubble that made life difficult for both motorists and pedestrians, and everyone was at the mercy of the weather: if it rained heavily, the streets became a mudbath; if there was a little rain, weeds sprouted between all the cobblestones; and if it was dry, the wind raised clouds of dust that got into balconies and apartments and brought the housewives to despair.

Poveda lived in an old, soot-covered building with narrow balconies. The only sign of life in the porter's lodge was a mangy cat asleep in the empty chair. Prullàs climbed the stairs and rang Poveda's bell. From inside he heard a well-known voice: "I'll go, mamma!"

The door opened an inch or two, then Poveda jumped back in alarm. "Don Carlos!" "Poveda, I have to talk to you and I didn't know where else to find you. Can I come in?" He could see a tiny woman feeling her way along the corridor, her arms outstretched. "Who's there, son?" "A friend, mamma, don't worry," Poveda replied in a tremulous voice. The woman had reached the hall where the two men stood, and was stroking the air, trying to touch her son. "Why don't you ask him in?" "Yes, mamma, I was just about to do that," Poveda said; and then, to Prullàs he added apologetically: "As you know, my mother is slightly blind." "I'm sorry," Prullàs said. "Oh, you can't imagine how well she gets on, don't you, mamma?" "My son never brings friends home," the blind woman lamented; "it's obvious he's ashamed of having an invalid for a mother." "Goodness, mamma, what a thing to say!" Poveda complained, more pained than angry.

As Prullàs' eyes got used to the gloom in the hall and corridor, he realised Poveda was wearing a pair of striped pyjamas which made him look like a comic-strip jailbird. "Your son has always spoken of you with great affection," Prullàs told the blind woman. A gleam of gratitude shone in Poveda's eyes.

"Come in, Don Carlos, and forgive the untidiness; mother's right, we never have visitors. This way, please."

The air in the apartment was stale and stuffy. A disgusting smell of vinegar hung everywhere. At the end of a long, narrow corridor there was an equally gloomy dining-room. Poveda switched the light on, and a dim bulb shone from the ceiling. "We always keep the shutters closed in here during the daytime because the sun shines straight in; I'm always in my room, and having light or not makes no difference to my poor mother," Poveda explained.

He took another bulb out of the sideboard and screwed it into an empty socket. "When there aren't any visitors I take it out to save on electricity," he said; "we have to try to live within our limited means."

Prullàs was examining the flaking walls and rough furniture: a pine table, dresser and sideboard, and some paper roses in a clay vase. Presiding over this gloomy room from a set of shelves was a photograph of the Head of State dressed as Admiral of the Fleet. "Yes," Poveda said, swelling with pride, "some years ago I sent some heartfelt verses to the Pardo palace, and to show his gratitude he sent me his portrait. But do sit down, Don Carlos, my house is your house."

Prullàs sat on a broken-backed chair. "From the prices you charge us, I thought you must be rolling in it, Poveda," he said. The blackmarketeer spread his hands dramatically. "Oh, Don Carlos, you only say that because you don't know how complicated the market can be! You'd be amazed if you knew how expensive the goods I buy are; I have to pay out a lot just to make a modest living; I have to work with ridiculous profit margins and I can never guarantee I'll place everything. It's ruining me, Don Carlos!"

Prullàs agreed, and added: "And of course every now and again you have to give the authorities their share so they turn a

blind eye, don't you?" "Not at all, Don Carlos!" the other
man hastened to reply. "The authorities of our New Spain are
transparently honest!" "And does the same apply to Don
Lorenzo Verdugones?" The blood drained from the blackmarketeer's face. "I am very small fry, and Don Lorenzo has
always been generous towards me," he muttered. "And you're
even more generous in return, aren't you, Poveda?" Prullàs
said, raising his voice. "Don't lie to me."

"Excuse me a moment, Don Carlos," Poveda whispered;
then, out loud, he said to his mother, who was still following
their conversation closely from the threshold of the room:
"Mamma, why don't you go into the kitchen and start washing
the dishes? I'll be along in a minute to put them in the racks.
She finds that a bit difficult because of her problem," he
explained, speaking to Prullàs once more.

The blind woman edged her way back along the corridor
and Poveda switched on the radio. After the valves warmed
up, a soupy tune could be heard in a storm of crackling interference. "I prefer my dear mother not to hear us," he said,
sitting at the table, "and you know what sharp hearing blind
people have . . . Now, where were we, Don Carlos?"

Prullàs didn't know how best to intimidate someone for
whom he felt a mixture of pity and contempt, but not dislike.
"You find your way into everyone's homes," he said with
feigned irritation; "you go to all the parties, and then you tell
Verdugones what you've heard, isn't that right?" Poveda started
to snivel: he was an easy catch. "I've never harmed anyone,
Don Carlos, least of all you, you're like a father to me!" Prullàs'
anger dissolved in the face of the blackmarketeer's spinelessness.
"Let's forget it, Poveda," he said; "I've got nothing against you:
we all have to live. All I want to know is what Don Lorenzo
Verdugones has been up to recently."

The blackmarketeer wrung his hands; sweat threatened to

dislodge his false moustache. "He doesn't explain anything to me, Don Carlos, as you can imagine; I'm no more than a humble pawn." "Last weekend the Civil Guard was out searching on the Costa Brava, Poveda. What were they looking for?" "I don't know, Don Carlos, nobody owes me any explanations; all I do is repeat what I hear, and then Don Lorenzo draws his own conclusions. I'm just a pawn in this chess game!"

"Poveda, don't make me lose my patience!"

The blackmarketeer leapt back, taking his chair with him. "Don't get angry with me," he groaned; "I only listen to bits and pieces, or rather, to loose ends. I don't have any idea of the whole picture, Don Carlos. But . . . " he added quickly when he saw that Prullàs was about to rise from his chair: "I've heard a rumour that they're worried about a plot." "A plot?" "As I say, it's only rumours; rumours and speculation, but there must be something to it; after all, there's no smoke without fire." "A plot!" Prullàs said again; "Poveda, that's strong stuff!" "Oh, Don Carlos, people are ungrateful and soon forget how much we owe him!" Poveda said, pointing to the great leader's portrait on its shelf. "What kind of plot?"

The howls and whistles from the radio made Poveda's hesitant mumbling difficult to grasp. Prullàs stood up and tried to tune the set in properly. "What an awful radio!" he said exasperatedly. "A few months ago, you were trying to sell me a wonderful Marconi: couldn't you have kept it for yourself? Or for your mother at least! A radio set that works isn't much to ask for a poor blind woman, is it?"

"Not so loud, Don Carlos, please!" "What kind of plot, Poveda?" Rolling up his eyes and covering his face with his hands, the blackmarketeer mumbled: "Early this summer various monarchist and socialist groups met in San Juan de Luz; just imagine, only a short distance from where the Government of Spain takes its vacations!" "What for, Poveda?" The

362

blackmarketeer sighed a deep sigh. "The details go beyond my incompetence," he said, "but they say there are some high-ranking officers in league with the king in Estoril. They want to set the demons loose on us again, Don Carlos!"

There was a sudden crash of broken plates from the kitchen. "What's wrong, mamma?" "Nothing, son, I dropped a tray, that's all!" "Don't worry, mamma, just be careful you don't cut yourself!"

"Poveda, if you help me I'll buy you a whole new plexiglass service," Prullàs said; "do it for her." "Don't force me, Don Carlos, it's a serious business: heads will roll!" "But not yours, Poveda; none of this will leave these four walls; and a bit of money never did anyone any harm." This new twist in the conversation seemed to be to the blackmarketeer's liking. "Whatever you say, Don Carlos." "Does Vallsigorri's death have anything to do with this? Was he linked to the plot? Did they kill him to keep him silent?"

Poveda stood up and began to walk around the room. "They're only rumours, Don Carlos, rumours and speculation; but a lot of people are mixed up in it." "Who, apart from military people?" "Important people, Don Carlos." "Bankers? Industrialists?" "Yes, and others too." "Priests?" "Don Carlos, wherever there's rumours there are bound to be cassocks." "I want names, Poveda, names!"

The blackmarketeer stopped pacing and threw his hands up. "That's asking too much!" "Poveda, don't leave me in the lurch like this!" "They're only rumours and speculation!" "Poveda, I don't want to have to punch you!"

When he heard this, Poveda flung himself on the sideboard, opened a drawer, pulled out a revolver, and lifted it to his temple. "Don Carlos, you're driving me to a fatal deed!" he shouted, staring straight at the other man.

"Poveda, put that thing back and come and sit down again!"

Prullàs roared at him, "who are you trying to impress? Anyone can see from a mile away it's a toy gun!" "It's not, Don Carlos! It's a nine-millimeter Star made in Eibar and it's loaded." "All the more reason not to play around with it then, Poveda!" "I'm not playing, Don Carlos," the blackmarketeer retorted, his face suddenly turning as red as a lobster. "I may not know how to fight, but at the hour of truth my hand will not tremble," he announced. "I'm a poet, Don Carlos, and I'll be happy to meet my end like Don José María de Espronceda!"

"Don't talk such nonsense," Prullàs replied. "You're not a poet or anything like one; you're a second-rate smuggler, a police informer; in short, a scoundrel. So put that pistol down: you know it's the devil who loads the bullets. If there's an accident, your mother will be sent straight to a home, and I'll have no American tobacco. And the poet suicide was Larra, not Espronceda."

Poveda put the gun back in the drawer, locked it and wiped the sweat from his face and neck with a yellowing handkerchief. "What's the matter, son?" his mother asked from the dining-room doorway. Neither of them had heard her approach. "Nothing's the matter, Señora," Prullàs said. "Your son and I have had an amicable disagreement; it happens every day." He stood up, took the blind woman by the arm, and guided her to the chair he had just vacated. "Here, sit down," he said. "I was just leaving."

On the landing, Poveda said: "Not a word of this to anyone, Don Carlos; our lives are at stake." He had calmed down, and talked with the relaxed voice of someone who knows he's finally out of danger. Prullàs realised he wouldn't get anything more out of him. "Of course not," he said.

The heated argument had given him an appetite. He parked his car outside the Puñalada, found a table on the terrace, which was almost deserted at this time of day, and ordered risotto, roast beef and a carafe of chilled white wine. After that, he went inside the restaurant and phoned Mariquita Pons. The celebrated actress answered at once, as if she had been sitting waiting anxiously for just such a call. "Carlos, at last you've phoned! I've been waiting hours, where did you get to?" "To Poveda's," he replied. "Has something happened?" "It certainly has! But I can't talk about it on the 'phone; come to my place straightaway." "All right," Prullàs said. "I've just ordered a bite to eat; I'll finish it in no time, and be right with you."

When he reached his table, the first course was waiting for him. A waiter stood guard over his table, while a beggar at the far end of the terrace could not take his eyes off Prullàs' plate. Prullàs gave the waiter a few coins for the beggar, who walked away, and Prullàs, free from his embarrassing presence, unfolded the napkin, picked up his knife and fork, and enjoyed his meal under the loving shade of the trees.

There was a very tense atmosphere in Mariquita Pons' apartment. Prullàs was shown rapidly into the living-room, where the actress was waiting for him. "Would you like coffee, Señora?" "No, Carmen, thank you very much." "Tea, perhaps?" "No, Carmen." "A cool drink then?" The maid was sent off with a flea in her ear. "Be off with you, you numbskull! You're not needed here!" As soon as the poor girl had left, Mariquita explained to Prullàs: "She can't take her eyes off you since she first saw you, and every time you come here, she loses her head." "I'm very flattered," Prullàs said, "but we can talk of that some other time; for now, tell me what's happened."

Before she began, Mariquita made sure all the doors were shut. "This morning," she said, "Don Lorenzo Verdugones suddenly appeared here out of the blue." "What was he after?" Prullàs asked; "he can't have expected to find me at your place;

I phoned Sigüenza this morning myself and told him exactly what I was doing." Mariquita cut him short: "Don't be so big-headed, Carlos: it wasn't you he was looking for, it was my husband. And you can't imagine how furious he was when I told him Miguel had gone to Madrid." "Aha, so the circle of suspects is getting wider!" Prullàs laughed. "Don't joke about it," the actress chided him. "I'm not, Kiki; I know how things stand, and there's nothing funny about it; but I can't help taking a perverse pleasure in seeing the person who a week ago was giving me advice has got problems himself now. Did Don Lorenzo Verdugones say anything to back up his suspicions?"

Mariquita Pons sighed. "No, nothing; he simply got angry and told his assistant to get in touch with security headquarters; apparently he's going to mobilise all the police in Spain to capture poor Miguel. I told him it would be much easier just to go to his hotel: he always stays at the Palace. But Don Lorenzo Verdugones was acting as if Miguel were Public Enemy Number One." "Don't pay him any attention: he was just trying to impress you." "Well, he succeeded."

"D'you know if Miguel is mixed up in politics at all?" Prullàs wanted to know. "No," she replied. "No, he's not mixed up in it, or no, you don't know?" "Both: I mean, I've never heard him say anything about it." "Kiki, I don't want to pry into your private lives, but if Miguel was involved in something danger-ous, would he tell you?"

The actress thought this over. "I guess not," she said finally. "Well, it's natural for him to want to spare you any worry," Prullàs said gallantly. "More likely he doesn't feel he can count on me for anything," she replied. She lit a cigarette and began to smoke in a leisurely fashion, staring up at the ceiling mouldings. "I don't hold it against him," she said after a while. "I've always tried very hard to show I'm independent, and he probably took that distance as a sign that I was indifferent towards him. We actresses are naturally very self-centred, and some of us can be a bit heartless." "But you're not like that, Kiki!" Prullàs protested.

She received this protestation with a cold silence. "Why did you ask about any political activities Miguel might have been involved in? D'you really think my husband is a subversive?" Prullàs laughed. "Not one of those who goes up into the mountains with a rifle and a couple of cartridge belts like Pedro Armendáriz," he said. "What sort, then?" "My dear Kiki," he said, "you're old enough now to be aware of these things: in Spain, there are some people who are against the regime; people who would prefer to see the monarchy restored . . . or any other system less *sui generis* than the current one. If all the countries of the world agree on not letting us into the United Nations, there must be some reason for it." "Well, I can assure you Miguel doesn't give a fig for the United Nations," Mariquita said. "But sweetheart, Miguel spends his life coming and going from here to Madrid," Prullàs went on patiently; "perhaps it's not only business and chasing after skirts that takes him to the capital, as you suggested the other day. Perhaps without us knowing it, he's acting as a go-between." "A go-between," she repeated doubtfully, as if this was the first time she had ever heard the word.

Prullàs decided to change tack. "What were relations like between your husband and Ignacio Vallsigorri?" "Fine," she said. "Miguel and Vallsigorri had done some business together a few years earlier. I don't know what kind of business; I only remember hearing some snatches of conversation, but I didn't pay much attention. Vallsigorri used to come here quite frequently, but he and Miguel used to shut themselves up in the study and talk about their own affairs for hours. Sometimes I heard them shouting, but I never thought they were violent arguments, more like disagreements, which seem to me perfectly normal when decisions, risks – in short, money – are at stake. About a year or a little less ago, this business relation came to an end, without any fights or recriminations. Miguel never said what had happened, and I didn't ask. Vallsigorri stopped coming here. To tell you the truth, they had never been friends in the sense of going to football matches or bull-fights together, or going to the same social events. That didn't mean they got on badly, quite the contrary; even after their business relationship ended, whenever they met at a gathering somewhere they would greet each other like old friends, and chat and laugh together. I myself never knew Vallsigorri very well, despite his disinterested passion for the theatre and young actresses." "Did you tell Don Lorenzo Verdugones all this?" "More or less," she said. "When is your husband due back from Madrid?" "In mid-week, if the Civil Guard doesn't bring him back earlier in a chain-gang." "Don't worry, Kiki," Prullàs said to reassure her; "it'll all blow over: it's nothing really. Anyway, I'll talk to Don Lorenzo Verdugones and try to find out what he's thinking. As soon as I know anything, I'll call you."

Mariquita Pons accompanied Prullàs to the door. He was in a hurry to fulfil his promise, but she kept him in the hallway for no apparent reason, as if she wanted to comment on some-thing that had nothing to do with what they had just been discussing, but couldn't bring herself to because it did not seem appropriate or convenient. Prullàs, who had noted this kind of indecision in the actress before, waited for a while but then, seeing that the situation could go on forever, he said: "It's getting late, Kiki, I have to go." "Thanks for everything, Carlos," she whispered. "Think nothing of it." "Who told you all that, all about the plot and the United Nations and so on?" "Poveda," said Prullàs.

Mariquita Pons stared down at her hands. "Don't believe a word he says; a fortnight ago he sold me a miracle cream that was supposed to get rid of spots on my skin. I put it on my hands, and now I've got more spots than ever. If I'd carried on with it, I'd look like a leopard by now. Poveda is a liar and a cheat. And remember you promised to take me to the cinema," she added in a more light-hearted tone; "I'll be here after rehearsal." "I haven't forgotten, and I'll keep my promise," Prullàs said, "but not tonight."

6

He got out of the taxi opposite the imposing building just as two guards were lowering the flags on the balcony. He had to give lengthy explanations and show several identity cards before they let him in. He was finally shown to the anteroom of Don Lorenzo Verdugones' office, where Sigüenza received him with his habitual, ineffective disposition to please.

"Don Lorenzo cannot see you at the moment, but if you would be so kind as to wait, I'll tell him just as soon as he finishes his current appointment. I can't tell you when that might be. It could be a few minutes or a couple of hours, perhaps more."

Prullàs nodded in assent. "I'll wait as long as it takes." "In that case, I'll show you to the waiting-room," Sigüenza said. "No thank you, I prefer to wait here," Prullàs replied firmly, and sat down in an uncomfortable chair with a stiff back. "You carry on working, Sigüenza, and don't worry about me."

The obsequious official racked his brains for a way to get rid of Prullàs without seeming to be impolite, and when he couldn't think of anything, decided with obvious embarrassment he had to accept the other man's presence. Through the connecting door to the governor's office they could occasionally hear his voice barking orders, followed by long periods of silence. "Has his visitor been in there long?" Prullàs enquired.

"I don't know," Sigüenza replied. "I've been out several times and haven't seen anyone go in; it could be there is no-one in there with him." "Is Don Lorenzo Verdugones in the habit of shouting at himself then?" The official shook his head. "The fact is that because of his duties, Don Lorenzo has to give a lot of speeches; he hates empty rhetoric, and tries to include a proper amount of dogma in all his public utterances; this means he has to prepare thoroughly." "I understand," Prullàs said; "and now is one of those cases." "I'm not sure," the other man said. "It may be he has a visitor."

The last rays of the setting sun flooded into the room, breathing a faint glow of life into the ashen mounds of furniture. As the street noises died away, all that could be heard was the scratching of Sigüenza's pen across paper. An hour went by like this, at the end of which the obsequious official placed his pen in the inkwell, stood up and said: "Excuse me." He went across to a cupboard, took out a bottle of water, removed the cap, and emptied the contents of a sachet into it. The water immediately started to effervesce. Sigüenza closed the bottle again, then shook it to help the bubbles. After this, he took a picnic tumbler from the same cupboard and filled it with the water. "Would you care for some?" Prullàs declined the offer courteously, and Sigüenza drank the contents of the tumbler in one. He shuddered, his face became contorted, and a silent belch marked the end of this small-scale transformation.

"Don Lorenzo can't be much longer," he said as he returned to his desk; but then, taken aback by his own rashness, he added: "On the other hand, he could be." Then without making any further predictions he sat down, turned on his lamp, and immersed himself once more in his tasks.

Prullàs was trying to appear calm, but inside he was becoming increasingly despondent. If my luck runs out and I have to leave without being seen, I'll lose the last scrap of dignity I have in the eyes of these cretins, he thought; but if I have to wait much longer, I'll go mad. He tried to use the time to reflect on the most recent events and sort out his ideas, but the overwhelming sense of routine and boredom emanating from the office in the sad twilight, far from helping him concentrate, produced in him an exasperated, sterile torpor.

He was about to admit defeat when the inner door opened and a man backed out of the governor's office, bowing repeatedly as he did so. Before he turned round, a polite cough from Sigüenza warned him there was a stranger in the room. Deeply embarrassed, the man covered his face with his hat in a grotesque attempt to avoid recognition, and shot out of the door. Sigüenza's voice brought Prullàs out of his stupor: "Don Lorenzo will see you now."

Don Lorenzo was in his shirtsleeves and was obviously in a grim mood. "Such a bore, Prullàs my friend, a real bore!" he shouted as Prullàs came into his office; then went on, accompanying his words with a sweeping gesture: "Not you of course. I've already told you, I like the look of you, and I never mince my words. Don't forget: my word is my bond! I was talking about the messenger who's just left. A bore from start to finish! And you waiting as if for Santa Claus all that time, it's unforgivable! A glory of our Spanish theatre having to wait his turn. Unforgivable! Sigüenza, this must never happen again, d'you hear?"

The obsequious official bowed his head in submission and the governor picked up a packet of cigarette papers and a tobacco pouch from his desk and began to roll a cigarette. The operation was not a success: the paper came unstuck, and several tobacco shreds remained stuck to his lips. The governor growled, tore the cigarette apart, and threw it on the floor. Prullàs offered him an American one. Don Lorenzo grimaced, but accepted the offer, and even signalled Sigüenza to help himself too. For a short while, the three men smoked in silence, savouring the delicious aroma of the contraband goods.

Prullàs left the packet on the desk, then said: "That bore of yours . . . "

"Do you know each other?" Don Lorenzo asked. "I don't know, there was something about him that seemed familiar, but I couldn't really see his face," Prullàs confessed. "He hid it as if his life depended on not being recognised." The governor gave a scornful smile. "Nobody wants to be seen coming in or going out of this office, as though it might tarnish their reputation; yet you'd be amazed if you knew how many of the most upright citizens of Barcelona have warmed their buttocks on this chair. A parade of models that would do that chap Christian Dior proud! Isn't that so, Sigüenza? You of course are the exception," he said without changing his facial expression. "What brings you to these parts?"

Prullàs coughed. The lengthy wait he had been subjected to meant he had almost completely forgotten why he had come. "Don Lorenzo," he eventually said, "I'm here to intercede on behalf of Miguel Fontcuberta. I've been told you have had him brought in. Naturally," he added, "I have no idea of your reasons, but I've known Miguel Fontcuberta for years and I'm convinced he's a perfect gentleman, incapable of committing murder."

The governor slapped the desk with a thud; the writing case lifted into the air, and the blotter swayed to and fro. "Fontcuberta!" he shouted, "a fine mess! Have you come to tell me where we can lay our hands on him?" "As far as I know, he's in Madrid; try the Palace Hotel: that's where he always stays." "Don't talk rubbish!" Verdugones replied; "it's been over a year since he set foot in the Palace, or any other hotel in Madrid, at least using his real name; we haven't found out yet if he's using false papers, but we're on his trail. In fact, we don't even know if he goes to Madrid, all we know is that he says he's going there, and brings back sweets from La Pajarita. A fine mess! When did you hear he'd gone?" "A few days ago," Prullàs admitted, surprised at what he had just learned. "You should have told me immediately; didn't I tell you to keep me informed? Some detective you are!" "But how was I supposed to know Fontcuberta was a suspect? I didn't even know he was under surveillance," Prullàs grumbled. "As long as we don't have the guilty person behind bars, everyone is under surveillance," the other man shouted. "Even my own father!"

Prullàs sat in silence. The air in the office was unbreathable. "Sigüenza, take this ashtray out of here!" the governor shouted. "There's nothing worse than the smell of a cigar." The obsequious official quickly removed the offending ashtray. As he walked past the fan, he disappeared in a cloud of ashes. Prullàs plucked up the courage to ask: "How d'you think Fontcuberta is implicated in Vallsigorri's murder?"

"Murder? Who mentioned murder?" "Ah, so you're not looking for Fontcuberta in relation to Vallsigorri's death?" Prullàs exclaimed. "No, of course not, you're the one taking care of that blessed murder! I'm after much bigger fish." The telephone interrupted him. Sigüenza's voice could be heard from the outer room. "Hello? Yes sir, Lieutenant-Colonel sir! I'll tell him immediately, Colonel sir!" Then his head appeared round the door: "Don Lorenzo, it's Lieutenant-Colonel Vergara for you."

Don Lorenzo quickly picked up the telephone extension. "Vergara? Vergara, dammit, what can I do for you? No, dammit, no; me for you! What? Yes, I can hear you perfectly; yes, dammit, as if you were in the next room. Yes, I can hear you clear as a bell, dammit! What's your news? How's the family? That's good to hear, dammit! And the little one? She must be a real rosebud by now. No, dammit, a rosebud! A rosebud!

What? In January? Well congratulations, dammit! Yes, Vergara, yes, they're on the up and up, we're on the slide, dammit, what can you do? That's life! What? Ha ha ha, that's what I say too: always keep your weapon greased, Vergara, that's the main thing. You don't change Vergara, dammit! And here, as you'd expect: struggling with day-to-day problems. Don't say a word, dammit, not a word! You know how the saying goes: all tradesmen are rogues, and all Catalans are tradesmen, so you can see how the syllogism goes. Yes? Really? Well, I'll be damned! Who? No, not him. Yes, my lad, hard going. But it's done. Yes, of course, the complete list. No, no-one: four queers and a couple of bankers. No, it was a lawyer who told me. Yes, I've just said goodbye to him. Yes, of course, if you want something you have to pay for it. Yes, dammit, as soon as you show your teeth they sing *La Parrala* if it saves their skin. No, not now anyway. What's that? I can't hear you, dammit. Interference. What sentences? I couldn't say. Death penalties? No, dammit, there's no need. At any rate, we'll see what Madrid says. Yes, of course. What? You don't say! Dammit, dammit, dammit! Aha . . . aha . . . I see, yes . . . aha . . . aha. Well, I'll be damned! Right. Right. Right. Of course, dammit. No, dammit. Right. Aha, aha. No, that's all for now. Yes, I'll keep you posted. Thank you, Vergara, thanks for everything, and don't hesitate. Send your daughter a kiss from me, and start getting ready to be a grandfather, dammit! Goodbye then. My very best, Vergara!"

He hung up and, a smile still on his lips, explained: "That was Lieutenant-Colonel Vergara; a comrade from the old days! A fine man, very cultured! A good man! Sigüenza, have I ever told you what happened that time Vergara and I went to talk to General Mola?" "Yes, Don Lorenzo, you've told me the story several times, but it's so interesting and you tell it so well that I never tire of hearing it," Sigüenza replied. "Thank you,

Sigüenza," Don Lorenzo said coolly. "But to get back to business, Prullàs, I've just learned from Vergara that Fontcuberta has been spotted in Seville getting out of a horse-drawn carriage. It seems he's on a tourist trip. Sigüenza, send a request to the Civil Governor of Seville, and to police headquarters. Not by telephone; first of all by telegraph then through official channels. Let's see if just this once we can do things properly, dammit!" "Yes sir."

The official scribbled in his notebook and then left to carry out his orders. Prullàs and the governor were left alone again. The light bulbs flickered as if they were about to go out; then came back on. "It's a bad sign when they start like that; there's sure to be a power cut," Don Lorenzo said. "Sigüenza, stop what you're doing and go and fetch an oil lamp. We have our own generator, but it takes a while to warm up." Just as he finished saying this, the lights went off altogether. Outside the window they could still see a patch of dark-blue sky. The electric streetlamps had also gone out, and the motorists started to sound their horns.

The governor settled back in his chair; in the gloom his bulky shape merged with the leather upholstery. Only his deep voice and the faint glow from his cigarette testified to his presence. "At the start of this year," he began, "as proof of the fraternal ties between our two countries and as a token of the esteem their president holds us in, a ship arrived here from Argentina loaded with wheat, beans and other raw materials, destined to help alleviate the serious supply problems we are experiencing in Spain as a result of the unjust blockade our enemies have imposed. As I say, they were basic goods intended to provide food for our workforce. The bread of our motherland! A few months later, President Perón's wife, that incomparable lady, honoured our shores with a visit. I went to Madrid to meet her. Imagine my astonishment and sense of shame – shame at being

375

Spanish! – when none other than His Excellency the Argentine ambassador informed me he had learned from a good source that some Catalan businessmen, in conjunction with the Flour Board of Madrid, had managed to get hold of several tons of wheat behind their compatriots' backs and had sold them here in Barcelona to the pastrycooks' guild, so that they could make cakes for Easter and the feast of Saint John! The bread of our motherland, Prullàs! I was ashamed to be a Spaniard!"

As the governor said this, the lights came back on, and simultaneously Sigüenza appeared in the doorway carrying an oil lamp. "Ah, here comes the foolish virgin!" Don Lorenzo said irritably, as if the light had surprised him revealing his most intimate secrets. Sigüenza left with the lamp, and Prullàs asked: "And was Fontcuberta one of them?" "Of course," the governor said. "And Vallsigorri?" "We've no proof, but I wouldn't be surprised; did you know Fontcuberta is a freemason?" "No, no I didn't have the slightest idea," Prullàs admitted. "Well he is, and his chum Vallsigorri as well. They were associates for a while in various swindles; then they separated but kept in touch, perhaps through the lodge." "I thought there weren't any more masons," Prullàs said. "That shows how little you know," the governor snapped; "masons never disappear; just when you think they've all been wiped out, they break out again like lice."

Prullàs thought this over for a while. "If both Fontcuberta and Vallsigorri were freemasons," he said, "that means Fontcuberta can't be on the list of murder suspects." "Why so?" Don Lorenzo wanted to know. "Masons don't kill each other; they come to each other's aid," Prullàs said. "Masons have souls as black as pitch," Verdugones said. "What about Mariquita Pons," Prullàs asked, "is she one of them too?" "Don't be such a clot, Prullàs; the masons won't have women in their organisation. Not even the devil wants them."

Sigüenza put his head round the door. "Excuse me, Don Lorenzo; they've just rung from headquarters in Seville. A person responding to the description of Miguel Fontcuberta booked in yesterday at the Alfonso XII Hotel under the name of Miguel de Casabona, Marquis of Ampurdán. He was with a young lady who claims to be his private secretary. She is in the room adjoining the marquis, and goes by the name of Charito. Is there any reply for them?" "Not for now, Sigüenza; we'll see to it later; it's late and we've kept Señor Prullàs here a long time. Show him out, would you, and then come back, I have a speech I need to dictate to you."

7

Prullàs got home exhausted. "Draw me a bath, Sebastiana, and then prepare me something to eat, would you?" "How about an omelette and some croquettes to follow?" "Yes, that'll do fine. Did anyone call?" "Only that gentleman with the voice like a crow," Sebastiana said; "I reckon he's a bit cracked." "Did he say he'd phone again?" "He didn't exactly say so," the maid replied, "but you can be sure he will."

At that precise moment, the telephone rang. "See what I mean, sir?" Sebastiana said, scuttling over to pick it up. Prullàs stopped her. "I'll get it." He picked up the receiver and roared into it: "Who is this?" "That's no way to start a conversation, Carlos," an amused voice answered. "Who am I talking to?" "It's Doctor Mercadal here." "Ah, I'm sorry I was so rude, I didn't recognise your voice," Prullàs said in apology; "there's this inconsiderate fellow who keeps ringing and I thought it was him; how are things with you?" "As well as can be expected in the circumstances," the surgeon replied. "In fact I was calling because I'm in Barcelona and don't feel like dining alone; if you've no other plans, I'll see you in half an hour and we can go and have a bouillabaisse at Can Solé." "Make it three quarters of an hour, and it will be on me," Prullàs replied. "O.K. to the first suggestion, no chance to the second," the other man replied.

Prullàs called Sebastiana. "It wasn't your crazy friend," he said; "and don't bother with the bath or dinner. I'm going out; while I have a shower, put out some clean clothes, would you?" A short while later, Prullàs was admiring the cut of his English wool suit in the mirror; in the background appeared the plump shape of Sebastiana staring at him adoringly.

The massive hull of a cargo ship docked at a pier stood out against the evening sky. Leaning against the bridge rail, an officer was smoking his pipe. Sounds of scraping metal came from the hold, and in the quiet between waves crashing against the breakwater, the distant, muffled notes of a melancholy accordion could be heard. At their table by the restaurant window, Prullàs and the doctor ate cockles and mussels while waiting for their main course. The surgeon was staring out into the darkness. An engine on the dock railway blew its whistle and the doctor's expression changed, as if this had set in motion some mechanism inside him. He began to speak: "I'd promised myself not to spoil your dinner with my worries, but I consider you a good friend and it doesn't seem right to put on a show which doesn't correspond to reality."

Prullàs dabbed his lips with the napkin, drank a little beer, and said: "I'm all ears." Doctor Mercadal also took a drink, then said: "It's Marichuli again; she gets worse every day; she's obsessed with the idea of death. She thinks of nothing else day or night. Considering what happened in her family and the situation with Alicia, that may seem logical, I must admit, but no-one can live like that! We all have to die, so what sense does it make to waste the years we're given out of fear of something which nothing can prevent, which is bound to happen? I tell her: live now, and keep the obsession with death until after you've died. That's reasonable enough, isn't it? Death, after all, is nothing: one fine day we stop eating bouillabaisse and become bouillabaisse for the worms. That's all. I tell her this over and over, but it has no effect: my philosophy doesn't seem to comfort her."

"Is that so bad?" Prullàs wondered. "It is, if it means denying the evidence," the surgeon replied. A waiter came and placed a magnificent soup tureen in the middle of the table, then filled their dishes to the brim with a ladle. "*Bon appétit!*" he said when he'd finished. As soon as he had gone, the doctor went on: "In the past few days, the situation's got worse. Now it's not just her pessimistic view of life, but there are signs her mind is going."

"Heavens!" Prullàs exclaimed, "that's terrible!" He wasn't really surprised at the news, however; deep down he had always thought Marichuli was deranged, and the embarrassing episode with the hypnotist had seemed to him the final proof that she was mentally unstable. "What are the symptoms?" Doctor Mercadal blew on his soup before trying it. "She's forgetful," he said, "she constantly loses track of things. Not like you or I might do, but in a way that's almost pathological, close to amnesia. And she's started hallucinating. For example, in the middle of the night she cries out your name in despair; she's done it several times, yet as far as I can tell, she's always been fast asleep. When she wakes up she can't remember having had a dream, let alone talking."

"Hmm, and apart from my name, does she say anything else?" Prullàs wanted to know. "Yes, lots of things, although they're not always comprehensible," the other man replied; "odd phrases like 'don't leave me', or things like that; in general, she seems to think that directly or indirectly, you're to blame for all her misfortunes. I know it's absurd, but it's exactly as I'm telling you. I've consulted a former student friend of mine who went on to specialise in psychiatry, he's an excellent person, and he gave me a typical psychiatrist's answer. According to him, in dreams it's common for someone to replace a distant, forgotten or lost person towards whom we have aggressive feelings with a closer, harmless figure; in this case, it's Marichuli's father, who, as you know, died when she was still a child. He abandoned her, as it were, just when she most needed his care and protection. So now in her unconscious mind, two opposed emotions are in conflict: one of hostility towards the father who abandoned her, the other of love and admiration. As children we all idealise our fathers, and then as we grow up we strip away the myth. But Marichuli lost her father in childhood, and so has not had the opportunity to consider him more soberly. Now, when she is in trouble, she calls out to him, convinced that if he only came back, he could solve all her problems with a wave of his magic wand."

"I get it," Prullàs said. "And this wonderful man, in her dreams, takes on my appearance." "So it seems," the surgeon agreed. "As loyal husband to Martita, whom she feels very close to, you are a typical father figure for Marichuli."

"Well, to me your friend's diagnosis seems spot on," Prullàs said, mightily relieved at the direction their conversation had taken. "It doesn't to me," Doctor Mercadal replied; "I'm a man of science, and I mistrust Freudian psychoanalysis. It may in some cases have helped alleviate some specific complaints of the mind, at least temporarily, but in general it seems to me a fraud. Psychoanalysis makes the dreadful mistake of reducing human conduct and its disorders to the evolution of infantile sexuality. That's to over-simplify. The latest advances in neurology refute this hypothesis categorically. The life of the mind is entirely based in the brain and its extremely complicated convolutions. To put it simply, the brain appears to function like the control panel of an extensive electric network, which is the nervous system. This network carries our sensory impulses, up and down, up and down, from skin to brain and back, zip, zap. Action and reaction, action and reaction, bing, bang. D'you follow?" "Yes," Prullàs said. "Well, that's what our feelings are," the other man concluded: "Love, desire, memory, passion for bullfighting, devotion to the Holy Father. Whether we like it or not, that's all they are. Nothing more."

Prullàs nodded in agreement, but did not pause in his meal. He wasn't concerned in the slightest about the scientific aspect of the problem, and anyway, felt that Doctor Mercadal only wanted from him a bit of attention and understanding.

The waiter came over to the table, and asked: "Well, how's the soup?" "Excellent," Doctor Mercadal replied; "a bit heavy for my taste, but still excellent . . . In any case, we're facing a polyneurotic breakdown, an acute upset." "Hey, what was that you said?" the waiter butted in. "What's it to you?" Prullàs asked. "Nothing, but I thought you were talking about the soup, and couldn't follow what you were saying." "No, we weren't, we were talking about the nervous system." "Oh, I don't give a damn about that!" the waiter replied. When he had slouched off, Prullàs said: "I don't want to contradict you, but I don't see the fact that she confuses me with someone else as a sign of madness, especially in dreams. If she did so while she were awake, that would be disturbing, but when we're asleep we're not responsible for what we say, what we dream, or anything else for that matter."

"Oh, no?" the surgeon responded; "so you wet your bed, do you? No, of course you don't. Nor do I, and I bet that our waiter, however uneducated he might be, doesn't either. Why? because an inner watchdog, to give it a name, takes it upon itself to wake us up at the critical moment. No, Carlos, not even in our dreams can we escape responsibility for our thoughts or feelings. I'm not talking about the moral aspect: that doesn't concern me. But however painful it may be, Marichuli is a sick person, and sooner or later I'm going to have to take a drastic decision. I hate the idea, but can't see any other solution." "You'd put her in an asylum?" Prullàs asked. "There's no need to exaggerate," Doctor Mercadal said. "There are other ways."

He ate in silence for a while, finished his glass of wine, and then went on: "Have you heard of Korsakov's psychosis?" "If my memory serves me right, Korsakov is a Russian musician, but I didn't know he had a psychosis." "No, of course not!" the surgeon laughed, dropping his spoon and splashing soup onto his tie. "Korsakov was a Russian doctor with a name similar to the composer of *Scheherazade*. The Korsakov I mean, the doctor, discovered the mental illness that has his name at the end of the nineteenth century. People suffering from it have frequent mental lapses and disorders, and replace the events they've forgotten with fantasies they make up. I'll give you an example to help you understand: Suppose you went to see that film *Scheherazade*. I mean the Technicolor version, of course. Then the next day, or the next moment even, you've forgotten everything about it; the Kursaal cinema, the plot of the film, the actors, the images, everything. All that remains in some corner of your memory is how impressed you were by Yvonne de Carlo. So to make up for all you've forgotten, your fantasy creates a false but satisfying story: the previous night, you went out with Yvonne de Carlo, you asked her to share a bouillabaisse in Can Solé, you had a wonderful conversation and when you said goodnight you agreed to continue your friendship by letter. From that day on you start saying: I haven't had a letter from Yvonne de Carlo in a long while: I wonder if something happened to her!"

"I understand," Prullàs said. "And can this illness be cured by medication?" "No, not with medication," the surgeon replied, "it takes a lobotomy. It's a painless and non-invasive operation. And it leaves the patients as right as rain."

On a tiny, mountainous island in the Azores, after several hours' efforts, US Marines had finally succeeded in taking a Japanese non-commissioned officer prisoner. This man, unaware that the Second World War had ended with his country's unconditional surrender, was stubbornly defending this unlikely bastion in the name of the Emperor, whom he considered a true god. The capture had been successful thanks to the use of asphyxiating gases, which had knocked out the soldier before he had been able to turn his own weapons on himself and commit the famous hara-kiri. When he came round, the valiant soldier, who stank terribly because by his own admission he had not had a bath since spring 1942, expressed his astonishment on learning through an interpreter that Japan and the United States were no longer adversaries, but allies and friends. The article on this strange event did not specify how a Japanese non-commissioned officer came to be in the Azores, though the mostly likely explanation appeared to be that there had been a mistake in transcribing the news-agency cable. In Nuremberg, the court was still deliberating behind closed doors, while the accused was locked up alone in his cell until the verdict was known. For the first time in several weeks, that morning the whole world was deprived of news about Krupp.

Prullàs folded *La Vanguardia* and called Sebastiana. "Sebastiana, if I told you that last night I had dinner with Yvonne de Carlo, would you think I was mad?" "As a hatter." "And if I told you someone can commit a murder and then forget it completely and believe they were somewhere else, doing something completely different, would you believe that?" "No, master, in that case I'd think you were making fun of me. But you shouldn't pay me any attention," she said hastily, "I'm just a iggerant woman. And please, don't say any more about crimes, because I take them all to heart, and I don't get a wink of sleep at night."

CHAPTER SEVEN

I

ENRIQUE: Cecilia, come here and sit down, there's something very serious I have to tell you. Something dreadful has happened, truly horrible . . .

CECILIA: Oh goodness gracious, Enriquito my love, don't scare me; it can't be so bad.

ENRIQUE: I'm afraid it can. You see, it's to do with Todoliu.

CECILIA: (*worried*) Todoliu?

ENRIQUE: Yes, Todoliu. Your relative Todoliu.

CECILIA: Oh, Todoliu! What can have happened to him? Why, this morning he set off on a journey, happy and contented after spending a few precious days here with his beloved nephews and nieces . . .

ENRIQUE: That's just it: he didn't go off on a journey as you think.

CECILIA: (*increasingly worried*) What . . . he hasn't gone?

ENRIQUE: Oh yes, he's gone all right; I mean he's not gone. He's gone, but he's not. What I mean is your relative Todoliu has gone, but not on a journey, except to the other world. I mean, he's dead.

CECILIA: (*feigning surprise*) Dead! Now there's a surprise! Poor Todoliu! That's incredible. When he said goodbye to us this morning, he was as fit as a fiddle.

ENRIQUE: He didn't have a health problem, my love.

Todoliu has been murdered.

CECILIA: (*feigning even greater surprise*) Murdered! That's impossible! How could anyone murder poor Todoliu? Everybody adored him! It must have been a mistake.

ENRIQUE: There's no mistake, Cecilia. However hard it may be, you have to get used to the idea: Todoliu has been murdered. (*Pause*) But there's something more I have to tell you.

CECILIA: Something . . . more?

ENRIQUE: Yes. Todoliu was murdered . . . a month ago.

CECILIA: (*genuinely surprised this time*) What! A month ago! But that's impossible, Enrique, impossible! (*Gives a sideways glance at the wardrobe*) Because if as you say Todoliu died a month ago who did we . . . I mean . . .

ENRIQUE: Yes, my love, I know what you mean. And you're right: the person who spent the past few days in your home . . . wasn't Todoliu, but his murderer!

CECILIA: I think I'm going to faint! (*Faints*)

Mariquita Pons gave a start when she walked into her dressing-room and found Prullàs already there. "Your assistant helped me get in without being seen," he explained. The actress sent her assistant on her way. "I didn't expect to see you today," she said, sitting at her dressing-table mirror. In among all the make-up pots, Prullàs could see a candlestick with a stub of candle in it. "Isn't that Bonifaci's candlestick?" Prullàs asked. "I haven't the faintest idea. My dresser brought it the last time the lights went out, and left it here for any future problems. Apparently in this hot weather everyone has their fans, refrigerators and air conditioning going at full blast, and the power lines can't cope. Every five minutes either a fuse goes or a condenser explodes, or the devil gets up to his tricks and we all suffer as a consequence. It doesn't matter how it happens, but that's why the candlestick's there anyway. Are you doing an inventory of the theatre fittings?"

"No," Prullàs said; "I'm investigating a murder, and in my spare time I'm trying to solve burglaries, thefts, and other minor misdemeanours."

Mariquita started to fiddle with one of the pots, uncertain where to begin. Her face betrayed the fatigue of someone caught between the twin evils of worry and insomnia. Prullàs too was unsure of how to begin. "Yesterday evening I went to see Don Lorenzo Verdugones as I'd promised you," he said finally. She fluttered her hands at him. "Thank you for that, but you needn't have bothered," she said cheerfully. "Miguel called me last night from Madrid; he couldn't find a room in the Palace so he went to another hotel, whose name escapes me. I told him about Don Lorenzo's visit and he laughed out loud; then he said that this morning he'd go to police headquarters, where he knows lots of people, and sort out all this misunderstanding." "Did he also tell you when he was thinking of coming back?" "He wasn't sure," the actress replied. "Apparently there was a possibility he might make a lightning trip to Seville to sort a few things out. If he did, he told me, he'd be sure to go to the bullring; he was as thrilled as a little boy at the idea of seeing a good bullfight at La Maestranza."

Prullàs didn't reply. After a while though, he said: "I can imagine. How are the rehearsals going?" Mariquita finished wiping her make-up off with a wet towel and rubbed her forehead and cheeks with moisturising cream. Her good humour evaporated. "Worse and worse," she said. "Gaudet's in a real trough; I'd almost say he was trying to undermine us. He doesn't hear anything, or see anything; he forgets just about everything and confuses the actors with the characters they're playing, and sometimes he confuses the play with other plays – which of course is inexcusable, given the extraordinary originality of 'Arrivederci, pollo!'" "Bah, you're just cross because the stutterer will get more laughs than you," Prullàs said. "You ought to be ashamed, using our friend's crisis to get at my play; d'you really think it's so bad?" Mariquita shrugged. "I haven't the faintest idea. Perhaps it's just nerves and this dreadful heat. Nothing works properly: the electricians complain about the power cuts, the costume designers are way behind, and a certain member of the company can't remember her lines," she said, pointing at the dressing-room door. "But that's not it," she said even more sombrely; "whether Gaudet is ill or is having a spiritual crisis, you ought to be thinking about replacing him with another director." "Replace Pepe?" Prullàs exclaimed. "You can't be serious!"

The actress was now busy powdering her cheeks. "It would be cruel, I know," she said, "but it would be even more cruel to make him do something that's beyond him at the moment." "If that's the case, we won't put the play on," Prullàs asserted; "without Gaudet there's no 'Arrivederci, pollo!'" "Your loyalty does you credit," she said, "but it's not your decision to make." "We'll see about that. I'll write to the Society of Authors!"

"It may not be a question of that," Mariquita Pons said. "After Vallsigorri's death I don't know what sort of financial backing there still is for the play." "Bah, he can't have invested that much in it," Prullàs replied, slightly worried, "and anyway, he must have already paid up."

Mariquita laughed lightly once more. "Don't be such an optimist; perhaps he only offered some promissory notes, in which case honouring them would depend on his heirs." "Hmm, I hadn't thought of that," Prullàs admitted; "d'you know how much he'd put in?" "Enough to impose conditions on Gaudet," the actress said. "Who told you all this?" Prullàs asked. "Oh, walls have ears, and people never stop talking!"

Mariquita said, still as cheerful as ever. "Are you taking me to the cinema tonight, or will you stand me up again?"

Prullàs looked at his watch. "I'll call by your place at half past nine. Beforehand I'd like to have a little talk with our friend Gaudet. Choose a film, but make sure it's a cowboys and Indians one. How!" She laughed, and then added in a more serious tone: "Be careful when you talk to Gaudet; if he's got things wrong lately, make sure you put the blame on his mother's death, or his health, or his age, but not on other things." As she was speaking, she took a small key out of her bag and opened one of the dressing-table drawers. She took out a bottle of perfume and used the stopper to dab the scent behind her ears and on her wrists. Prullàs spotted the name of the perfume. "Where did you get that bottle of *Arpège*?" he asked. "Where d'you think? Poveda sold it me some time ago. He swore there was only one bottle in the whole of Barcelona, which meant – according to him – I absolutely had to buy it, and that he couldn't lower the price at all. Naturally I fought like a tigress and managed to get it for half the original price." "Why d'you keep it locked up?" "Because the first bottle I bought from him disappeared. I brought it here, and while I was gone, some light-fingered man came into my dressing-room and stole it. Some light-fingered man or woman," she said, with an amused lack of concern.

After leaving the actress's dressing-room and making sure no-one saw him, Prullàs headed for Lilí Villalba's room. He was determined to clear things up once and for all. He walked in without knocking and immediately collided with the young actress who had just been about to leave. To avoid falling on the floor, they became locked in the parody of an embrace. Lilí reacted with unusual vehemence. "Who d'you take me for? It's been *weeks* since you even spoke to me, and now you throw yourself on me without so much as a by-your-leave. I'm not your plaything!"

"I didn't mean to attack you; I came in quickly to avoid being seen," he said by way of apology. "You come and go as you please in the dressing-room next door," she complained, adjusting the strap on her sandal; "why am I different?" "It is different: nobody would think anything strange of my relation with Kiki." In the flickering light of the electric bulbs the young actress's eyes flashed and then turned sullen: "Oh, of course, our relation is different because people will think there's something wrong, because I'm good *for only one thing*," she muttered.

Prullàs went over to the dressing-table, picked up a comb and tidied his hair. "Don't exaggerate. You're a young and highly attractive woman, and that has its drawbacks, but it also has its great advantages. Would you prefer to be ugly and hunchbacked?"

"No," she replied, less aggrieved. "Anyway, the world is unfair, and men are even more so. Why did you come?" "To invite you to dinner if you don't have a prior engagement," Prullàs said, still looking at himself in the mirror. To hell with Gaudet, he told himself, to hell with that dratted perfume and to hell with Kiki and her blasted films; I'll call and cancel our arrangement with some excuse or other.

The young actress was staring at him in astonishment. "Would you really do that for me? Take me to somewhere *public* . . . ? Ah no, it's impossible . . . anyway, I don't have any clothes to wear," she murmured. "You're fine as you are," he said, turning round and staring at her intently.

The light went off then came back at once, stoking the fire in his eyes. "Don't say that!" Lilí blushed, then laughed for no apparent reason. "Wait; a neighbour of mine could lend me a dress; she's a bit plumper than me, filled out more *here* and *here;* but it's easy enough to alter a summer dress. I'm very good at that: give me a couple of hours, and when you see me you won't believe your eyes."

"All right," Prullàs said. "It's seven o'clock now; I'll pick you up in that small square by your house at nine; don't be late."

The telephone was ringing as Prullàs entered his apartment. "Oh sir, you get it please, if it's old crow voice again I think I'll have an attack," Sebastiana said. Prullàs closed the door to his study, sat down unhurriedly, got a piece of paper and a pencil, and answered the call.

"At last you're there," a strange voice said at the far end of the line. "You're playing hard to get, as if this business was nothing to do with you." "Who am I talking to?" "To someone who has something of great interest for you," the crow voice said, "as long as you're willing to pay for it." "I'm not going to pay or even continue listening unless you tell me who you are right now," Prullàs exploded; "who the devil are you?" "A true friend; and don't lose your temper with me, Señor Prullàs; if you insult me, I'll hang up, I won't call again, and we'll all lose out: you more than anyone."

"Don't let's beat about the bush then," Prullàs said; "what's this all about?" "Not on the telephone," crow voice said. "Face to face just the two of us; like the French say, *tay a tay.*" "And who's to tell me you're not a madman or a practical joker?" "Me, a joker? Come off it! Look, I'll give you an example to show I'm serious: D'you remember the other night? You were in a bar with another gentleman, and that other gentleman accidentally lost his wallet. The bar is called the Taberna de Mañuel. Am I correct or not?" "You're quite correct," Prullàs had to admit; "that's what happened."

"And wouldn't you like to get it back?" "The wallet?" "The contents of the wallet," the other man continued, lowering his crow's voice. "A compromising document that would draw the cops' attention away, and leave certain people free from suspicion, if you follow me . . . if you're interested, meet me tonight and bring some money with you."

"How much?" Prullàs asked. "Ten thousand pesetas ought to do it," the stranger said. "Ten thousand pesetas!" Prullàs exclaimed. "Even if I were interested in the deal, I couldn't lay my hands on that much money so quickly!"

"Try, Señor Prullàs; the document is well worth it. Some people you are acquainted with would pay a lot more to get hold of it and prevent our excellent Don Lorenzo Verdugones reading it. But when all's said and done, it's your money: if it seems too much to you, don't come."

"Wait! I'll try to get the money, but I don't promise to hand it over; at any rate, before I give you the cash, I want to see the document."

"But of course! This is an honest deal. Now listen: go back to the Taberna de Mañuel tonight at nine sharp, not a minute before, and not a minute later. Stay at the bar, and don't talk to anyone: I'll come and join you and give you the password. And come alone: you're not in any danger, but if you decide to tell the cops, then you can kiss the document goodbye."

2

Undaunted by the harsh blows of fate, unconscious of the inexorable passage of time, untouched by discouragement, La Fresca still hoped she would triumph in the world of flamenco. Tonight, as every night, she was getting ready to put her heart and soul into her performance, when the public clamoured for her to appear. She had already washed the plates and glasses, swept the floor, put out the tables and chairs, unblocked and mopped the toilet, filled the jugs of water and tuned all the guitars in the Taberna de Mañuel. The clock on Nuestra Señora del Pino church was just striking nine when Prullàs entered the bar. Seeing nobody else there apart from La Fresca, he hid his astonishment behind a false friendly smile and sat at the bar, where the extraordinary creature was staring into the depths of a glass of cheap anisette, getting her strength back by soaking a crust of bread in a bowl of ersatz coffee.

La Fresca pursed her scarlet lips. "Goodness, sweetheart, you're here early," she said sarcastically. "I've brought the money," Prullàs said in a determined manner; "but first I want to see the goods. And I'm warning you: I've only brought four thousand." "Four thousand?" La Fresca exclaimed, raising her eyebrows until they almost cracked the thick layer of make-up she used to cover the wrinkles on her forehead. "My, my, sweetheart, there's no need to exaggerate; for a hundred pesetas I'd not only show you the goods, but make a new man of you."

Prullàs considered this reply. "Aha, didn't you and I talk just now on the telephone?"

"No."

Prullàs burst out laughing. "Forget what I just said," he guffawed, "there's been some confusion; I didn't mean to offend you. Have another drink on me." "Thanks," La Fresca said, "and you didn't offend me, dearie; at my age, I've got an elephant's hide. But if the business that brings you here is as important as you said, I'd better warn the owner." And before Prullàs could protest, she shouted towards the back of the bar: "Come on out, Mañuel, someone's looking for you!"

The person she was calling to appeared a few moments later, buttoning up his flies and shouting: "Who's looking for me?" Prullàs recognised in this uncouth individual the bar-owner who on the night in question had first of all served them and then thrown them out so unceremoniously. Entrenched behind the bar, as if he wanted to protect the bottles lined up there against the intruder, the barman asked gruffly: "Whaddyou want?"

"D'you remember me?" Prullàs asked. "I was in here a few nights ago, with a man who looked like Bing Crosby."

The barman threw up his hands in horror and said yes, the police had already questioned him about it; he'd answered all their questions and had nothing more to add, he added. "This is a decent, law-abiding place," he concluded. "Be on your way, and don't cause any more trouble."

"I don't doubt you're a law-abiding citizen," Prullàs said, "and I haven't come to cause any trouble. I've got nothing to do with the police; I'm a playwright, I write comedy thrillers; perhaps you've heard of me, I'm Carlos Prullàs. I'm in the same position as you: I'm mixed up in this without knowing why."

"Go on, Mañuel, be kind to the gennleman," put in La Fresca, who seemed to have been stirred out of her lethargy by their conversation. "Yeh can see he's not to blame." "Like hell!" Mañuel replied. "He's to blame for everything. Who asked them to come? They could have gone to Rigat's! What were they doing here? Laughing at us? Seeing if we ate with our fingers and scratched our backsides with the forks? What's it to them? After all, we are what we are, and that's all there is to it. But as soon as this stuck-up pair poke their noses in here, we all become criminals. Get out of here!"

"Don't pay him any heed," La Fresca said, laying a fat, sweaty hand on Prullàs' sleeve. "Is it true yeh's a theatre writer?" "As I told you, I write comedies," Prullàs said. He withdrew his arm, smoothed down the sleeve, and added curtly: "But I have nothing to do with the variety theatre."

"But yeh could write a little part for me in one of yeh's plays," La Fresca suggested, oblivious to Prullàs' gesture and the sense of his words. "Only a little one, but appealin' loik: I comes on, sings, and dances; people always like that, and then who knows, someone might discover me . . . " "What did you say yeh name was?" "Prullàs," he said reluctantly.

"Look, Prullàs, I'm an artiste," the creature went on; "if yeh seen me hact, you'd have realised; the t'ing is, I never had no proper treachers, thats what I needs: all I know, I've learnt for meself; I sings and I dances with all me heart, but what I need is technique. With the other flamenco dancers we tells each other about the mistakes loik, and gives advice, but I don't care what the others say: they don't have singing and dancing in their blood like I does. They has the souls of grocers. I'm different: I were born an artiste. Go on, Prullàs, dearie, yeh has to give me a chance!"

"Ah, shut up you ragbag, and get back to work!" Mañuel shouted at her. "You waste all your energy blabbing with the customers, but when it comes to polishing, just look at those glasses! D'you call that cleaning? Not even a pig would drink from them!"

La Fresca set about cleaning the glasses with a filthy cloth. While she was doing this, without bothering with water or soap, she carried on talking to Prullàs: "Oh, sweetheart, this is such a miserable country. If I could, I'd be off today, even if t'was to China. But what would I lives on? There's not much call for flamenco in China, so I hear." She lifted a glass to the light, spat in it, wiped it with the cloth, and went on: "But here there's absolutely nothin' either. If one day I had money, say I won the lottery, d'yeh know the first t'ing I'd do?" "No," Prullàs said. "Well the very first t'ing I'd do, dearie, would be to catch the Madrid hexpress and at the Puerta del Sol I'd have a drink at the zero kilometer post. Ha! Right in the middle of Spain I'd get as drunk as a lord. That's all we needed," she suddenly said interrupting herself, "what mischief brings yeh here, Pretty Face?"

The lottery vendor's crutch rang out like a doorknocker on the wooden floor. Pretty Face leaned against the bar, propped up the crutch, and wiped the sweat from his brow with his sleeve. "Give me a beer, Mañuel," he muttered, "I'm dead beat."

The barman stood frowning at the cripple. "Come on, serve our friend a beer," Prullàs said; "it's on me." "Don't do that thug any favours, sweetheart," La Fresca cut in; "he's evil through and through."

"Don't pay her any attention, Señor Prullàs; it's plain to see you're an honest sort," the one-legged man said, fixing his one good eye on the would-be artiste with obvious rancour; "not like others I could mention." "How d'you know my name?" Prullàs asked him. "I'm the one who brought you here," Pretty Face said. "I arrived late because of the damned trams; public transport gets worse by the day; unless his excellency the governor does something about it soon, there's going to be a real uproar and no mistake."

Prullàs was amazed that a cripple like Pretty Face could get on and off a tram without breaking his neck, but said nothing. "I'm not serving a beer or anything else," Mañuel growled; "my customers are about to arrive, and I don't want you here. Nor you neither, Señor whatever your name is. Clear off, the pair of you."

"That's fine by me," the one-legged man said, replacing his crutch under his armpit and lurching up off the bar. "No, wait a minute," Prullàs interjected. "I've got the money, so if you've got the document we can finish our business here and now. I'm sure Señor Mañuel will give us a few moments." "Ah, but I haven't got it with me, Señor Prullàs!" Pretty Face said. "I'm only a poor invalid – I can't defend myself or take risks. Anyway, someone else has got the document, I'm just a go-between. If you want it, you'll have to come with me. It's not far."

La Fresca gripped Prullàs' arm again. "For the love of God," she begged him, "don't leave before yeh give me your details. I've never had a chance like this and most likely never will again. Yeh can help me a lot, I can see it in yeh face. Go on, sweetheart. I's not asking fer a contract nor anythin'; just ha audition. If I'm no good, yeh doesna lose anythin', but if I am, yeh's the one who's discovered me."

Prullàs thought for a moment. The cripple had struggled as far as the door, and was making urgent gestures to him from there. On an impulse, Prullàs took a visiting card out of his wallet and scribbled a name and address on the back. Then he handed it to La Fresca. "Go to this address tomorrow morning and ask for José Gaudet. He's bound to open the door himself; tell him I sent you. Then on the spot, before he can react, make sure you sing and dance just like I saw you do the other night. He might be a bit surprised at first, but he's a director and is used to fits of genius. He's also good at discovering true talent. I'm afraid I can't do any more for you; the rest is up to you . . . and Señor Gaudet."

La Fresca stared at the card as if she couldn't believe her eyes. The dim light in the bar glinted in a tear welling in her eye. "May God reward yeh kindness, Prullàs," she said hesitantly; "I'll never forget this, and yeh'll never regret it. Success will never go to me head; I'll always be what hi am now: La Fresca! They gave me that sweet name on account of how I'm always cheerful . . . and because I never say no to a good-lookin' boy."

She clasped Prullàs' hands between hers and printed the scarlet grease of her lips on it. The cripple was shouting at them from the doorway. "Let him go, you trollop! Can't you see he's no catch for you?" "Go get stuffed!" La Fresca replied, with a swirl of her skirts. Then, lowering her voice so that only Prullàs could hear her, she added: "Don't trust that Pretty Face an inch, sweetheart; he's capable of anythin'."

But Prullàs didn't heed her warning.

"Ah," the cripple exclaimed, taking a deep breath of the damp, fetid air in the squalid street outside the bar; "there's nothing in the world like the sea, nothing so beautiful! I'm from the interior, a long way away, the other side of Barbastro. Until I was twenty, I'd never seen the sea! You can imagine the impression it made on me! So much so I swore then and there I'd always live beside the sea, in a port and near a beach. I really love the beach! As often as I can I escape to Sitges, because the beaches here in Barceloneta are full of junk. I don't mean the swimming pools, but an invalid like me . . . well, you get the picture."

"I can imagine," Prullàs agreed, still uncomfortable despite these friendly overtures. He tried to memorise the route they were taking, in case he had to find his way back along it all on his own, but soon had to give up: at each and every corner, the cripple invariably turned right, but instead of going round in circles, this method took them ever deeper into a mysterious district where the streets got ever narrower and meaner. All the shops were locked up, and the houses looked uninhabited, with not a single lighted window. It was only every now and then, at the corner of a square or on a piece of waste land, that the black market was visible in its crudest form. Foodstuffs, medicines, spare parts for cars, radios, wind-up gramophones, electric kettles, toiletries, crockery and knives and forks, coal and tobacco were all for sale at every imaginable price. Also for sale were identity papers, certificates, and more or less skilfully forged ration books. None of those buying or selling deigned even to look in the direction of the odd couple presented by Prullàs and Pretty Face, who soon disappeared once more down a dark alley. In the corners, mangy cats fought over the scraps of rubbish. "Aren't you afraid of walking alone in these vile streets?" Prullàs asked him.

Pretty Face cackled unpleasantly. "What on earth could happen to me?" he said; "I've nothing more to lose, except my crutch, and I can get by without that. I've already lost it several times, but here I am, still alive and kicking; once some kids stole it just for fun; then a drunk took it out of spite, and a third time a crook snatched it to bash in the ribs of the man he was fighting with because he had nothing else to hand."

"And what did you do then?" Prullàs asked. "What could I do? Get along as best I could on one leg. But there have been some advantages," he went on; looking the way he did, it wasn't hard for him to move people and sell his lottery tickets, which helped him keep body and soul together even in hard times such as these. He'd found an old medal in a junkshop, and usually wore it on his coat; so that even though in fact all his numerous injuries were the result of illnesses and accidents that had occurred in childhood and adolescence, others took him for a war hero and let him ride for free on the trams or the metro, and even allowed him into cinemas. He often went to the cinema, he said, especially on cold, rainy days; if he liked a film he went back to see it again and again. And he could recite the dialogue of these films word for word, without omitting a single line. That was all he needed, he said: one good meal a day, a bit of sun to warm his bones, and from time to time a good film, preferably with Hedy Lamarr in it. He couldn't ask any more of life. At this stage in the proceedings, he concluded, it was all the same to him. And if for example God suddenly came down from heaven and asked him: "Pretty Face, would you like the leg, the arm, the eye or the ear you're missing restored?" he wouldn't hesitate to answer him: "Thank you, God, but I don't need them, save yourself the trouble." "Seeing you're such a stoic," Prullàs said, "I don't understand how you get yourself into so much trouble over money."

"Oh, everyone has their weak spot!" Pretty Face said with

a horrible grimace. He closed his good eye in a parody of what Prullàs assumed was a wink, and added: "Whenever I manage to put a few coins aside, I get myself a gypsy woman and get her to dance and sing for me in the nude. I love their gleaming skin, that's the truth. Don't you?" "I wouldn't know about that," Prullàs said. "How much further do we have to go?" "It's right here, like I told you. In fact we're not far from Mañuel's place. We've just come a long way round to get you lost and to make it look as though I've done more work," laughed the cripple. "I'm not going a step further," Prullàs protested. "Well, you'll never find your way back: this area is a maze if you don't know it. But don't worry, Señor Prullàs, we've arrived: can't you hear the din?"

Prullàs came to a halt: nearby he could hear voices and a gramophone blaring out. He caught up with Pretty Face and they walked on in silence.

They came out into a short street lit by garish neon signs. On their right the street was separated from a waste lot by a wall three metres high. The wall was covered in torn, faded posters, and several individuals were urinating against it in a relaxed, leisurely way. "That's it, enjoy your piss!" the cripple shouted at them. "And don't forget to shake your dicks when you've done!"

On the other side of the street ten or a dozen dark entrances opened beneath neon signs. On the top floors red lights shone behind shutters. In the middle of the street a crowd of silent men shuffled by, some of them idiots, others driven by a secret vice, still more the victims of terrible congenital deformities or ghastly diseases. Every now and again, dishevelled whores like something out of a bad dream stuck their bony chests out of the brothel doors and called to the men in filthy, mocking tones. Prullàs and Pretty Face found themselves in the midst of a swarm of beggars. Prullàs could not understand why such wretched creatures would want to be in such a poverty-stricken place. "Why don't they go and beg out on the Diagonal?" he asked. "I've no idea; maybe the people here are more generous," the cripple laughed.

A few yards further on, Pretty Face suddenly stopped in front of a dosshouse. Prullàs protested. "You're not going to get me in a place like that!" he exclaimed. "It'll only take a moment, Señor Prullàs. The person we're looking for is in here."

Prullàs reluctantly followed the cripple into a long rectangular room with flaking walls and a beamed ceiling. At the far end, a raffia curtain hid a dark corridor. Sitting on the edge of their wicker chairs, four sweaty whores caked in make-up were laughing outrageously at the antics of a cadaverous old man dressed in black who had rolled his trousers up above the knee to reveal milky-white smooth calves, wrapped his mourning jacket round his waist, and stuck a large carnation behind his ear without removing his beret. "Come on my lovelies, come on!" the aged fool bellowed. "Don't pay any attention to him," Pretty Face whispered in Prullàs' ear. "That's Don Eduvigis: he comes here every night to entertain the troops, hoping he'll get a free ride."

The old fogey flung his calloused hands up towards the yellow bulb hanging from the ceiling. As the bulb swayed, all the shadows swelled and shrank. "What rhythm the old goat's got!" the whores cackled. Still laughing, they lifted their petticoats and drove away the flies from between their legs with a cheap fan. Seeing the newcomers arrive, their laughter turned to wheedling flattery. "Who's this little gem you've found, Pretty Face?"

"Keep your hands off him, he's not for you, you old sow!" the cripple said, trying to impose his authority. "That's what you think," the woman replied. "As the saying goes: when it's sex you need, no-one's safe, not e'en the dead."

Disturbed by their intrusion, Don Eduvigis redoubled his efforts to keep the women's attention. "Come on, come on!" Pretty Face spat disdainfully on the floor. "Get back to the workhouse, you dried-up old prick!" "And wouldn't you just love it up your arse, faggotface!" came the old man's retort.

The whores celebrated this exchange. "That told the cripple all right! Oh, what a cunt!"

Soon, though, Don Eduvigis accepted defeat with dignity. The whores slowly calmed down: they pushed their sagging breasts back in, straightened their petticoats, pinned up their straggling hair. "Isn't Antoñita la Espatarrá here?" Pretty Face asked. "She's in the back room," they told him. "On her own?" "No. Niño de la Doctrina is with her. And in a bad mood. Oh, shit!"

Prullàs was still standing in the doorway, ready to run out at any moment; from time to time he surreptitiously raised a perfumed handkerchief to his nose, to ward off the stench from the fetid atmosphere. "Is something wrong, Pretty Face?" he wanted to know. "No, not at all. Come with me, Señor Prullàs, make yourself at home."

The corridor was flanked by several narrow, gloomy rooms. They had no windows and were separated from one another by thin partitions. Grimy sacking curtains hanging from a rail in the doorways offered the only possibility for intimacy. At this time of night, there was no need for that: the curtains were drawn back, and the rooms empty. Inside they contained a flimsy bed with sunken springs, a bowl of slimy water with a soiled sponge floating in it, and a chair to put clothes on. In one of them, the two men stumbled on a tender scene: in the cone of light from a bedside lamp, a still youthful woman was sitting on the edge of the bed, giving suck to a skinny child; another scrofulous child sat clinging to her skirts chewing on a stick of liquorice.

Prullàs paused to look in at them, and when she saw him, the emaciated mother gave him an exhausted smile. "Spare a few coins for my little treasures, poor things!"

Pretty Face spun round on his one leg and growled: "Who told you to have them?" "No-one asked my permission," the woman complained. "You could've drowned 'em at birth, like they all do!" "It's you they should drown in a bucket of spit, you leech!" Then turning back to Prullàs, she said sadly: "You have them without meaning to, but then you get fond of them, you see."

There was more sorrow than anger in her voice. Prullàs took some coins out of his wallet. The cripple grabbed his arm. "Don't encourage begging," he snarled. "Listen, I do as I like with my money!" Prullàs said. "Not here. Give to charity in your own church." "Why are you so much against that poor woman?" "She's only got what she deserved," the cripple said. "And anyway, those kids don't have much future: just look at them! They're like living corpses! Don't waste your money on them."

All of a sudden they heard shouting and crashing at the far end of the corridor. "That's Niño de la Doctrina and his trollop," Pretty Face said. "Is he the one who has the documents?" Prullàs asked. "Him? No. It's Antoñita la Espatarrá who's got them." "Did she steal the wallet?" Prullàs wanted to know. "No! Stealing is wrong, and here no-one does wrong. But as you know, things can change hands."

"And who is Niño de la Doctrina?" "He's Antoñita's pimp, of course," said the other man. "He must have heard about the deal, and naturally enough wants his share. They must be sealing the bargain right now. Can't you hear the blows?" "So he hits her?" "Only when he's in a good mood. When he's drunk, he gets really nasty. Then anything's enough to make him blow his top, and if he's got a knife in his hand, he's his own worst enemy. He's been in the can twice, but only for short spells:

403

the women he cut up were whores, and the beaks took that into account. Otherwise he'd still be inside come Judgment Day."

When they reached the curtain pulled across the door of the end room the noise ceased. The silence was even worse than the stream of insults and slaps that had preceded it. Prullàs turned on his heel. "Let's go," he said; "I've got more than enough trouble with one dead body." "Don't go on so, this is nothing. Don't you teach your wife a lesson every now and then?" "Never!" "God knows how you ever get her respect!" Pretty Face said. "Let's call them."

The cripple pushed his face close to the curtain. "Is anybody in?" A woman's voice replied: "Is that you, Pretty Face?" "Yes, and with company."

"Come in!"

The room's lampshade was torn, so a harsh slanting light shone on one wall. Lying back on the bed, they caught a glimpse of Antoñita la Espatarrá's thighs, covered in varicose veins and bruises, before she wrapped the bottom of her petti-coats around them. In the darkened corner of the room stood a sallow, sunken-cheeked man with plastered-down hair, dark lips, a pencil moustache and a receding chin.

"We don't want to interrupt," Pretty Face said. "You're not, we were only having a little chat," the pimp said. "And getting some exercise by the sound of it," the cripple replied.

Niño de la Doctrina struck a match on the sole of his shoe and lit a cigarette. "Just billing and cooing," he hissed. The whore grimaced. "Some cooing!" "Some bill!" the pimp replied.

Prullàs felt more and more ill-at-ease. "Let's finish our business." "That's up to you. Have you got the dough?" "I've brought four thousand." "It's worth three times that." "Everything is worth what someone is willing to pay for it," Prullàs said. "My offer is what I've just told you. If you're not satisfied, find another buyer."

Niño de la Doctrina glanced furtively at Prullàs and smiled, showing a row of broken teeth. "It's not my style to haggle over cash," he said. "Show us the four thousand."

"The document first."

"Antoñita, show the gentleman what you have for sale."

"It's at home, so I don't lose it."

"My God," Prullàs exclaimed, "how many places do I have to go to for this damned document?"

"It's just next door," the cripple said soothingly, "right round the corner."

Antoñita la Espatarrá began to put on a pair of filthy stockings. Prullàs folded his arms. "I'm not going anywhere," he said firmly. "If it's as close as you say, let her go for the document and bring it here."

Niño de la Doctrina rolled his eyes. "Look here, friend," he growled; "with all due respect, I'm going to tell you something: this isn't the Ritz; it's a simple, modest place where honest people come to dip their wick; if any of them wants something special, they pay for the service. But apart from that and in all other matters, it's yours truly who gives the orders here, O.K.? So, let's go! And you, stop picking at your lice and get a move on!"

"They're crabs I get from the clients," Antoñita la Espatarrá complained. "My cunt's all sore from the flyspray I put on it!"

The pimp threw his cigarette on the floor and stubbed it out with the sole of his patent- leather shoe. The cripple laughed his noiseless laugh, opening and closing his toothless mouth. "What a princess! She'll only put out for Charles Boyer!"

The pimp sighed: "Lazy as a pig! Just as well yours truly is there to stir his stumps when need be."

Antoñita la Espatarrá finished doing up her print blouse, and hung from her pimp's arm. "I don't know why I loves you so much, you brute!"

"Shut your mouth, you slut! After you, sir," he said, drawing back the door curtain, "because when it comes to manners there's no son of a bitch can teach a shite to Niño de la Doctrina."

4

This strange group retraced their steps, crossed the dank entrance hall without exchanging a word, and emerged into the street. The late-night customers leered at them and promptly forgot them. If anyone wanted to string me up, they'd all offer to join in, Prullàs thought to himself, horrified by the ghastly appearance of these dregs of society, but if my life was in danger, not one of them would so much as lift a finger to help me. Really, he reflected, solidarity is an illusion. He was increasingly aware how stupid he had been to bring the money with him, convinced he would only be meeting one person, and in the Taberna de Mañuel. All this is Gaudet's fault, he told himself somewhat illogically; *he* would have known how to deal with this. I'll never forgive him for leaving me in the lurch. While he was pondering in this fashion, they left behind the noisy bustling streets and once more found themselves in dark alleyways. Soon the only sound to be heard was their footsteps on the uneven cobbles of this disreputable district. The three of them stepped as lightly as possible over the uneven ground, while the one-legged man struggled along behind them. "Is it far?" Prullàs asked.

Niño de la Doctrina came to an abrupt halt, peered all around, and declared that they had arrived. Prullàs looked about him in surprise. "What, here?" "This is as good a place as any," the pimp replied, pulling a large jackknife from his trouser pocket. "What are you staring at, dummy? Never seen a stick-up before?

Well now you can tell everyone you have! And hurry up with the dough if you don't want me to slit your gullet."

"What's this? You're robbing me?" Prullàs moaned. "Got it in one!" the pimp cackled like a hyena. "But you don't have to put your hands up, dummy, we're not going to dance a jig!"

"Pretty Face, what's this? What's going on here?" Prullàs asked the one-legged man, who had just joined the others, huffing and puffing. "Sweet Jaysis, Niño, couldn't you wait for a poor lame old man?" he complained. "Buy yourself a roller skate!" the other man mocked him; "and tell your friend here to behave if he values his hide."

"Don't get mad now, Niño, and be careful what you're doing with that thing," the one-legged man said, dodging to avoid the blade the other man was twirling as he spoke. "As for you, Señor Prullàs, you heard him."

"What about the wallet you were going to give me? And the document?"

"What wallet and what document are you talking about?" Niño de la Doctrina roared. "Here *you* pay 'cos I sez so, and if you don't get a move on, I might just cut your ears off and then make a start on your guts, geddit?"

"Calm down, for God's sake!" Prullàs said in a faint whisper. "I'll give you all the money and the valuables I have on me, but don't hurt me."

"You'll give us! Give us! Like shite you will! You're not going to give us anything, sweetheart, we're going to take all we want from you, including your smart arse pants: d'you get that at least? Antoñita, empty this skunk's pockets; and don't worry about him, anyone can see he's more scared than ashamed!"

The whore obeyed his instructions with trembling fingers; her chubby hands groped at Prullàs' legs through the lining of his trousers.

407

"Are you going to take all night weighing his nuts?" Pretty Face muttered. "Hurry up, you bitch!" Antoñita la Espatarrá struggled to remove Prullàs' possessions from his pockets and hand them one by one to her pimp, who assessed them with casual expertise: "One cambric hankerchief for his lordship's snot! Not worth shite!" Then again: "One Parker fountain pen with gold top! Five hundred pesetas at least! What's this? One Homega wristwatch with crocodile strap, plus cigarette case also crocodile, for his lordship's pleasure, containing ten Lucky Stroik fags! Shite, all o' it! Where's the money?" "Calm down, Niño, I'm just getting it," Antoñita said.

The pimp grabbed the banknotes with his free hand, spread them like playing cards and gave a long whistle. "Holy shite! Seven grand! See that, Pretty Face? Didn't he say he'd only brought four thousand? Why, he was trying to cheat me! Me! Niño de la Doctrina!"

The crook's cockiness grew as the amount of money he was holding sunk in; he thought he was on top of the world. "There's nothing more, Niño," the whore shouted, showing her two empty hands. "Stow the money and let's get out of here!"

Niño de la Doctrina was about to take her sensible advice when the one-legged man squawked, pointing at Prullàs: "What about him?" The pimp shrugged. "He ain't got any more," he said; "unless you want to smother him in kisses . . ." "What are you going to do with him?" Pretty Face insisted, "leave him here so he can go to the cops and make a statement? You're not thinking straight, Niño!" "So what d'you suggest? What else is there?" "Kill him." "Hey, steady on, you can't be serious!" Prullàs shouted.

The pimp thought it over, frowning deeply and with his chin sunk on his chest. His tiny eyes jumped from the money to his knife and back again, as if these inanimate objects could tell him how to act. "What's the matter, Niño? You scared or something?" the one-legged man croaked.

"That wasn't part of the deal, Pretty Face. Holy shite! It's one thing to pick someone's pocket, and another to slit his throat!"

"Hey, you two," Antoñita said; "if there's going to be violence, yours truly here is off." "You stay right where you are, or you'll be the first to get it!" her pimp threatened her.

"Yes, yes," Prullàs wailed, "stay here and tell them they're wrong to be worried about me: I haven't the slightest intention of reporting this to anyone."

He seemed to be speaking lightly, as if all their display of verbal threats was nothing more than a farce designed to persuade him not to put up any kind of resistance, but in fact his legs were giving way under him, and his shirt was sticking to his skin with sweat. Niño de la Doctrina was trying to weigh up the pros and cons of his fateful decision; his dull mind was swirling with images of blood and terror. Seeing him still reluctant, Pretty Face whispered to him, insidiously: "Go on, Niño, finish him off. He's no good to you, can't you see? He's just a toff!"

"But sweet Jaysis, Pretty Face, like this, in cold blood . . . !"

The two rogues were busy wasting their time in an interminable discussion full of verbal cut and thrust. "They weren't being serious, were they?" Prullàs whispered to the woman, taking advantage of the momentary respite. "About killing me, I mean, they can't be serious about it, can they?"

"Don't be scared," she reassured him. "Niño won't hurt you: he's all bark and no bite. He's a little lamb really. But Pretty Face is a different matter: he's evil through and through. If he weren't crippled, he'd gouge your eyes out with his bare hands, tear out your tongue and wring your neck for good measure." "All that for seven thousand pesetas?" "Pretty Face hates every living soul; and the rich more than anyone. He's a true bolshervick," she added in a low whisper. Then she sighed and went on, as if to herself: "But Niño only wants money so's he can spend it on gut-rot and whores."

"And you?" Prullàs asked desperately, noting a sense of bitterness in what she had just said; "what are you going to get out of this senseless adventure?" "Huh," she replied, holding out the empty palms of her hands to him in an almost begging gesture, "I'll get something, and God knows, I need it! I've got a girl boarding with the Mercedarias nuns, and that costs an arm and a leg."

"Listen, Antoñita," Prullàs interrupted her hastily, speaking as close to her as he could, "don't get carried away by the money you saw. That might seem a lot to you, but it's nothing to me: I've got much more. Help me escape: if I get out of here alive, I'll pension you off. On my word of honour, I'll get you off the streets. An apartment and an allowance, Antoñita, apartment and allowance. Think of your daughter, and don't let her life and yours be ruined for such a paltry amount. Help me escape!"

"What! And betray my man?" the trollop roared, arms akimbo as if she was about to burst into song. "Never in my life!" Then, turning to the pair of thieves who were still arguing loudly, unaware of their victim's efforts to get away, she shouted at them: "Hey, you two, stop all that bleating and look out, this fine gennleman here's trying to give you the slip."

Alerted by this warning, Niño de la Doctrina and Pretty Face immediately put an end to their bickering. Returning to the business in hand, Niño came forward making his blade dance a tango, with the one-legged man urging him on in his hoarse croak: "Slit his throat! Mince his liver for him! Don't let anyone have the chance to say Niño de la Doctrina didn't have the balls for it!"

Prullàs clung to Antoñita la Espatarrá, seeking protection behind her sagging flesh. "Help me, Antoñita," he begged her, "don't let him touch me! Tell him what you already know: that he's risking the garrotte for a few miserable pesetas! Antoñita, if you really love him, stop him committing this madness!"

The pimp came ever closer, flourishing his blade. "Antoñita, get out of the way and leave him to me! Now you'll see how Niño de la Doctrina despatches a bull!"

"Antoñita! I'm a father too!" Prullàs sobbed. "Think of your daughter! I could give her a future! I have friends who are professors at the university!"

The pimp was becoming more and more enraged at Antoñita getting in his way, and Pretty Face spun round like a top on his one good leg, not for a moment letting up in his bloodcurdling cries: "Kill him! Kill him!" "Get out the way, you sow!" the pimp roared.

The whore struggled to free herself from Prullàs' grasp. As she did so, he could feel his limbs refusing to obey any rational commands, and he fell on his face in the gutter. He burst into sobs. "Don't hurt me, I beg you!" he wailed. "Let me live and I swear you won't regret it! I'll give you money! More money! All the money you want! You say how much, I won't even try to make a bargain! But for the love of God, don't kill me! Listen, I know people. I can get you pardons, help you start new lives, free of guilt . . . and I'd pay you a wage, so you wouldn't have to work. I'll do whatever you want, whatever you want, if only you let me live! Look, look at me, I'm on my knees to you! Pretty Face is right: I'm worthless, I'm a good-for-nothing, I'm not even worth the effort of killing me, let alone the risk . . . Have pity on me!"

These pleas and promises had little effect on the minds of the two ruffians, being almost unintelligible anyway amidst all Prullàs' choking sobs and quaking terror. The knifeblade caught the dim glow of a streetlamp as it described its mortal half-circle through the air. Prullàs shut his eyes. There was a confused tussle, and blood began to flow. In a fraction of a second that seemed to him an eternity, he felt a painful blow to his chest, sensed a warm fluid soaking his legs, and collapsed forward on the ground. Before his head hit the cobbles, it collided with a soft form. He heard someone curse, and a dying groan. When he opened his eyes again, he saw the front of his coat covered in blood, and thought: I'm badly wounded, but I'm not dead; if I got to hospital quickly enough perhaps they could save my life; I'm in desperate need of a transfusion, if not, I'll bleed to death like poor Vallsigorri: now there's a coincidence!

"Well I'm damned," the one-legged man croaked. "You're so ham-fisted you've gone and stuck your whore, you idiot!"

"Holy shite! How was I to know she'd step in to try to save that queer!"

"Well, it's no great loss," the other man said; "she was pretty dumb anyway." "Don't say that," the pimp protested. "Poor Antoñita! She spent all her life putting it out to pay for me, and now I've killed her! I didn't mean to! Poor Antoñita!" "This is no time to start getting sentimental, Niño," Pretty Face said. "Finish the job and let's get out of here." "I didn't mean to, Pretty Face, you saw that. She brought it on herself! Spilling guts is men's business! Why did she have to get mixed up in it?"

"That's not going to bother the judge, Niño," the one-legged man replied; "if the cops find you not even sweet Jesus can save you from the garrotte." "What shall we do then?" the pimp asked him. "Right now, you've got to get rid of the witness, and then beat it."

From all this Prullàs deduced what had happened: either to save his life, or to prevent her man from doing something he would regret, Antoñita la Espatarrá had pushed in between them and received the knife thrust aimed at him. Now the self-sacrificing woman lay lifeless before him. It was her blood soaking his clothes and hands; and her body was the bulky mass on which his head was cradled. This offered him only a brief respite: Niño de la Doctrina was already preparing to accede to Pretty Face's goading, and was waving the bloody knife as a prelude to employing it once more on its fateful mission.

5

At that very moment not far from there in the Tasca del Tío Ciruelo by the dim light of a candle stub, two middle-aged, rough-looking men, one of them a gypsy, the other a workman of some sort, were whiling away their time drinking liquor and risking their scant savings in a card game.

"Six pesetas," the gypsy said to open. "Only six? *Peccata minuta!* Here's ten, to make it more interesting!"

The gypsy shuffled the cards and stroked his chin with scrawny fingers covered in cheap rings. "You're very free with your money recently, friend," he growled; "I reckon you've found that daughter of yours another rich boyfriend."

Before replying, the bulky individual facing him scratched his midriff through a hole in his vest and then stared down fascinated at the black fingernail he withdrew. "What's a man to do? You can't live on air. But it's not a man's work selling pussy, especially not his own flesh and blood. No, my friend, we earned every cent of the money you see here, son of a bitch that I am! Him as is ready to shift it and take his shirt off can always find ways of making it. Son of a bitch that I am! The thing is, Spain's a country full of lazy good-for-nothings, my friend. Disciplin' an' culture, that's wha' we needs!"

Roused by his own words, he tossed down his glass of cheap rum and rounded off the fiery swigging with several noisy belches. The gypsy covered his face. "Hey friend, can't you turn your gob in another direction, we don't want to risk anythin' with the candle, does we?"

At that point, an outlandish figure loomed up and filled the bar doorway. It hesitated for an instant, then headed straight for the two men; the choice cannot have been all that difficult, as they were the only two in the dive. "You must be Villalba," the figure hissed.

The burly man stared from head to toe at this strange apparition, which was bent forward over him so as not to scrape the ceiling with the comb on top of its head. The gypsy instinctively raised his hand to his waist; he was a bony, sallow-faced man who made his money clipping dogs and was expert in the use of the enormous pair of scissors he kept in his trouser sash. Villalba stopped him with a gesture. "There's nothing to cut off here," he said slyly. "A tongue perhaps," the gypsy said.

"Stop trying to be funny, there's no time for that," the artiste pronounced, shaking the cockroaches off the tail of her dress. "I has to be on stage in five minutes. If I'm not there, theyse'll cancel my contract an' then what will I's eat? Singin' is a dog's life."

Without more ado, she leaned over and whispered into the fat man's ear. When he heard what she had to say, he thumped the table with a giant fist. Then he leapt up, knocking over his chair, and shouted to the gypsy in commanding tones: "Forward march!"

The three of them burst into the alleyway just as Prullàs was preparing to receive the coup de grâce. Somewhat relieved, Niño de la Doctrina interrupted his thrust at the very last moment. The one-legged man protested loudly: "What's the matter? Why don't you finish him off?"

"Time to retreat, Pretty Face! We're outnumbered!" With that, the pimp ran off and disappeared down the dark alleys. "You could at least wait for me, you lily-livered son-of-a-bitch," the other man groaned.

Pretty Face vanished round the first corner, hotly pursued by the gypsy and his scissors. He knew all the ins and outs of these slums like the back of his hand, and was no mean opponent on his home ground; the gypsy soon gave up and came back to join the others, who were clustered around the dead woman. Prullàs was sobbing and hiccoughing uncontrollably, his face buried in her opulent bosom. "Oh, it was horrible, horrible!"

"Calm down, sweetheart, it's all over now." The gypsy stuck his scissors back in his waistband and brought them back to reality. "We have to beat it," he said; "the cops could be here at any moment, and if they catch us standing around with this little bundle, we're in trouble." "That's true," Prullàs said. "Poor Antoñita, she gave her life to save mine!"

"Bundle o' shite, more like!" Antoñita la Espatarrá suddenly howled from the ground. "I's not dead yet! But I will be if yeh don't get me to 'ospital quick!" "No chance!" Villalba cut in. "Our friend here is right, we have to get out of here." "But surely," Prullàs objected, "we can't just leave this poor woman here to bleed to death on the asphalt!"

"We've no choice," the fat man replied. "We can't show up at a 'ospital with a trollop like that and her guts 'anging out, can we? If yeh want to try, good luck to yeh, but the likes o' me and my friend have done enough for one day."

"He's right, he is," La Fresca pronounced. "Someone'll come and help her; if not tonight, then tomorrow mornin', you'll see. And don't worry, her sort has nine lives, like cats."

Antoñita la Espatarrá clutched at Prullàs' ankle. "Don't leave me, Holy mother of God, don't leave me! I's goin' to die, and I have a daughter boarding in the Mercedarias!"

The four of them hurried off down the narrow streets, and soon the whore's pleas and curses faded on the night air. Prullàs was so weak they had to drag him along. Villalba suggested they take him home, but Prullàs would not hear of it: he didn't want anyone to see him at that time of night, with companions like them, and with filthy and bloody clothing. They walked on for a while with no idea of where they were heading, when suddenly Prullàs saw the streetlamps of the Ramblas and had an idea. "We can't be far from the Hotel Gallardo," he said. "It's a discreet place and they know me well. You can leave me there and get me some clean clothes. But you'll have to lend me some money," he quickly added, "because those thieves stole everything I had." "I suppose you're good for it," Villalba replied loftily.

As they made for the hotel, La Fresca told them how when she saw Prullàs leave the Taberna de Mañuel with Pretty Face, and knowing he had a large amount of money on him, she sent a pickpocket to follow them. The man had come back a short while later to tell her what he had seen: La Fresca had realised Prullàs was in grave danger, left the bar and started to ask where she could find help. It had been easy enough to locate Villalba, because he had spent the last few days boasting of his lucrative association with a fine gentleman. When she had finished her story, La Fresca ran to get back to the Taberna de Mañuel, because she was already late for her show.

The receptionist with the gardenia in his buttonhole raised his eyebrows when he saw Prullàs and his team entering the hotel. He looked very frightened, and seemed unable to decide whether he should hide behind the counter or run off up the stairs. Prullàs reassured him: "My friends will be leaving straightaway, and I only want to have a bit of a rest," he said. The receptionist's hand trembled as he gave him the key. As soon as Villalba and the gypsy had left Prullàs in his room and gone to get him some clean clothes, Prullàs tore off his trousers and flung them at the far wall: the large dark stain and the penetrating smell were more than enough evidence of his lack of manliness. His jacket, shirt and tie soon followed his trousers across the room. He was too exhausted to wash, so he merely collapsed onto the bed and lay staring up at the ceiling until he was interrupted by a knocking at the door. "Come in," he said.

Lilí Villalba came in, carrying a large bundle. "My father told me you needed some clothes, and I thought you might need *me* as well," she said. "Oh, Lilí, I'd have preferred you not to come!" Prullàs exclaimed. "I'm so ashamed that you're seeing me like this."

Lilí undid the bundle and spread out the clothes at the foot of the bed, then tied up the dirty clothes in the same cover. When she saw the state of Prullàs' trousers, she couldn't help laughing. "Don't be ashamed," she said tenderly, "my father told me what happened. It's a natural reaction: nobody says you have to be a hero. These things happen to *everyone*. Perhaps not in your circles, but in mine they do. In any case, nobody need find out: it will be our secret; *yet another one*. Look, I've brought a clean towel. You just lie back and leave it to me. If you'd come to meet me like you promised, you wouldn't be in this state, and you wouldn't have had such a fright. You might *at least* say you're sorry to me. Look, I'm still wearing the special dress I told you about; d'you like it?"

Meanwhile in the street below the window, the gypsy was passing the time as he stood guard singing an old song:

> God it was give him a weapon
> And the heart of a lion
> Only so he might prove
> Your love he could rely on.

CHAPTER EIGHT

I

Prullàs gave Sebastiana a long and complicated explanation for the cheap clothes he was wearing and the bag of dirty ones, which the faithful maid pretended to accept completely. "I'm going to have a shower," he went on. "Put out some clean clothes for me, and throw away all this rubbish. And my dirty clothes as well: Don't send them to the laundry – I wouldn't wear them again for anything in the world. Did anyone call while I was out?" "No-one," Sebastiana told him. "But this morning," she continued, "shortly before you arrived, a boy brought a package. He didn't say who it was from, he simply gave it me and rushed off."

An hour later, once he had taken his shower and done the crossword in *La Vanguardia*, Prullàs felt clean and relaxed, safe once more in his own home; it was then he remembered the package Sebastiana had mentioned. He found it on the hall sideboard, propped against one of the candlesticks. It was small, and carefully wrapped in brown paper with a string round it; there was no sign of any mention of who had sent it. Prullàs shut himself in his study and opened the package; he at once recognised what it was, though he had never seen it before. A shiver ran down his spine. How on earth can this have finally reached me? he wondered. His fingers trembled as he opened Vallsigorri's wallet, the search for which had very nearly cost him his life. Several business cards, a photo of its former owner

418

and the lottery tickets they had bought in the Taberna de Mañuel all testified to its authenticity. In a sleeve for banknotes he found a piece of paper folded in four. Prullàs unfolded it and read its contents. After reading it three times and weighing up the consequences of his discovery, he folded it again, put it back in the wallet, slipped it into his pocket, and left his apartment.

"This was why you did it, wasn't it?" he exploded after reading the letter out loud. Gaudet shrugged and spread his arms wide, as if to say he was not denying the charge, but couldn't accept the accusation behind it. Once again Prullàs put the piece of paper back in the wallet, and the wallet in his pocket; he stared angrily at his friend. "You knew about all this!" he shouted.

"Yes," the director admitted; "but I only learnt about the letter recently. How did it get to you?" "I haven't the faintest idea," Prullàs said, "and I'm not interested. Oh Pepe," he said more in sorrow than in anger, "how could you do this to me?"

He crossed the living-room and pulled back the curtains. The harsh noon light flooded into the room, revealing its peeling walls; dusty, battered furniture; the floor littered with books, magazines and manuscripts; Gaudet's faded, dirty pyjamas, covered in greasy stains; his sallow face and the emaciated, hangdog look of his face. "You've no right to accuse me like that," he said. "And shut those curtains, would you?"

Prullàs felt sorry for his friend and did as he asked. The room was submerged in darkness once more. Prullàs sat down again, and neither spoke for some time. Eventually Gaudet said: "Miguel Fontcuberta always was a fathead. He married Kiki on a whim; he didn't even consider the consequences of the sacrifice he was demanding of someone who up to then had only lived for her art. Perhaps she should have seen that, and refused him. But those were difficult days for everyone. Like the idiot he is, he soon got tired of the novelty. Kiki suspected he had another woman in Madrid, and it was probably true. But she needn't have looked so far away: here in Barcelona he's had at least two mistresses and several affairs, and that's without counting the number of times he's been seen visiting brothels. He's passed on quite a few disgusting infections to his wife. And besides, as you know, malicious gossip is the favourite pastime here." "I never heard anything," Prullàs interrupted him. "You never hear anything; you're only concerned with yourself," the director said. And without giving the other man a chance to reply, he went on: "In all likelihood Vallsigorri was no better than Miguel Fontcuberta, but at least he treated her well, and by betraying her husband with him, Kiki thought she was getting revenge for her humiliation. But women – especially such a highly-strung artist as her – never really calculate what they're doing." "When did you find out all this?" Prullàs wanted to know. "Oh, only a few weeks ago," Gaudet said. "When Vallsigorri came to see me at the theatre, I hadn't the heart to hide it from Kiki, and she told me everything. She was desperate. Her age is beginning to tell, and she finds it harder and harder to play the roles of scatterbrained women you write for her so remorselessly, and which she feels obliged to perform day and night, day after day, on all the stages in Spain . . . you can't imagine how nasty provincial critics can be. And every attack makes it more obvious to her how her charms and the advantages of youth are slipping inexorably away from her."

"So you're saying I'm to blame for everything!" Prullàs exclaimed.

"Poor Kiki," Gaudet went on, ignoring his friend, "she couldn't find respite or consolation. She used to come here often on the excuse she was looking after me and straightening out my chaotic bachelor life, when in reality she would pour out all her troubles and anger to me. In spite of myself, I became her confidant, and that meant I could see just how great her distress was. Then when Vallsigorri was killed, I refused to jump to any conclusions, not even to myself. My trust in her as a friend meant I was bound to hope that in the end it would be discovered that a third person had committed that terrible crime."

"Someone like me, for example?" Prullàs said. There was no rancour in his voice. The director replied that of course he had never for a moment doubted Prullàs' innocence. "But you refused to help me," Prullàs replied, "just when I most needed you, when the circle of suspicion was drawing tighter and tighter around me."

"I had no other choice," Gaudet replied, visibly exhausted. "After Don Lorenzo Verdugones had interrogated us both, Kiki told me of the existence of the letter. She said she'd written it in a moment of madness, and had taken advantage of the housewarming at Brusquets' to slip it to Vallsigorri unnoticed. I was caught in the middle: I couldn't go on helping you without incriminating Kiki, or pretend I was on your side, and still keep such an important clue from you. I decided to keep out of it, in the hope that your investigation would lead nowhere, and that the affair would slowly be forgotten. Contrary to what happens in films, in real life lots of crimes go unpunished." At this point Gaudet paused, looked his friend up and down, then went on, weighing every one of his words: "And I still hope that's what'll happen in this case."

"What d'you mean?" Prullàs asked.

Gaudet leaned back in his armchair and stared up at the ceiling. "We don't really know who it was who killed Vallsigorri," he said calmly. "It's true there's a compromising letter, but you can use that in your favour. Verdugones cannot know of its existence, or he would have arrested Kiki already. In fact, Verdugones knows nothing whatsoever: he's relying on you to solve the mystery. And if you don't allow yourself to be scared by his threats, things won't get much further, and everything will return gradually to normal . . . " "But Vallsigorri has been murdered!" Prullàs interrupted him. "Unfortunately, nothing can be done about that," Gaudet replied. "D'you really want more blood spilled? That wouldn't achieve anything. You know the person who killed him acted without thinking, in a moment of madness and without any criminal intent. And there's no reason to believe that person would commit another crime, because the circumstances which caused the fit of passion will never be repeated."

"That's fine, but what about justice, Pepe?" "What justice?" Gaudet cried, his face flushed as he leapt out of his chair, as though propelled by the springs sticking out through the upholstery. "What justice? The kind that not only condones but celebrates men's lack of morality while condemning women without appeal whenever they commit the slightest indiscretion, blinded by their emotions?"

"Pepe, please, that's enough!" Prullàs shouted. "You're talking like a radio soap opera. And a murder isn't a slight indiscretion, drat it!"

"I'm sorry, it's just that things like this take it out of me," the director replied.

2

Mariquita Pons told her maid to ask him to be so kind as to wait a few minutes in the reception room. "Madam has not finished her toilette," the girl said, blushing and attempting an awkward curtsy. What a shame things are so complicated, Prullàs thought as he sneaked a glance at her legs; she's certainly a prime specimen.

She left him on his own. He paced nervously up and down the room, noticing with distaste how solid and expensive all the pieces of furniture were, and how valuable the collection of objects in the showcase was. The clock on the mantelpiece chimed twelve. It's noon, he said to himself, and Kiki's still in her bath. What a life of luxury! And yet she still complains! A lot of women would put up with anything if they could live in plush surroundings like this, but she feels cheated. Of course, who knows, he answered himself, it may not all be selfish and premeditated.

By the fireplace he saw the tongs, the shovel and the poker for the fire: implements that appeared so often in the thrillers he was fond of. He was reaching down to touch the burnished handles of these tools when suddenly the maid came into the room again, carrying a tea service on a tray.

"I put another cup on in case you would like some tea too," she murmured, her cheeks burning. Then she said more firmly: "Madam is just coming."

Just as she was saying this, Mariquita made her entrance, dressed and made-up with great care. She looked as if everything had been specially chosen to convey a perfect image of respectability. The maid withdrew, and they sat down at the table with the tea tray on it. Mariquita picked up the teapot and the strainer, and carefully served herself a cup of tea, to which she added half a slice of lemon and a lump of sugar.

"Well, what d'you have to say?" she whispered finally, without raising her eyes from her teacup. "I suppose Gaudet's phoned you already," Prullàs said. "It was him on the phone when you arrived; that was why I had you wait. You can't think I'm still getting up at this time of day. But let's get down to business: what d'you want to know?" "Kiki, my love, it's me who is asking the questions," Prullàs said. "And I warn you, I'm in no mood for games."

He took the piece of paper out of the wallet, unfolded it, showed it to Mariquita, and then put it away again. The actress merely gave it a cursory glance, and calmly returned to her tea. "That letter doesn't prove a thing," she said. "I won't deny I wrote it, but that's no crime. At the very most, it's a release of passion and a rash act. Thousands of letters like it are written every day. This might come as a surprise to you, because you always choose dummies who can't read or write, but we women are passionate creatures."

"That perfume on Vallsigorri's clothes was yours, wasn't it? You were with him on the day he was killed, perhaps even in his apartment."

"That's possible," she replied, and after an awkward pause, she added in a firmer voice: "that evening, I did go to his apartment. I realised how stupid I'd been to give him that letter. What I'd seen as wounding and threatening became a weapon against me. I rang to tell him I was coming; his assistant answered. I didn't say who I was, but she probably recognised my voice: it wasn't the first time I'd called, and maids are born gossips. I didn't care. I went to see him, and asked him to give me back the letter. He told me he didn't have it any more. He invented some cock-and-bull story about how he had never even read it, that a pickpocket had stolen it the night before in a flamenco bar, no less. Of course, I didn't believe a word of it, but what could I do? I summoned up my last dregs of dignity and left then and there. There was no-one else in the apartment, and no-one saw me arrive or leave, but Ignacio Vallsigorri was still alive when I left. May I die on the spot if I'm telling a lie. Would you like some tea now?"

Prullàs accepted. I'd prefer a whisky, he thought, but I must keep a clear head. He picked up his cup, and the two of them drank their tea without saying anything more for a while.

"When I heard Ignacio had been killed, I forgot about the letter. I forgot everything after that terrible shock; it was devastating, and the worst thing was I couldn't even show it openly.

And don't take my apparent calm now as an admission of guilt. If I seem in control, it's only because I've cried so much all alone. I've no more tears to shed. But I did not kill him. I wouldn't have harmed him for anything in the world; I could have forgiven him anything. In any case," she added, putting her cup down on the tray and heaving a great sigh, "I'm too old to kill. I don't mean I haven't the strength, but I don't have the will. I don't think there was ever really a time when I could have killed someone, because I hate violence, but there was a time when out of rivalry or jealousy or the desire for revenge I've wished someone dead. But now I've lived too long to wish any harm to anyone, even my worst enemy. I've seen a lot of people die, and I'm scared of the loneliness ahead of me. Besides, I loved Ignacio. At first I wanted him just for myself; I fought and lost that battle; then I got used to the idea of sharing him with others, as long as he went on loving me. By the end I accepted anything, just to know he still existed."

"But in the letter you threaten to kill him: it's written here in your own handwriting!" Prullàs said. "Oh, words, words, what would our grey lives be without words?" the actress retorted, placing a cigarette in her mother-of-pearl holder and leaning forward for Prullàs to light it.

Prullàs did so, then stared down at his lighter and said: "The fact is, Kiki, I don't understand you: how could you fall in love with such a rogue, at your age and in your position? If your husband didn't fit the bill, you might at least have found something a bit less complicated. There are dozens of handsome young actors who would have been happy to oblige . . . we know lots of cases, don't we: Maruja Ribera, Rosario Besaragua, Lolita . . ."

Mariquita Pons silenced him with an imperious gesture. "Please," she said, "I'm a decent, married woman!" Then almost immediately she added, in a lower voice: "At least, I've tried to be. That was my biggest mistake. My mistake and yours, Carlos. We should never have allowed wealth to corrupt us!"

She filled their cups a second time, and went on smoking unconcernedly. Prullàs was thinking: anyone who has seen another person stabbed can never talk about it so calmly afterwards; I know that now from experience. Perhaps then she's telling the truth; or perhaps she killed him and doesn't remember, as Doctor Mercadal explained to me. Or perhaps I'm simply seeing proof of what a talented actress she is.

He had got up and was walking around the garishly decorated room. All of a sudden a mirror hanging from the wall caught his attention: in the looking-glass room framed in gold he saw the reflection of Mariquita Pons' face as she followed his movements, unaware she was being watched. Her features had relaxed, and betrayed the effects of the passing years: her skin was wrinkled, her neck looked scrawny , and her eyes were dull and lifeless except for a gleam of fear and need. This sight touched his heart. "If I only knew how," he said, "I'd write different kinds of play, more suited to your talents and your artistic merit. Sometimes I wonder whether I shouldn't try, even if it's a failure; but it's not because I'm frightened that I don't do it. I simply can't. I'm not Ibsen, Kiki, I'm sorry."

"Don't apologise, Carlos; your comedies are excellent, and the public likes them a lot. Why wouldn't they, with their stutterers and corpses in cupboards?" "Oh yes, you're right," Prullàs burst out; "and all those who prefer Jean-Paul Sartre can go boil their heads!"

Mariquita crushed her cigarette in a cut-glass ashtray and immediately put another one in the holder. "You can't imagine," she said, "what horrible things the press says about me."

Prullàs came back over to the sofa and lit her fresh cigarette. "That'll teach you to read reviews. Isn't the public's applause enough for you? On the first night of *Un puñal de quita y pon* we came out to take bows at the end of each act, and when the play was over, we had to come on stage eight times, d'you remember? And what about *Merienda de negros?* Six months' run in Madrid, and two in Barcelona, not to mention the tour round Spain! What does it matter if the critics savage us?"

The actress stroked his hand and gave him a melancholy smile. "I appreciate your effort, Carlos, but it's no use. We've made a mistake. Whether we like it or not, things are going in a different direction. We'll soon be redundant and faintly ridiculous. We already are. We can carry on as long as we have a public, but as soon as the last of our audience dies of old age, we'll disappear in a puff of smoke." They stared at each other. Then Mariquita said, in the same tone of voice: "I'm not guilty, Carlos, but I'm not completely innocent either. I've committed unforgivable mistakes, but what else could I do?" She dropped her gaze to her hands, then added in a murmur: "If only you'd paid me some attention all these years, Carlos!" She drew her hands across her face, and repeated: "I didn't kill him, Carlos: D'you believe me?" "Of course I do," Prullàs replied. He got up and made to leave the room. When he reached the door, he turned back to her again. "It was you who sent me Vallsigorri's wallet with the letter in it, wasn't it, Kiki?" Mariquita did not deign to reply: she was blowing perfect smoke rings. "How did you get it?" "The way you can get everything in this world, Carlos: by paying for it." "And was the person who sold it you a cripple?" Mariquita Pons smiled. "That's putting it kindly: it would take about four like him to make one complete man. Do you know him?" "Yes," Prullàs said. "He tried to sell me the wallet too . . . but we couldn't reach an agreement. Why did you send it me?" "In thrillers, the heroine always helps the detective, doesn't she?" "That's true," Prullàs said. "By the way, is your husband back yet?" "Yes, he arrived early this morning from Seville – he was so done in, he went straight to bed. He brought some special cakes; do you want one?" "Not just now, thank you," Prullàs replied.

3

Sebastiana opened the study door, her eyes rolling with terror; she could hardly speak. "That fellow is here with two heavies," she announced. "Who? Don Lorenzo Verdugones?" Prullàs asked. "No sir, the other one, the one with the pencil. I told them to wait in the hall, and there they are, with their shotguns and everything." "O.K., I'll be right out; while I'm talking to them, prepare my bag, would you, with a toothbrush, my razor, some spare blades, soap, a shaving brush and all the rest. And several changes of clothes." "Shall I put some winter things in as well, just in case?" Sebastiana asked. "There's no need to exaggerate!" Prullàs replied. "Or to pull faces like that; everything will be fine in the end, you'll see."

In the delicate surroundings of the hall, in among drapes, mirrors and candelabra, the two uniformed policemen looked out of place and threatening. "Have you come to arrest me, Sigüenza?" Prullàs enquired. The obsequious official consulted his notes stony-faced, and said: "Señor Prullàs, this is an unfortunate situation." "But you know I'm innocent, Sigüenza," Prullàs said. "I am only carrying out my orders, Señor Prullàs." "Ah, so that absolves you from all responsibility, does it? Haven't you been following the Nuremberg trials?" Prullàs said. "I'm not one for subtleties, Señor Prullàs," the other man replied, "but if I didn't carry out the orders I'm given, everything would be chaotic, and besides, someone else would come and do them anyway, so in the end it would come to the same."

Prullàs decided to avoid the quicksands of the theory of duty, and asked instead: "What evidence do you have against me?"

"Don Lorenzo will inform you of that in due compliance with the legal process, Señor Prullàs," the official said. "Very well, I'll go with you voluntarily: I've nothing to hide. May I make a phone call first?" "As many as you wish," Sigüenza replied; "this isn't the Soviet Union."

Prullàs shut himself in his study without anyone following him. Nobody in my plays would be so careless, Prullàs said to himself with satisfaction as he took out Mariquita Pons' letter and burnt it in the flame from his cigarette lighter. Once the piece of paper had been reduced to a black, greasy ball, he cleaned his fingers on his handkerchief and returned to the hall. "Gentlemen," he said, adopting an almost arrogant pose, "I'm at your disposal."

They met Don Lorenzo Verdugones in the corridors of the court building. "The investigating magistrate will see us straightaway," he said. A secretary disappeared behind a door to inform the magistrate, who came out an instant later, accompanied by a man dressed in black with a face as sour as vinegar. After lengthy exchanges, this sour-faced man left and the magistrate, turning to the little group formed by Don Lorenzo, Prullàs and Sigüenza, said to them: "That gentleman I've just said goodbye to is none other than the Valladolid hangman. He's visiting Barcelona and dropped in to pay his respects. He's a good man – very serious, as you'll have noticed, and very attentive; and he's also someone who had the merit to rise above his humble beginnings and make a name for himself, all by his own efforts." "Let's get on with it, shall we?" Don Lorenzo said, cutting in. He was in a foul mood.

The atmosphere in the magistrate's office was stifling, and smelt vaguely of sweat. Apart from that, it was solemn and dark, appropriate to a place where every day decisive words were spoken and opinions formed which could ruin the lives of many people. A huge crucifix hanging from the wall added the inevitable pious touch. "Please be seated," the magistrate said, "make yourselves at home."

"As I have publicly stated on several occasions," the governor began, "Señor Prullàs here has always inspired in me respect and admiration for the important literary work he has accomplished, as well as a certain sympathy for him as a person. But no consideration or feeling, as you will be the first to recognise, can be allowed to interfere with the accomplishment of my duty. I am here to serve the state! Señor Prullàs' behaviour, in general and in particular in the days before and immediately after the event which has brought us here, together with the circumstances surrounding this grave affair, leave me with no choice: the facts themselves force me to follow the path I have chosen."

"May I ask with all due respect on what factual elements you are basing these conclusions, Don Lorenzo?" the magistrate asked, and, before the other man had the opportunity to reply, went on: "The reason being that, in view of your assertions, perhaps we should give this interview a more binding legal character, if you allow me to say so. Light and stenographers! as the saying goes. There's a secretary in the next office ready to take down the accused's statement."

"We'll come to that," Don Lorenzo said, "when I'm good and ready." The magistrate went pale, and bit his lips. Don Lorenzo turned to Prullàs and went on: "While you were rushing about complicating matters and playing the fool, the police were carrying out an exhaustive and fruitful investigation, thanks to which the case is now closed. We had our suspicions from the start, but the day before yesterday we got the conclusive proof."

He took out his tobacco pouch and cigarette papers and began to roll himself a cigarette with his habitual clumsiness. Prullàs pulled out his packet and offered it to the governor. "Keep it," Don Lorenzo said, with a touch of irony, "you'll need it in the jug." These words destroyed all Prullàs' self-assurance. "Are you really going to lock me up?" he stammered. "There's nothing else for it, my friend," the governor replied. "I'm a servant of the state!" "But what evidence have you got against me?" Prullàs wailed. "The best!" Don Lorenzo said. He signalled to Sigüenza, who swiftly took some typed sheets out of his briefcase and handed them to his chief. Don Lorenzo waved the sheets of paper in the dense air of the office. "The witness sang like a canary!" he said triumphantly. "The witness?" Prullàs queried, stretching out his hand to take the papers. Don Lorenzo dropped his arm to prevent him reaching them, then in a grave voice started to declaim, with an occasional glance down at the transcript: "Is it or is it not true that the accused, when questioned by me, declared that he had spent the evening on which Vallsigorri was murdered strolling in the streets of Barcelona, and in response to further questioning, declared he had not been seen by anyone he knew? And is it not also true that these declarations are false, given the fact that on the day and time in question, the accused was not 'strolling' but was in a hotel of ill-repute, situated in Calle de la Unión, where, as the accused himself told the receptionist, 'he had arranged to meet someone'? Is it not equally true that the accused then left the aforementioned hotel and directed his steps towards a public bar also situated in the Calle de la Unión, where he proceeded to imbibe alcoholic beverages?"

"One small beer!" Prullàs protested. "Is that what you call 'alcoholic beverages'? One wretched draught beer – which, by the way, made me feel very ill."

"Would it not be more exact to say," the governor went on in the same pompous tone, "that what made you 'feel very ill' was not 'one small beer' as you claim, but 'a considerable amount of highly alcoholic drink, such as La Asturiana anisette and Negrita rum, as reported in the statement made by the lady in charge of said establishment."

"That's not true!" Prullàs shouted, "that woman's lying to conceal the lack of hygiene and the criminally disgusting state of the products she sells, the old sow! But even if it were true, is it a crime to get drunk? Is that the conclusive proof you're basing my guilt on?"

"All in good time," Don Lorenzo said. "Now listen, and don't interrupt. While you were getting drunk in the bar on the corner, as has been proven, another gentleman arrived at the said hotel. After asking for a room and paying for it in advance, as is the custom in this kind of establishment, he went up to it, previously informing the receptionist that 'he was expecting someone' and asking him 'to show her up as soon as she arrived'. Naturally, the receptionist did not ask this man to enter his personal details in the hotel register, something he had not done either with the accused – an omission for which the appropriate authorities would have closed the establishment down were it not for the intercession of the bishop, due to the fact that apparently, several individuals close to His Lordship, and even higher up in the Church hierarchy, have their savings invested in this lucrative business. What I've just told you is to go no further than these walls." "Have no fear, Don Lorenzo," the magistrate quickly assured him.

"Once this new gentleman was installed in his room," the governor went on, "the accused reappeared from the bar 'in a very agitated state', asked if during his absence the young lady he had arranged to meet had turned up, and after being told that she had not, then said: 'I'll wait upstairs, if she appears, send her straight up.' Is that what happened or is it not, Señor Prullàs?"

"Yes, things happened as you have just described them," Prullàs said, "except that I was not 'in a very agitated state'. I was simply hot because of the summer heat, like now, and perhaps rather annoyed at how unpunctual the person I was to meet had been, and also because of my upset stomach from the beer. As far as the other gentleman is concerned, I haven't the faintest idea of who he might be. As magistrate, could you please take note of my objections on this point?"

"I'm sorry, Señor Prullàs, but these allegations are outside my jurisdiction," the magistrate replied. "I'm just here as a spear-carrier, if you'll permit the theatrical comparison."

"At some unspecified time later," Verdugones went on, ignoring their interruption, "a young lady entered the aforementioned hotel. She was someone who, according to the receptionist 'he had seen often' on previous occasions, and was someone he considered 'of lax habits' and of 'loose morals'. This young woman told the receptionist she had come to see 'a relative of hers who was visiting the city' whom she had promised to 'call on'. Would the receptionist be so kind as to show her which room her relative was staying in? The hotel employee did not know how to answer this question, since both the accused and the other gentleman 'had been relatives of the young lady in question on previous occasions'. Not wishing to favour one client over the other, or to put himself on bad terms with either of them, the receptionist decided simply to tell the young lady the numbers of the two rooms, without saying who was in which one, or that there was a different gentleman waiting in each of them. Without asking him for any further clarification, the young woman then went up to the first floor, where both the rooms were situated. A short time later, she came back downstairs and left the hotel without saying a word. When the receptionist was asked how long the young woman had stayed in the room or rooms, he replied that he had not paid attention at the time, but that her stay in the hotel had been 'short and fleeting'. When pressed on this point, he had guessed it could have been no more than five minutes. Was it normal for her to make such a fleeting visit?

433

No, rather the opposite, since in the receptionist's opinion, the young lady was 'one of those who offer an excellent and full service'. Did the receptionist have any idea which of the two rooms she had visited? Reply: No, he had no idea, because the rooms, as he had said, were on the upper floor. Nor had he heard any noise of doors that could have helped him identify the different rooms. What happened then? After a similar length of time had gone by, the second gentleman had appeared, apparently 'rather disturbed'. At first, the receptionist put this down to the fact that the young lady must have visited 'the other room'; but a short time later, the 'first gentleman' – that is, the accused – also came down, in an 'even more disturbed' state. In fact, in the words of the receptionist, he looked 'like a madman', with 'bloodshot eyes' and so terrified him that, fearing he might be attacked, he told him that 'he had only done what you had told him to do'. Doubtless appeased by these words, the accused desisted from his violent intentions and staggered out of the hotel.

"I scarcely need add," Don Lorenzo went on after a pause, "that when the corresponding photographs were shown to the hotel receptionist, he had no difficulty identifying Señor Prullàs, the deceased Señor Vallsigorri, and a young woman who goes by the stage name of Lilí Villalba, and who is the daughter of a well-known crook – in whose company, let it be said, the accused returned to the same hotel a few days later with blood-stained clothes and an equally disturbing and suspicious attitude as that previously described."

The governor handed the sheets of paper back to Sigüenza, folded his arms across his chest, looked Prullàs full in the face, and said: "Having heard the detailed reconstruction of events as evidenced by the sworn statements of the witnesses, does the accused have anything to declare, or is he willing to make a proper confession?"

"A confession?" Prullàs shouted in alarm. "But I haven't done anything!" "Phew!" the magistrate said, "he's going to give us a hard time." Then he added in a persuasive voice: "If you confess, it'll help your case." "Come on, Prullàs, we have more than enough proof that it was you who killed Vallsigorri! Don't make us waste any more time!" Don Lorenzo urged him. "It's not true!" Prullàs insisted. "I didn't kill Vallsigorri and you don't have a shred of proof; all you have is a statement by a hotel receptionist that on one particular evening three people were in a cheap hotel at the same time. He doesn't know if those three people met each other, nor if any of those three people knew of the presence of the other two in the building. He only saw the three of them enter and leave the hotel separately. That in itself makes it weak evidence. But on top of that, the receptionist does not know any of us personally, he never checked our identity, and sees many people in the same situation day after day. How can he be so sure he saw Vallsigorri that particular day and not someone else? And the same could be said for Señorita Villalba. How many similar young ladies must have passed before his eyes?"

Verdugones dismissed Prullàs' arguments vehemently. "How dare you say my evidence is weak? The receptionist's deposition clearly establishes the relationship between you and Vallsigorri and an irrefutable motive for the crime; that's clearer than a poorhouse broth. And you still say there's not enough proof? Well let me tell you, Señor Prullàs, that I've taken the trouble to read all your plays, and in not one of them have I found such a solidly based argument. And if that's good enough for you, it's good enough for me. In my view," he went on rather more calmly, addressing himself above all to the magistrate as if Prullàs' opinion no longer interested him, "the events took place as follows: The accused and Vallsigorri had a violent argument in the Hotel Gallardo over Señorita Villalba, after

435

which the accused returned home, told his maid he was going to Masnou, then went instead to the apartment of the deceased, who at that time was still alive, rang the doorbell, and once he was shown into the living-room, attacked Vallsigorri with a kitchen knife, killing him instantly. After which, having wreaked his revenge, he set off for Masnou, which he reached in the early hours, without being seen by anyone. Weak proof! I'll give you weak proof!"

The magistrate spoke up again: "I advise and indeed call on you to speak now; if not, the full weight of the law will be brought to bear on you." "Speak?" Prullàs retorted. "I've nothing to say: you are the ones who have to prove my guilt." "You don't understand," the magistrate insisted. "Your guilt has been established, at least sufficiently for me to be able to order your arrest. The only thing that could avoid that, and the preventive measures taken as a result, is if you gave us a different, more convincing version of what happened that day. Are you in possession of any facts which contradict the allegations made against you? Are you aware of any other person or persons who might have had a motive or motives for wishing Señor Vallsigorri dead, and had the opportunity to bring this about? If so, speak now and we'll set you free; if not, I'll have to wash my hands of the affair, as it says in the Holy Bible."

Prullàs clenched his teeth and shook his head. Don Lorenzo got to his feet. "Your honour!" he cried, lifting his forefinger towards the ceiling, "given the authority vested in me, and taking into account all the evidence collected against the accused, namely Señor Carlos Prullàs here present, by profession playwright, but considering furthermore the sacrosanct principle of the independence of the judiciary, as laid down in our national political constitution, I hand over to your jurisdiction this womanising rogue to be judged for having butchered

Ignacio Vallsigorri, according to the terms of the Penal Code and the corresponding articles of Criminal Trial Procedure, and forgive me if I have not employed the correct legal terms, but I am a soldier and not a lawyer."

"For heavens' sake, Don Lorenzo, you are a past master in legal jargon! What a pity you never felt called to the profession: what a great legal expert you would have made! A real Cicero! A Puffendorf!"

"That's that then," the governor replied. "And hurry up with all the details, Sigüenza, I'm keeping the mayor of Tarrasa waiting."

In an impossibly stuffy windowless office, a perspiring secretary placed several layers of paper and sheets of carbon paper in her typewriter. Once this operation had been completed, the magistrate asked Prullàs to state his full name, that of his parents, his date of birth, marital status, home address and profession. Had he on any occasion had personal contact with one Ignacio Vallsigorri y Fadrí, now deceased, previously an inhabitant of Barcelona? Prullàs replied that he had. Could the accused give the exact date of this personal contact? Of course, it was the ninth of August. For what reason? A social gathering. Had he seen the aforementioned individual on any occasion after the ninth of August? No. And prior to the specified date, that is, the ninth of August? No again. Did he wish then to declare, on his own responsibility, that he had not seen the aforementioned now deceased Ignacio Vallsigorri Fadrí when still alive except for that one specified occasion and subsequently on the afore-mentioned date and not otherwise? Unsure he had properly understood all this, Prullàs hesitated and finally said no.

At this point, the secretary stopped typing because, as she explained, she had written "yes" where she should have put "no". After she had corrected her mistake, she read out the clarification she had added: "The amended word is to be considered replaced by the one which follows, this new one being valid as is the crossing out corresponding to the word replaced above, both of them which are valid in the terms of the current statement. Does that cover it?" she asked. When everyone agreed, and the magistrate had declared he was satisfied with the proceedings, she took the sheets out of her typewriter, carefully put away the carbon paper in her drawer, and gave him the original and copies. The magistrate read the declaration carefully, then handed it to Prullàs.

"Read it and sign at the bottom if you're happy with it," he said. "Isn't it a rather summary statement?" Prullàs asked. "We're still at the inquiry stage," the magistrate replied. "We have to proceed according to the law. As far as this deposition is concerned, you can see for yourself: it doesn't compromise you in any way. Sign here."

Prullàs signed where he was told to do so. Then both Don Lorenzo Verdugones and Sigüenza added their signatures – as witnesses, the latter explained. The secretary put one copy in a file, gave the magistrate the original, and used the third copy to fan her face and under her arms. The magistrate read the deposition again, and once more expressed his satisfaction at a job well done.

"We mustn't get ahead of ourselves," he pronounced. "And now, Señor Prullàs, if you'd be so kind as to follow me."

They went into a small office where two guards were dozing on wooden chairs. When they saw the magistrate come in they stood up and put their helmets on. "Take the prisoner to the cells," the magistrate said. One of the men took a pair of handcuffs out of a drawer. "A mere formality," the magistrate explained, "it's just a precaution. And now you'll have to excuse me, Señor Prullàs, but other matters less pleasant than chatting with you await me. It's been a great pleasure to meet you, and I wish you every success with your new play. My wife and I are great admirers of Doña Mariquita Pons. So long!"

Handcuffed and with a guard on each side, Prullàs went out into a corridor thronged with the worst kind of rabble. Seeing him walking so elegantly to the cell, several of these wretched creatures burst out laughing. "Mind how you go, sweetheart!" a fat old woman shouted at him. Prullàs walked along with his head hung low, like a scene from Christ's passion painted by Esparraguera.

4

They descended a broad staircase to the basement, then walked along a gloomy corridor with a jumble of pipes running along the ceiling. At the end of the corridor one of the guards opened a heavy metal door, and they entered a square room. A guard was sitting behind a table reading *Dicen*. When he saw his colleagues come in, he lifted his gaze and blinked at them as if emerging from profound thought.

"This one's for number three," one of the guards told him. To Prullàs he said: "Put everything from your pockets on the table." Prullàs did as he was told, and the guard seated at the table made a note of all the objects and the money, and put them in a box. Then they made Prullàs hand over his tie, belt, and shoe-laces, after which the seated guard took a huge bunch of keys out of his drawer, and flicked through them slowly one by one until he found the right one. Then he stood up and led the way to one of the cells. The clunk of the key in the lock and the creaking of the cell door on its hinges made Prullàs' flesh creep.

"In you go," they told him roughly. Once he was inside, they took off the handcuffs, left the cell and locked the grille.

Prullàs found himself in a rectangular, windowless room, with walls covered in tiny, laboriously scrawled inscriptions. The only furniture was a narrow bunk bed attached to the far wall by a plank of wood. "Do you have any idea how long I'll be in here?" he asked. "That depends," came the reply. "Couldn't you lend me a paper to make the wait more bearable?" "Only if the magistrate gives permission," the guards replied as they left.

Prullàs sat on the bed and waited. From another cell he could not see into came the sound of loud and regular snores. There's a wise man, Prullàs thought; a true stoic. Since they had removed his wristwatch, and the only light in the cell came from a feeble bulb in the corridor ceiling, he soon lost all notion of time. He had not eaten for several hours, and was feeling extremely weak. But when the guard eventually reappeared with a bowl full of hard, cold chick peas, he could not force down even one mouthful. "I'm sorry, but couldn't I be brought a roll from a bar near here? A ham one maybe, or sausage, or whatever." "If you have the money, we could try," the guard answered. "My money's in the desk, where you put it," Prullàs said; "just take what you need." "Oh no, sir, if I used a prisoner's possessions like that without written permission, I'd be in deep trouble." "I could sign you an IOU," Prullàs suggested. "Where would that get me?" the guard replied. "If they give you thirty years, it's not worth the paper it's written on."

Some time later, this guard was replaced by another one. Prullàs tried to re-open negotiations. By now he wasn't worried about the poor food or the uncomfortable conditions, but about the uncertainty surrounding his future. "I'll reward you handsomely if you get a note to Señor Gaudet," he told the night guard. "As you can see, I don't have any money on me, but I'll tell Señor Gaudet himself to give whoever delivers the message a tidy sum."

But his promises and pleas fell on deaf ears. "Come on," the guard finally said, "it's time for sleep, not for chatting." One by one, the prisoners were taken out to a muddy latrine where the stench made it impossible to breathe, and then led back to their cells. "This is intolerable!" Prullàs protested. "Don't complain," the guard replied, "nobody's laid a finger on you, have they? You must have good connections! And anyway, don't worry, tomorrow or the next day they'll transfer you to Modelo prison, and you'll be as right as rain."

The next morning a third guard, whom Prullàs had not seen take over from his night colleague, opened his cell door and shouted: "Hey you, come out of there!" Prullàs picked up his jacket, which he'd folded and used as a pillow in a vain attempt to sleep, put it on, and did as the guard ordered. Sigüenza was standing out by the desk. "Collect your belongings," the obsequious official said with a deference that seemed at odds with their surroundings: "You're a free man." "My, my!" Prullàs said sarcastically, "and how did you decide that?" Sigüenza did not flinch. "The law is the law," he said. "The guilty are put in jail, the innocent are set free." Then he added in a whisper, as though he were giving confidential information: "Vallsigorri's murderer was arrested during the night."

It took Prullàs a few seconds to react. "What did you say?" "The real murderer," Sigüenza repeated: "He was caught last night, and at this very moment the magistrate is taking his statement. If you wait a few minutes, they'll be bringing him in here." "No, no," Prullàs quickly replied, "the sooner we're out of here, the better; who is it?"

Sigüenza shrugged. "No-one in particular, a cheap crook." Behind his glasses, his forlorn eyes moistened, as though he was profoundly disappointed at this news. The guard had put all Prullàs' personal effects on the desk. "Sign here to say you got everything back." Prullàs signed. "Can I go now?" he asked. "You're in luck, Señor Prullàs," Sigüenza said. "The magistrate was called away unexpectedly last night and didn't have time to make out an arrest warrant; that means there won't be any need to obtain a stay of proceedings. I suppose you'll want to clean up and have breakfast. If you'll permit me, I'll give you a lift home: I have an official car, and should you wish, I can give you some idea of what has happened."

5

As he had promised, Sigüenza told Prullàs the following: Two days after Vallsigorri's death, a man claiming to have evidence in the case turned up at the police station in Calle Enrique Grados. He justified his delay in coming forward by saying he was naturally averse to meddling in other people's affairs, especially by giving possibly false evidence, but also because in his youth he had made the mistake of belonging to a group that was now illegal, and as a result, despite the fact that he had been acquitted by a tribunal after the Civil War, he was on police files, and this made him act very cautiously at all times. This, Sigüenza explained, was what the man had said. But both his sense of civic duty and his fear of being accused of withholding evidence had impelled him to come forward. After all this preamble, he went on to state that for several years he had been living in an apartment on Calle Aribau, from which he could clearly see the deceased's home opposite; that on the night of the crime he had been unable to sleep because of the heat; that he had gone out onto his balcony to try to cool off; that while he was out there he had seen someone leave the doorway to Vallsigorri's building, someone whose appearance and attitude seemed to him highly suspicious; that at that moment he had not attached any particular importance to the incident; and that he had only managed to get a fleeting glimpse of the individual because he was a long way away, it had been dark, and there had been foliage in the way. When shown photographs of known criminals, he was unable positively to identify the man in question, but did point to several whose faces looked to him, as he said, especially sinister, Sigüenza told Prullàs. When the photos selected by this eyewitness were shown to the porter at the building where Vallsigorri had lived, he quickly pointed to one of them as someone who had been a frequent companion of one of Señor Vallsigorri's maids – precisely the one he had dismissed a few months earlier because her behaviour did not reach the high moral standards expected of someone working in an honourable and decent household. As if this were not enough, the said individual had already been imprisoned twice for theft and once for attempted burglary. Thanks to an informer, the police learnt of his latest domicile, and went there to question the neighbours. One of them swore that he had seen the suspect return home in the early hours of the night of the crime, and that despite the distance and the lack of light, he had clearly seen blood stains on the man's right hand. A twenty-four hour watch was kept on the building. As night fell, the suspect appeared, walking along hurriedly, hugging the walls and constantly looking round to make sure he was not being followed. When arrested and questioned, he denied any knowledge of the crime he was accused of: he claimed never even to have heard the name Ignacio Vallsigorri. On the other hand, he could give no clear account of his whereabouts on the night of the crime. He said he had been to the cinema, where he saw a very good film, with a famous actor in it whose name he had forgotten, as he had also forgotten the film's title and its plot; all he remembered was that there were lots of horses, and shooting, and the main actress was very beautiful but it was plain to see she was a bad lot, although she came round to the actor's side by the end. The police found a small amount of money on him, which he could not explain either: he claimed he had been working as a delivery man, but could not remember what he had been delivering, or where, or who he had been working for. Finally, when he saw it was useless to persist, he yielded to the police's persuasion, and signed a full confession although still insisting on his innocence to all and sundry. So now the case was closed, Sigüenza said, finishing his account.

Prullàs, who had not slept a wink, and in recent days had been through more emotional shocks and upheavals than in all the rest of his life, could scarcely take in what the other man had said. "But why should this fellow have killed Vallsigorri, if he didn't even know him?" he asked. "What was his motive?"

"He didn't have one," the official replied. "In all likelihood the criminal had been helped at some point by his friend the maid to make a wax impression of the keys to Vallsigorri's apartment. Then on that summer night, believing the owner to be out of town on vacation, he had got into the property using the forged set of keys. Before he could even begin to steal the valuables, he had been surprised by Vallsigorri's unexpected return. In a panic, he had tried to escape, but Vallsigorri had prevented him doing so. The thief had a knife in his hand with which he intended to force a lock. The two of them collided, with such unfortunate consequences."

The car came to a halt outside Prullàs' home. "But if you were on the suspect's trail all the time, why didn't you tell me so?" he asked before getting out. "Why did you let me go on with my investigations, putting my life at risk like that?"

"We couldn't have known you would leap into the lion's den so foolishly," Sigüenza said; "as you can imagine, Pretty Face's little scheme wasn't part of our plan. That was when you were really foolish. But Niño de la Doctrina wouldn't have harmed you anyway; he's a good lad. He helps us from time to time, and in return we don't give him any trouble. He's not stupid, and knows who it pays to keep in with. And besides," Sigüenza added, shutting the car door behind Prullàs, "he wouldn't have dared touch such an eminent figure in Spanish letters."

"What about all the rest? The scene in the magistrate's office, the night I spent in the cell, what was all that for?" Prullàs insisted. "Oh, that . . . Don Lorenzo must have had his reasons; he never tells me what they are, and naturally, I don't pry," Sigüenza replied.

The chauffeur started the car. Prullàs lent down to Sigüenza's window. "What about the letter?" The car was pulling out, and he had to let go. "What letter?" But the car was already picking up speed, and his voice was lost in the noise of traffic. The porter roused Prullàs from his stupor. "Don't stay out in the sun, Señor Prullàs." With his crumpled, filthy clothes, his unshaven face and dishevelled hair, all the passers-by were staring at him.

6

He thought he was awakening from a long, deep sleep that had lasted several days, but when he checked the time and date, realised he had slept for only two or three hours. He was in his own bedroom, and the last rays of the evening sun were slanting through the shutters. He struggled to get up. He still felt very tired and drained, but he was determined not to go back to sleep again. He had had the most dreadful nightmares. It seemed to him it would be a long time before he could recover his previous peace of mind: all kinds of horrors had installed themselves in his unconscious. He had a shower, put on clean clothes, and left the apartment. He felt too weak to drive, so hailed a taxi and got it to drop him at the theatre door.

When he saw him come in, Bonifaci rushed out of his box. Respectful as ever, he enquired after Prullàs' health. Since he had not been in for the past few days, and had not left any messages, Bonifaci said, he had wondered whether perhaps he was ill. And looking at him now, he added, brandishing the lantern aloft like a sceptre, he could see he didn't look well, it must be the heat . . . By now they had made their way down the corridor to the stage. He was very pleased to see him again, Bonifaci confessed in a whisper as he manoeuvred a way through all the props. It was a good thing he'd come back: now everything would go a lot better; and the change he'd made had been a huge success. "Everything'll go smoothly now, you'll see; and this play will be as big a success as all your other ones, Don Carlos."

Prullàs nodded. He didn't need to see with his own eyes to guess what change Bonifaci was talking about.

JULIO: Good God! So it turns out we didn't have just one murderer in the house, but two!

CECILIA: Who would have thought it! She looked as though she wouldn't hurt a fly!

LUISITO: Boohoo!

CECILIA: Don't cry, Luisito. She wasn't for you. It's better to find out sooner rather than later. Just imagine if you had married her, then one fine day wham! You find yourself chopped up in little pieces.

LUISITO: Boohoohoo! What a sha . . . sha . . . shame!

JULIO: That's enough blubbing, my lad! There's no reason to cry, my boy: you'll have all the girlfriends you want, and more! All you have to do is set your mind to it! All young girls think about these days is getting married! What's harder is to find another maid to iron my poplin shirts!

LUISITO: Boohoo!

CECILIA: Didn't you hear? Don't go on crying like that, you numbskull! (*Slaps him*)

LUISITO: Ow!

MAID: With all due respect, I must tell you you're making a big mistake. What happened to poor Señor Todoliu was an unintentional accident. And the Countess of Vallespir, three quarters the same. Just imagine how upset we were when we saw the countess's head on one side, and her body on the other, one leg over here, and an arm over there! Because I may be poor, but I've always been a tidy person, and as decent as anyone you care to mention. Not like some others, stealing from the groceries.

ENRIQUE: (*handcuffing her*) That's enough, my girl, to the police station with you! They'll make you confess your crimes soon enough!

At the end of the rehearsal, Prullàs, Gaudet and Mariquita Pons met up in the actress's dressing-room. All the morning newspapers had carried stories about the successful outcome in the Vallsigorri case, and both the director and Mariquita were relieved and delighted. The ghastly nightmare was finally over, they commented in one voice. "We've been calling you since early this morning," they said, interrupting each other in their haste, "but Sebastiana refused point blank to pass on our calls; at first she said you weren't at home, and then that you were asleep. She's a real dragon."

Prullàs did not share their satisfaction. "What happened?" he wanted to know. Gaudet understood what he meant and quickly brought him up to date: Señorita Villalba had called him first thing that very morning to inform him of her irrevocable decision to break her contract with the theatre; she had to leave Barcelona at once for family reasons, she said. Although the excuse seemed a feeble one, Gaudet had detected a note of genuine alarm in her voice, and had agreed – what else could he have done? Coming such a short time before their first night, he went on, this would have been a terrible blow if it had been anyone else involved in the play. But since she was such a ninny anyway, her withdrawal had been a real godsend, he said flatly. Before mid-day they had already found an understudy willing to take her place. She wasn't as pretty or shapely as her predecessor, the director had to admit, but what a difference in talent! She had learnt the lines of the last scene in a couple of hours, and without ever even having rehearsed it, she had performed much better than Lilí Villalba after a month of rehearsals.

Mariquita Pons patted Prullàs' shoulder affectionately. "Come on, don't be sad; there are thousands more like her." "You ought to be glad you've seen the last of such a deadweight," Gaudet said; "I never liked her, and this ending only confirms my suspicions." Prullàs didn't respond. Gaudet and the actress glanced at each other in dismay.

"Since you're so depressed," Gaudet suddenly said, "I'll tell you something funny that'll make you laugh. Yesterday evening I had the most extraordinary visit. The person came on your recommendation, or at least she had your visiting card. All at once, without any warning, she started singing and dancing out on my landing. All the neighbours came out to see what was going on, and I didn't know where to put myself. Then when the show had finished, this person told me she was an artiste, with a lot of experience and even more desire to triumph, but with no luck so far. Apparently, you told her I could open the doors of serious theatre for her, and that's why she came to see me. She told me she wasn't fussy, and would make do with bit

448

parts at first; then God would decide. And she ended by telling me an unlikely tale, according to which she saved your life."

"There's some truth in all of that," Prullàs admitted. "As far as her art is concerned, what can I say? La Fresca is no Margarita Xirgu, but she has more than enough enthusiasm. And she's not a bad person. Could you do anything for her?" Gaudet shook his head in surprise. "Why d'you always have to get me into messes?" he said. "You know only too well what the theatre is like these days. The blasted cinema is digging our grave. Hardly anyone can find work, let alone someone like La Fresca. In Spain the theatre belongs to the past, Carlos; when are you going to get that into your head? But," he said after a pause, "I told her that if she needed a job, and was really desperate to find something, I was looking for a home help: that if she could cook, wash and iron, and didn't mind taking on a crazy bachelor's household, I could give her a provisional contract." "And what did La Fresca say?" Prullàs asked. "She starts tomorrow," Gaudet replied. "And when are you off to Argentina?" Gaudet smiled a sly smile. "Well, if we get on, perhaps we'll elope there together," he said.

While he waited for a taxi on the corner by the theatre, Prullàs bought *El Noticiero* and *La Prensa*. Both of them had short and suspiciously similar accounts of the news the morning papers had carried, with a few extra details that added nothing new to the resolution of the Vallsigorri case. The arrested man was only identified by his initials: S.V. *El Noticiero* carried a short biography of Vallsigorri, and some sentences praising his character; this was obviously a clumsy attempt to disguise the fact that something had been pulled from the article at the last moment. Both newspapers were full of praise for the police's brilliant achievement. Pride of place in the two papers was given to the news that after lengthy deliberation, the

Nuremberg tribunal had sentenced Alfried Krupp to twelve years in prison for collaborating with the Nazi regime and had ordered the expropriation of his family firm's stocks and shares, which would become a limited company with state participation. The special correspondent in Nuremberg pointed out that the harshness of this sentence had led many to suspect that it was dictated by powerful economic interests, whose pressure had meant that the allegorical blindfold on Justice's eyes was kept well and truly in place in order to tip the scales of her balance in the required direction.

It was dark by the time a free taxi appeared. Prullàs took it and sorely tried the driver's patience trying to find where the Villalba family lived. He couldn't remember the name of the back street or how to get to it: he had only been there once, in a state of great nervous tension, and blindly following Gaudet's instructions. After lengthy detours around wretched streets peopled by swarms of extravagant-looking people, he finally recognised the small square where the gypsies had been camping. He stopped the taxi and told the driver to wait for him while he carried out some business. "Carry out whatever you like, but I'm not staying here a second longer," the taxi-driver replied. "I'll pay you double," Prullàs offered. "Ah well, in that case . . . but don't be long, and be careful how you go: there's a tribe of gypsies over there."

Once Prullàs was in the right alleyway, he found the doorway without difficulty. He climbed the stairs, and knocked repeatedly on the door. After a while, the door opposite opened, and a woman in a nightgown and slippers poked her head out. She had heard all the banging and come out to see what on earth was going on. She didn't seem upset or even surprised at all the noise.

"You'll wear out your knuckles knocking like that," she told Prullàs, "but it won't do any good. The Villalbas have flown the nest; the father, all the women, that tart of a daughter of his, and the children as well: the whole lot of them. The flat's empty. They've even taken the cobwebs, if the state of their handcart was anything to go by. They could scarcely push it," she went on; "they all had to lend a hand, except for the little one, who sat on the back in tears."

They cleared out in a hurry, without telling anyone where they were going, or why they were leaving so quickly. Someone said that the night before Villalba had been visited by a man in a suit who seemed like someone in authority. Several of the neighbours reckoned this must have been the reason for their sudden departure. But the woman was having none of this: whenever something unexpected happened, people found odd reasons for it, she said; and then there was always someone who blamed everything that happened in this world on the secret plans of beings from other planets. "They'd seen too many films," she said; "but I reckon something put the wind up Villalba. He used to say," she added, "that he was thinking of emigrating to America: to Venezuela or Mexico, where apparently there were fortunes to be made without much effort." She'd never taken his fantasies seriously, though. "Villalba was a hopeless case," she said; "he could never settle to anything, but his biggest problem was the drink, which had brought about his downfall like it had so many others. Whenever he came back at night drunk from the bar – which meant most nights – he always caused an unholy row. Everyone in the Villalba household got their fair share of blows and curses." Not that she was surprised by that, she added sadly. She had gone through the same torture when she had been married; as long as her husband had been alive, she had lived in fear. That was why now, although her neighbours kept her awake with their arguments, she wasn't complaining: it was a thousand times better to hear all the hullabaloo through her wall than to have it at home. She did feel sorry for the Villalba children, though, she said with real commiseration; some of them were still tiny; and more than once she had taken them in behind Villalba's back and given them a wash and something to eat. "Now who knows what'll become of them?" she murmured.

Prullàs left the building and made for the gypsy camp in the square. It was eerily quiet, as though abandoned or as if all the gypsies were resting inside their caravans. Behind one of them, however, he found a wan-faced man with spreading white sideburns, busy reviving the fire in a clay oven with a pair of bellows. Prullàs asked him if he knew of a gypsy with a pair of shearing scissors; he needed to talk to him, and would handsomely reward any information he could give. The gypsy told him he and his group were not shearers but tinkers. They repaired people's pots and pans, he said; the oven, he went on, blowing the bellows on it again, was their forge: they used it to melt the copper they patched up worn-out utensils with. They also repaired umbrella spokes, he explained, but Prullàs wasn't listening. In among the dark shadows thrown by the caravans, he thought he could see the shape of a bear stretched out on the ground. Following his gaze, the tinker confirmed his impression: it was in fact a trained bear which had come, as had its master, from Bulgaria. The pair of them had crossed the whole of Europe on foot, dancing in streets and squares everywhere to earn a living. Now they were taking advantage of the tinkers' hospitality for a while. Prullàs thanked him for all this information and gave him a hefty tip. The tinker's face showed his surprise: he couldn't understand what he had done to deserve such a reward. "It's for you and the bear," Prullàs said in justification.

He told the taxi-driver to stop again outside the Hotel Gallardo.

"D'you want me to wait here as well?" the driver protested. "What's it to you, so long as the meter is running?" Prullàs said. "I get bored." "Buy yourself a comic, then."

The receptionist blenched when he saw Prullàs come in. "I swear on my mother's grave I didn't want to talk. I swear it! But you know what the authorities are like. And anyway, it's my job to look after the clients' safety." A gang of thugs had attacked several similar hotels in the past few months, he explained; they stripped the gentlemen they found of all their belongings, and of course none of the said gentlemen ever reported the thefts. The thieves always got away with it, the receptionist added; that was why he was obliged to be extremely careful, to take every precaution and to call on the police whenever necessary; that was why he told them at once of anything strange going on. "I live in constant fear," he concluded.

"Don't worry," Prullàs said: "I haven't come looking for trouble. I only want my usual room, if it's free." The receptionist handed him the key. Prullàs went up to the first floor, went into the room, and locked the door behind him. A window in the house opposite framed the reassuring spectacle of a family gathered around their kitchen table; a clay stewpot sat steaming in the middle of it, and a middle-aged man and a youngster were eating voraciously, their heads down over their plates as the spoons flew up and down; a woman entered and left the area Prullàs could see without any obvious purpose. Through the still night air came the artificially urgent advertisements on the family radio: Three bowls, five pesetas! Six Sindel pencils, five pesetas! A run-free nylon slip for only twenty-five pesetas! A colander and a funnel, only seven pesetas! Disturbed by all this shouting, the goldfinch hopped to and fro in its cage. Prullàs moved away from the window, and fell back onto the bed. He stared up at the crack in the ceiling and could barely withhold his tears. Who would have said less than a month ago that this cheap and nasty room would come to seem the height of happiness to me! he thought. The direction his thoughts were taking troubled him. All at once he realised he was giving in to an absurd and painful emotion, and also that he would never see the woman he so desperately wanted ever again. He leapt up: this room, imbued with the overpowering memories of the happy hours he had spent there, only made him feel all the more dissatisfied with himself. He ran downstairs, left the key on the front counter without a word, and rushed out of the hotel. The receptionist was relieved to see him go. He might have been a wealthy and polite guest, but his behaviour, even in a place designed to accommodate the most extravagant expressions of lust, had been strange to say the least.

CHAPTER NINE

I

As so often happens, the month of August ended with a series of spectacular storms, leaden skies and furious squalls, interspersed with brief, uncertain periods of blissful warmth. Bathing had become hazardous and unappealing: the sand was wet, and the storms had left a line of tangled greenish seaweed that gave off an unpleasant smell as it rotted in the sun. The sea was rough: its waves were white-capped and crashed against the breakwater; on some days, the undertow was so strong it scared off the bathers. Despite all this, as soon as the weather conditions permitted, the summer families rushed down to the beach to perform their daily rite. Whenever they did so, Prullàs went with them, promptly and uncomplaining, but did not join in; he did not even bother to put on his bathing costume. Dressed impeccably in white and wearing a brand-new Panama that Martita had bought him, he sat beneath their beach tent on a folding chair and tried with amazing application to read the daily press, struggling all the while against gusts of wind that tore at the pages and frequently wrenched them from his hands altogether, to the children's great delight. Occasionally, he would give up his fight against the wind, lift his gaze from the newsprint and stare out at the horizon, where a thin grey line already heralded the arrival of fresh showers and storms. Then he would be overwhelmed by a tremendous feeling of sadness, and seek any excuse to return to the house. When he got back there, he had no idea what to do with himself. Since he had given up reading thrillers and couldn't concentrate enough for any other kind of reading, he wandered from room to room in a daydream, his hands thrust in his trouser pockets, bumping into the maids and generally getting in the way of the household work. He was the last to get up in the morning, always took a long nap after lunch, and yet still went around half-asleep the whole day. For the first time ever, he devoted a lot of time to his children and, to their great dismay, had allotted himself the tedious task of helping them with their summer homework: an endless series of arithmetical problems or grammatical parsing which, outside the context of school, in this relaxed, lazy atmosphere, seemed to have been dreamt up by an insane mind.

Prullàs did not seek out others, but did not avoid them either. As ever, in social gatherings he was talkative and witty, and only fell silent when the general gossip turned to criticism of others, which he hated. But he was not the same. It was as though in his attitude now there was a mixture of happiness and irritability, interest and boredom; it was impossible to tell whether he was pleased or vexed by the presence of others, if his volubility was real or was simply part of a public image that little by little was taking over from his true personality. Those who knew him best sometimes saw the fleeting shadow of an intense emotion flit across his face.

He had had no further contact with Marichuli Mercadal than that offered by chance and proximity: on these occasions they greeted each other and exchanged only brief, inconsequential phrases. Nor did she try to get in touch with him. The rainy days and the foretaste of autumn, with its sense of melancholy, had visibly affected her daughter. For the first time in her short life, Alicia Mercadal seemed to have become aware of her condition. On the beach she too every now and then paused in her excited play and looked out at the horizon, as if in the dark clouds massing above the sea she could glimpse a presage of things coming to an end, of the imminent date of her own calling to account. During the daytime she joined happily in all the children's games, but at night she would weep disconsolately and Marichuli, however much her husband tried to play down this instability – which he saw, perhaps rightly, as a sign of the desires and disappointments of the first flush of adolescence – fell into despair herself at the thought there was nothing she could do to comfort her daughter.

Paradoxically it was this dejection, similar to Prullàs' state of mind, which allowed her to rein in a passion which, a short while earlier, her robust good health had only served to fuel. Now her heart was desiccated, her mind empty; not even the constant presence of the man who only a week before she would have sacrificed everything for was enough to drag her from the morass in which she was sunk.

Every day, as the afternoon drew to a close, Prullàs set off for a long walk along the deserted beach. He walked quickly, with no particular goal, lost in thought. From time to time, an object thrown up on the beach by the waves caught his attention: a rusty sardine tin, an empty bottle, a worn-out shoe like something from a Chaplin film. Prullàs would kneel down over these tiny remains of a false shipwreck, study them for a few moments, then set off again even more self-absorbed than before, as if these discoveries had given him cause for further reflexion.

One afternoon his steps took him right to the far end of the beach, near the breakwater. He sat down and stared, fascinated, at the waves sparkling in the last rays of the sun. An express train thundered by. The ground shook, a shower of sparks fell between the rails and a dark plume of smoke smeared the scarlet evening sky; the seagulls perched on the top of the breakwater flew off with screeching cries. Then a contrasting, oppressive silence appeared to take hold. This solitary spot, the twilight, the dark rocks, the lapping waves and the sad bird calls seemed to Prullàs the exact reflection of his own state of mind. Realising this brought tears to his eyes.

He recovered when he saw the distant figure of someone clambering down from the near end of the breakwater, jumping agilely from rock to rock despite his advanced years and his portly stature, and the fact that he was loaded down with fishing tackle. As the man approached, he realised the energetic angler was none other than his father-in-law. He went to meet him, and helped him down onto the sand. Then the pair of them set off for home. Prullàs' father-in-law was in excellent spirits; he paid no attention to his son-in-law's gloomy mood, but proudly showed him the fruits of his skill and persistence: three tiny fishes that were obviously too small to eat, and which lay gasping their last in the bottom of his basket.

"You can't imagine how happy it makes me to see you among us," he said impulsively as he clung to his son-in-law's arm. "I've never meddled in your affairs, and I understand that sometimes the oddities of your profession mean you have to lead a rather unconventional life, but whatever they say, I've always thought that a man's place is at home with his family. One of these days we must sit down and talk calmly. I'm thinking of retiring from business, and I'd like you to take over . . . not now of course, not immediately, and not all at once. Bit by bit. Everything is changing so quickly! When I started out, and always before that in the past, a business associate was a friend, almost a brother. You used to go to his house, you shared the pleasures and pains of his life, were godfather to his children, as he was to yours . . . you know what I mean. Today, though, it's all limited companies; in other words they're anonymous! You have no idea who you're risking your money with, who you can trust and who not; nowadays companies are machines run from anywhere in the world, from London or Wall Street. Look what happened to poor Krupp. But I don't want that to happen to my company. My grandfather founded it, and ran it until he died; after him came my father, and after him, me; our firm is part of Catalonia: it's a piece of the economy and history of this land, and after I'm gone I don't want it falling into the hands of some gnome of Zurich or anywhere else. That's why I thought . . . anyway, we'll talk about it."

Prullàs agreed in a mechanical fashion. For just a second the suspicion crossed his mind that there was a hidden meaning to his father-in-law's words, that this good-natured man knew more than his affectionate attitude revealed; but he immediately put this ridiculous idea out of his head.

As they were entering the village they met Roquet el dels Fems, who gave them some leaflets describing the activities for the saint's days' celebrations. A solemn Mass, a street carnival, puppet shows, a firework display, grand dances, games and competitions for young and old, with magnificent prizes! Roquet was hooting with laughter, already imagining all the fun there was to be had. Prullàs, on the other hand, was taken offguard by these festivities.

"Good Lord, my lad, where've you been the past few days?" his father-in-law joked. "My wife and Martita have both been into Barcelona twice to see their dressmakers and the hairdressers, and you didn't even realise! Some husband you are!"

"No, the truth is I didn't notice," Prullàs admitted.

"Ignorance of the law is no defence," the other man replied; "yesterday I saw them ironing our dinner suits."

On the second day of the festivities, at about five in the afternoon, something extraordinary happened. Prullàs was dozing
in his deckchair under a pine tree, *La Vanguardia* balanced
precariously on his lap, when his sweaty, excited children came
to disturb him. "Papa, please please can we have some money
for the shooting range!" "More money?" Prullàs grumbled.
"But your grandfather gave you a hundred pesetas only this
morning!" "We've spent it already! Please, papa, please!"
Prullàs handed over a twenty-five peseta note. "Don't buy
ice-creams or any other rubbish with it," he said; "and above
all, no candyfloss!" The children agreed, but could barely keep
straight faces: they knew they had to pretend to pay attention
to someone who let himself be fleeced so easily. Before they
all dashed off, they told him: "Oh, papa, there's a man at the
door for you." "A man? Why didn't you say so before? We're
sorry, papa, but we forgot." "Didn't he say who he was?" "Yes,
but we've forgotten that too. 'Bye, papa."

Prullàs struggled up to go and see who the caller was. As
he folded his newspaper he saw from the headlines that a court
of appeal had quashed the sentence against Alfried Krupp
because of irregularities in the trial procedure. The German
magnate had been set free, and all the shares in his industrial
empire had been returned to him. All that hard work for
nothing, Prullàs thought.

Out at the gate in the fierce afternoon sun stood Don
Lorenzo Verdugones. "Don Lorenzo, you here again!" Prullàs
exclaimed. "What a surprise! But come in, do; you'll fry like an
egg in this heat." "Don't worry," the military man replied, "I
can withstand hardships." "I'm sorry to keep you waiting, but
the children forgot to tell me . . . " "Children," Don Lorenzo
interrupted him, "are the seed of our future; the first fruits of

our New Spain." "So you won't come in?" Prullàs insisted. "I'd prefer to take a stroll round the village; I've seen the bunting in the streets and I know it's the festival. Ah, the old traditions of Spain!" "All right, we can walk up to the club," Prullàs said, interpreting the other man's suggestion as a desire for privacy.

The two men walked along the deserted streets, seeking out the shade of trees and high walls. Neither of them spoke. On this occasion however, unlike previous ones, it was Don Lorenzo who was uncomfortable with the silence, while Prullàs found it suited his frame of mind: neither the curiosity nor the fear nor the rancour he might have felt at the governor's unexpected visit were enough to lift him out of his despondency.

"It's possible," Verdugones eventually said, with obvious effort, "just possible, that I might owe you an apology for what has happened over the past few days. In the hypothetical case that this is so, I want to make it very clear that I didn't come here to do so."

"Don Lorenzo, whatever you may think or do is all the same to me," Prullàs replied. "Ah, so you don't want to know what brings me here?" "No, I don't want to know, but if you want to tell me, go ahead."

Don Lorenzo cleared his throat before speaking. "In fact, I've come to say farewell. Two days ago, I was informed I was being transferred. It was . . . a sudden decision, to tell you the truth; quite frankly, I wasn't expecting it. Of course, I'm not in the least concerned. Anywhere will do to serve our fatherland!" "Yes, you're right," Prullàs said; "what you do can be done anywhere."

They walked on a little way in silence. As they approached the club, they were enveloped in the greasy smoke from a fritters stand. Don Lorenzo took a deep breath of the dense air and exclaimed with delight: "Ah, doughnuts, fritters, cakes and buns! The delights of Spanish cookery, so simple but so tasty!" "Don Lorenzo, stop all this tomfoolery and tell me why they've got rid of you." "Got rid of me?" the other man murmured, frowning. "I don't see it like that." "You can see it in whatever way you like, Don Lorenzo, but the fact is, they've turfed you out: who are you trying to fool? Come on, let's go into the club; there won't be a soul in there at this time of day, so we can talk quietly and cool off a bit."

Everyone in the village was having their siesta, so the club bar was completely empty. They clapped for attention, and Joaquín appeared, rubbing his eyes. "I never have a sleep in the afternoon," he said, "but with these festivities going on, whether you like it or not you get to bed very late. Not that I'm complaining; business is business. Soon all the holidaymakers will leave, and we'll be stuck here broke for the winter," touching the end of his nose with two fingers to dramatise the situation. "Let us have two whiskies with ice and soda," Prullàs said. "Make mine a double," Verdugones said.

He took a gulp of his whisky, then dabbed his pencil moustache with an almost transparent triangle of paper. Prullàs observed him curiously. What a specimen, he thought; when he was in a powerful position, I thought he was a clown, and now, stripped of his power, he looks like a clown to the nth degree. Then he said out loud to his silent companion: "Don Lorenzo, no-one can hear us, so tell me the truth: were you mixed up in the San Juan de Luz plot?"

The official placed his glass on the table and stared Prullàs up and down. "Why do you ask a question like that?" "For no reason," Prullàs replied. "I thought that might be why you were removed so suddenly." "My transfer, you mean? No, not at all," the other man quickly replied, "my loyalty to the regime is rock solid! And anyway, that San Juan de Luz affair was a farce. Just imagine: the old provincial aristocracy, a bunch of syphilitic pisspots! And while they were pretending to conspire and getting fleeced at the baccarat tables, on board the *Azor* the head of state and Don Juan de Borbón were sorting out their differences man to man." He waved to Joaquín for another double whisky, and went on: "It's official; within a month His Royal Highness Prince Juan Carlos is coming to Madrid to start an education that will prepare him for his historic role. Spain's future is in safe hands!" Joaquín brought the whisky, Prullàs handed out American cigarettes, and the three of them lit up. After a while, Joaquín withdrew tactfully.

"I'll confess one thing to you," Verdugones went on after a while. "I'll be sorry to leave Catalonia. Yes, contrary to all expectations, I've ended up very attached to this beautiful and noble land: the busy energy of its industry, the elegance of its Romanesque churches, its sun-kissed beaches, the fertile fields of Lérida . . . and Barcelona, that happy, hardworking and cosmopolitan city immortalised by Cervantes! It's a wonderful region! Such a shame about the Catalans, they spoil it all."

He sat smoking in silence for a while, ruminating on how they had offended him, and at length went on: "I can't bear Catalans. I've spent years praising them in all my speeches; now at last I can say what I really think." "Don't worry, Don Lorenzo, I'm sure they feel the same about you," said Prullàs, secure in the knowledge that the other man wasn't listening to a word.

"When I was posted to this corner of the peninsula," the ex-governor said, "I came reluctantly but with the best intentions. I did all I could to solve the serious problems here, or at least to mitigate them. And now look how the Catalans have repaid my sleepless nights! A race of Judas Iscariots is what they are! They agreed to everything to my face, and then went off and did just as they pleased. They all kowtowed to me, but nobody liked me. I've learnt how lonely power can be, Prullàs my friend! But nothing I ever did could win them over: resolving the problem of the cost of foodstuffs or raw materials for their factories, encouraging the building of publicly funded homes, stamping out banditry in the Sierra del Cadí, authorising the *sardána* to be danced! And what did I get in return? Nothing! Every man for himself, and for the common good, not a thing. The economic powers in Catalonia act to the detriment of their own people. How backward it is, how backward! It's the out-of-date liberalism of the nineteenth century, the serpent of mercantilism once again raising its poisonous head to attack Spain's prosperity! Over and over again, we have to fight the same old enemy, just like Ramiro the First, who refused to pay the despicable tribute of a hundred maidens; like Don Pelayo or Racaredo and Wamba, or El Cid, Count Fernan González and Don Gonzalo de Córdoba, better known as the Great Captain."

Prullàs let him get it all off his chest. When Don Lorenzo had finished the rollcall of national glories, the playwright returned him quickly to his own concern: "Well if it wasn't the monarchist plot, what happened, Don Lorenzo? Who had you thrown out?" Don Lorenzo shouted for another double whisky. "Can't you work it out, my fine detective friend?" he said, in answer to Prullàs' question. "Those bastards on the Flour Board!"

"Ah, I get it," Prullàs said; "the wheat thieves won the battle. Is that it? And Fontcuberta really was the brains behind the operation, as you said."

"Oh, Fontcuberta – he's merely a pawn in the game, nothing more than a puppet. There are lots of people involved, in Catalonia and elsewhere; well-known people."

"Vallsigorri?" Prullàs asked. "I suppose so, and that legal shyster too . . . " "The lawyer Sanjuanete?" "Yes, and lots more. They were all at the trough! Do you remember the night we met, at Brusquets' place? A hornets' nest of cheats, swindlers and racketeers! In that Ali Baba's cave, with their glasses of champagne, Cuban cigars and canapés, they were busy stealing from the hungry common people under our very noses! They've cooked up their fortunes with the bread of our beloved nation!" Joaquín came and placed another glass of whisky on the table, then vanished as quickly as he could, worried at the harsh words the ex-governor was yelling. Don Lorenzo swallowed half the whisky then added forlornly: "If only they'd let me, I could have cleaned this country of the leeches, Prullàs my friend; I could have cut out this rotten cancer if they hadn't dashed the scalpel from my hand. But they got in before me: they have very powerful protectors, very high up indeed, if you get my drift." "In the Pardo palace itself?" Prullàs suggested. "Don't even mention the caudillo!" the other man replied; "all I said was 'very high up'. Even in the Last Supper there was a traitor, and Jesus himself had chosen all of them! Oh, but I could have amputated that gangrenous leg. But just as I was about to do so, when I set my trap for them, they got in first. Someone gave me away. Can you guess who?"

"Don't tell me. Poveda."

"No, Poveda always worked for me," Don Lorenzo laughed. Then his face clouded over again. "Sigüenza! Who would have thought it! I put all my trust in that scoundrel, Prullàs my friend, and he turned out to be a rat. I treated him like my own child! With people like that, how are we ever going to save Spain from its centuries of backwardness?" The old warrior's voice trembled close to tears, and his eyes were misty with sentiment as the drink began to take hold.

"To tell you the truth, Don Lorenzo, I couldn't give a damn about your problems," Prullàs said. "I reckon you got what you deserved for trying to sort out the world when nobody asked you to." The heroic ex-governor stared at his companion more in sorrow than in anger. "Ah," he retorted, "it's easy enough for you to say that, because you spend your time writing rubbish and living off your father-in-law's money. But I've devoted my entire life to my country, goddammit. I've risked my balls in the Montaña barracks, at the Alto de los Leones in Castille, and at Teruel. These balls here, Prullàs my friend! And it's sad to see how a life consumed in the fire of an ideal can end up in the filthy puddle of theft and banditry! Goddammit, my whole life up in smoke! I'm pissing myself, Prullàs, where's the bathroom?"

Prullàs pointed to the door, and Verdugones quickly downed the rest of the whisky, ground out his cigarette in the ashtray, and stood up. "I'll be straight back, Prullàs my friend; don't run away," he said. "I've got one other important thing to tell you. It doesn't matter where one serves the fatherland! Where did you say the bathroom was?"

A short while later, the heroic ex-governor came staggering back and sat down again. "We've run dry," he muttered, staring down perplexed at his empty glass. "You shouldn't drink any more, Don Lorenzo," Prullàs said; "especially if you're driving back to Barcelona." "Oh, don't worry about that; I still have my official car and a uniformed chauffeur; they wouldn't dare take them away from me. I've been awarded the San Fernando Cross; I'm not travelling by train. Anyway, I'm not drunk. But perhaps you're right, we shouldn't drink any more. We have to keep our heads clear because we still have something important to talk about, Prullàs my friend; clear heads and steady hands. Prullàs, I've already said this on several occasions, and I'll repeat it now: I like what I've seen of you. A steady hand! I've taken a liking to you; I don't expect you to feel the same, but it's true. We've had our disagreements, I know, but in spite of everything I've taken to you. Consider me your friend. A sincere and steady friend . . . steady as a rock. That's what I came to tell you. No, wait, don't interrupt. I've something more to say. Look, now that Sigüenza has done the dirty on me, I've been thinking and I've come to the conclusion you might be interested in coming with me, not as my secretary, but more as my confidant. You're discreet, loyal, and you get on well with people. You on my left, and a steady hand, Prullàs my friend; the two of us could work well together. Think about my offer: what d'you say?"

It took Prullàs some time to find adequate words to reply. "Don Lorenzo," he said finally, "I've never been made a less interesting proposition." The heroic ex-governor sighed. "The truth is, I didn't think you'd accept, but I felt I had to give it a try. Don't worry, you haven't offended me by turning me down; in your shoes I'd probably have done the same. There's absolutely no reason why you should give up the theatre: a bohemian lifestyle, the public's applause, fame . . . not to mention all the pretty girls. That's why, isn't it?"

"No, Don Lorenzo, it's not that at all," Prullàs replied. "In actual fact, in the last few days I've taken the decision to leave the theatre and devote myself to business. I've talked to my father-in-law about it, he has welcomed the idea, and so I'll start working in one of his companies this autumn. 'Arrivederci, pollo!' will be my swansong. I turned down your offer because that's how I feel, that's all. And do up your flies, would you?"

"All right, all right," the heroic ex-governor said, struggling with the buttons on his trousers, "you've every right to laugh at me. Go on, strike me while I'm down! When all's said and done, it's my fault: I'm behaving in a grotesque and undignified way, I know. I'm a bit dizzy; it's this ghastly heat and the smell of fritters which is making me feel queasy. I've also realised I've said some foolish things. Everyone has their weak point, as Frederick March said. No," he hastened to say when he saw

467

Prullàs' amused reaction to this, "I'm not a cinema-goer: films seem to me like flashy nonsense; but I occasionally go, to forget my worries . . . oh well, it's quite possible I came here to be humiliated exactly like this; God only knows the workings of our subconscious. But none of this should make you feel superior to me, Prullàs my friend. You would be silly to think you were. And I'll tell you something else for good measure: you might think you've got it easy, but you won't be able to sit on the fence for ever. If you don't take sides, others will do so for you. It's possible they've already done so, without you're knowing it. Look, I've done it," he said, pointing down at his flies.

"You're right, Don Lorenzo," Prullàs replied; "your behaviour is truly grotesque. And there's one last thing I'd like to make clear: you began by saying you hadn't come to apologise for all that's happened in the past few weeks. Well, I'd like to say that if you had come to apologise, I would never have accepted it. I don't think I'm superior to you, Don Lorenzo, but it's quite probable that I am. And I think there's nothing left for us to say."

"Suit yourself," Don Lorenzo said, struggling to his feet again. "Waiter, the bill!" "No, no, Don Lorenzo," Prullàs said; "you paid me this visit, so it's for me to pay: no falling-out between us should go against the sacred laws of hospitality. Joaquín, put the drinks on my account, would you?"

Verdugones headed for the door, with Prullàs at his side. Before stepping outside, he said: "The Interior Ministry has named as my successor Colonel Vergara, whom you heard me talking to the other day on the telephone. He's a good man; if ever you should need anything, don't hesitate to get in touch with him. Even though the Vallsigorri case is closed, you still may have some slight problems. If you do, both Colonel Vergara and Sigüenza will be only too pleased to help. Anyway,

I wish you every success with your play; don't forget to offer my warmest wishes to your wife, and do one thing for me: get rid of that stutterer." He stepped forward resolutely across the dividing line between the cool shade in the bar and the scorching sunlight out in the street. "Goodness," he said, shielding his eyes with his forearm, "I must have left my sunglasses in the car. Oh well, bring on the bull!"

Prullàs stretched out his hand, which the other man shook quickly and vigorously. "Make sure you have a nap on the journey," said Prullàs. "Thanks, I will," the other man said. He walked on a few steps, stopped in the middle of the street, turned round and shouted in his thunderous voice of old: "If you change your mind, let me know. Our country needs people like you and me, Prullàs my friend. Somebody has to take the lead, shape everyone up and encourage the fainthearted!"

He straightened up, clicked his heels and raised his arm in a salute that baffled an old woman who had just set up her stall of peanuts and lupins on the pavement.

3

The crowd's eyes were still glittering from the splendour of the rockets, Catherine wheels and cascades of the firework display; the loud bangs of the final firecracker still hung in the air; and the sea breeze wafted the smell of gunpowder to every corner of the village when the holidaymakers, in their best evening dress, perfumed and bejewelled, made their entrance into the Social Club. All the villagers were thronging the streets to witness yet again this display of elegance and social standing. Despite the lateness of the hour the holidaymakers' children had also taken advantage of the festive spirit to come out with the servants to see their parents go by. Out of the corner of his eye, Prullàs spotted his children perched on a wall on the far side of the street, from where they could get a good view of proceedings. This sight stirred him out of his apathy. Many years from now, he thought, when most of us are already dead, they will still remember these happy years; perhaps only that remote possibility can excuse us for the futility of our lives.

In the main bar, which was festooned with streamers and pennants, Joaquín and his children, all of them dressed up in dark grey suits, greeted each couple as they came in with a ceremonious and increasingly heated bow from the waist. In the garden, the orchestra was playing a waltz. The sky had been clear all day, and there seemed to be no risk that a sudden shower would put an end to the celebrations. It was a warm night; but the ladies had taken the precaution of already leaving their shawls, wraps and capes in the club cloakroom in case it turned cold.

Prullàs left Martita and his in-laws busy with a laborious exchange of greetings and compliments to other summer visitors and sought refuge at the bar. With Joaquín and his children absent, this was attended by an inexperienced young girl who looked very flustered. Doctor Mercadal was scolding her as Prullàs came up.

"Ah, Prullàs, take a look at this. I ordered a whisky, and this young lady has served me a ridiculously small amount, as if I were asking for cough medicine . . . or a laxative! Come now, give me the bottle and I'll show you how it should be done. And serve my friend here another glass with some ice."

The surgeon poured himself a copious amount and another similar measure for Prullàs. They toasted the end of summer and drank deeply. Marichuli Mercadal joined them, extremely worried: as she came in, she had seen Alicia in the crowd, and thought she wasn't wrapped up warmly enough. "I told her to wear her angora cardigan," she said, "it's really warm and suits her perfectly, but she insisted on putting on her maroon blouse, and that's as thin as cigarette paper. She never listens, she's as stubborn as a mule."

"Let her be, will you? Nothing will happen to her," Doctor Mercadal complained. "I've told you a thousand times not to be so obsessive with poor Alicia. It doesn't do any good, and by being over-protective you'll only create a counter-transference which could affect her character development." "I think I'll have a whisky too," Marichuli said, with an irritable wave of her hand; "but don't pour me so much, please." "I didn't know you drank whisky," Prullàs said. "This is my first time," she replied. She swallowed some and did not so much shudder as have a convulsion. Her eyes flashed with the mad gleam Prullàs had noticed on earlier occasions. "Shall we dance?" he suggested.

They walked down the steps into the garden. The dance floor was lit by dozens of Japanese lanterns. "Thanks for taking me away from there," Marichuli whispered; "I can't stand that imbecile, I really can't. One fine day, I'm going to murder him." "Don't say that even as a joke," Prullàs exclaimed, grasping her round her waist. He smelled the perfume on her hair, and said: "What a lovely scent you have. What perfume is it?" "*Arpège*," Marichuli replied. "My husband bought it from a blackmarketeer and gave it me as a gift some time ago; why do you ask?" "Oh, curiosity, that's all; how are you feeling?" "Dreadful," she said. "When we go back to Barcelona they want me to have an operation. They say it'll help me feel better." "Yes, your husband already told me." "And d'you think I should do it, Carlos? Should I really have a lobotomy?" Prullàs hesitated. "Frankly, I haven't the faintest idea," he said after a while. "But if your husband is suggesting it, there must be something to it; he only wants the best for you."

The orchestra was playing a Cuban waltz. It was still early, and only a few other couples were dancing. Nobody paid them any attention. Prullàs could feel the warmth from Marichuli's shoulders, and the tautness of her body under her dress. He began to feel intoxicated by the whisky, the dance rhythm, and the sweet night air; he wanted to stay like that forever, for the waltz to go on without end. Marichuli would not look at him, but he understood that a single word, a simple gesture from him would be enough to demolish the wall that had grown up between them. Martita passed by, dancing with an acquaintance of theirs, and smiled and winked at him; he did the same in return, responding to her collusion and affection. The tune finished, the dancers applauded, and the man who had been dancing with Martita asked Prullàs if he could dance the next one with Marichuli Mercadal. Prullàs let him take over and left the dance floor. He felt thirsty and decided to return to the bar.

As he was climbing the steps up from the garden, a stranger greeted him with a mixture of timidity and familiarity. "Don't you remember me, Señor Prullàs?" "No, I'm afraid I don't." "That doesn't matter," the stranger said. "It's only natural; but you'll remember as soon as I tell you my stage name: I'm the diabolic Doctor Corbeau," he explained, raising his hand as if to hypnotise someone. "Ah yes, of course, and what brings you here again, Corbeau my friend?" The magician's face lit up with a smile of satisfaction. "I've been hired to put on a show for the children," he said. "I was really lucky. They had an agreement with Li Chang, but at the last minute he couldn't come because of illness, and I had given my details to Joaquín just in case, so with time pressing, they called on me . . . and here I am, with my false-bottomed chests and my magic powders."

"Well, I'm really pleased for you, Corbeau my friend," Prullàs said. "Thank you," the magician replied; "summer's on its last legs and until the First Communion parties next May

472

I've got some lean months ahead of me, so a juicy contract like this is just what I need. I truly didn't expect it, especially after that regrettable incident . . . Fortunately," he said with a contented sigh, "people forget and forgive everything, provided they see a show that takes them out of themselves, even such a banal one as Doctor Corbeau's. All of us in the business know we may have hard times, but we can always be sure of one thing: people would prefer to go without food than give us up. Don't you agree, Señor Prullàs?"

By now, they had reached the bar, where one of Joaquín's sons had taken over from the unfortunate young girl, who was clattering about red-faced, washing and drying up plates, cups and spoons. Prullàs asked for a glass of water, drank it down at a gulp and then, turning to Doctor Corbeau, said to him: "There's a lot to what you say, Corbeau my friend; and that conviction is the only thing that keeps us going; order what you like and tell them to charge it to my account."

He shook the magician's limp hand and went back to the garden. He looked around for Martita but couldn't see her.

At the musicians' feet on the edge of the bandstand sat Roquet el dels Fems. Even though the dance was open to anyone who bought a ticket, by a tacit agreement dating from no-one knew when, this was the summer holidaymakers' ball, the ceremony with which they marked the end of the season. The only exception to this rule was Roquet, who by virtue of his special position and thanks to an equally tacit and unchallengeable understanding was allowed to come, even though no-one actually agreed with the idea. Now he was sitting watching the couples go by, mindless but happy, the whites of his eyes showing as he moved his head back and forward against the music, laughing hilariously whenever the saxophone blared out. Prullàs sat next to him. The orchestra struck up another tune,

473

and the couples started to whirl round again. Prullàs and Roquet sat looking for a while at this island of content in the midst of all the violence and uncertainty; it was a world apart, condemned no doubt to perish, but still intact, the precarious but obstinate survivor of its own past. Seeing this pleasant spectacle after all the upheaval of the previous weeks and the terror of the last few days, Prullàs finally felt at peace with himself. For the first time, he understood that everything could be reduced to a simple proposition: that the years had not gone by in vain, that he had reached maturity and that this had been the last summer of his youth. Now he could see himself as he really was: an adult with nowhere to go, with no other future but nostalgia. He was nothing more than a cog in this huge machine, with no merit or blame attached to him, simply the inheritor of a past he had played no part in constructing, but whose consequences he was bound to accept. He realised now Gaudet had been right from the start: his theatre career was over. His jokes, plays on words and *double entendres* no longer satisfied the public's sensibility, because everything was on the verge of change in society, everything except this island of peace, won with such difficulty and stubbornly defended against all ambush. He understood once and for all that this was the life he had been destined for, and that unless circumstances proved otherwise, any effort he made to change it was bound to fail.

To ward off these thoughts he took out his pack of American cigarettes, lit one, and offered another to Roquet el dels Fems. Roquet took it gratefully, and put it behind his ear for later. "Go on, smoke it," Prullàs said. "They don't let me smoke," the boy said. "You only live once," Prullàs replied.

THE END